"PUT ON YO〇 〇〇
H〇

Hanratty go〇
swirling ma〇
firing at the〇
watching me〇〇〇〇

Around him was the whirling, roaring
confusion of a major battle. Shouting and
shooting and bugles. Grenades and
mortars were exploding until it was almost
impossible to hear single detonations.
Tracers burned through the night.
Artillery roared overhead to land on the
southwest slope until it seemed that the
entire mountain was on fire. No one could
live in the inferno, and yet the enemy kept
coming, pouring out of the trees and
overrunning more and more of the base,
trying to kill all of the Marines before help
could arrive.

VIETNAM: GROUND ZERO

Shifting FIRES

ERIC HELM

A GOLD EAGLE BOOK

London · Toronto · New York · Sydney

*First published in Great Britain 1990
by Gold Eagle*

© Eric Helm 1989

*Australian copyright 1989
Philippine copyright 1989
This edition 1990*

ISBN 0 373 60502 1

25/9003

Made and printed in Great Britain

VIETNAM: GROUND ZERO
Shifting
FIRES

PROLOGUE

The six men appeared out of the gloom at the western end of
the airstrip, walking slowly toward the interior of the combat
base. They were outside the wire, well away from the perimeter. They came from the direction of the rock quarry, where
there should have been no Marines. The ARVN and the local
RFs were never in that area. Six men, dressed in the jungle fatigues of the U.S. Marine Corps, were walking along as if they
were at a stateside camp, heading back to base after an evening of drinking in the closest tavern.

There was nothing distinctive about the men except that
they were smaller than the average American, but with the
number of Hispanics and Orientals in the Marine Corps, even
their size wasn't that far out of line.

The men vanished as the terrain dipped, but they soon
reappeared, closer to the wire and at the end of the runway.
They didn't appear to be armed, and didn't seem to be returning from a patrol. They certainly weren't following established procedures as they walked toward the combat base.

Calvin Jones, a Marine new to Vietnam, picked up the field
phone in his bunker and twisted the crank. He squeezed the

handset and blew into the mouthpiece to make sure it was working.

"I got movement out here," he whispered.

"Identify yourself and state nature of movement."

Jones crouched near the firing port of his bunker and squinted into the darkness, not believing what he saw—six men wandering around outside the perimeter as if they owned the place, as if they didn't fear the Vietcong, or the Marines.

Jones gave his call sign and said, "Five, six men, walking along the perimeter."

"You sure?"

"Roger. Six men at the edge of the runway, just walking along." He wiped the sweat from his forehead with the palm of his hand and then rubbed it on the front of his fatigue jacket.

"Roger."

Jones cradled the field phone and took a few steps to the left. He sat down on an ammo can, and reached for his rifle, propped against the sandbagged wall of the bunker. Six men didn't make an assault, but six sappers could blow a hole in the wire for a pending assault, and anything outside the wire was considered unusual.

The six men continued to approach, not crawling, not walking one behind another as a patrol would. They came forward, almost as if sweeping toward Khe Sanh on line, except they were bunched too close to one another for that.

From the camp, half a dozen Marines moved forward. Even in the faint light created by the glow from the camp, it was obvious that the Marines were Americans—big burly men, carrying M-16s.

The Marines stopped when they were thirty feet from the mystery men. The officer shouted a challenge, but there was no response. Keeping his eyes on the men, he used his thumb to flip off the safety on his weapon.

"I said eight," he repeated.

Still there was no response, but this time one of the strangers grabbed at his side. His hand came up. He seemed to be yanking at the pin of a grenade.

The Marines opened up as one. The M-16s stuttered, firing on full-auto. The muzzle-flashes lit the ground and the jerking men like the strobes of cameras. In the glare, the enemy twitched and danced as the rounds hit them. There was a piercing scream and a low moan. One of the men turned to run, leaping up and down, disappearing in the dark.

Five of the six men were down. The Americans advanced on them and checked the bodies for weapons. Each of the dead carried a pistol and a grenade. They wore American uniforms but weren't Americans. Blood stained their clothes, and the face of one had been shattered by the M-16 bullets.

The American patrol retreated, taking the dead with them. They were worried that they had cut loose on a South Vietnamese patrol that no one had bothered to coordinate with the Marines, though the few weapons, of Soviet manufacture, suggested otherwise.

In the morning they learned the identity of some of the men. One was the commanding officer of a North Vietnamese regiment, another was his operations officer and the third was a communications officer.

In Marine headquarters it wasn't hard to figure out what the officers of a North Vietnamese regiment were doing at the end of the runway, dressed like American soldiers. The answer was obvious: they'd been checking the defenses and approach routes for an attack. The enemy had been on a recon mission.

1

KHE SANH COMBAT
BASE January 20, 1968

KHE SANH sat nestled in the northern hills of South Vietnam, only a few klicks from the Laotian border, and not far from the DMZ. It was a kidney-shaped base about a mile long and half a mile wide, looking like a gaping red wound in the deep greens of vegetation on the surrounding hills. On the northern side was the surfaced runway. A series of roads divided the base into sections, with the main ammo dump and the artillery batteries on the eastern and southern sides, away from the majority of the hootches assigned to the Marines stationed there.

Life at Khe Sanh wasn't bad in late 1967 and the first few weeks of 1968. The coming of the monsoons, with the heavy rains that turned the hard-packed roads into seas of gumbo and huge pools of stagnant water, was the worst threat. The tropical heat and humidity sometimes oppressed the men at Khe Sanh, but they ignored the minor discomfort, thinking only of the thirteen months they had to remain in Vietnam before they could return to the World.

Many of the hills around the base had been the scenes of recent battles. Marines had fought their way up more than one of them and established small camps on the summits. From there, on clear days—which were becoming less frequent with the approaching monsoon season—they could look down into Khe Sanh.

The base was east of the town of Khe Sanh and the small Special Forces compound at Lang Vei. Marine patrols into the jungles around Khe Sanh met most of their resistance in the heavy vegetation that grabbed and tore at their uniforms. The undergrowth was as dense as steel wool in some places, requiring days for men to advance a few klicks. Razor-sharp elephant grass covered the plateaus and clearings. Wait-a-minute vines and other creepers strangled the life from some of the trees, whose branches reached two hundred feet into the air to create a canopy as thick and solid as the dome over a football stadium.

Khe Sanh was situated on Route 9, which stretched from Cambodia into Vietnam and on to the eastern coast. Viewed by many military men as the cork in a bottle, it had been built where it was in order to stem the flow of supplies from the North into the South.

But the strategic location didn't matter to the Marines stationed at Khe Sanh. They saw it as a fairly quiet base from which they sortied into the jungle on operations designed to trap and kill the enemy. Operations Crockett, Ardmore and Scotland One had met with varying results.

That had been the quiet before the storm.

Corporal William Dobson sat in the guard shack, his feet propped on the thin wood of the siding. His steel pot was on the dirty plywood floor next to him and his M-16 was leaning against the wall. Although his only activity was to flip the pages of the magazine he was reading, he was sweating heavily. The underarms and a strip down the back of his fatigue shirt looked black from moisture. His dark hair was plastered to his head and perspiration was beaded on his forehead.

Occasionally he glanced up and out into the perimeter wire and the deep greens beyond it—tangled scrub that had been cut back for killing fields so that enemy assaults would have to cross open ground. For most of the day he had been looking through waves of heat rising from the ground, causing the vegetation to shimmer slightly. When the white flag suddenly appeared out of the undergrowth, Dobson's first reaction was to think he was seeing something that wasn't there.

His feet hit the floor with an audible thud and he stood up. He wiped his sweaty hand on his fatigue jacket and picked up the binoculars from a shelf near him. As he focused the glasses, a man appeared, a short, thin man dressed in black pajamas, holding the flag in his left hand and an AK-47 over his head with his right. Without waiting for a response from the base, he came steadily forward toward the eastern end of the runway, waving his flag and holding his weapon high.

Dobson grabbed his M-16 and helmet and stepped out of the tiny guard shack into the bright afternoon sun. He wondered exactly what he should do. The situation wasn't all that common.

The answer was given to him. A jeep appeared from the south, racing along the road that skirted the perimeter of the camp, raising a cloud of choking red dust. An M-60 machine was mounted in the back of the speeding jeep, and one man clung to it.

As the jeep approached the gate, it slid to a stop, wrapped in the dust that slowly drifted away on the light breeze.

Dobson joined the men in the jeep—two sergeants and a lieutenant with a bad sunburn, who now stood with his hands on his hips. He wore new jungle fatigues, and a pistol belt that held a Colt .45 and a single canteen. In his flak jacket and steel pot, he looked uncomfortable, not like the men who had been at Khe Sanh for several months. He had a boyish face, short hair and peach fuzz on his chin.

"What we got?" he asked.

"Guy appeared in the bush. Don't know who he is or what he wants."

The lieutenant nodded and snapped his fingers. The sergeant behind the M-60 worked the bolt and swung the barrel around, aiming at the chest of the approaching Vietnamese, who didn't hesitate. He just grinned widely and continued to hold his weapon high over his head to show that he wasn't going to use it.

"Get on the field phone and alert the intel boys that we've got a gook coming, armed with an AK."

"Aye-aye, sir," said Dobson, nodding. He walked back to the guard shack. While watching the show outside, he lifted the handset of the field phone, spun the crank and asked to be connected with the intel section.

The enemy soldier had reached the wire. The lieutenant and one of the sergeants were walking out to meet him. The lieutenant's hand was on his pistol, though he hadn't drawn the weapon. The sergeant carried an M-16 in the crook of his arm, looking like a hunter strolling the cornfields of Iowa searching for pheasant.

As they approached, the Vietnamese stopped and bent at the waist. He set his weapon on the ground and stood there waiting, the white flag catching the light breeze and flapping gently.

The sergeant picked up the AK while the lieutenant searched the man, running his hands over the loose-fitting black pajamas. Satisfied that he had no other weapons, they escorted him back toward the camp.

Dobson got his call through finally and said, "We've got a man in the wire, possibly Vietcong. He's being brought in."

"Where are you?"

Dobson told him and then said, "There's a lieutenant out here picking up the guy."

"You have them hold right there. Someone will be out to look over the situation."

"You better hurry," Dobson advised, "because I don't think the lieutenant's going to hang around here very long."

"Then you tell him to wait until we get someone over there. Be about five minutes."

"Yes, sir," said Dobson. He cradled the phone and stepped back out. The men were moving toward the jeep. The sergeant was already back behind the wheel.

"Sir," Dobson called as he hurried toward the jeep. "You have to wait here for a moment."

"And give this guy a good look at our side of the perimeter?"

"There's a team from intel coming to pick him up. They want to look at him before they do anything else."

The lieutenant took off his helmet and dropped it onto the dusty canvas seat in the jeep, then wiped the sweat from his face with the sleeve of his fatigues. He looked disgusted and shook his head, then said to Dobson, "All right, Corporal." He looked at the Vietnamese. "You, sit down."

As the Vietnamese hunkered down in the red dust, another jeep appeared, heading toward them. It slowed, and one man stood and jumped onto the ground, taking a couple of running steps to keep his balance. He slid to a halt as the jeep stopped behind him.

"I'm Sergeant Burns." He glanced at the lieutenant but didn't salute. Saluting was avoided in the field because it identified the officers for the enemy. "What do we have here?"

"One Vietnamese armed with the AK there. He walked up to the perimeter."

"Who are you?" asked Burns, pointing at the Vietnamese.

"I am Lieutenant La Than Tonc, commander of the Fourteenth Antitank Company, 325th C Division."

"What?"

"I have come to surrender to you. To defect to you. I have brought my weapon."

Burns took a step back and stared at the slight man. Black hair cut short, oval brown eyes in an oval face. A young face bathed in sweat from the tropical sun. Black pajamas smudged with dirt and stained with oil.

"I have information for you," Tonc continued. "Important information. Your camp will be attacked tomorrow at 0530."

"Sure," said Burns. "I believe you."

LIEUTENANT COLONEL Samuel Lockhart sat in his darkened office, the only light from a tiny lamp in the center of his desk, and read the latest reports from South Vietnam. Lockhart was a career soldier who had graduated near the middle of his class at West Point and who had had an undistinguished career. He'd skipped the chance for flight school after the Point, figuring that helicopters were not the wave of the future, and followed too many of his fellows to jump school at Fort Benning. That had been three weeks of hell, but when he was through, he was awarded the jump wings that marked him as a paratrooper. It was the glamour move dictated by Army tradition and afternoon movie matinees.

The smart money had been on the helicopter. The men who had earned the wings of a helicopter pilot found themselves commanding combat units in Vietnam and earning valuable points toward promotion to full colonel and then general, while Lockhart sat in the bowels of the Pentagon reading intelligence estimates written by captains and majors who couldn't understand the big picture with the enemy shooting at them.

Without pilot's wings and combat command time, Lockhart's only hope for promotion was to be the best man available in Washington, D.C. He had to hope he found something others overlooked, or that he was able to appease his bosses and the President.

Now he stood up, stretched and strolled around his tiny office. The battleship-gray desk had seen better days; it was serviceable, but one of the bottom drawers stuck. He had a metal bookcase on one wall, filled with black binders holding the documents and regulations covering the operation of his office. In a corner he had a single visitor's chair—a big brown leather hand-me-down from a brigadier general who'd ordered better furniture. The green curtains hid not a window but a blank wall. Lockhart found it pleasant to pretend he had a window; it sometimes threw visitors off balance as they tried to figure out why he rated an office with a window when they didn't.

Finally he sat down again and pulled a cigarette from the pack in his unbuttoned shirt pocket. He lit it, blinking at the flare of the match, then tossed it into the overflowing ashtray. His mouth tasted like hot sand, and his eyes burned from the long hours of work.

"Okay," he said out loud just to hear a human voice, and then turned his attention back to the report he had been reading. From the hallway outside he heard the quiet tap of footsteps as someone walked by, probably one of the guards. Lockhart was tempted to go out to talk to him, but knew he was merely avoiding the work he'd promised himself to finish.

The intel estimates coming from Saigon, Da Nang, Nha Trang and each of the Corps headquarters showed a marked buildup in enemy forces throughout South Vietnam. Troops and supplies were pouring into the country, and the command structure was worrying about a surprise attack, possibly during the Lunar New Year called Tet.

Lockhart, a political animal, remembered the atmosphere at the Pentagon a few weeks earlier when Westmoreland had said he expected a radical switch in North Vietnamese strategy. There had been a lot of unhappy people running around, because that wasn't what the President wanted to hear. He didn't want to hear about enemy troop buildups and supply increases; he wanted to hear that the tide in the conflict was turning and that the war was being won.

In fact, in his State of the Union address, the President had failed to mention any of the negatives. According to him, the war was being won; no one wanted to hear anything different.

Lockhart took his cigarette from the ashtray and drew on it, the tip glowing a brilliant orange as he tried to decide what to do. Too often the messenger who brought the bad news had his head handed to him.

He made his decision, and stubbed out the cigarette. For now he would sit on the report. There were no indications that the enemy would launch its attacks in the next twelve hours, so he had time to prepare a report requesting merely that

Vietnam be watched carefully. That couldn't be construed as alarmist. His bosses would be happy and his ass would be covered. Covering his ass was the important factor.

LA THAN TONC sat in the lone chair in the center of the bunker. With a bright light shining in his eyes, he couldn't see the Americans hovering around the perimeter of the room, but he knew there were four of them, big men in perfect uniforms. They didn't seem to sweat and they didn't care if he could speak English or not, because they could speak Vietnamese. They were frightening men who sometimes shouted questions at him. He smiled at them when they did that, answering each of their questions as completely as he could, though he knew they didn't believe him. Still he sat quietly, giving the Americans everything they wanted.

Tonc had spent fourteen years in the field, fighting the enemy, whether they were dressed as French Paras or American Marines. He had been in ambushes and firefights. He had led his men in raids against the Americans, always doing as he was told, always believing all he was told.

There had been terror-filled nights when the American airpower had swooped through the sky above him like birds of prey. He had huddled in the bottom of his inadequate bunker, feeling the concussions of bombs detonating around him, sure that he was about to die. He had heard the screams of his fellows as the hot shrapnel had cut through them and he had listened to the moans of his friends as they had died.

And each day, after the Americans were gone and he could claw his way out of the smoking ruins, he had been sure he was on the right side.

He had suffered through the cold monsoon rains and the hot tropical summer. He had sweated in the humidity of the deep jungle, where the enemy was more likely to be the hundreds of poisonous snakes, or the rats, or the big cats that didn't care if the prey was human or animal. He had done all that had been asked, had sacrificed his men in meaningless attacks, and for what? So that someone else could get the promotion he had deserved.

So now, when the Americans asked him questions, he gave them the answers, telling them everything he knew. He rattled off dates, locations and times, displaying a knowledge of the battle plans that was truly remarkable. He had been briefed on everything, and he gave it all away for the promise that he would be protected and given the opportunity to fight as a Kit Carson scout.

STANDING WELL BACK in the gloom of the bunker were Lieutenant George Korski and Sergeant James Goddard. Korski was a man of average height, but he was burly with a thick chest and huge thighs. He had an air of power about him until you looked into his face. It was a baby face—pudgy cheeks, sunburned skin and bright blue eyes—a face that made him appear to be a fun-loving man who just happened to head one of the intelligence units at Khe Sanh.

Beside Korski, Sergeant Goddard seemed small. He was a gaunt, wiry man with thinning brown hair and a deep tan on his face. He had lost weight thanks to the poor food and the pressure of living in a combat environment. His too-big fatigues were a dull green, almost gray, and his boots, though black, were badly worn. Goddard had spent his adult life in the Marine Corps and was looking forward to winding up his tour in Vietnam.

They watched and listened to the interrogation as the two other men circled La Than Tonc and shouted questions at him, then stood still and asked them again in quiet tones. One of the Marines crouched in front of the man to look directly into his eyes. That was something that interrogators rarely did. They tried to maintain the superior position, looking down on the prisoner.

"You believe all this?" Korski asked Goddard.

"Don't know, sir. It's a little too pat, if you know what I mean. Zip strolls in and hands us their battle plans for the next six weeks."

Korski touched Goddard on the shoulder and nodded toward the door. They stepped out of the bunker into the bright afternoon sun.

The air was hazy. The nonthreatening smell of burning garbage was typical of the almost relaxed atmosphere of the base. No pressure on it from anywhere, and although it took mortar rounds and rockets occasionally, they were such a hit-and-miss proposition that no one worried about them. Some of the men just listened to the mortars to determine the direction they were moving and then rolled over and went back to sleep. It was almost as if they were on a training exercise.

Korski sat down on a stack of sandbags that someone had failed to place around a bunker. There had been no reason to rush, so the sandbags sat, filled but not stacked, while other, more pressing matters were attended to. He pulled his sunglasses out of his pocket, carefully put them on and stared up at Goddard. "What'd you think?"

"Christ, sir, he has a lot of information. If it's right, the shit's going to hit the fan very soon."

Korski stared off to the northwest where the hills rose into the sky. On top of them were small outposts. Tonc had told them that attacks would be launched at those outposts just after midnight. "Seems to me we'll have an answer in about ten hours," he said. "I can't see him making up stories that would unravel so fast."

Goddard crouched and scooped up a handful of red dust. He let it dribble through his fingers, the wind tearing at it, pulling it away from him. "As a lieutenant, though, you wouldn't think he'd have access to the whole plan. He's talking about the North Vietnamese overrunning us here and then sweeping out to attack all the provincial capitals on their way to the sea, not to mention their assaults south toward Saigon. Why would he have all that information?"

"Right," said Korski, nodding. "That's too much for him to know, but it ties in with what we've gotten from the Special Forces and our own recon people." He stopped talking and glanced around, but there was no one within earshot. No one cared what the two of them were discussing.

"Those guys at Lang Vei are talking about the enemy massing in Laos as if preparing for an attack."

"Yes, sir," said Goddard. "But the guy's only a lieutenant. Do *you* know what's being planned in Saigon? Or in Da Nang, for that matter?"

"No, but then I'm not being told of the great battle we're about to fight to drive the enemy from our country. The political officers might be doing that."

"So what are we going to do now?"

Korski wiped a hand over his chin and then idly rubbed his chest. "I think we just give the colonel what we have and let him pass the information on. If we're right, then the men on the mountaintops will have a few hours to prepare. If not, they'll have sat up all night for no reason."

"Makes us look like chumps."

"Not really, and only if the enemy doesn't materialize. If he does, those guys are going to be buying us beers for the rest of our tours."

"That's true, sir."

"If his story was the only thing we had, I'd say pass the information along to our people but hold off on alerting the units up and down the line. But there's too much else going on out there for us to ignore it."

"Still," Goddard said one more time, "this guy's only a lieutenant, and even his reason for coming over sounds too good to be true."

"Yeah, doesn't it?"

2

NORTH OF CO ROC
MOUNTAIN ALONG THE
XE PONE RIVER LAOS

Feeling a growing sense of horror, Army Special Forces Sergeant Michael Hobbs lay in the tangled vegetation on top of the ridgeline. Below him, along the trail that bordered a wide stream, stretched an almost endless line of North Vietnamese soldiers. Through a thin place in the jungle canopy, he had watched them since late morning—hundreds of men moving steadily to the east, their AKs, RPGs and RPDs sometimes visible in the patches of sunlight. They were not what Hobbs had wanted to see.

Slowly he raised a hand to his head and dabbed at the sweat covering his face, sweat caused by the hot sun overhead and the horror that was spreading from Laos to Vietnam. His muscles ached from lying absolutely still for hours, his stomach rumbled due to lack of food, and his throat was dry because he refused to drink from his canteen.

Hobbs let his hand drop to the soggy ground and tried to estimate the number of troops streaming past. They were more than a battalion, probably more than a regiment and climbing toward a division.

Hobbs was a professional soldier who had volunteered for jump training and then for the Special Warfare School and finally for the unconventional warfare school. During the training, he had added a layer of muscle to his stocky frame. He was six feet tall and had weighed two hundred pounds when he had arrived in Vietnam. The stress of the war and the lack of good food had stripped nearly thirty pounds from his body, though he still looked robust. Hobbs had blond hair that was so light that he had taken to using camouflage paint on it before the mission. His once-round face now looked angular.

He slipped to the rear, off the ridge and into the shadows of the dense vegetation. He could smell the rotting leaves of the jungle floor. Around him he could hear the buzz of mosquitoes and the flicker of gnats as they darted at his eyes.

In the deep shadows he detected a movement as Corporal Richard Quinn shifted. Quinn's hair was brown and his eyes were blue. The tropical sun had tanned him deeply, giving him the look of a Chicano. He was smaller than Hobbs, and thin, having lost weight during an illness he'd contracted just after arriving in-country. The military diet and jungle conditions had never given him the chance to gain back any pounds. His heavy beard made it obvious he had spent several days in the jungle.

Quinn was the RTO and was crouched by the radio now, next to the smooth trunk of a teak tree. Using hand signals, Hobbs told Quinn to pick up the radio. He then gestured toward the trees where he knew that Privates David Rogers and Martin Lawrence were hiding. They appeared a moment later.

Rogers was a small man, only slightly larger than the Vietnamese. His dark hair hung straight, and from a distance he could have blended into the local population. His face was round and his eyes looked slanted, but they were a light gray. He had delicate features and a number of shrapnel scars.

Beside him was Lawrence, who was almost his exact opposite, a huge man with light-colored skin and hair. He had excelled in high school football, and he probably would have received a college scholarship if he hadn't twisted his knee late in his senior year. The colleges suddenly lost interest, but not the Army. They were only too happy to draft him.

Without saying a word, Hobbs ordered Lawrence to take the point. Quinn would be next, then Hobbs and finally Rogers. They would work their way back to Vietnam, only a klick or so to the west, and then try for a helicopter pickup. Failing that, they would attempt to raise net control to pass on their information, and if that failed, too, they could retreat to the Lang Vei Special Forces camp.

They slipped silently through the jungle like a fog, barely in sight of one another, which sometimes meant they were no more than two or three feet apart. Each of them stepped carefully, watching for trip wires and booby traps, but also trying to keep from leaving signs that they had been there. A broken twig, a limp blade of grass or a scuff mark in the rotting vegetation could tell the VC that Americans had been near within the hour.

But the jungle also became a friend. The thick veils of lacy ferns, the broad-leaved trees and the hanging vines combined to hide them from the enemy. If the going was rough, finding the enemy was even rougher. Now that Hobbs and his men wanted to get out, that curtain of vegetation, an almost solid wall of plants, bushes and trees, hid them from the prying eyes of the Vietcong and the North Vietnamese.

The jungle was both friend and foe, a sanctuary from the enemy, and a place where a thousand different deaths stalked a man. There were snakes that could kill in seconds and there were traps that took days to kill. There were rats, some the size of cats, that carried rabies, and there were huge insects that might not have the power to kill but could make you wish they did.

Making conditions worse, if that was possible, was the effort of keeping quiet, of trying to walk carefully and not make any noise that would alert the enemy. There was a trick to it, but it strained the leg muscles, causing knots and aches so bad that it was nearly impossible to keep from screaming. Sweat, whether caused by the sun where it could penetrate the thick canopy or by the humidity that hung in the jungle air like an invisible fog, stained and then soaked the uniform, turning it black. Salt rings formed and progressed outward as the body fought the heat and humidity. Cotton formed in the mouth, demanding water, but there was only so much available, and it had to be saved for later.

Hobbs kept the men moving, even though they had spent three days in the jungle, sleeping only fitfully at night as they waited for the enemy to find them. Each man was tired, dirty and hungry, but although each yearned to be clean again, they were glad to be dirty in the jungle. The first night there they always suffered the most from the insects. By the second day the accumulation of dirt and sweat kept the insects away. The next man might smell bad, but that odor combined with the other odors of the jungle to hide him. To bathe in a bomb crater or a stream was to invite the enemy to attack. The layers of dirt and sweat that itched were also protective coloration necessary for survival.

All this passed through Hobbs's mind as he edged carefully among the plants. There was a crash to the right that he ignored. One of the big, broad leaves of a tree had filled with water and had finally spilled it. Monkeys swung through the trees around them, and a few birds darted among the branches. A good sign. The birds were bright splashes of color that stood out vividly against the greens and blacks of the vegetation.

In front of Hobbs, Lawrence was crouched on one knee near the rotting trunk of a fallen tree, his rifle cradled in his arms as he stared into the distance. Quinn was to his left, watching the jungle in that direction. Hobbs approached slowly and knelt next to Lawrence. He didn't have to ask why he had halted. The evidence was in front of them.

It was a small clearing created by a bomb. The center was a red hole with the dirt folded back, crushing the grass and bushes. The trees, blown down by the concussion, were scattered, spreading outward like the spokes of a wheel. At the lip of the crater were four men, two in black pajamas and two wearing khaki. All four had AK-47s and all four wore chest pouches holding their spare magazines. A splashing came from the bottom of the crater and a fifth man, dressed only in black shorts, emerged dripping.

There was a babble of voices and one of the men pointed, laughing as the man in the crater stumbled and fell. He scrambled up the mud-slick side on his hands and knees, and once he was out, another of the men stripped and entered the crater.

Slowly, cautiously, Hobbs raised the back of his hand to touch his lips as he kept his eyes focused on the enemy around the crater. He felt the sweat drip, running down his back and sides. Insects buzzed around him and monkeys chattered overhead. There was a peacefulness to the scene that belied the location.

Hobbs took a deep breath and exhaled slowly. His eyes burned from lack of sleep. His muscles ached from the strain of moving through the jungle without making noise and without leaving traces. It felt good to crouch there in the shade of the jungle, watching the enemy.

He knew they should get out now while the five soldiers were bathing. He glanced to the right where Quinn knelt. He could barely see the man, concealed among the bushes and trees and patches of light and dark. Hobbs didn't want to move; they needed the few moments of rest. He didn't want to kill the VC, because that would alert the enemy to their presence.

He was about to back off, away from the artificial clearing, when there was a long, sustained burst from an M-16. The rounds poured from the jungle and slammed into the dirt of the crater, creating geysers of dark red dust. The five bathers caught in the hail of fire, jerked and danced and collapsed. One tried to get up, his hand pawing at the ground, but a single shot took him in the head, exploding it like a ripe melon.

There was sudden quiet. The insects were gone and the monkeys had stopped their chattering. The sound seemed to have an aftershock, a quiet, distant popping that was almost like the echoes of the gunfire, and yet different, unreal.

Hobbs lifted his weapon and snapped off the safety but didn't fire. He watched the men at the crater, sprawled in the grass and on the dirt, unmoving. Splotches of red stained their clothes and the dirt around them, turning it into thick mud.

Without a word to the others, Hobbs stood and moved toward the bodies, his eyes focused on them. At the edge of the clearing he hesitated, his weapon held in both hands, the barrel pointed at the dead men. He took a step forward, stopped and then hurried toward the dead. At the first body he crouched and picked up the AK-47.

The man's eyes were still open but were glazed over, looking almost like the glass eyes used in stuffed animals. Hobbs had seen enough blank, staring eyes to know that he was looking into the face of a dead man. A dead man who might not have reached his twentieth birthday, who might have had a wife, and probably had brothers and sisters. A man whose family would never know what had happened to him.

Quinn and Lawrence swept out of hiding to check the bodies of the others. Hobbs shot them a glance, but both shook their heads, telling him that they hadn't fired. Rogers remained in the jungle.

Hobbs stepped closer to the crater and looked down into it. One of the enemy soldiers was at the bottom, floating facedown. His blood was turning the surface of the water a bright crimson.

"Throw the other bodies into the crater," Hobbs whispered.

Quinn slung his weapon and picked up one of the dead VC. He tossed him over the edge of the crater so that the body slid down the dirt, stopping just short of the water. Lawrence did the same with another.

While the two of them worked at concealing the dead, Hobbs moved toward the jungle, halting at the edge and staring into the kaleidoscopic pattern of greens, browns and blacks until Rogers revealed himself.

"Why?" Hobbs asked.

Rogers shrugged, as if he didn't have the answer.

"You could have compromised the mission." Hobbs turned and saw that Quinn had disappeared over the edge of the crater. A moment later he reappeared and nodded. The knees of his uniform were stained a rusty brown. Hobbs didn't know if the color was from the blood of the dead or the dirt of the crater.

Hobbs said, "Rogers, take the point."

Rogers turned and moved into the jungle. As he did, Quinn joined him. Lawrence followed and Hobbs brought up the rear. As he stepped back into concealment, he realized that the whole incident had taken ten minutes, if that.

THE MARINE RECON PATROL moved quietly along the slopes of Hill 881 North. The enemy was out there. They knew it because the intelligence reports for the past three weeks told them that the enemy was moving into position to hit the combat base. Thousands of Vietnamese, under the command of General Vo Nguyen Giap, were massing. Tens of thousands whose job it was to turn Khe Sanh into another Dien Bien Phu.

The point man, Corporal Amos Hanratty, clutched the stock of his M-16 so tightly that his fingers were white. The weight of his flak jacket and steel pot was a burden that he refused to give up. He carried extra ammunition, and four canteens to fight the effects of the tropical sun and the high humidity, which could kill a man as easily as the poisonous snakes and the Vietcong booby traps.

Hanratty was typical of the Marines at Khe Sanh. Just out of high school, he'd joined the Marines to avoid the draft, and because he thought the Marines were the best and he wanted to be the best. During basic the Marines had put muscle on his thin body, and had fattened him up. The baby fat on his face had melted away, leaving his features sharp—a small nose, thin lips and a pointed chin. The outdoor life, the exercise and the scarcity of candy had cleared his complexion.

As he moved now, stepping carefully, feeling his way along with his foot, testing the ground almost like a swimmer about to dive into a cold pool, his head swiveled back and forth. He was looking for signs that the enemy was close. He was listen-

ing for the sudden sound that would signal the beginning of
the enemy attack.

Strung out behind Hanratty were the other eight men of the
patrol, each man a picked veteran who'd spent six months or
more in Vietnam and who had survived jungle patrols and enemy mortars. They were no longer rosy-cheeked youngsters
spirited from high school to Marine boot camps by recruiting
sergeants who filled their heads with stories of heroics on the
beaches of Iwo Jima, Tarawa and Pelileu. They were men who
had tasted war and understood what it was all about.

Hanratty stopped once, glanced right and left and thought
about the water on his hip. It was too soon after the last drink.
He tried to swallow the cotton that had formed in his mouth
and continued forward.

The thick jungle opened up slightly, making travel easier,
but the humidity seemed to be trapped by the thick canopy
overhead. Hanratty felt the sweat bead and drip but ignored
it. Instead, he watched a lizard scramble across a huge leaf and
disappear into a shadow.

Charlie was out there. He knew it. He could feel their eyes
on him as he walked around the trunk of a giant teak, stepping over the gnarled roots that stuck up through the thin earth
of the jungle floor like arthritic fingers.

The explosion was behind him—a loud, flat bang. Hanratty dived to the right and rolled over so that he was next to
the tree's root system. The rippling fire of an RPD tore
through the jungle over his head. The rounds slammed into
the trunk of the tree. Shredded bark and bits of leaf rained
down.

There were more explosions. Chicom grenades popped and
American grenades exploded. The hammering of the RPD
was joined by the chattering of M-16s and AK-47s. The
rounds snapped through the jungle, ripping the leaves from
bushes.

Hanratty poked the barrel of his weapon over the top of the
root but didn't shoot. He stared into the patches of black and
green, searching for the enemy. The sound rebounded from

the hills and the jungle, confusing him, making it hard to spot the Vietcong of the ambush. Behind him were the shouts of his fellow Marines, trying to organize the defense.

The firing tapered off. Hanratty rolled to the right again and then crawled over the top of the root, dropping to the ground. Oddly he noticed the odor of the ground, a musty, dirty smell, like that of an open grave.

Hanratty crawled around and managed to get into a sitting position, his back against the tree that separated him from the enemy ambush. He hit the release button to drop the still-loaded magazine from his weapon, jammed the fresh one home and chambered a round. Then he didn't move. He tried to think of what to do but couldn't force himself into action.

The rest of the patrol was shooting again. The sergeant was shouting, directing the fire of the men, but Hanratty couldn't get back to them. He heard commands in Vietnamese, as the enemy tried to overrun the tiny patrol.

Hanratty was about to move when he caught a flicker to the left. He whirled and fired, holding his finger on the trigger, emptying the magazine. When the bolt locked back, he dived to the ground again and rolled onto his left side. With his thumb he dropped the spent magazine and slammed another into the well.

Before he could get the round chambered, there was a loud warbling sound overhead and the jungle erupted. The explosion shook the ground and threw dirt into the air to rattle back to earth. White-hot shrapnel spun across the jungle floor and buried itself in trees already thick with it.

Hanratty tried to bury himself between the huge roots of the tree, keeping his face pressed against the soft, moist soil. It filled his mouth and nostrils, but he didn't care. He wanted to scream as the mortar crews at one of the bases kept dropping rounds on the suspected enemy positions.

The explosions walked through the jungle, smashing trees and bushes and people. The shrapnel ripped at the leaves and branches, cutting them off and dropping them onto the ground until the jungle looked like the scene of a ticker tape parade.

The firing from the RPD ended abruptly, and the AKs fell silent as the mortar rounds continued to fall.

And then they stopped, too. The jungle was left in silence until the voice of the gunnery sergeant cut through. "Point! You okay?"

Hanratty climbed to his feet slowly, listening to everything around him. Then, like a man hunched against a stiff breeze, he ran back to where the rest of the patrol waited. He hurtled over the body of one Marine, whose weapon was broken in half and whose cleaning kit lay in the dirt near his outstretched hand.

Among his fellows again, Hanratty hit the dirt. The lifeless body of another Marine lay near him, with blood on the flak jacket and the helmet and the stock of his rifle.

"You okay?" the sergeant asked again.

"I'm fine," Hanratty said. "How badly we been hurt?"

"Three dead and two wounded," said the sergeant. He grinned then and collapsed facedown on the jungle floor.

The RTO lay near him and picked up the handset. He jammed it up against his ear and began mumbling into it. Hanratty crawled toward him and waited until he had finished with the radio traffic. Then he asked, "Aren't we going to sweep the ambush site?"

"You go fucking right ahead," the man said. "I'm going to wait until we get some more people in here."

Hanratty crawled away and found Davis sitting near another tree, his hands around his calf. Blood stained his fingers and clothes and his face was a pasty white, but he was grinning.

"I'm getting the fuck out of here before it happens," he announced. "You assholes will be pinned down and shot at and I'll be drinking beer and eating steaks in fucking Japan."

Hanratty tried to see the wound, but Davis wouldn't let him. He kept babbling about getting out of Vietnam. His weapon lay near him, broken in half. The cleaning rod was in the dirt beside it.

"What happened?" asked Hanratty.

"Fucker jammed on me. Burned through the magazine too fast and the fucker jammed. I about had it cleared when I got hit. Fucking million-dollar wound."

Hanratty didn't know whether to congratulate Davis or to console him. Instead he asked, "That hurt?"

"Fuck, yes, it hurts."

Sweat was rolling down Davis's face and soaking into his uniform collar. He rocked back then and said, "I'm the fuck outta here and that's all that counts."

Hanratty moved on, suddenly afraid that the VC would be back to overrun them. The mortars might have driven them from the field, but that wasn't likely. Charlie could be waiting for the opportunity to ambush the relief, or he could be trying to get into position to kill the rest of them. No one seemed too concerned about it, with the sergeant lying facedown on the trail.

Then, in the distance, came the pop of rotor blades. Davis turned to look, though the jungle hid nearly everything. "Fucking evac chopper."

As the aircraft came closer, there was a burst of fire, heavy fire from a hidden 12.7 mm antiaircraft gun. A second burst and then nothing. The chopper flashed past, suddenly stopped in midair, then dived toward the ground. Someone yelled, "Let's go! Let's go!"

Hanratty grabbed Davis under the arm and helped him to his feet. He retrieved the M-16, leaving the cleaning kit in the dirt. Together the two of them ran and hobbled toward the helicopter, which had landed in a tiny clearing twenty yards away. As they burst out of the jungle, Hanratty realized that it wasn't a Marine helicopter, but an Army chopper.

They ran toward it, and Hanratty helped Davis into the cargo compartment. Almost as soon as Hanratty's foot hit the skids, the pilot sucked in pitch and the chopper rose a few feet off the ground. The rotor wash flattened the grass and sucked up the loose debris, spinning it around, creating a miniature storm.

Then they were climbing slowly into the sky. The trees became bushes and they were out of the jungle, skimming the canopy. It flashed by, a green blur that had the texture of sculptured carpet.

Firing came from below, as the enemy tried to knock the chopper out of the air, but the rounds weren't close. Davis sat on the troop seat, hunched over so that he could hold the battle dressing in place. Hanratty looked into the faces of the dead men and noticed that they looked the same as the enemy dead: pasty skin and glazed-over eyes, blood on the uniforms and holes in their bodies where there should have been none.

He glanced over toward the sergeant, who sat on the gray metal deck, blood dripping from his elbow onto the floor. The man grinned and held up one thumb, telling Hanratty that he was getting out, too. Getting out before the enemy came rolling out of Laos, shooting and shouting and trying to kill every Marine at the Khe Sanh combat base.

In that moment Hanratty thought about putting a round through his own foot. Firing just once. A flash of pain and then no more worries. Out to Japan and maybe out of the Crotch, because he wouldn't be able to walk right. Not after taking a round in the foot.

But he didn't do it. He couldn't see it. Somehow shooting himself in that fashion would be letting down his friends—those who were stationed in the tiny outposts on the hills around the Khe Sanh plateau, and those who were at the combat base. It wasn't fair to them, nor was it fair to the poor SOB who'd have to take his place. Hanratty wasn't stupid. He'd watched as Marine after Marine arrived at the base, filling it up until many had no place to sleep, some had no place to sit and a few had no place to stand. The military was getting ready for a big push. Everyone knew it was coming and everyone wanted to get out and miss it, but none of them was willing to shoot himself to do it.

At least not yet.

3

WHITE HOUSE
SITUATION ROOM

Lockhart sat in a long, dark hallway, a briefcase holding the latest classified material from Khe Sanh on his lap. He watched as men, civilians and military, entered the situation room. When the President appeared, Lockhart stood, but the man paid no attention to him. Lockhart sat down again and kept his eyes on the carpet at his feet. Even with the air-conditioning, he was sweating. It wasn't every day that a lieutenant colonel had the kind of information that could pull the President of the United States from meetings and the general staff from their homes.

Without looking Lockhart fiddled with the clasp on the briefcase and wondered again if he had jumped to conclusions. His boss, and his boss's boss, and finally General Wheeler had decided that the information had to be given to the President as quickly as possible. But in the final analysis it was Lockhart's butt on the line.

He wanted to pace but he had been told to have a seat and wait. He wished he could get something to drink, preferably something strong, but he would have settled for water. His stomach was tumbling, and he told himself to relax. It wasn't the first time he'd had to brief important people. He'd ap-

peared on Capitol Hill several times, had briefed foreign dig-
nitaries, military leaders and even the Vice President once.

The difference was that in all those other cases, he'd been
asked to appear; this time he had initiated the meeting. It was
the information that he'd gotten from the message center that
had prompted him to make a half-dozen phone calls.

Finally he couldn't sit there any longer. He stood up and
glanced at his shoes, which gleamed like black mirrors. His
uniform fit perfectly, and his ribbons, a bit of bright color,
were stacked above his left breast pocket, topped by his jump
wings. His tie was choking him and there was dampness under his arms.

The door of the situation room opened and a civilian in a
light gray suit with a dark tie and white shirt leaned out.
"Colonel Lockhart, we're ready for you."

Lockhart plucked his briefcase off the chair and took a deep
breath. He stepped through the door, and was surprised by the
interior of the room. It wasn't quite what he had expected.

There were bright lights recessed in the ceiling. One wall was
covered with a huge map of Khe Sanh made from aerial pho-
tographs. The Marine combat base was outlined in bright red.
The smaller outposts on Hill 881 North, Hill 881 South and
Hill 861 were also marked. The town of Khe Sanh and the
Special Forces camp at Lang Vei were marked in blue. Route
9 looked like a long red line.

In front of the map was a podium, which faced the long table surrounded by military officers and civilian leaders, many
of whom Lockhart recognized from their news photos. No one
bothered to introduce him to anyone, and Lockhart knew
better than to ask. The President, dressed in a dark suit, sat
at the head of the table, with piles of file folders and reports
spread out in front of him. Behind him was an American flag
and the Presidential flag.

Each of the others had a single leather folder in front of him.
They sat quietly as Lockhart entered and walked toward the
podium.

The President looked at Lockhart. "Whenever you're ready, Colonel," he said.

Lockhart retrieved the classified documents from his briefcase and set them on the podium. He straightened them out, leafed through them, then turned to look at the map. He knew he was keeping the President of the United States waiting, but he wanted to have everything ready.

"Colonel," General Wheeler prompted.

"Mr. President, General Wheeler, gentlemen, we have come into possession of information that suggests a major buildup of enemy forces is taking place in the northern regions of South Vietnam."

"Colonel, we already know that," said the President. "Don't waste our time with the bullshit."

"Yes, sir," Lockhart said. "Earlier today, Vietnam time, a North Vietnamese soldier, a member of the 325th C Division, walked out of the jungle and surrendered to our Marines at Khe Sanh. Lieutenant Tonc then proceeded to tell the Marines that a massive attack was going to be directed at their combat base."

"Damn!" the President said.

"Normally we wouldn't take the word of one man as the truth," Lockhart went on. "The North Vietnamese and the Vietcong would be unlikely to give their whole battle plan to such a low-ranking officer. Or rather, that is what we believe. But in the past few weeks there has been a considerable buildup of enemy forces in the hills around Khe Sanh. Marine and Special Forces patrols have been making contact with the enemy almost within sight of the wire of their camps."

General Wheeler interrupted them. "Mr. President, you might remember that a similar incident of an informant defecting occurred just prior to the North Vietnamese attack on the Special Forces camp at Dak To in the Central Highlands. At that time the conventional wisdom was that it was some kind of a blind, but the attack came off just as the defector claimed it would."

Lockhart waited until all eyes were back on him, then said, "The defector also claimed that plans were being made for countrywide attacks on the eve of the Lunar New Year."

"I don't want to hear that shit," the President snarled. "I want to know what's happening at Khe Sanh. I don't want another damned Dien Bien Phu."

"If I might, Mr. President," said General Wheeler, "we're not in the same position as the French at Dien Bien Phu. Unlike them, we hold the high ground, and Khe Sanh isn't in a valley, but on a plateau. Unlike the French, we have air power to call on, as well as artillery support. There are thousands of reinforcements available in the immediate vicinity. We can resupply by air."

"I've heard all that before, General," said the President "and it doesn't make me feel any better. The French didn't think they had a thing to worry about, either, and they were finally forced to surrender."

"But, Mr. President—"

President Johnson held up his hand and stared at the chairman of the Joint Chiefs of Staff. "You think about this, General. What if those little bastards pull it off and overrun the Marines at Khe Sanh? Six thousand Marines dead—"

"To do that the enemy would have casualties exceeding ten or twelve thousand dead—"

The President leaned forward, his face suddenly red. "Don't you ever, *ever*, interrupt me again, General," he roared. "Never again. Now, I don't give a shit if there are twenty thousand dead Vietnamese, if we lose that base. I don't care if there are a hundred thousand, because it would mean the end to all we're doing here."

"Mr. President," Wheeler said. "We're not going to lose the base. The enemy can't overrun it. Operation Niagara alone could stop it."

"I'm not interested in your assessment of air power, General," the President said. "At least not now." He turned back to Lockhart. "Colonel."

Lockhart flipped through his notes, not knowing what he was supposed to say. Obviously, and logically, the President and the chairman of the Joint Chiefs would know everything that he knew, with the exception of the very latest intelligence data. He glanced at the last page of the report. "There is, of course, a way to check the accuracy of the information provided by Lieutenant Tonc."

"Yes, yes," General Wheeler snapped. "We have the reconnaissance planes and patrols out. We have sensors in the area that will tell us about troop movements. We have the information gathered when those six men probed the Khe Sanh perimeter a couple of weeks ago."

"Yes, General, all that's true," said Lockhart, "but there's an even quicker, simpler way. Lieutenant Tonc said that the first assault would be made on Hill 861 just after midnight. If that happens, then we'll know."

HOBBS DIDN'T LIKE IT. True, they had gotten away with killing the Vietnamese soldiers at the bottom of the crater. The sudden rush of enemy soldiers hadn't taken place, and after an hour he was convinced that they were in the clear. At least from that.

But the enemy was still everywhere. Thousands of them prowling the hills and jungles as they slipped closer to the combat base at Khe Sanh. Night fell, but Hobbs refused to stop. They couldn't afford to stop now. They had to get out.

He had hoped that with the setting of the sun it would be cooler, but the heat didn't dissipate. The heat, combined with the humidity that was dripping from the trees and bushes, made movement through the jungle feel like sneaking through a sauna wrapped in wet towels. His uniform was soaked through. He had finished all the water in one canteen and refused to drink from any of the others. It was too early for that.

The darkness had slowed them. They had to move carefully, avoiding the trees and bushes and trying to miss the booby traps. Hobbs kept them off the trails and away from the paths, routing them through the thickest parts of the jungle, where the undergrowth grabbed at them and tore at their clothes. He did it because he was convinced that the enemy wouldn't be there. The enemy now controlled the jungle trails and paths. To avoid them was the mission.

Ahead of him was the black shape of the point man, Quinn, little more than a moving lump against the blackness of the jungle. Hobbs watched him and stayed close to him as they continued to penetrate deeper into South Vietnam, deeper into the protection of the thick undergrowth.

Quinn stopped periodically, using his compass to maintain the heading. At the moment they weren't worried about pinpoint navigation. The trick was to get into South Vietnam and then turn south until they came to Route 9. From there it would be easy to find either the Special Forces camp at Lang Vei or the Marine base.

But the sudden, quiet rattling of equipment cut through the night like a knife. Hobbs went to one knee, frozen, as he listened. He heard a rustling of cloth against the leaves of the trees and knew they weren't alone.

The Americans halted, then collapsed in on the center, forming a loose ring, turning their backs to the inside. No one spoke or moved, except to flick off the safeties of their M-16s. Hobbs touched the grenades on his harness. A grenade was the best weapon at night. It didn't give away the position with a muzzle-flash, and it didn't require the accuracy of a rifle bullet.

He stared into the night, trying to see out of the corners of his eyes. The low-hanging clouds of the monsoons blotted out the little light from the moon and stars, and there was no random light on the ground. Only the Marine combat base had multiple lights. It was so bright there that the Special Forces called it Coney Island.

But there was also an arrogance in all that light. It said that the Marines didn't fear the Vietcong and North Vietnamese gunners. With their own artillery they were ready to counter anything the enemy could throw at them.

In the jungle it was the opposite. There was no light, but the enemy no longer moved with the quiet of a phantom. He was so confident in his presence, in his numbers, that he didn't fear the American patrols. It was an odd contrast, and the irony wasn't lost on Hobbs.

He crouched in the thick undergrowth, in the wiry elephant grass, and studied the shifting shapes around him. The shadows danced and swayed, giving the jungle a life it didn't normally possess. There were the animals, lizards, snakes and monkeys, and even tigers roaming the hills, looking for food and shelter. Insects filled the night with their buzzing and chirping. The sounds of that jungle life concealed the quiet movements of the Vietcong as they slipped closer to their targets in the hills around the combat base.

Hobbs wished he could call for a helicopter evacuation, but knew it was too late. The choppers wouldn't be able to get in because of the dark and the low clouds. There was no place for them to land, and with the enemy suddenly as thick as fleas, they couldn't use the jungle penetrator. A hovering chopper would be shot out of the air in a matter of seconds.

Hobbs stayed where he was, a knee on the soft, moist jungle floor, his head slowly turning right and left as he tried to detect enemy movement. He reached up to finger the hilt of the knife taped to his harness near the grenades. His fingers were wet, his hand slippery.

There was nothing he could do about the enemy now. He could only crouch there and listen as they worked their way closer to his tiny patrol. In the dark the two forces could pass within inches of each other and never know it. That was if he got the breaks. Now that he and his men weren't moving, the enemy could walk over them and not know it. The jungle hid so much from everyone.

The enemy was coming closer. Now Hobbs could smell burning tobacco as someone smoked. He had told his men that the danger from a cigarette wasn't the tiny glowing orange tip, because that could be effectively concealed, but the smell of it. Nonsmokers could detect the odor over long distances, and in the jungle, smoking was like singing out loud or lighting a beacon. It was one of the quickest ways to let the enemy know your position.

There was a quiet burst of laughter and then a hushed voice giving orders in Vietnamese. Hobbs looked in the direction of the sounds, but saw only the black shapes of the trees and bushes and the blacker smudge of the jungle. Nothing to see and very little to hear. But the sounds meant that Charlie was close and that Charlie felt safe in the jungle. That wasn't a very good sign for the Americans, either on Hobbs's patrol or at the combat base at Khe Sanh.

ARMY SPECIAL FORCES Captain MacKenzie K. Gerber had known all along that hanging around in Saigon, in places where he could be found easily, was a mistake. In the Army, when you were off duty, you got out, because there was always someone looking for warm bodies to fill out a patrol or detail, and if they found you, you were volunteered.

Gerber, a tall, slender man just over thirty, was feeling relatively safe because he was a captain, had ignored the unwritten law, and now found himself wearing clean fatigues, a fresh shave and sitting in a large conference room that at least had air-conditioning. He sat there quietly, taking in his surroundings and wishing he had listened to Sergeant Anthony B. Fetterman when the diminutive master sergeant had suggested they catch a flight to Vung Tau. There was nothing pressing in Vung Tau except white beaches and the deep blue waters of the South China Sea. They could have spent the day in the sun, watching the bikini-clad girls romp in the surf. Now he sat with twenty-five other men, waiting for a briefing.

It wasn't that he could have gotten out of the briefing altogether, even if he had been in Vung Tau. Eventually the Army would have caught up with him. It was just that he wouldn't have had to be there at that moment.

The conference room was one of the finest he had seen during his latest tour. Paneled in dark wood, with watercolors of local scenes hung on the walls, it demonstrated that the

American officer corps knew how to spend taxpayers' money.
The massive mahogany conference table gleamed under the
recessed ceiling lights. High-backed chairs ringed the table,
and there were leather folders with notepads in front of many
of the chairs. The low-ranking men had been told that those
were reserved for the colonels and generals who would be arriving for the briefing.

At one end of the room was a blackboard, a bulletin board
and an American flag that had been tucked into the corner. At
the opposite end was a slide projector on a small table. A sergeant in a khaki uniform sat near the projector, jealously
guarding a tray of slides.

"Told you we should have gotten out of here," said Fetterman, leaning close to Gerber.

Gerber turned to look at Fetterman. The master sergeant
was relaxed, looking as if he was about to go to sleep. During
his years in the military, Fetterman had learned how to use the
random and sometimes lengthy periods of inactivity to relax.
He could sleep standing up, waiting for his stick to tumble
from the rear of a cargo plane, if he had to.

Before Gerber could respond, the door flew open and a
lieutenant who looked as if he had arrived in-country sometime earlier that day yelled, "Ten hut!" His voice was high and
strained.

The generals swept into the room, almost in formation.
They peeled off and slipped into the chairs that had been reserved for them. The commander took his place at the head of
the table and waved a hand. "Be seated, gentlemen."

As everyone sat down, the general said, "This briefing will
cover the current buildup of enemy forces throughout South
Vietnam, though the emphasis will be on the two provinces
just south of the DMZ and east of Laos. Colonel Miller, if you
please."

Miller was a tall, thin man with a receding hairline and a
sunken chest. He was deeply tanned, from afternoon tennis
at the Cercle Sportif, not from patrols in the field. He held
several file folders, the top one with a red cover and Secret

stamped on it in large, black letters. As he moved to the blackboard, the slide projector was turned on. Miller pulled down the screen and watched as the sergeant in the khaki uniform focused the first slide.

"Gentlemen, this briefing is classified secret and should not be discussed outside the confines of this room."

With that said, Miller picked up a pointer and nodded once. The slide changed, focused and Miller began his briefing.

"What we have here," he said, "is a photograph of the central plateau just a couple of miles east of the Laos border. Surrounded by mountains, and along Route 9, is the Vietnamese city of Khe Sanh. A mile away, guarding Route 9 and the cities to the east, is the Khe Sanh combat base, home of nearly six thousand Marines. It's a target the enemy won't be able to resist."

The map faded and changed to a picture of the combat base seen from the air. And then that was gone, replaced by one of that corner of Vietnam showing the DMZ, Laos and the hills around Khe Sanh. Finally that was replaced by a map of all of South Vietnam.

"The general idea here has been that the enemy is concentrating troops in the Khe Sanh area for a massive push against the Marines. General Westmoreland and the staff here in Saigon have been preparing for this for the past several weeks. Plans are on the drawing board to support the Marines. Everything from massive air raids to tactical nuclear weapons is being considered."

Miller held up a hand and added hastily, "And that last will not be mentioned outside this room under the threat of court-martial. No one must know that such a contingency is being discussed."

Fetterman leaned over and whispered to Gerber, "Christ. The nukes would bring the whole world down on us."

Gerber nodded but thought that the use of a tactical nuclear weapon was preferable to having Khe Sanh overrun. Either event would be a political nightmare for the Administration.

"Now a battle developing in I Corps has little impact for us down here, except for the men moved north to support that battle. I could tell you the philosophy behind it, the desire to get into a massive battle with the enemy, but I'm sure that you all know the advantages of that. I'm also sure you agree that in that kind of battle, we'll come out on top."

There was a mumbling of agreement around the table. For months the conventional wisdom had been that the enemy, even when holding a numerically superior force, couldn't defeat the Americans. The defense of Dak To showed that. A huge enemy force had been held outside the camp and cut up by American firepower. Everything from air strikes to artillery barrages had been thrown at the attackers.

"Now," said Miller, "the reason you are all here is because of new rumors coming out of Khe Sanh." He consulted his notes unnecessarily, letting the tension in the room build. He was playing with the emotions of the men, working them as a barker would work a crowd outside a carnival tent. When he decided they were ready, he gave it to them with both barrels.

"A captured Vietcong soldier has told the intelligence unit at Khe Sanh that the battle shaping up there is only the beginning. They look to overrun everything there, including the Special Forces camp at Lang Vei, to open Route 9 and give them clear sailing to the coast."

Now Miller held up his hands to stop the men from talking. "As I said, that's only the beginning. The prisoner also told of attacks being launched throughout South Vietnam, attacks designed to cripple the South Vietnamese government and to allow the people to rise up, joining the Vietcong. The intention is to begin the revolution that will put the Communists in power."

There was a moment of quiet and then one of the men said, "We've heard all this before."

"And that's why you're all here now. According to the information, we have a week, ten days, to prepare. We have a week to learn the truth. Each of you will be sent out or are being asked to go out into the countryside to see what you can learn. Unofficially, of course.''

"Of course," said Fetterman.

"We'll need to have daily reports, and if you come up with anything hot, we'll need to know about that, too. Individual assignments will be discussed in a few minutes. If anyone has an idea, that will be the time to bring it up. Any questions?"

"Just one," said Gerber. "How reliable is the source at Khe Sanh?"

"Currently he holds the highest rating available. By midnight we'll know just how good he is."

4

AIR FORCE BRIEFING
ROOM DA NANG

Air Force Lieutenant Lloyd Whitmire sat in the back row of
the aircrew briefing room and wished the major would finish
talking so that he could get back to the club where the USO
was being held. Whitmire was a copilot on a C-130 and had
been in-country for just over three months. In that time he had
flown missions to bases all over South Vietnam, and a few into
Laos and Cambodia that no one cared to talk about.

Whitmire was a college graduate in his early twenties. At six-
one and 160 pounds he was taller than average, but didn't look
big. His black hair was longer than it should have been, so
everyone was always telling him to get it cut, which he refused to do. He tried to stay out of the sun because he burned
badly and easily. As usual, he was in a bad mood.

He was no longer paying attention to the briefing because it
was too hard to hear over the roar of the floor fans in the corners of the room. The briefing room had been closed up because of the nature of the briefing, and although the sun had
set earlier, heat still radiated from the tin roof, trapped by the
sandbags and the bamboo walls. Now the plywood shutters
had been closed so that the Vietnamese couldn't see into the
room or eavesdrop on the briefing.

The pilots sat in rows, facing a raised stage that held a screen. One officer sat in a chair directly in front of the stage, flipping the slides as the major talked. The major strutted in front of them, looking like a bantam rooster. He was a small, dark man in a tailored flight suit that showed the signs of a tropic environment.

Whitmire sat with his flight suit unzipped to the crotch. He didn't bother with a T-shirt, although regulations demanded it; it was just too damned hot for that. Sweat had soaked his hair, making it hang down his face. His uniform had dark stains on it. He wanted to get up and run out of the room, but the major would see him and another black mark would be added to his already bulging file. War certainly wasn't anything like they showed in the movies.

Whitmire caught the gaze of one of the flight leaders and sat up, leaning forward as if trying to hear what was being said. It wasn't as if they were being briefed on an upcoming mission. This was just a preliminary so that they would know what was happening in case they had to go.

"Marine Corps estimates put the absolute bottom line of supplies into Khe Sanh at 160 tons a day. Got that, men? The minimum is 160 tons, and that is only food and ammo. That gives us quite a task."

"Christ," Whitmire whispered to his aircraft commander, Bill Carson, "that's going to keep us flying all day long."

"They're bringing in planes from Japan and the Philippines to pick up the slack," said one of the men in front of him, looking over his shoulder.

Carson, an older man with nearly twenty years in the Air Force, shrugged. He was a shade under six feet tall, had salt-and-pepper hair and a potbelly that he fed beer as often as possible. He'd been around long enough not to worry about much of anything. He didn't have that long until retirement, when he could get out and find a real job. He wasn't sure he liked Whitmire. The kid just couldn't roll with the punches.

Whitmire shook his head and looked toward the window, which was still covered. As he'd walked toward the briefing, he'd seen the clouds forming overhead, suggesting that the monsoon season had arrived. They were low-hanging clouds that would make an approach into the mountainous regions around Khe Sanh next to impossible. Low-hanging clouds would keep them from landing, could keep them from even seeing the airfield.

With the roar of the fans, it was difficult to hear. With the heat and humidity, it was hard to concentrate. With the constant droning of the major, it was hard not to fall asleep. Whitmire sat up, opened his eyes wide and tried to focus on the screen, even though the briefing room was the last place he wanted to be.

As the major talked, Whitmire studied the slides and got a feel for what the combat base looked like. The runway was nearly east-west and laid out on the northern edge of the base. High hills to the north and west were fortunately held by the Marines. Whitmire saw enough to know that he wouldn't accidentally land at the wrong place. There weren't many other places to land around there, accidentally or otherwise.

Then his thoughts moved to the cute little raven-haired beauty in the USO troupe who had spent the greater part of one show smiling at him. She was a petite girl who sang sometimes and told a few jokes and who wandered among the GIs, flirting with them. She seemed to concentrate on him more than any of the others, though. He hadn't figured out whether she liked him or just liked the fact that he was the pilot on a C-130 and could help her and her friends get around in-country.

Not that it mattered, because he was going to milk it for everything it was worth. She was a real round eye, with real long hair and real long legs. She was taller than the majority of Vietnamese, and she smelled better than ninety percent of them. He really couldn't care what kind of shit the Marines at Khe Sanh had stepped into.

The major was now leaning on his podium, talking to them about the need for interservice cooperation, which Whitmire thought was a crock. The Marines had no use for the Air

Force, except when it was time for the Air Force to save their butts. Whitmire didn't give a shit about the military significance of the combat base or how many Vietcong and North Vietnamese were in the area. All he needed to know was which heading to fly for how long and what he had to take with him.

"If we need to make resupply into Khe Sanh," the major was saying, "we'll get a full intel update on the ground situation. As it stands now, there's no evidence of anything in the area larger than a 12.7 mm antiaircraft gun. On the ground they'll have mortars and rockets to contend with, but airborne it's just small arms."

The major stood there for a moment, his hands clasped together, and stared at the assembled pilots. He finally grinned. "If there are no questions..."

Whitmire was almost on his feet to leave when one of the pilots stood and asked, "How soon can we expect things to get ugly out there?"

"Inside a week," said the major. "Tomorrow I want to start a series of flights into Khe Sanh just to familiarize ourselves with the terrain around the base."

Whitmire rubbed a hand over his face and hoped that no one had any more questions. The major didn't move for ten, twenty seconds, then nodded once. "Check the scheduling boards before you leave the squadron area and get too drunk. That's all I have."

Whitmire jumped from his seat and nearly pushed two pilots out of the way to get to the door. He was outside in a moment, standing on the boardwalk that led from their area to the officers' club. As he stepped through, he had expected it to be cooler outside, but that wasn't the case. The humidity and heat seemed to be trapped around them without the benefit of a cooling breeze from the coast. Whitmire decided that with very little effort he could learn to hate Da Nang, the major and even the Air Force. He wished he'd never seen the ad in the paper offering money to attend classes. It was a lousy trick to play on an unsuspecting college student.

And to make his mood worse, by the time he got back to the club, the USO show had ended and the girl was gone. He decided that Sherman had been right. War was hell.

WHEN THE EVAC HELICOPTER landed, Hanratty thought he would spent the night in Khe Sanh and then be returned to Company K stationed on Hill 861. Instead, within an hour, he was back on the hill trying to get something hot to eat.

In the hours that he'd been gone, something had changed on the hill. No longer were the men walking around stripped to the waist, wearing shorts made from ragged jungle fatigue pants. They were all wearing flak jackets and steel pots and many were carrying M-14s. Too many of the M-16s had jammed at critical moments, leaving Marines undefended. The men had traded the new weapon for the heavier, older and more reliable M-14.

As soon as he jumped from the skids, the helicopter launched itself into the air, climbing out rapidly until it was only a speck ten thousand feet above him, well outside small-arms range.

Hanratty stood on the pad for a moment and then hurried along the wire, looking for his platoon sergeant. He was told that the enemy was going to hit them that night, sometime after midnight, and if he planned to eat or sleep, he'd better do it now because later he wouldn't have a chance.

Hanratty didn't need to be told twice. He headed down to the quarters he shared with another man. His bunker was a sandbagged wooden structure that had been dug into the ground. It had thick beams that formed the roof, which was covered with more sandbags. The wood had had to be flown in by helicopter, for the jungle around the camp had been shelled by so much artillery and bombed so often that the trees were full of shrapnel. It was nearly impossible to cut them down because the metal would foul the blades of the chain saws used by the engineers.

Hanratty ducked and crawled into the hot, humid darkness of the bunker. It smelled of sweat and dirt and rotting food. A dim light burned, a flashlight sitting on its end. His bunker-mate, PFC Jerry Rowley, lay on his poncho liner, which had been spread out on an air mattress.

Rowley looked up from the comic book he was reading. "You're back."

Hanratty dropped his steel pot onto the floor and sat down on it. He propped his M-16 against the sandbags and nodded. "I'm back."

Now Rowley sat up and picked up a can of Coke. He drank deeply. "I heard it was a rough one."

"Couple dead and a couple wounded."

"Shit. Who got killed?"

Hanratty unbuttoned his shirt and plucked a towel from the tangle that was his bed. He wiped himself down and tossed the towel onto the flooring, which was made of thick, rough-cut planks. The loose construction let the moisture drip through during the rainy season.

Hanratty gave him the names, and Rowley shook his head. "Didn't really know any of them."

"Good men," Hanratty said. He punched at the sandbags, causing a cascade of dirt to fall onto the floor. "Shit. Gooks won't come out and fight."

"Tonight," said Rowley. "They're supposed to come out and fight tonight."

"You believe that?" Hanratty leaned over and unlaced his boots. He pulled the laces out completely, then slipped off one boot. He experienced immediate relief as the pressure was reduced. His foot felt warm and was discolored by the boot, the wet and the climate. Hanratty retrieved his towel and wiped his foot carefully, making sure he dried between his toes.

Then he realized just how silly that was. Two hours ago he'd been thinking about shooting himself to get out of Khe Sanh, and now he was practicing the foot care that the Marines required. But it was true that he didn't want the foot to rot off. A bullet wound could earn him a medal, but foot disease would get him into trouble.

Rowley flipped the comic onto the stack of others in the corner of the bunker. He shook his head. "I think they've got it right this time." He waved a hand. "Red alert tonight and orders to wear our flak jackets and to carry our weapons everywhere."

"Sure," said Hanratty. He dropped his other boot onto the floor and wiped his right foot dry. Then he stretched out on his poncho liner, an arm over his eyes. "Sure," he said again.

Hanratty knew he had slept, although when Rowley reappeared and said, "Rise and shine," he had been awake for a while.

Without using a light, Hanratty dressed himself, then slipped into his flak jacket and put on his steel pot. Rowley was at the firing port, looking out over the strands of wire that guarded the camp from the enemy. In the distance a half-dozen flares swung down through the low-hanging clouds.

Hanratty ducked down and laced his boots. He touched the supplies of spare ammunition and grenades so that he would know where they were in case there was an attack. There was a single burst of firing, the heavy chug of a .50 as the crew cleared the weapon again. The red tracers flew out and bounced into the night sky or disappeared into the trees.

Then there was silence except for the distant boom of artillery or bombs. Hanratty leaned forward, an arm on the dirty sill of the firing port, staring into the night. A little light reflected off the wires, but there was no movement in the grass that ringed the camp. A black smudge that was the jungle seemed to be quiet, almost friendly.

Hanratty turned to say something to Rowley when the first mortar shells dropped into the field in front of him, mushrooming fire and flame. It was followed by hundreds more. Explosions blossomed all over the Marine camp as the rockets and mortar rounds rained down. Shrapnel whined overhead, burying itself in the sandbags of the bunkers, cutting through the fifty-five-gallon drums set up to catch the monsoon rains, slashing through the thin plywood of the aboveground structures. There were screams and shouts as more enemy shells fell. The ground in front of the firing port flashed and sparkled like a photographer gone berserk.

Hanratty ducked back away from the opening, then waited. Waited for the stray piece of shrapnel to slice open his flesh, spilling his blood. Waited for the round that would land on top of his bunker, caving it in. Waited for the rocket to hit it, destroying it and killing him.

The sound built: first just the sporadic explosions of the enemy weapons, joined by the truck horn that alerted the camp, then the almost continuous detonation of mortar shells, rockets and RPGs as the enemy gunners hammered at the Marines. The sound was continuous, punctuated by the mortar rounds that fell the closest. Over that sound was the noise of dirt and shrapnel rattling against the sides of the bunker.

The odor of gunpowder overwhelmed the stench that had previously permeated the bunker. It was an almost festive smell, reminiscent of Fourth of July fireworks, except these fireworks were deadly, designed not to entertain, but to kill. Hanratty risked a glance out the firing port, but the enemy wasn't visible. He knew that the attack wouldn't come until the artillery barrage stopped. Suddenly he didn't know if he wanted it to end, or to continue. He didn't know which was worse.

For thirty minutes the enemy artillery, joined by heavy machine guns, slammed into the hilltop. The jungle around the camp flashed like the coming of a monsoon storm. The booming of artillery was like the thunder.

And then suddenly it all stopped. There was a single, lone explosion and then silence. The calm before the storm. From the jungle came the sound of bugles and whistles and shouted commands. Someone at the command post called for American artillery, and the shells began to fall in the trees to the southwest.

Up the slope, ignoring the American mortar rounds and artillery barrage and the sudden firing of the machine guns, came a force of NVA soldiers. They swarmed from their cover, using the thick elephant grass to conceal the attack. The Dac

Cong led them to the wire, ignoring the withering fire from the Marines, ignoring the net of ruby-colored tracers flashing over them and ignoring the mortar shells that were falling among them. They came on, heads bent as they ran toward the wire. At the last moment they threw themselves onto the ground, and the wire exploded. As soon as their charges detonated, they were up and running for the next obstacle.

Hanratty, staying back from the firing port, raised his weapon and began to shoot. He fired single shots, picking his targets as they appeared in front of him. He burned through one magazine and replaced it with a second.

On the opposite side of the bunker Rowley was using his M-14. The muzzle-flash reached out through the firing port. The hot brass kicked out to the right and bounced up against the sandbags. Some of it fell onto the floor. The smell of cordite was thick.

Even with the firing from the Americans, the enemy came on. They threw satchel charges, destroying sections of the wire. Some of the sappers died, but others ran forward. They threw bamboo ladders across the punji moats and tried to scramble up the berm and into the camp.

With pathways through the wire cleared, the assault troops rushed across the open ground. Flares exploded overhead, lighting the scene with a sickly green light. Shadows danced and weaved, adding to the confusion. The firing increased into a roar. Enemy soldiers dropped, but there were more to take their places. AKs were hammering, answering the M-14s and M-16s. Mortar rounds began to drop on the far side of the camp.

Hanratty ducked away from the port and leaned against the sandbags. The breath rasped in his throat as he tried to get enough air. Sweat had soaked him and the air tasted foul, full of acrid smoke and a little dust. He swiped at the sweat on his face and then changed the magazine in his weapon. He felt bullets hit the bunker and saw a tracer burn through the firing port to embed itself in the sandbags. It sputtered and went out.

"Christ," yelled Rowley over the sound of the firing. "Christ on a stick."

Again Hanratty jammed the barrel of his weapon out the port and opened up. He snapped the selector switch to full-auto and began squeezing off the bursts.

"Fire low," he told himself. "Fire low."

When he finished the magazine, he reloaded and did it all again. There were hazy shapes, dark shapes, moving outside his bunker. The flares were burning out too fast now. Hanratty wanted to shout at them, order them to keep burning. He fired his weapon, aiming at the shapes as they dodged and jerked and dived. The enemy's weapons flashed. Green tracers and red. Explosions of fire and flame and sparks that blotted out the landscape. Shouting and shooting and bugles and whistles. Men were screaming and cursing and somewhere a group was belting out the Marine's Hymn, yelling the words so loud that they could be heard over the shooting.

The enemy was getting closer. The Marines in the trenches at the edge of the perimeter were overrun. The NVA jumped in with them, forcing them to retreat or to die. Firing there was intense and then it was sporadic. Men leaped clear, scrambling for safety toward the center of the camp.

Now the Vietnamese were closer, the shape of the AKs easy to see in the half-light of the flare-dominated landscape. A single sapper ran toward Hanratty, the satchel charge in his hand resembling a briefcase carried by a student. Hanratty fired at the man repeatedly, but he came on, seeming to have a charmed life. He stopped short and wound up to throw his weapon. Hanratty fired again, the bullet hitting the man and spinning him. He threw the satchel charge to the left and fell onto his face. An instant later an explosion filled the bunker with smoke and hid the enemy behind a cloud of dirt.

Rowley reached to the right and grabbed a bandolier. "Let's get the fuck out of here!"

Hanratty didn't want to leave. He felt safe in the bunker, protected from the hail of lead and steel that was crisscrossing the camp.

"We've got to get out!" yelled Rowley. He reached the back and scrambled into the night.

Hanratty stayed where he was for a moment. Another sapper loomed out of the smoke and dust, running at him, head down. Hanratty fired and fired. The enemy stumbled once and then went to his knees. He tried to throw his satchel charge, but there was no strength left in his arms. It exploded only a foot in front of him.

With that man dead, Hanratty followed Rowley. But the Marine lay on his side, his rifle not far from his fingers.

"Fuckers shot me," he gasped. "Shot me."

Hanratty grabbed Rowley under the arm and lifted him to his feet. He helped the wounded man run, remembering that he'd done the same thing earlier that day. It was suddenly getting hairy to be in the area.

They ran toward a knot of men who were firing at the enemy. Together they leaped over the barricade. Hanratty rolled onto his side and then scrambled around, aiming at the NVA. As he did, the bunker he had been defending exploded in a bright orange flash. The heat and sound rolled over them like a wave on the beach. Debris rained down.

Rowley sensed what had happened. "Shit! That was close."

Before either could catch his breath, the enemy came on, running across the open ground. They were shooting and shouting. One of the NVA was repeating over and over, "Put on your helmets, Marines. Here we come!"

Hanratty got to his knees and aimed at the swirling mass of the NVA. He kept firing at them, watching men fall, watching men die. He pumped out the rounds, not wanting to fire on full-auto. It burned the ammo too quickly and there wasn't that much left.

Around him was the whirling, roaring confusion of a full-scale battle. Shouting and shooting and bugles. Grenades and mortar rounds were exploding until it was almost impossible to hear single detonations. Tracers burned through the night. Artillery roared overhead to land on the southwest slope of the hill until it seemed that the entire mountain was on fire. No one could live in the inferno, and yet the enemy kept coming, pouring out of the trees and overrunning more and more of the base.

"Where's the sun?" demanded Hanratty, knowing that daylight would give them some advantage. "Where's the sun?"

But the sun didn't come up. There was only more of the enemy, trying to kill all the Marines before help could arrive.

5

KHE SANH COMBAT BASE

Dobson sat in his bunker, on the remains of an ammo crate, and stared into the darkness to the north. Directly in front of him was Tiger Tooth Mountain, now lost in the darkness. Off to the right was the small camp on Hill 950, and to the left were the twin camps on Hill 881 North and 881 South. Between them and the base was Hill 861, where two hundred Marines waited for the enemy to attack.

Ever since he had watched the single Vietcong soldier walk out of the shimmering heat at the end of the runway that afternoon, Dobson had been scared. He'd overheard enough of what the man had said to be scared. Coupled with the unusual orders that had been issued, Dobson knew things were about to pop.

On the thirteenth the order had been passed that every Marine had to wear his flak jacket and carry his weapon at all times. Then the movies had been canceled and the camp had been put on red alert. In the movies, red alert sounded good, but at a combat base it meant that enemy action was expected in the near future. The very near future.

Dobson crouched in his bunker, wondering if it would stop a mortar round or a rocket. He could almost feel the red-shot shrapnel ripping into him. He could almost feel the concussion of the explosion as the rockets detonated. The bunkers and flak jackets were designed to protect them from shrapnel, not from the effects of a direct hit.

Dobson squirmed around, peered into the night and then reached out to touch his rifle. Reassured, he continued to watch. He saw a few flashes on the hills, nothing spectacular at first, quiet pops of bright orange. For a moment he thought it was the Marines on 861 firing on the enemy.

He slapped the man beside him in the bunker on the shoulder and pointed. "Our boys are pouring it on someone."

The man sat up and glanced out. "Asshole. That's incoming. Our boys are taking it."

Dobson stared and realized he was watching the detonation of mortar rounds and rockets. "Maybe we should tell someone."

"Don't be an ass. Command knows it already. First thing they'd do is call in."

"Shit." Dobson watched as the mortars and rockets continued to slam into the camp. There was a continuous flash, bouncing all over the mountaintop as the rockets and mortar shells exploded. A flickering seen in the distance like a light about to burn out, leaping around on the darkened hilltop.

For thirty minutes Dobson watched the show, glad he was inside Khe Sanh with six thousand other Marines and not on a hilltop with only two hundred. Ten thousand, twenty thousand enemy soldiers were supposed to be hidden in the jungles around them, and Dobson couldn't understand how two hundred Marines were supposed to withstand an enemy attack if the enemy threw everything he had into the battle.

Then, suddenly, the guns at Khe Sanh began to fire. The artillery, brought in during the fall, opened up. Firing across the runway and over the bunker line, their shells began to fall on the slopes of Hill 861. It wasn't a normal barrage of five or six volleys, but a continuous flow of high explosives into the suspected enemy positions.

It was quite a show. Again Dobson was glad it was happening at Hill 861 and not outside the wires at Khe Sanh.

JERRY MAXWELL, dressed in his normal uniform of rumpled white suit, black tie pulled down and stained white shirt, sat in the communications center beneath the sprawling MACV compound in Saigon and listened to the radio messages. The room was air-conditioned and brightly lighted, filled with rows and rows of radios, teletype and secret communications gear, manned by a hundred technicians, some military, some civilian. The brightness, although artificial, gave the impression that it was the middle of the day. So did the level of activity; the technicians, clerks, watch officers and observers were all rushing around.

Although Maxwell's normal function was to control some of the MACV-SOG activities and to oversee the CIA's role in the conduct of the war, he had been drafted for radio watch. For him, a man who hated the tropics and tried to stay out of the sun as much as possible, it was good duty. He could sit at his battleship-gray desk near the front door, which resembled a bank vault more than anything else. It was designed to prevent the VC and the NVA from gaining easy access, if they ever got a foothold in Saigon.

Maxwell sat and watched the ebb and flow of activity, much as a sunbather might watch the ebb and flow of the tides. In front of him was a logbook where he was to note the time of each important message, along with a brief description of it—a simple, mind-numbing task that he had to perform once or twice a month, depending on the duty officer rotation system.

He rocked back in his chair, which squeaked every time he moved, and put his feet up on the desk. Overhead, the fluorescent lights burned. There was green tile on the floor. The cool air was filled with chirps and clicks and static bursts from the dozens of radios.

Maxwell laced his fingers behind his head and stared at the backside of one of the female operators. She wore a green sundress that left her back bare, and Maxwell was fascinated with the rippling of her muscles under the skin. He didn't know when he'd seen a more erotic back and was trying to figure out what it was that attracted him to it. Backs weren't supposed to be erotic.

He glanced to the right where a clock was ticking off the hours, and realized it would be a long time until his shift ended. He dropped his feet onto the floor and picked up the can of Coke sitting on his desk. It was empty.

Before he could get someone to go buy him another, an army Spec 4 stepped up to the desk. He was young, probably not out of his teens, heavily tanned from the sun and wearing jungle fatigues that had been starched. It was rare for starched fatigues to hold their creases in the humid climate of Saigon, but the humidity was all sucked out of the air-conditioned communications center. The man looked fresh, as if he had just broken starch.

"Yeah," said Maxwell, looking up.

"I think it's started, sir."

Maxwell wasn't sure what the man was talking about. "What's started?"

"Attack at Khe Sanh. Radio traffic has picked up quite a bit."

Maxwell knew that most transmissions from Khe Sanh would be on the relatively short-range FM band, but Air Force planes orbiting over Laos intercepted the signals, boosted them and retransmitted them to the communications center. It allowed the generals in Saigon to have instant communications with field commanders hundreds of miles away, enabling them to feel that they were part of the war.

Maxwell stood. "Take me to your station."

The young man turned and threaded his way through the complex of radio consoles and monitoring stations. He pulled out his chair and sat down, and then reached over to turn up the sound on his radio equipment.

Suddenly the walls of the communications center seemed to vanish. Maxwell was transported to the battlefront where the radio procedures were no longer precise. The language deteriorated and there were sounds of fighting in the background. Maxwell stared at the dancing needles on the vu meters and listened to the drama developing around Khe Sanh.

Over the radio came calls for artillery support, demands for assistarce and orders to the various units. There was shouting and cursing and calm responses. The detonation of mortar rounds and machine gun and small-arms fire drowned out some of the words.

"You have a feel for what's happening there?" asked Maxwell.

"One of the outposts around Khe Sanh is being hit hard by the VC and NVA. They want support. Some of the other bases have refused to fire their weapons, afraid they'll need the ammo when the enemy hits them."

"Details, man," snapped Maxwell. "I need specific details of the battle."

The clerk pulled a map from the stack of papers on his desk, studied it, then said, "I don't know which camp is being hit."

"It's the Marines and not the Special Forces at Lang Vei?"

"Oh, yes, sir. Radio procedures for the Marines differ slightly from the Army. It's the Marines, all right."

There was a burst of static and the demand came through. "I want the six, actual."

"Negative," a tense voice replied. "Six is down."

"Five actual."

"Five is down." There was a burst of machine gun fire and the crump of an exploding round.

"Christ, who's left up there?"

Maxwell looked at the Army specialist. "You stay here and monitor everything that goes down. Keep a list. If that position is overrun, you let me know immediately."

"Yes, sir."

Maxwell turned to his desk at the front of the room, leaned on it and felt his head spin. Earlier in the day he'd heard the reports that the VC and NVA were massing to move against the combat base at Khe Sanh, but he had assumed, like many others, that it would never really happen. The only thing he didn't know was if the enemy was swarming up Hill 861 or

881. Not that it mattered. He'd have to alert Westmoreland so that the general could make some decisions. Maxwell didn't envy him.

LOCKHART HADN'T LEFT his office in the Pentagon, because he knew that if anything happened in Vietnam as predicted, it would begin about noon. He didn't want to be out of the office when the message came through. He sat at his desk, thumbing through a copy of *Time* magazine. He wasn't concentrating on it, just looking at the pictures and wishing he could get the hell out of there before something happened.

He stood up and walked to the curtains where the window would have been if he'd had one, and stared at the cloth. Suddenly he was sick of the whole charade. Everything around him was make-believe—boys and girls pretending they were all grown-up and out to better the world in some mysterious fashion. Everything was for show, but there was no substance. It wasn't the best general who won battles; it was the one who fucked up the least. In the end that was what it boiled down to—you fucked up the least, and then convinced the historians that you'd known what you were doing at the time.

There was a tap at the door and a captain entered. The captain was a young man whose tour in Vietnam had been cut short by enemy gunners who had accidentally dropped their mortar round at the edge of a base camp. A fuck-up for them. Seconds before, the captain had decided he had to go to the radio room. Shrapnel had hit him in the arm, back and leg, causing a lot of superficial, but very bloody, damage. A fuck-up for him. Still, he'd earned a Purple Heart and a Bronze Star for Valor because he'd been wounded trying to do something brave. He'd also gotten a ticket home. Lockhart hated him and his fucking medals.

He glanced at the man and saw that his face was white, a chalky, sickening shade of white. Lockhart felt his belly go cold and his skin crawl. He actually felt the skin of his neck and back rippling, creating goose bumps. "What is it, Mansfield?"

"The worst, sir. They overran the place."

Lockhart thought he was going to collapse. His knees were weak, and he didn't trust himself to move. Six thousand Marines and they couldn't hold the goddamned place? "Khe Sanh? You mean they overran Khe Sanh?"

"No, sir. One of the outlying bases. Hill 861, I think. Radio traffic is somewhat confused."

Lockhart suddenly knew that he could walk. He stepped to his desk and dropped into the chair. "Tell me what you've got. I trust you confirmed the information."

Mansfield referred to the folder he carried. Its red cover announced that the document was classified as Top Secret. "We've made a number of inquiries, but at this moment, here is all we know. The outpost on Hill 861 was attacked just after midnight, just as the defector captured earlier said it would be. There was a massive rocket and mortar attack and then a ground assault. The marines held as long as possible and then retreated, giving up the camp."

"Casualties?"

"Bad, I'm afraid. We know that the commander and his exec were wounded and maybe dead. The gunnery sergeant was killed outright, and from the information we have, the senior surviving sergeant was directing the battle."

"Then there are survivors?"

"Oh, yes, sir. We just know that they lost the base."

"Fuck!" said Lockhart. He glanced at the clock on his desk. "Who's been briefed on this?"

"You, sir, and of course, the Joint Chiefs."

The phone on Lockhart's desk buzzed. He hesitated. He knew without having to pick it up who it was. It was going to mean a quick trip to the White House to brief the President on the situation. He could still hear Johnson snarling, "I don't want another damned Dien Bien Phu."

Lockhart picked up the phone. "Colonel Lockhart here." That was the last thing he said, as General Wheeler began giving him hurried instructions, and then finished by ordering him to the White House.

"But, General—"

"You do as you're told, Colonel. I'll have a car waiting for you. Then you stay right there as a liaison between us here and the President. Office space will be arranged."

"But I have order duties," Lockhart objected.

"As of now, you have no other duties. You are a direct pipeline between us and the President. Your only concern is with the developing battle around Khe Sanh. Nothing else matters to you. Understood?"

"Yes, General."

Lockhart hung up and stared at Mansfield. "All right, Captain, I'm going to need a copy of everything you have on what's happened at Khe Sanh. I have to brief the President."

"Christ, sir!"

"Exactly. He's not going to be thrilled with this."

THE POUNDING on the flimsy door finally penetrated the alcoholic fog that infected Whitmire's brain. He held up a bare arm in front of his eyes and tried to see the tiny glowing numbers on the face of his watch.

The pounding started again, and he sat up. "I'm awake, dammit."

"Sir, your presence is required in the briefing room."

"Now?"

"Yes, sir. Major's orders."

Whitmire looked at the naked back and bottom of the woman lying next to him—a young blonde with the USO show, whose name he'd now forgotten, but who had performed above and beyond her duty, making the lonely soldier feel better.

She rolled onto her back, not bothering to cover her breasts. They were two white globes visible in the little light slipping into the hootch. "Whatzat?"

Whitmire wished she would just get the hell out. She was pretty enough but didn't seem to have much brain. She could sing a little, wiggle her butt a lot, and she hadn't wanted to talk. She'd just wanted to climb into bed. Whitmire wondered why that irritated him: she had all the qualities of the perfect woman for a war zone. All he needed was a bar, and he'd have it made.

By now Whitmire was sitting on the side of the bed. The woman rolled closer to him, her breasts pressing against him. She kissed his back and reached around to grab his crotch. "You ready?" she asked.

"Good God! I've got a briefing."

She moved one leg around him, rubbing her thigh against his. Her hand felt him respond, and she giggled. "Briefing, huh?"

Whitmire pulled away and got up, keeping his back to her as he slipped on his shorts. Then he whirled and stared. She had kicked the covers away and was reclining, her legs spread and her hands behind her head. Whitmire was tempted to leap onto her and do what she wanted. Ten minutes would be enough, he was sure. Fifteen at the outside.

But there was a briefing and the major wouldn't tolerate his tardiness, even if the cause was a good one.

"Come to bed," she cooed.

His heart hammering, Whitmire turned from her and grabbed his flight suit. The green Nomex was hotter than hell, but regulations forced him to wear it.

"Come to bed."

Whitmire wanted to punch her now. Punch her in the stomach and then see if she felt like teasing him. He spun and took a step toward the bed, his hand curled into a fist, his eyes on the target. He could see her rib cage in the light. Her breasts and her vulnerable belly. A single punch in the stomach would be enough.

But then the irrational rage subsided. He sat down next to her. He pawed her breast and bent to kiss her, aware that he hadn't brushed his teeth. Bad breath was the least of his concerns.

"After the briefing," he said. "We'll have time after the briefing."

"I might not be here," she said, pouting.

"You will be." Whitmire stood. "There's no place else for you to go." At the door he picked up his boots, slipped them on, zipped them up. Regulations said he wasn't supposed to have boots with zippers, but everyone did.

As he opened the door, he looked back at her. She hadn't moved. Bitch, he thought, but he didn't say it out loud.

He walked across the compound toward the briefing room, where light was bleeding out through the shutters. There were flares hanging in the sky overhead, their descent marked by the twisted smoke trails they left. The distant boom of artillery was so ever-present that Whitmire rarely heard it anymore.

As he entered the briefing room, an MP closed the door, locking it. Whitmire made his way to his seat with the rest of his flight crew. He noticed that the major was on the stage, looking as if the news was bad. Then, around him, he saw the strained faces of the other pilots, men who only hours before had been singing and dancing with the USO girls, trying to talk them into bed.

The major nodded at the projectionist. The lights dimmed and the screen was filled with the aerial photograph of the Khe Sanh combat base they had seen in the earlier briefing.

"Gentlemen, about forty minutes ago forces of the Army of North Vietnam made a push to take one of the Marine outposts around Khe Sanh. The assault we've been expecting there for the past few days is now under way."

The major stopped talking, letting what he'd said sink in, letting the men realize that the contingency plan for airlifting in the 160 tons of supplies was now going to be put into effect. It meant they would be flying into a base surrounded by hostile soldiers who wanted very much to shoot them out of the sky.

Whitmire's desire to get back to his hootch evaporated in the few seconds it took him to realize what was going on. He felt limp and sweaty and not very happy.

"Oh, shit!" was all he could say.

A PRESIDENTIAL AIDE met Lockhart at the door and waved him into the hallway. The hall was huge, carpeted in red, with a giant chandelier hanging overhead. The aide looked at the briefcase and then at Lockhart.

"The President cleared two appointments to see you. He's giving you thirty minutes, but don't take all that time. We have to move quickly because there's so much else he needs to do today."

Lockhart nodded and wondered if he should tell the aide that the President wasn't going to be happy when he heard the news. Ten minutes would do it.

They hustled down a wide corridor that had paintings of former Presidents hanging on the walls, with ornate chairs and long narrow tables scattered here and there. The lighting was bright, but all of it was artificial.

They stopped outside a door in front of which an Army warrant officer sat quietly. He held a black briefcase on his lap, and didn't bother to acknowledge either man.

"Wait just a moment," said the aide. He disappeared inside, and a moment later, reappeared. "The President will see you now."

Lockhart entered the office, overwhelmed by the sense of history. Dozens of men had sat in that office, making decisions whose ramifications had changed the face of the globe and affected millions of lives. He was aware of the massive rosewood desk, the powder-blue carpeting with the Great Seal woven into it, the leather visitors' chairs and the flags. There were curved windows behind the President with a view of trees and gardens.

"Mr. President," Lockhart began, suddenly unsure of the protocol. Should he salute and report? Should he stand at attention?

The President solved the problem. He waved at one of the visitors' chairs. "Take a load off."

Lockhart knew enough to realize that anything the President said took precedence over everything else. He dropped into the chair and sat stiffly, feet flat on the floor, his briefcase held in both hands.

"All right, Colonel, what do you have for me?" President Johnson leaned forward, both elbows on his desk.

Lockhart fumbled with the clasp on his briefcase and then opened it. He drew out the classified documents. "We have some information about Khe Sanh."

"General Wheeler called to inform me that you were coming. He indicated that the news isn't very good."

"No, sir, it's not," Lockhart said. He flipped over the cover and began to read slowly, letting the information sink in. A disaster was building up around Khe Sanh, and Lockhart didn't know how to tell the President about it. He kept his eyes on the paper, not wanting to see anything other than the parade of words. He listened to the sound of his voice, trying not to hear the mumbling from the President.

When he finished he closed the report, but didn't look up. He kept his eyes on the red cover.

"Let me have that," said the President.

Lockhart handed over the document. He noticed now that the President seemed older, more tired, than when he'd walked into the room. His skin color was bad. Lockhart thought about the man who had cheerfully displayed his operation scar to news photographers, and realized this man resembled that one only superficially. It was as if two men were President—the younger, fun-loving man who had picked up his beagles by the ears, and this older man, who looked sick.

"You're familiar with the battle at Dien Bien Phu, Colonel?" asked the President.

"Yes, sir."

"Then you know that one of the first things the Communists did was take out all the outposts so that the French were trapped down there in that little valley."

"Yes, sir."

"You see the parallels with this?"

Lockhart didn't want to admit it, but he saw them. Just as every other military officer in the American army did. It would be stupid not to see the parallels.

"I have just one question for you, Colonel. What the hell is going on over there?"

6

SOUTHWEST OF THE
MARINE CAMP HILL 861

The jungle around Hobbs was alive with people, hundreds of them, slipping through the trees, heading to the northeast to climb the hill there. Hobbs and his tiny band pulled closer together, slipped to the ground in a defensive ring and then tried not to breathe. He could feel the toes of the other men against his feet—physical contact necessary in case the enemy slipped up on one of them.

They had been lying there for a couple of hours when the first of the dull pops from a hidden 60 mm mortar drifted to them. Moments later it seemed the whole world was shooting. Mortars, rockets and RPGs were being fired, directed uphill, at the tiny Marine outpost at the summit.

As the mortar shells and rockets began to detonate, Hobbs dropped his head into his hands. He closed his eyes and breathed deeply. Humidity hung in the air. The sweat that he had worked up during the day didn't dry, but lingered, forming a sticky film over his skin. He ignored it, as he did much of the jungle's discomfort.

He looked up then, hearing a sound not far away. There was a quiet command in Vietnamese and a clicking of metal against metal. The flash and the pop came next. A mortar tube had been set up not more than fifty yards from his position.

Hobbs wanted to crawl back, deeper into the jungle, because the mortar tube was bad news. It meant that Charlie was all around him, and it meant that the Americans on the hill, if they, too, spotted the flash, would try to drop countermortar rounds on it. Either way, Hobbs and the patrol were in danger. They no longer had the luxury of lying quietly in the jungle and letting the enemy walk around them. Now they had to get out.

Slowly, carefully, Hobbs withdrew from his part of the circle until he was sitting in the center of it. In sequence, he touched the foot of each of the other men, drawing them to the rear. After an agonizing ten minutes, the patrol sat nearly nose to nose. In the jungle darkness, Hobbs could barely make out the shapes of the men around him. The low cloud cover, now nearly down to the summit of the hill, reflected the ground light but kept the moon and starlight out.

There was a flash behind him as the mortar fired again. For a moment he could see his men clearly. The afterimage was burned into his eyes so that he believed he still could see them even when the light had faded.

Leaning in close, he whispered in a voice that was barely audible, ''Mortar.''

Quinn stared over Hobbs's shoulder as another round was fired, and nodded.

Without speaking, Hobbs set up the ambush. They would take out the mortar and then slip off the hillside, heading down to the south and west toward the Special Forces camp at Lang Vei. Once there they could arrange for a chopper ride out so that they could report to their intelligence people.

Quinn nodded his understanding of the hand signals and tapped Rogers on the shoulder. Rogers moved closer to Quinn. Lawrence knew that meant he was paired with Hobbs. Hobbs pulled at the camouflage cover on his watch, checked the luminous dial and then held up one finger, telling the men they would launch their attack at one in the morning.

After each man had nodded, Hobbs slowly climbed to his feet. He stood still for a moment, listening. The usual jungle sounds were absent. Animal life had fled from the influx of men. The blasting from the mortar near them and the other weapons around them drowned out the chirp of insects.

From the hilltop came the sound of mortars and rockets exploding—dull, quiet crumps from the small mortar rounds and louder, flatter bangs from the rockets. Hobbs turned once and glanced up the hillside, but the vegetation was too thick and he could see nothing. He could smell the battle, though, smell the burnt gunpowder. And he could hear the small arms returning the fire.

He moved out then, circling to the south and then to the east, trying to outflank the mortar tube. With the number of NVA and VC that had been moving about earlier, he doubted the enemy would have security out. They felt as safe in the jungle as they did in the streets of Hanoi. The Marines hadn't ventured far on their patrols in the past few weeks. Hell, they hadn't had to. The enemy had been creeping up on their camps all around the Khe Sanh area.

Hobbs turned, moving toward the weapon. The flashes as the rounds were fired made it easy for him. He got in close and then dropped to one knee, his left shoulder against the smooth bark of a teak tree. The roots stuck up through the soil, and Hobbs reached out to touch one. He shifted his M-16 to his left hand and pulled a grenade.

Next to him Lawrence did the same thing. Hobbs checked the time and then dropped back, resting on the heel of his right foot, his knee on the ground. He closed his eyes once, trying to build his night vision, and then opened them.

Through the gaps in the vegetation he could see a single human shape. It moved once, bent at the waist and then straightened, as if it was picking up a mortar round and handing it to one of the gunners.

Hobbs checked the time again and then pointed at Lawrence, one finger extended, telling him that there was a minute left. When thirty seconds had elapsed, he doubled the finger and then pulled the pin from his grenade, letting the pin drop onto the jungle floor.

When the time expired, Hobbs threw his grenade at the shape he had seen. As he released it, he dropped to the ground. He heard his grenade smash through the jungle. Silently he counted to himself.

A moment later there was one explosion, a second's hesitation and then two more, another hesitation and a final one. The shrapnel ripped through the trees, sounding like the beginning of a rainstorm. There were screams and then shouts. A single AK opened fire on full-auto. The enemy held the trigger down, spraying the bushes and trees all around, the muzzle-flash strobing in the blackness.

Hobbs pulled another grenade and tossed it at the enemy soldier. Either Quinn or Rogers had the same idea, for there were two quick explosions and then nothing. No return fire. No more screaming. Just the sounds of the battle as it developed higher on the slopes of the hill.

Lawrence reached out and slapped Hobbs on the shoulder, then retreated, moving away from the mortar tube. Hobbs didn't move right away. He wanted to check on it, make sure they had damaged or destroyed it, but knew that he couldn't. Lawrence was right. The smart thing was to withdraw, to get off the hill while they still could.

Before he could move, there was a rushing overhead that sounded like something running through dry autumn leaves. An instant later came the explosion, a bright orange-yellow flash, as the artillery from Khe Sanh or one of the surrounding bases hammered the enemy.

Hobbs dropped to the ground and waited, but there wasn't another shot. He was up then, moving downhill rapidly, ignoring noise discipline now. With so many enemy soldiers, so much firing and so many outgoing and incoming rounds, a little noise from him wasn't going to be a problem.

He and Lawrence stopped and then worked their way back to the original hiding place. Quinn and Rogers were already there, waiting. Again, without an order, Quinn took the point, moving directly downhill, trying to get them out of the area.

ON HILL 861 the Marines had been forced to retreat to the crest. They had given up the outer perimeter wire, a series of trenches and several bunkers, falling back to the hilltop. In the retreat the enemy had overrun the helipad. During all this, the firing hadn't tapered off and the mortar rounds had continued to fall. The Marines tilted their tubes again, trying to drop their rounds on the bunker line and perimeter wires.

Hanratty had dropped onto his belly, his head in his hands, his weapon propped near him. For a moment, a single moment, he had tried to ignore everything around him. He had to ignore the smell of the burnt gunpowder and the burning sandbags and bunkers. He had to ignore the sounds of rifle fire and automatic weapons. He had to ignore the exploding of Chicom grenades and enemy mortar rounds. For just a moment.

Then he was up, staring into the flashing, flaming darkness as the enemy tried to overrun the rest of the camp. Hanratty flipped the selector switch to full-auto, turned the weapon on its side as he'd seen John Wayne do in the movies, and pulled the trigger. There was a quick ripping sound like cloth being torn and the bolt locked back. Hanratty had no idea where his bullets had gone, other than toward the enemy.

Again he ducked, reloaded and opened fire. Around him the other Marines were doing the same, putting out rounds just as fast as they could. Others, running between the ammo bunker and the line, dropped off bandoliers of ammo. In the safety of the rearm bunker, a half-dozen men worked feverishly to reload magazines. Their fingers were ripped and bleeding, but they kept at it, jamming the 5.56 mm rounds into the twenty-round magazines, trying to keep up with the demand.

Even with the wall of lead the Marines were throwing out, the enemy came on, dodging from bunker to bush to fifty-five-gallon drum, working their way closer to the Marines. They fired their AKs and ducked, only to pop up again.

But then artillery from the combat base and from the tubes on Hill 881 South opened fire. The rounds hit low on the southwest face of Hill 861, huge fiery explosions as the artillery searched for the enemy reinforcements, trying to chop them up.

At about dawn the Marines had taken enough. As one they rose from hiding and swarmed out of their positions, attacking the enemy. Hanratty and Rowley were swept along, jumping from their hiding places, charging downhill.

Hanratty leaped over a fifty-five-gallon drum lying on its side and stared into the face of a Vietcong soldier. He saw the eyes as he fired. The face was illuminated in the muzzle-flash, and then the enemy was tumbling, falling to the rear. Hanratty jerked at the trigger of his weapon, pumping bullets into the enemy. He then leaped over the body, running toward a ditch that had been captured.

Hanratty reached the trench and dropped into it. As he did, a Chicom grenade bounced in after him. Without a thought, he fell onto his side and curled in a fetal position, his hands between his legs to protect his balls. He didn't hear the grenade detonate, but felt the shrapnel slam into his flak jacket and heard some of it bounce off his steel pot.

A second later Hanratty was on his feet. He saw an enemy soldier running away and opened fire, holding the trigger down. The rounds caught the man in the back, smashing him to the ground. He rolled once and was still.

Hanratty whirled, running down the trench. There was firing all around him. He could hear grunts and shouts and the wet slap of bullets striking flesh. In front of him a VC was aiming at the back of another Marine. Hanratty leaped, feet-first, driving the soldier to the ground. Hanratty rolled and kicked. There was a flare of pain through his foot and a groan from the enemy. As the soldier struggled to sit up, Hanratty kicked him again. He fell back and Hanratty scrambled to his feet. He snapped the stock of his M-16 down into the soft flesh of the throat of the enemy soldier. He slammed it home again and again until the soldier vomited blood.

All around him was a roaring that overpowered the sounds of the battle. Men screaming their rage as they attacked the enemy. Bursts of fire from M-14s, M-16s and AKs. Explosions from grenades inside the wire and artillery on the outside. But it was the screaming that surprised Hanratty. He'd never heard anything like it except in the movies, when the Rebels assaulted the Union lines in the Civil War.

Then, as he rushed downhill, pulling at the trigger of his weapon, he realized that he was shouting, too, screaming as loud as he could. The roar that came from deep within him seemed to give him courage.

He roared right up to an enemy soldier who was kneeling with his head down. Hanratty shot him once in the face and then leaped over the body.

He kept running downhill. He fired his weapon, and when the magazine was empty, he dropped it free. He crammed another one home as the last of the VC and NVA fought to hold the trench they had captured.

Hanratty jumped in among them, swinging his elbows and rifle butt. He knocked two of them down. He shot one and felt his leg grabbed. He fell forward and put out his hands to stop the fall. As he touched the loose dirt, he spun and kicked out but missed.

Now the enemy was up, holding an AK with the bayonet extended. He feinted to the right and then thrust back toward the left. Hanratty rolled right, and the bayonet sank into the dirt at the side of the trench. The American grabbed the barrel, hot from firing, and held on as the enemy soldier tried to jerk the weapon free.

Hanratty used the momentum and launched himself at the NVA. He rammed his shoulder into the man's chest, knocking him back with a grunt of surprise. Hanratty used his fist, hammering at the man's body, first his chest and then his face. Bones cracked and snapped, and the enemy soldier slipped to the bottom of the trench, but Hanratty wasn't through with him. He pounded on him, driving his fist into the man's neck, smashing the larynx. The enemy thrashed, clawed at his throat and then was suddenly still.

Hanratty crawled out of the bottom of the trench. He picked up his weapon and worked the bolt, ejecting a live round. Then he leaned forward, elbows on the surface of the ground, and watched as the last of the enemy fled the perimeter. There were sporadic shots and one of them fell.

The artillery, now just the American tubes from Khe Sanh and the summit of Hill 881 South, continued to slam into the slopes below him. But the shells were walking away, out of the killing zones and into the trees that surrounded them.

Satisfied that the enemy had been cleared from the camp, Hanratty dropped into the bottom of the trench. He sat with his back against the side, his knees up. He held his weapon between his legs and let his mind go. He was numb, unable to even think about the battle. Already it had blurred into shifting images and dancing shapes.

Moments later the last of the artillery rounds fell, and it was quiet for a moment. There was sporadic firing around the perimeter, and a few shots sounded from the crest of the hill, but nothing like the din that had rocked the base only moments before. A single voice penetrated the quiet, calling softly, "Medic! Medic!"

Hanratty got to his feet. He could see a few men moving up the slope from him, some of them carrying the heavy bags of medical supplies of the corpsmen. Others had weapons and were checking the bodies of the dead. Only a few enemy soldiers had been left inside the perimeter. Charlie, as he always did, managed to carry off the majority of his dead.

SITTING IN HIS TINY new office in the basement of the White House, Lockhart read through the message traffic coming in from Khe Sanh. A Marine ran the stuff from the White House communications center directly to him so that he could screen it before talking to the President. Some of the messages were so garbled it was difficult to figure out exactly what was happening over there.

Lockhart closed the file folder and leaned back. He was sweating heavily, even though it was cold in the basement office. Not an office, really, but more of a cubicle, it had a small desk, a chair and room for nothing else. There were a couple of pictures on the wall, left by the former occupant, who had been jerked out within five minutes of the President's saying he wanted Lockhart to remain close at hand.

Lockhart had expected something more luxurious at the White House than a cinder-block cubicle painted bright blue. There were two phone lines. He had been cautioned never to touch one unless it rang. It was a direct line from the President, and only the President could initiate a call on it. If Lockhart had a problem or needed to see the President, he was to use the other phone to schedule the appointment.

"Everyone here is at the beck and call of the President," he had been warned. "If he wants you, you drop everything and run up to his office."

"No problem," Lockhart had said, but as soon as the aide disappeared, Lockhart had thought of a dozen questions. He wanted to know when he could go home, and if he could tell his wife about the new arrangement.

That was the funny thing about Washington. Everything in the city ran at the whim of the President. If a member of a family was missing from a wedding, a birthday or some other gathering, the absence was accepted without question after the simple explanation, "He's at the White House." It was the perfect cover for a man or woman who was having an affair. It was difficult, nearly impossible to call someone at the White House, and absence on short notice, even all night, wasn't suspicious.

The Marine appeared at the door again and handed Lockhart another batch of papers from the teletype machines. Lockhart signed for them and thanked him. As the man disappeared, the colonel realized that he needed a safe. He couldn't leave classified material lying around, even in the basement of the White House.

Fearing the worst, he read the message and realized that earlier reports had exaggerated the situation case at Hill 861. The Marines were now in full possession of the camp. Only part of it had been overrun. The Marines had taken some casualties, but they had pushed the North Vietnamese and the Vietcong off the hilltop.

Slowly Lockhart reread the message, looking for anything he might have missed on the first pass. Things were now quiet around Khe Sanh. This was the news the President had been waiting for. Lockhart picked up his phone and called the aide, telling him he needed to see the President. He was told to hold on.

As he waited, the other phone buzzed. He grabbed it immediately. "Yes, Mr. President."

"What've you got?"

Lockhart hesitated. All through his military career he had been drilled that classified information was never discussed over the phone. Regulations didn't allow it. With the improvements in intercept techniques, even some shielded phone cables could be penetrated.

His body grew clammy, and he wished he was still at the Pentagon, sweating over mundane statistics. The hot seat was the last place he wanted to be. The only solution was to try an end run.

"Would you like me to bring it up to your office, Mr. President?"

"No, I want you to tell me what you've got. I don't have all day to waste on this."

Lockhart hesitated again and finally decided that what the President wanted he got. Besides, the information wasn't that vital to national security. If the Russians somehow intercepted it, they would learn that Hill 861 still belonged to the Americans.

"Sir, our early messages were slightly garbled in the transmission. Apparently only part of the camp on 861 was overrun. Our people have recaptured it."

There was a moment of silence and then a long, loud whoop. "Hot damn, Colonel! Hot damn!"

"Yes, sir. Apparently everything is quiet for the moment. First round goes to us."

"That's fantastic, Colonel. You get more news like that, you let me know immediately."

"Yes, Mr. President."

The line went dead and Lockhart hung up. He stared at the secret reports in front of him and wondered how long the crisis would last. They had known the attack was coming, and still it had been a close thing. And the information was that there would be more assaults, culminating in the destruction of the Khe Sanh combat base. If the enemy did as well in that assault as they had done at 861, the Marines were going to be in big trouble.

7

KHE SANH COMBAT BASE

Korski stood well back, outside of the circle of light that surrounded the Vietnamese officer. Tonc sat in a chair, his hands in his lap, and waited. His face was drawn and his eyes ringed in black from his sleepless night. Within minutes of the launching of the attack on Hill 861, the intelligence section had dragged him back into the interrogation room, demanding to know everything that was going to happen.

At first Sergeant Goddard had raged at the Vietnamese, then he had slipped into a conversational tone. Korski had been about to say something to Goddard when he realized that nothing they did would shut off the spigot of information. Tonc wanted to tell everything he knew.

So while Goddard quizzed the man, Korski stood in the background, almost out of sight, scribbling notes. He kept at it while the artillery at Khe Sanh fired in support of the defenders on Hill 861. He kept at it even as Marines poked their heads into the interrogation room and told him that it was grim on the hilltop. He wanted to be out there with the men, fighting the Communists, but he knew he could do more damage to the enemy if he could figure out when Tonc was telling the truth and when he wasn't.

At 5:15 a.m., after a long night, one of the Marine sergeants entered and said, "We've pushed them out."

Korski drew the man aside. "Anything from any of the other
camps?"

"Everything's quiet."

"Thanks." Korski put the cap back on his pen and stepped
into the circle of light. He stopped in front of Tonc and looked
down, staring at him for a long time. Finally he looked at
Goddard. "It seems our friend isn't sharing the whole truth
with us."

"It is truth," Tonc said. "It is whole truth."

Korski shook his head. "It is not. We've had the men at a
number of the camps on full alert all night, waiting for these
attacks. No one's storming the wire. No one's dropping mortar rounds. Hell, man, we haven't even had a single shot fired
at us here."

"You wait," advised Tonc. "Attack come. I know. I tell you
truth. Attack come."

Korski bent so that his face was only inches from the Vietnamese. He glared at him, sucking in air through his mouth,
faking a rage he didn't feel. "Well, mister the attacks you predicted for just after midnight haven't materialized. There have
been no assaults."

"No true," said Tonc. His face had gone pale. "You lie to
me. You try trick."

Korski straightened up and shook his head. "Afraid not,
pal. The enemy just hasn't bothered to attack. You've done a
hell of a job getting us to jump through hoops, but the information you gave us just didn't pan out."

"It come. You wait. I not lie."

Then, as if to prove that Tonc wasn't lying, the first of the
enemy rockets slammed into the combat base. Though the
prisoner and his interrogators were inside a heavy bunker, it
was obvious that an enemy rocket had landed.

"It start now," Tonc said.

Korski was going to respond when the salvo smashed into
the base. There were a few small explosions and then a huge

crash that shook the ground. Korski staggered like a drunken sailor. Dirt from the sandbags overhead cascaded, creating a cloud of dust in the bunker.

Goddard fell to his knees. "What the fuck was that?"

Then firing broke out all around. The artillery opened up, trying to suppress the enemy. The bangs from the tubes firing outgoing combined with the explosions of the incoming.

"Shit!" Korski said. He spun and ran to the bunker entrance, where he crouched and looked to the west where the main ammo dump had been. A massive cloud of black smoke and red dust hung over it. Explosions still rippled from it as the base's ammo supply destroyed itself after the direct hit from a Communist rocket.

Still kneeling there, one hand up on the sandbags, Korski glanced to the rear where the prisoner now sat on the floor. He was grinning broadly. Korski's first instinct was to punch the grin off his face. Then he realized Tonc was smiling at the vindication. He'd said the enemy would attack. The rocket barrage was only the beginning.

DOBSON CROUCHED in his bunker as the first of the enemy rounds fell on the camp. When the ammo dump exploded, he was thrown off his feet, landing on his side. He felt the concussion wash over him, like the pressure of a dive to the bottom of a swimming pool. There was a dry heat, like that of a fire, and a rolling, crashing, vibrating roar that seemed to build and then disintegrate into a thousand smaller detonations.

Dobson got off the planks at the bottom of his bunker, muttering, "What in the fuck was that?"

He scrambled to the rear and looked out along the runway, toward the east. A huge cloud of dust and smoke hung over the eastern end of the camp, drifting slowly to the west.

"Christ!" he said.

But then he scrambled back into the bunker as the rockets and mortar shells continued to fall. Hundreds of them landed all over the camp, destroying small hootches, tents, bunkers and other structures. Trucks and jeeps were hit and destroyed. Fires broke out, roaring through the plywood hootches. Bunkers began to smolder as the fuel oil the Marines had poured on them to discourage the rats caught fire.

The fires burned uncontrolled, for the men who would have been fighting them stayed crouched in their bunkers. Too many enemy shells were falling on the camp too quickly.

Dobson spent the first hours of the mortar attack watching the hills and jungle around him, waiting for the assault. Massive enemy barrages almost always gave way to a ground assault, but that didn't happen this time.

At noon Dobson let Bill Conica take over his post at the firing port, but he didn't run for the mess hall closest to them. Instead he opened a box of C-rations, eating them with the plastic spoon included with the box.

He sat on the plank floor of the bunker, his back against the wall of sandbags, and tried to ignore the shelling while he ate. Hundreds of mortar rounds had already fallen. There would be a temporary lull, and then another barrage would drop on them, blowing holes in the runway, knocking down hootches and destroying the supplies the Marines would need to survive.

When he finished eating, he moved to the front of the bunker to look out. The monsoon clouds hung low, obscuring the tops of some of the hills around the combat base. A drizzle had started about midmorning, had stopped and now started again.

"Fucking weather," Dobson said.

"Yeah," Conica agreed. He was a young Marine who had arrived less than three weeks earlier. The chin strap of his steel pot was buckled so that the helmet wouldn't slip off his head. He had traded the M-16 he'd brought with him for an M-14.

"This going to last long?" he asked.

Dobson shrugged, feeling like an old salt. "Never had this happen before."

"Christ, I gotta take a piss."

"Not in here you don't," said Dobson. "You crawl outside and do it."

Conica crouched in the entrance to the bunker, glancing outside. Columns of smoke from the fires were hanging over the base. Men were running along the side of the runway, heads bowed, weapons held up. There was a fine mist blowing over the field, keeping the aircraft away. It should have burned off, but it refused to.

Conica, his hand gently squeezing his crotch, waited until there was a lull in the barrage. Then he leaped from the bunker and ran to the side, unfastening his fly. Just as he began to relieve himself, a rocket roared by and hit the runway not far from him. As it detonated, he threw himself to the ground.

From inside the bunker, Dobson yelled, "Hey! You okay?"

Conica, lying on his side, finished his business, but it was already too late. The sudden arrival of the rocket and then the explosion so close had surprised him. When he'd dived for cover, he'd landed in the pool he'd created.

Conica stayed where he was for a moment and then scrambled around into the bunker. When Dobson saw the stains on Conica's uniform, he burst out laughing. "You could have stayed in here and pissed all over yourself."

"Yeah. Well, I didn't get killed."

"Not yet, anyway," Dobson said. Then he wished he'd kept his mouth shut.

WHITMIRE SAT in the right-hand seat in the nose of the C-130 Hercules cargo plane as they circled in the bright blue sky. Underneath them was a thick, boiling soup of cloud. Somewhere below the clouds was the runway for Khe Sanh. An approach through the clouds to the runway wasn't that big a problem. In the World, at any of the civilian airports, they wouldn't have thought twice about it. But here things were different. There were people who would try to shoot holes in the airplane.

Whitmire looked out the windows, but he didn't see anything. He felt slightly sick, probably from too much to drink the night before, and hoped he wouldn't throw up.

He tuned out everything that was going on around him. He ignored the radios that were filled with messages from a hundred sources. He didn't listen to the men behind him as they talked about the weather and the enemy and the stupid Marines who had managed to get themselves surrounded on the plateau hidden by the thick clouds.

He leaned back in his seat, then reached up over his head and opened the vent so that air could blow right into his face. Fresh, cool air sometimes settled a queasy stomach, but this time it did little for him except dry the sweat on his face and make him feel clammy.

"Drinking," he said without benefit of the intercom. The roar of four huge engines overwhelmed the sound of his voice. Out of the corner of his eye he could see the AC, Carson, hands on the wheel and feet on the rudder pedals. Carson was looking out the window, to the left, searching for the other C-130s orbiting above Khe Sanh.

"Drinking," Whitmire repeated, using the intercom this time. "I am through with drinking."

That brought a bark of laughter. Then someone said, "You give it up for good, or just for the rest of the flight?"

Whitmire knew what the man was talking about. He swore off drinking at least once a week, especially if he had to fly the next day. Then he thought about the woman who'd been in his bed, and he wondered if the drink had been so bad. The woman hadn't been bad-looking, and the alcohol had helped him ignore her one major flaw. She didn't have a brain in her head. But then who really cared? He closed his eyes again and gulped at the cool air blowing in his face.

"You want to take it for a while?" asked Carson.

Whitmire sat up and glanced at the instruments. "I'm not feeling all that well."

"No problem," Carson said. "Just thought you might like to see what it was like to actually pilot the aircraft rather than sit there waiting to get sick."

Whitmire reached out to take the controls, and his stomach rebelled. He felt the sweat bead and drip. His armpits were clammy. He willed himself not to throw up.

"You going to need a sick sack?"

"Yeah, I think so." His stomach flip-flopped. Then suddenly he knew he was going to be fine. "No. No, not at all."

He straightened up and wiped a gloved hand over his face. He checked all the instruments and then stared outside the cockpit at the other orbiting aircraft. It looked like the sky above the busiest airports in the World. Cargo planes were stacked up, waiting for an opportunity to land, but with the damage to the runway, no more than one could get in at a time.

Finally, after two hours, the AC decided it was time to get out. "Can't waste the whole day here. Marines will just have to wait for the cargo. We're heading for the barn."

"Won't they need it on the ground?" asked one of the voices on the intercom.

"If the Marines needed it, they'd get the fucking runway repaired so we could land. Fuck 'em if they can't take a joke."

LOCKHART SAT in his tiny office and waited for the President to call him. He'd managed to get a two-drawer safe, though there was hardly enough room for it. He had to tiptoe around it, squeeze by the corner of the desk and only then could he sit down.

For the past few hours the message traffic had slowed. A sergeant in the communications center was screening the messages given to Lockhart so that the colonel could screen the information bumped up to the President.

Everything was ready for the President now. Lockhart had arranged the data, created a couple of files and made written notes on a yellow legal pad. Then he sat there, waiting for the phone to ring.

It was after midnight when it finally rang and he was ordered into the White House situation room. Lockhart retrieved his notes, grabbed his files so that he would have all the information at his fingertips and headed out of his office.

The interior of the situation room had changed since the last time he had been there. On the table was a scale model, in full relief, of Khe Sanh and the surrounding area. The model was painted green. It showed the Laotian border, the hilltop Marine outposts, the city of Khe Sanh and the Special Forces camp at Lang Vei, identifying the locations with white labels.

A dozen people, including the President, were gathered around the model. Most of them wore dark suits, though a couple of military officers in uniform were present. They were colonels and brigadier generals, not the chiefs of staff who were usually with the President.

Johnson looked up as Lockhart entered and waved him forward. He turned his attention back to the model as he said, "Give it all to me now."

Lockhart stepped forward and oriented himself on the map. He put the file folders down and flipped over the first page on his legal pad.

"As you know, Mr. President, we were successful in the defense of Hill 861." He glanced at the model and pointed. "That's it right here, northwest of the combat base. The other major outposts, here and here, weren't attacked. Just after five-thirty, Vietnam time, a major rocket attack was launched against the combat base. One of the first rounds took out the ammo dump, destroying some fifteen tons of ammunition that had been stockpiled. Colonel Lownds, the Marine commander on the scene, now claims that ammunition is critically low."

Johnson waved a hand like a studio director trying to speed up the slow-talking host of a late-running show.

"Air resupply, designed to bring in literally dozens of loaded C-130s, has failed so far. Only six planes have landed at Khe Sanh."

"What the hell is the problem there?" asked the President.

"Weather and the enemy gunners. The base is literally surrounded, and although there's no indication of sophisticated antiaircraft, there are plenty of small arms and Soviet-made 12.7 mm weapons."

Johnson stared at the man in the Air Force uniform. "I thought you said there would be no problems with aerial resupply, General. Your people promised we could get everything into that base that was needed."

"Yes, Mr. President. Just a few unforeseen problems that we'll get worked out quickly."

"You damned well better get them worked out. Six planes, and the Marines are already running out of ammunition."

"There is some other news," Lockhart went on, "though I'm not sure that it's all that bad."

The President waited expectantly. All other eyes were on Lockhart.

"The city of Khe Sanh has been abandoned," he said dramatically.

"Which means?" the President asked.

"Enemy forces attacked the city first thing in the morning. That assault was repulsed. They were shelled for the remainder of the morning. Late in the afternoon several hundred North Vietnamese tried to overrun the city again, but with the aid of air and artillery support the defenders easily beat back the attack. A Marine fighter pilot claimed about a hundred kills as the enemy was driven into the jungle."

"That's the best news you've given me all day," said the President.

"But the bad news is that the commander at Khe Sanh decided to abandon the city after the last attack. He was afraid they would get cut off and the Marines at the combat base wouldn't be able to lend support."

"Dammit!" snapped the President. "There any good news out of there?"

Lockhart shrugged. "I would think that it's all fairly good news. The enemy hasn't made any significant gains. We still hold everything we started with except the city of Khe Sanh, and that isn't much of a victory for the enemy since we gave it up for tactical reasons."

Johnson turned the full force of his gaze on Lockhart. He stared at the colonel for nearly thirty seconds, his eyes flicking from the rows of ribbons above the left breast pocket to Lockhart's face and back again. Finally he dropped into the huge chair behind him and rubbed a hand over his face.

"Colonel, let me clue you into the facts of life on this. First, we nearly lost that hilltop base. In fact, it was reported at first that we had lost it. Then the ammo dump at the combat base is destroyed and the resupply planes haven't been able to land. Now you tell me that we've given up the defense of Khe Sanh, even after we successfully defended the place. I thought one measure of victory was who held the field after the battle."

"Yes, sir, that's the traditional rule."

"Then we lost at Khe Sanh because the enemy holds the field."

"Yes, sir," said Lockhart. He wanted to point out again that it had been decided that the Marines would pull out of Khe Sanh *after* the fighting was over so that technically the Marines had won. But he knew better than to argue with the President.

"And we knew in advance that the enemy was coming," the President continued. "We knew that the attacks would be launched, and even with that the enemy came close to overrunning Hill 861."

"Yes, sir."

"Then our performance today has been something less than sterling."

"Yes, sir."

Johnson turned his attention to the Air Force officer. "I think it's time we unleash Operation Niagara."

"I believe General Westmoreland has already put those orders into effect."

"Damn it, man, I don't want to hear what you believe. I want to know what's going on. You make sure that Niagara is going ahead and report back to me."

"Yes, Mr. President."

Johnson closed his eyes and pinched the bridge of his nose. Finally he looked up at the men still gathered around the mock-up of Khe Sanh. "Gentlemen," he said, "this has been a very unsettling day. If the enemy's plans can be so hope-lessly compromised and we still only hang on by our finger-nails, think of the results when he unleashes the ten to twenty thousand men assembling around Khe Sanh. Tell me that after today's performance that doesn't concern you.''

No one spoke.

8

THE JUNGLES OUTSIDE
KHE SANH COMBAT
BASE

It had been a hard, tiring, frightening day. The dawn hadn't brought the relief it usually did. Instead, it highlighted Hobbs and his tiny force of Green Berets. The daylight, which in other parts of Vietnam forced the VC and NVA to take cover, did nothing to frighten them around Khe Sanh. They were now the dominant presence, chasing the smaller American forces, making them hide in the jungle and fear the coming of the sun.

After they had killed the enemy soldiers at the mortar tube, Hobbs and his men had tried to get off Hill 861. American artillery fell on the slopes, trying to eliminate enemy forces attacking the Marines, and Hobbs found himself dodging that, too. They fled downhill until they were in a vegetation-choked valley where the underbrush was almost impenetrable. Wiry plants resisted them, plants with razor-sharp branches and leaves slashed at them, and gigantic trees blocked them. The jungle floor was spongy and covered with vines that grabbed at their feet and shins. Outcroppings of rock hindered their progress. Perfect places for the enemy to hide, the rocks provided some protection from American artillery or bombs, but were just one more obstacle in their line of retreat.

Hobbs had taken the point from Quinn. At about sunup he halted them. Usually dawn was signaled by a riot of sound as birds screamed and monkeys screeched, but during the night, the birds, monkeys and other animals had gotten out, fleeing from the battle zone. Now the jungle was strangely quiet with only the distant boom of the artillery, sounding like thunder in the next county on a summer evening, to keep them company.

They found cover near a small stream that fed into the Song Rao Quang, which eventually skirted the Marine combat base. Hobbs filled one of his canteens and then moved back deeper into cover. He poured the water over his head, letting it cool him and wash away some of the sweat and caked dirt. For a moment he felt good, almost happy, but then the water was gone and the heat and humidity swirled in around him.

Hobbs sat with his back against a giant stone that seemed to be radiating a heat of its own. The sun had risen, but there were low-hanging clouds slipping down the mountains to clog the valleys, black and gray clouds that threatened rain but produced nothing. They held the humidity in without benefit of a breeze to blow it away. There was a mist rising from some sections of the jungle, a clean white fog that looked like woodsmoke, though it was too damp for anything to burn.

Quinn and Lawrence were sitting on the ground, their uniforms stained black by their sweat. Their faces had been painted green and black at the beginning of the mission but were now streaked, giving them a bizarre, unnatural look. They blended into the surroundings, though, and if they sat perfectly still, it would be difficult to see them.

Rogers was at the stream, brushing his teeth with a leaf ripped from a bush. He filled a canteen as Hobbs had done and poured the water over himself for the little relief it supplied.

In turn, each of the men went to the stream and then came back to the tiny camp. They were sitting there quietly, watching for the enemy, when the first of the enemy rockets roared over them, destroying the Marine's ammo dump in an explosion that shook the ground, even as far away as they were.

They sat there throughout the morning, listening to the barrage, listening to the American response, mostly artillery, but a few fighters. They didn't speak, except in whispers, and then only about their mission. The intelligence they had gathered on the Ho Chi Minh Trail was no longer of any importance. The enemy attacks on the Marines had outdated it, so there was no reason to hurry toward the combat base.

But Hobbs knew that with the enemy swarming over the hills and in the jungle around them, it was only a matter of time before someone stumbled over them. Still he didn't want to leave. He was tired.

Quinn moved close to him in the middle of the afternoon and whispered, "Someone's coming."

Hobbs used hand signals to get the men under cover and then waited as a platoon of NVA soldiers marched by, heading away from the battle on Hill 861. A ragged bunch of men, wearing torn, dirty uniforms and carrying a couple of wounded, they looked like a defeated enemy.

As they passed, Hobbs considered his options. A firefight would bring the enemy down on them quickly, hundreds of the enemy, and Hobbs couldn't hope to shoot his way clear. Grenades might be mistaken for mortars or artillery, but they would have to stay close to the enemy to use the grenades, and that would invite counterattack.

Still, the platoon presented an inviting target. Hobbs finally took the handset of the tiny URC-10 radio, extended the antenna and whispered, "Any American arty base, I have a fire mission, over."

There was a loud burst of static and Hobbs quickly turned down the radio. But the enemy was too far away to have heard it, and the other sounds, the thin dripping of the drizzle and the crashing of the rockets and mortar shells directed at the combat base, covered it up.

Hobbs put his lips to the radio and whispered the instructions, asking for high explosives to drop on the enemy unit that thought it was safe in the jungle, now nearly a half klick away.

He waited for a moment as the rest of his team crouched among the rocks, waiting for the artillery to fall. There was a crash overhead, like a train rushing past, then an explosion to the southwest, where the enemy patrol should have been.

"On target," Hobbs whispered, not sure that it was. He shut off the radio and ducked down. The rounds roared overhead and slammed into the jungle. The explosions threw clouds of dirt into the air and spun shrapnel into the trees, trees that were already so full of shrapnel that it was almost as if they were made of metal.

For fifteen minutes the artillery crashed into the jungle, then finally it stopped. When it was done, Hobbs got his men on their feet and they began threading their way among the trees and bushes, heading for the Marine combat base.

They moved quietly, maintaining noise discipline. There was no talking, just hand signals. Quinn had the point to begin but rotated out, letting Lawrence have it. Later, Rogers took over and then Hobbs, as they crossed the valley and finally reached the road that touched the western end of the combat base. Hobbs resisted the temptation to take the road and run along it. Instead, he took to the trees that paralleled the road, using their cover.

In the late afternoon they halted. Across the road, at the gate to the combat base, they could see a huge crowd of civilians. Hundreds of Vietnamese were standing there, arguing, shouting, screaming and waving their arms. Half a dozen armed Marines were keeping them outside the camp. The Marines were backed up by a couple of armored vehicles and several machine guns.

Quinn asked Hobbs, "What are we going to do now?"

"Cross the road and enter the camp. They won't keep us out."

"How do you want to go about it?"

"I want both Lawrence and Rogers to hang back ten or twelve yards as a rear guard and I'll take the point. We'll cross the road and push our way through to the gate. The Marines have to let us in."

"Says you," said Quinn.

"Don't worry about it. Let's not get stupid now that we're this close to safety."

As he spoke, a volley of rockets dropped out of the clouds and exploded near the center of the base. The flat bangs were dulled by the distance, but it was obvious that the enemy was still shooting at the Marines.

"You call that safety?"

"It's better than wandering around out here." Hobbs glanced to the rear. "Everyone ready?"

He was greeted with nods and one thumb up. He stood and worked his way out of the trees. Once clear of them, he jogged over the broken ground, leaping the boulders as he broke a trail through the elephant grass. He stopped at the edge of the road, a wide dirt-and-gravel track that splintered off Route 9 and disappeared to the north, passing Tiger Tooth Mountain and finally reaching the DMZ. He crouched on one knee, glancing both right and left, but there was no sign of the enemy. They were hiding from the fighters that were searching for them, hiding from the helicopter gunships that worked the lower slopes, and from the artillery spotters at the combat base.

A moment later he was up and running again. He reached the rear of the crowd outside the gates and began to shoulder his way through it. Vietnamese grabbed at him, screaming, "Hey, GI, you help. Hey, GI, I follow."

Hobbs pushed past them. Then he was stopped by a white man, about thirty-five or thirty-six, tall and lean with black hair. He looked as if he hadn't slept much the night before. In English with a heavy French accent he said, "You must help me and my wife get into the base. Tell Colonel Lownds that we're out here."

Hobbs glanced at the woman and was surprised. He had expected a matronly lady with blue hair who would take no shit from anyone, a tower of power dominating everything and everyone around her. But that wasn't the case. The woman was tall and slender, wearing a dress of silk that was dirty and stained. Her long hair hung down straight. She looked badly frightened, and Hobbs couldn't blame her.

"Okay," he said. He shifted his weapon to his left hand and pointed toward the front where the crowd was the thickest. "Follow me."

The man waved to the rear and his children assembled around him. "Thank you, Sergeant."

"Come on." Hobbs started pushing through the crowd again. To his right were five nuns from the Catholic school in Khe Sanh. They joined the party as Hobbs, his men now forming a cordon around the civilians, worked to get through the crowd of angry Vietnamese.

They reached the gate where the armed Marines stood, ignoring the shouting Vietnamese. Hobbs yelled, "Open up and let us in."

The Marine looked at him. "Who the hell are you?"

"Hobbs, Army Special Forces. You going to let us in?"

The Marine waved. "Sure. Come on."

As Hobbs came closer, the Marine stopped him and demanded, "Who do you have with you?"

Hobbs turned and looked at the man, who said, "I am Felix Poilane. I own one of the coffee plantations south of Khe Sanh. The others are my wife, Madeleine, and our children, and the teachers from the school."

"Satisfied?" Hobbs asked.

The Marine, a big, burly man, stood his ground. His uniform was sweat-stained, and he didn't look happy about facing the hundreds of Vietnamese crowding around the gate. "I don't know," he said.

"Sir," said Poilane, "your commander has been to my home many times. I have given him and your officers much coffee for their mess. We are friends. I am sure he would want us to enter your camp."

"I was told to keep all the locals out," the Marine said.

"Maybe so," said Hobbs, "but these people are going to be identified as Westerners, maybe even as Americans, which means they're in danger."

"My orders are specific."

"I'm sure they are, but I don't think your commanding officer would want you turning away our allies. There aren't that many of them."

The Marine stared at Hobbs for a moment, then wiped his face with his hand and nodded once. "Okay. They can come in, too."

Hobbs waved to the others, and the small party entered the Marine combat base. They passed through the wire and walked around one of the Ontos, a squat little vehicle that held six 106 mm recoilless rifles. This one was helping the Marines guard the approach to the camp.

Just as they cleared the gate, a Marine officer came toward them. He held up a hand, telling them to stop, as he stepped up to Hobbs and said, "I'm Lieutenant Korski, one of the intelligence officers here."

"Ah," said Hobbs. "I had some information for you, but I'm afraid it's out of date by now."

Korski grinned. "That's the problem with intelligence. It's so damned perishable. Who all's with you?"

Hobbs introduced the others. Korski looked at the Frenchman as if he didn't trust him, but said, "We'll have to see about getting everyone quartered."

At that moment mortar rounds began to fall on the runway about a hundred yards away. The civilians dropped to the ground, but Hobbs and his men turned to look, listening, waiting to learn if the rounds were coming closer or moving away.

"Let's get under cover," said Korski.

"We'll follow you," said Hobbs. "And I'll need to make contact with New Control in Nha Trang to let them know we're out of the field."

"That shouldn't be a problem."

ALMOST AS SOON AS the plane touched down at Da Nang, Whitmire was out the door. He knew there were things that had to be done in the cockpit, rituals that needed to be completed, along with a variety of forms, but his stomach was rebelling again. The hot air that had blown through the plane as soon as they touched ground, made him sick. It was air thick with the odor of the sea and of burning rubber and burning shit. With the water table high, the product of a hundred latrines was covered with kerosene and set on fire. The black clouds created by the fires lingered over the base, heavy with a smell that wasn't quickly forgotten.

And that was what pushed him over the edge. He'd gotten over his queasiness while they orbited above Khe Sanh. After failing to land there, they had flown back and the rough air had brought back his nausea, started the rumbling in his belly that threatened to explode outward. But he had controlled it, telling himself it would look bad for the copilot to get airsick. Then they'd landed, coming down through the thick clouds into the basin where the hot, humid air was trapped, onto the base where yesterday's odors were undercut by new ones, but somehow still lingered like a bad debt. Whitmire's stomach revolted. He clamped his teeth shut and swallowed the bile, feeling he was about to pass out.

At last they rolled to a stop. As the AC worked shutting down the engines, Whitmire unfastened his seat belt. He scrambled out of his seat, banged his knee on the AC's seat and stumbled to the ladder. He climbed down and waited next to the hatch as the loadmaster came forward to open it. As soon as it was open, Whitmire was out. He ran to the rear of the airplane, avoiding the spinning propellers that could have cut him in half. Near the rear of the airplane, he fell on his hands and knees. As the prop blast tugged at his flight suit, he threw up once violently.

For a second he felt better, then his stomach started churning and he vomited again and again. His muscles cramped as he emptied his stomach. Finally the spasms tapered off. He turned away from the mess and looked up toward the spinning propellers, letting the wind wash over him like the breeze from a giant fan.

Then the dry heaves hit him, his stomach muscles contracting painfully. He tried to rock back on his knees, but it took too much strength. Instead, he dropped his forehead into his hands so that he looked as if he was praying.

"You okay, sir?" he heard someone ask.

Whitmire didn't answer right away. He took deep breaths, hoping that it was all over. Finally he sat up, his face covered with sweat.

"Christ, sir, you look terrible."

Whitmire nodded. "Thanks a lot, Finney."

Finney reached down and touched Whitmire on the shoulder. "You need a hand, sir?"

Whitmire got shakily to his feet and then straightened up. "I think I'll be all right now."

"Kind of bumpy back there," Finney said.

"It was the drinking last night," Whitmire said. "I had too much to drink."

"Yes, sir."

Whitmire returned to the front of the plane. All the engines were shut down. He climbed up into the cockpit. Carson was there, grinning.

"Can't handle the rough air, huh?"

Whitmire was going to respond, but knew it wouldn't do any good. The men would think what they wanted, and if he protested, it would only make matters worse. They would then be sure that Whitmire had gotten airsick. The best course was to ignore any remarks, and they would soon drop it.

"Are we through?"

"If you're still not feeling well, take off," said Carson.

"Yes, sir." Whitmire climbed out and then remembered that his helmet was on the flight deck. He retrieved it and left, walking across the ramp so that he could avoid riding in the crew van. He didn't want to be cooped up with the others, who would undoubtedly continue to make cracks about the rough air.

Fifteen minutes later he was back in his hootch, having avoided the intel debriefing, which he was supposed to attend. It didn't matter, because he hadn't seen anything of interest and the AC had let him go. The other copilots and flight crew members could hang around with the intelligence officer, who would ask all kinds of questions that would mean nothing to anyone anyway.

Whitmire grabbed a beer from the tiny refrigerator jammed into the corner of his hootch and washed out his mouth. He took a big mouthful of beer, swished it around, then spit it out. With the taste of vomit gone, he felt better still. Then he spotted the note pinned to his pillow: "We're at the Marine club tonight. Come and see me. Marie."

He smiled when he read it and then dropped onto his cot. Marie had left a souvenir of their night—a pair of bikini panties in the center of his bed.

He picked up the panties and threw himself on the bed, his head on the pillow, his feet on the metal rail at the end. He held the panties by the waistband, holding them up to the light as if they were a bottle of fine wine. They were small lacy things that did little to conceal.

"Yeah," he said and got up again. He tossed the panties onto his bunk and went in search of a towel and shaving kit. He could fly all day looking like a skid-row bum, but that night, at the Marine club, he'd have to look like an officer to impress the lady.

As he walked out the door, toward the officers' shower, he wondered why he should bother trying. Marie had already slept with him once and was promising to do so again. In a week she'd be gone, on her way to Cam Ranh Bay, and he'd probably never see her again.

He entered the officers' shower, hung his towel on a hook, left his shaving kit on the wooden shelf over the porcelain sink and stripped off his flight suit. Soap in hand, he stepped out onto the wooden-slat floor and turned on the hot water. It was the job of a Vietnamese worker to make sure that the huge drum mounted over the shower was always full of hot water.

Whitmire showered slowly, at first just letting the hot spray wash over him, cleanse him, relax him. He lathered finally, rinsed off the soap and still found it impossible to leave the hot water. After several minutes he at last shut it off and stepped into the other room to dry.

As he shaved and brushed his teeth, he thought about the panties and the fun he'd had slowly pulling them down the woman's thighs with his teeth. She'd giggled and he'd lifted his hands up her thighs, rubbing her carefully.

He realized where those thoughts were taking him and was glad there was no one else there with him. Forcing his mind onto the task at hand, he finished and wrapped his towel around his waist.

Back in his hootch he turned on the radio and lay down on his bunk. Rock music from AFVN filled the room. Whitmire knew he was ready for another night with Marie, just as long as she did her job and didn't talk too much.

He wondered how the Marines at Khe Sanh were doing, then decided he didn't care all that much. He had important things on his mind. He couldn't be bothered worrying about a bunch of grungy Marines and their minor problems. Marie was waiting.

9

KHE SANH COMBAT BASE

For several days Korski and Goddard had been interrogating Tonc. At first their approach had been adversarial, but Tonc was so willing to cooperate that the tone of the interrogations had gradually changed. Finally they moved from the intel bunker out into the open, though with the mortar shells and rockets falling at erratic intervals, they had to stay close to a bunker. Sometimes they sat at a table, drinking Cokes and eating sandwiches. Tonc never objected to the Americans' taking notes. On the maps they supplied, he pointed out everything he could remember. As an intelligence source, Tonc couldn't be topped.

Today the three of them gathered in a plywood-and-tin hootch not more than fifty feet from the mess hall. The MP had brought Tonc in and then left, though the others weren't there yet. Tonc was no longer felt to be a threat, not after his information had been proved right time and again. He sat with his hands folded on the table, waiting for Korski and Goddard to arrive.

The two Marines entered a few moments later. Korski sat down opposite Tonc, his elbows on the table. "Good news," the captain said. "You're going to get out of this hellhole."

Tonc sat back and blinked. "What do you mean?"

Goddard pulled out the other chair and sat down. "You've been so cooperative about telling all you know that you're going to Saigon."

"No. I will not go to Saigon."

"Why not?" Korski asked.

Tonc folded his arms across his chest. "I will not go." He sounded like a child refusing to take his medicine.

Korski sat back and hooked an arm over the rear of the chair. As he considered Tonc's reaction, he glanced at their surroundings. It was a typical hootch: dirty plywood on the floor, plywood walls that ended four feet from the ceiling where screening then filled the gap. The rafters showed, as did the tin of the roof. A single ceiling fan revolved slowly, stirring up a little breeze.

"Why not?" Korski asked again. "Saigon is a nice place to be. No war there."

"War is coming to Saigon. I tell you that. War is coming."

Korski waved his hand. "Yes, the war is coming, but not for a few days. Besides, you'll be in a safe place with military policemen to protect you."

"I not tell you anything if you make me go to Saigon."

Goddard reached out and touched Tonc on the arm near the wrist. He knew that some Vietnamese resented being touched. One of the biggest insults was to touch a hand to the head of a Vietnamese. But the beliefs differed depending on the region in Vietnam. It was hard to keep track of all the cultural variations.

"There's no reason not to go to Saigon," Goddard said. "You'll be treated well there, better than here, and it's a much nicer place."

Tonc didn't speak. He just sat there, his lips pressed together.

Korski shrugged. "Well, shit, I thought he'd jump at the chance."

"Will you go?" asked Tonc.

"I'd love to," Korski said, "but I have duties here, as does Sergeant Goddard. But hell, yes, we'd go if we could." Korski was silent for a moment and then added, "I get it. You're afraid. Better the devil you know than the one you don't."

Tonc didn't answer that, probably didn't understand it. He stared into space.

"Listen," Korski said, "you'll be better off in Saigon. First, you won't have to dodge the rockets and mortars of your own company. Second, you've already taken the biggest step. You walked in here without knowing what was going to happen. In Saigon you'll be kept with the Americans and not turned over to the South Vietnamese. You're too valuable to us. You'll be with others who have seen the light and come over."

"No."

"Women," Goddard added. "Some of the VC who have *chieu hoi*ed are women." He grinned broadly. "Good-looking women."

"Come on, it'll be good," Korski added. "Better food and more fun. Here you're taking the chance of getting killed with the rest of us."

Tonc suddenly realized they were begging him to go to Saigon, not ordering him. They could have just showed up with an armed guard and put him on an airplane. They hadn't done that. They'd warned him about the trip and left the decision up to him. Suddenly he knew that Saigon would be a better place. Saigon was where he should be.

"Okay," Tonc said, using the word he'd heard most often at the combat base. "Okay. I go."

"Great," Korski said. "You won't regret it. We'll get you on a plane this afternoon."

MAXWELL SAT in the conference room with a dozen other officers, waiting for General Westmoreland to arrive. With all the activity at the Khe Sanh combat base the past few days, Westmoreland had been getting little sleep. He called meetings at the unlikeliest hours, where he demanded all the information available. He warned that Khe Sanh wouldn't fall to the Vietnamese under any circumstances. He'd already moved more troops into I Corps to make sure the necessary force was there to protect the combat base. Then had come the information from a captured North Vietnamese about sweeping attacks during the Tet holidays. Westmoreland had tried to persuade the South Vietnamese to cancel the holiday celebrations and the leaves of the military, but they had refused.

Maxwell was tired, having spent most of the night consolidating the reports of the Special Forces men assigned to MACV-SOG, the Navy's SEALs and Marine Recon. Reports of heavier-than-usual traffic all along the Ho Chi Minh Trail. Reports of military-age men dressed in black pajamas infiltrating villages throughout Vietnam. Reports of major troop movements at night, when the enemy believed the American equipment was blinded.

There was no doubt among the generals, colonels and top civilians in Saigon and throughout South Vietnam. The storm was brewing and the clouds were about to open. The only question was when it would happen, and the North Vietnamese prisoner at Khe Sanh claimed that the beginning of Tet would mark the beginning of the battle.

The door opened and a major came into the room. He stopped just inside and announced, "Gentlemen, the commander."

As the men inside got to their feet, General Westmoreland entered. He looked tired, with a gray cast to his skin and dark circles under his eyes. His fatigue uniform looked freshly laundered and pressed, with no stains, spots or wrinkles. In one hand he carried a folded newspaper. On his face was a look of rage.

He waved a hand, indicating that everyone was to sit, and then slammed the newspaper onto the table. "It's becoming a sieve. Everything we have, everything we know, goes right to the press, who feel they have to print it."

Maxwell glanced at the paper on the table. It was the *Washington Star* but he couldn't tell what there was about it that had upset the general.

Westmoreland dropped into his chair at the table and shook his head. "Those assholes in the Pentagon or the Administration—feeding everything to the media so they can broadcast it to the world." He looked into each of the faces of the men around the table. "I know it isn't the fault of any of the men here."

The major picked up the paper and flipped it over so that everyone could see the story. The headline made it all clear. Each man understood exactly what the story meant.

Again Westmoreland shook his head. "We get a bit of intelligence that would allow us to stomp the Vietcong and the NVA into the ground, and the American press does everything it can to ruin that opportunity. If I didn't know better, I'd swear they were being paid by the other side."

"How did it happen?" asked one of the men.

"Who knows?" Westmoreland answered. "Someone in the Pentagon or at the White House let the information slip. I can't believe it would happen without some kind of sanction from on high, meaning either the President's office or the Chiefs of Staff. No one lower would have the nerve, and the media wouldn't believe someone lower."

Before anyone could speak, Westmoreland turned to Maxwell. "What does the CIA have to say?"

Maxwell looked down at the pad on the table in front of him. He picked up a corner of it but didn't look up. "Well, General, it doesn't seem that the traffic and infiltration that we've noticed has let up in the past few days. The enemy is still pouring troops and supplies into the South along a very broad front. That would seem to indicate the information received by the Marines at Khe Sanh is accurate."

"Your indications are that the enemy is either unaware of everything we know or doesn't care that we know."

Maxwell nodded his head and then looked at Westmoreland. "As you know, the prisoner came in several days ago. His information has been accurate. Although he must have been missed by the enemy, there's no indication they've changed their plans at all."

Westmoreland pointed at the newspaper, still held by his aide. "And with that?"

Maxwell shrugged and smiled briefly. "Hell, we have no indication the enemy reads the *Washington Star*. If the networks picked it up, then the enemy might have realized the extent of the information we possess. But they may not realize we have it all."

"Then your recommendation is what?"

"General," said Maxwell, "everything I've seen in the past week suggests the enemy is going to fall on us during Tet. Even after the man was captured at Khe Sanh, there has been no change in activity. He laid out the assault on the hilltop camp—" Maxwell consulted his notes "—861, and that happened. He predicted the mortar and rocket attacks, and that's happened. Each bit of intelligence he's given us has come to pass. My recommendation is that we ignore the press story and prepare for the coming assaults."

"Where is this man now?" asked the general.

Glancing at his watch, Maxwell said, "Arriving at Tan Son Nhut if we're lucky. We'll be able to talk to him in person in a few minutes."

"Good," Westmoreland said. He took the newspaper from his aide and tossed it onto the table.

Maxwell could read the headline easily: Major Attacks Predicted for Tet. Under that was a smaller headline: American camps and provincial capitals are targeted.

WHITMIRE ROLLED OVER and looked at the naked flank of Marie Osborne. Her long hair was spread across the pillow, and there was a light coating of sweat on her body. Her eyes were closed and she was breathing heavily.

As he reached down and touched the soft flesh of her inner thigh, he thought about the past several days. He'd been right when he'd thought she was interested in him. When he arrived at the show in one of the Marine clubs, she had smiled broadly, and at the first opportunity, when one of the other girls was at center stage, she had waved at him. A discreet flip of the hand, but he had known what it meant at the time.

As soon as the show ended, she came over and sat down with him. They talked quietly, sometimes having to remain silent as the jukebox blared with the latest rock and roll. Whitmire used the noise to his advantage, suggesting they find a quieter place to talk. It was as easy as shooting fish in a barrel; she was more than willing to return to his room.

Once there, it took no time at all to get her out of her blouse and skirt so that she was sitting on his cot in only her bra and panties. For a while he left her like that, playing with her, slowly teasing her until she nearly demanded that he finish the job.

The first night was a real test for it seemed he couldn't satisfy her demands. He used his fingers and his tongue, holding himself in reserve. She took each assault gratefully, spreading herself wide to receive him. Her gyrating hips nearly bruised his lips and her clutching fingers ripped into the skin of his shoulders. Each time she reached the peak, she groaned deep in her throat and went rigid, her hips thrust upward and her head thrown back, as if she wanted to study the wall behind where she lay.

Finally she seemed to be satisfied. She pushed Whitmire onto his back and then crawled atop him, her hips against his. Leaning forward, her breasts brushing his chest, her lips touching his, she began to rock slowly, forward and backward, only a fraction of an inch as she teased him.

It took a while, but he soon felt the pressure building. Reaching around, he grabbed her bare bottom, cupping the cheeks in his hands. Then he raised himself and pushed, increasing the tempo, thrusting himself at her.

"Oh, you like that," she cooed. "Well, we'll see what we can do."

When he finally exploded, he thought the top of his head would come off. He'd delayed for so long, and then let her control him for so long, that at his climax he nearly lost consciousness. It was an experience he'd never had before.

From that point on they'd spent every hour possible on his cot. Marie was rarely dressed, and when she was, it was in a jungle fatigue jacket that covered her to midthigh. She didn't bother with underwear.

The only diversion was when their work intervened. When Whitmire was scheduled to fly, he had to make the briefings, flights, and debriefings. Marie sometimes went to rehearsals, sometimes avoided them. She made the shows but never stayed around afterward, hurrying back to the hootch where Whitmire waited for her.

After several days of this, Whitmire wondered if he was getting tired of her. She was so open, so available, that he wasn't even sure he liked her.

Now, to find out exactly how much she would take, he shifted around and slid his hand higher. She moaned softly and turned her head so that she could look at him. There was a stupid smile on her face. Whitmire stopped moving his hand, and she pushed down, until his fingers made contact with her again. She rocked her hips, and he felt her wetness beginning again as she moaned deep in her throat.

Whitmire rolled onto his back and pulled her toward him. He forced her head down, toward his crotch. There was an instant of resistance, then she realized what he wanted and took him in her hand and her mouth. She stopped once, looked up and then bent back to work with her tongue and fingers. As he came, she didn't stop, and when he finished she smiled at him.

"You like?"

Whitmire nodded. He had liked it just fine. But now he wanted to go to sleep. He wanted her to get away from him because her body was hot and the air was hot and he was covered in sweat. He wanted to cool off and sleep before someone arrived with the announcement that he would have to fly again.

ALTHOUGH MAXWELL had felt confident when he had told General Westmoreland they should plan for the coming attack, he was less than confident now. In the conference he hadn't been aware that the intelligence had been compromised. It was funny how first the North Vietnamese had had their plan compromised, and then the Americans had had their knowledge of the plan compromised. Everyone seemed to know everything about the Tet attacks, and no one was doing anything about it.

But Maxwell had been around military and intelligence operations long enough to know these things sometimes took on a life of their own. Plans to change or kill an operation had a way of not reaching the right people, and stupid plans that no one wanted would somehow end up being executed.

Still, the intelligent thing would have been for the enemy to either delay or call off the attack. That would have given them some breathing room. It would have caused the Americans and the South Vietnamese, finding that their information was no longer valid, to relax. A surprise attack a week later would then be a much bigger surprise.

So, now that Maxwell had shot off his mouth, he was suddenly afraid the attack wouldn't happen. That would make him look like a complete jerk.

After meeting Tonc at Tan Son Nhut and moving him to quarters on the air base where other former NVA and VC were housed, Maxwell left without interrogating him. When the man was settled in his new surroundings, Maxwell returned to MACV headquarters, where he noticed there were now more guards, each of them armed with M-16s, and wearing flak jackets and steel pots. Several jeeps with M-60s mounted in the rear were parked in the lot. Apparently everyone was taking Tonc's information seriously, at least for now.

Maxwell wasn't hungry for dinner, even though the meal was better than most served in the cafeteria. He returned to his office to work, but that didn't seem the best idea, either. He pushed papers around his desk, but he hadn't been able to sit still. Each sound was a distraction that had to be investigated. Each noise seemed to be the beginning of the offensive, although he knew it wasn't supposed to start until after midnight. He wished he knew where Gerber and Fetterman were and what they had found out.

At midnight Maxwell left the office and wandered down the hallway to where the guard watched the iron gate. Tonight the man was in jungle fatigues, wore a flak jacket and had a steel pot sitting on the floor next to his weapon, along with two bandoliers for it. Outside the gate was a second guard.

"Looks like you're loaded for bear tonight," Maxwell said as he approached.

"Yes, sir. Taking no chances. I've even got a couple of grenades." He stopped talking, and looked around as if he suspected the VC had already penetrated the building. "Got some thermite, too. I'm supposed to burn everything if the enemy gets too close."

"You're expecting the attack, then?"

The guard smiled. "Hell, sir, you're one of them who told us it was coming. Beginning of the Lunar New Year and the beginning of the attack."

From outside came a burst of fire. Maxwell felt his heart stop and start again. His face drained of color. It was starting. It was finally starting.

The guard laughed. "You shouldn't stay cooped up in your office so much. That's been going on for an hour. The slopes are celebrating already. That was an M-60 firing."

"You sure?"

"Yes, sir. We've gone to check a couple of times. The sky downtown is alive with tracers. Don't know why they think it's necessary to waste their ammo that way."

"Yeah." Maxwell was thinking of the helicopters that were above Saigon day and night. With a thousand Vietnamese soldiers firing into the sky, it had to be dangerous for the men flying them. To the guard he said, "Be sure to let me know if anything happens."

"Yes, sir."

Maxwell was on his way back to his office when the first of the rockets slammed into Saigon. He heard the loud, flat bang, even over the other noise. He dived to the floor and rolled to the wall, wrapping his arms around his head. He was suddenly aware of the dirt on the floor and the smell in the cool air. For a moment he closed his eyes, and then opened them again. He glanced to the rear and saw the guard still sitting in his chair, laughing hard.

"Not going to get you down here, sir. Too much shit over our heads for them to get down here."

Maxwell got to his feet and brushed the front of his suit. "No, I guess not."

"Oh, by the way, sir, I think it's started."

10

THE WHITE HOUSE

Lockhart hurried through his lunch and returned to his office early. In Vietnam it was just after one in the morning, and the Lunar New Year was beginning. As he sat down behind his desk, he found he was nervous, just as a ball player might be before a big game. He knew something was going to happen, and he was worried about it.

Knowing that the President would want information as quickly as he could get it, Lockhart tried to concentrate but found his mind drifting. If the information they had was right, the Tet offensive would begin at any moment.

Lockhart worked his way out from behind his desk past the safe and walked to the door. He looked around the hallway like a man waiting for a check in the mail. For a moment he stood leaning against the doorjamb, wondering what was happening half a world away. Wondering if the enemy had decided not to attack.

He rubbed his face with both hands and realized just how tired he was becoming. He'd had too many late nights and early mornings, just enough time to go home, take a shower and change his uniform. His wife was becoming a stranger, though she wasn't complaining, now that she had the number that rang through the White House switchboard. She had no complaints about the nights alone, not with a husband working at the White House.

But it was all beginning to tell. Lockhart was tired. His eyes burned and his head hurt and he prayed that the President or the chief of staff would tell him to take a day off. All he needed was a single day so that he could sleep for twelve hours and then watch TV—anything but the news. Just one day off.

He glanced at his watch. If something didn't happen soon, they could all go home early. Lockhart, having studied the VC and the NVA, didn't believe they would launch their assaults with dawn coming. Charlie would want to take advantage of the night, no later than one or two in the morning, so that he would have several hours to consolidate his gains.

Lockhart returned to his desk and sat down. He picked up a file folder and opened it but couldn't concentrate on the report. It was like asking someone to read while the World Series was being played in front of him. No one could do it.

He closed the folder and pushed it aside. Rocking back in his chair, he laced his fingers behind his head and stared up at the ceiling. He told himself he would have to be patient because there was nothing else he could do. Patience was the name of the game.

The tap at the door caught him off guard. He had expected the messenger to arrive, but not for another hour or so. He waved the Marine into his office.

"Got a bunch of message traffic for you, sir," the Marine said. He set his clipboard on Lockhart's desk and added, "You'll have to sign for them."

Lockhart took the messages and checked the date-time groups on them, making sure he had everything he was signing for. All the messages were classified as secret, and to lose one would be the same as losing his career. A misplaced classified document had spelled the end to a number of careers.

Carefully Lockhart signed his name in each of the places indicated, and as the Marine left, the colonel pulled the cover sheet off the first document. Rocket and mortar attacks had been reported throughout South Vietnam. Every major base had been hit, including Tan Son Nhut, Khe Sanh, Nha Trang and Cam Ranh Bay. Ground attacks had been reported at a number of sites. Special Forces camps and base camps had been hit with probes, but nothing like that at Khe Sanh. Rockets were falling on Saigon, and there were reports of street fighting—VC and NVA shooting at MPs; snipers firing into crowds.

Lockhart was suddenly calm. The turmoil that had been boiling in his stomach was gone, and he relaxed. It was finally beginning, just as they had predicted, just as Tonc had told them it would. The NVA was coming out to fight. Lockhart had no doubt about the outcome of the battle. The enemy would be cut into little pieces.

He pulled a handkerchief from his pocket and wiped the sweat from his face. Stuffing the handkerchief back into his pocket, he picked up the phone and dialed a number. When someone came on the line, Lockhart said, "I need to brief the President on the latest from Vietnam."

"Can it wait?"

"Not this. It's the message we've been expecting for the past few days."

"Come on up, but it might be thirty minutes before I can squeeze you in. How long will it take?"

"Two minutes if the President doesn't want to ask questions. Longer if he does."

Lockhart hung up and then stood. He maneuvered his way out from behind his desk and then stopped at the filing cabinet to pluck his map of Vietnam from the top in case the President wanted to see the overall picture. Satisfied that he had everything he needed, he went upstairs.

An aide, a young man in a gray suit with a white shirt and a dark tie, met him as he got off the elevator. "The President said you were to go right in."

Lockhart stopped outside the door. The aide moved around him, knocked and then opened the door. "Mr. President, Colonel Lockhart is here."

Lockhart entered and stopped short of the desk. He waited until the President said, "What ya'll got for me?"

"If I may, sir," Lockhart said, unfolding his map.

"By all means."

Lockhart spread the map over the desk and then began to read from the first of the classified documents—the reports of the mortar and rocket attacks. He pointed out the cities and bases as he went along. The President nodded, and Lockhart wished he'd taken time to plot the information.

That finished, he started on the ground actions. He read through the list quickly so that the President would have an idea of the volume of activity, and then again slowly, pointing out the locations.

When he finished, the President asked, "Have they moved against Khe Sanh?"

"No, sir, not yet. Just mortars and rockets, as in the past. Lots of mortars and rockets, but no indication that there's any kind of ground action building around there."

"Thank you, Colonel. Please keep me informed."

DOBSON, WONDERING if there was a reason for a renewed order to wear the flak jacket and steel pot at all times and go nowhere without a weapon, sat in his bunker and waited. Sometimes he stared through the firing port, and the rest of the time he sat back, letting someone in another bunker keep watch. There was no way for the enemy to sneak up on them without someone seeing and shooting at them.

He could hear distant pops and crashes as one of the hilltop camps took some incoming, and three booms from falling bombs as the Air Force tried to find the enemy under the jungle canopy and destroy them. But in his immediate vicinity he was aware only of the tropical humidity.

"Shouldn't you be looking out?" Conica asked him.

"In a little while. Right now I just want to sit here and relax. Suck down a little Coke, even if it is warm, and not worry."

"Tonight's the big night."

"If you believe the scuttlebutt," Dobson said.

"It's been right more often than not," Conica reminded him.

At that moment they heard a series of distant pops as the mortars ringing the combat base fired. Conica laughed once, a single bark devoid of mirth. "Sounds like incoming."

Dobson looked out the firing port. There were still flares overhead, lighting the ground with shifting patterns of light and shadow. The light was an eerie greenish-yellow that reflected from the wire on the perimeter. He saw no indication that enemy soldiers were moving outside the wire.

The mortar rounds landed behind him, near the center of the camp, in the area occupied by Charlie Med. Dobson shook his head at the thought. When the camp was erected, it had been assumed that the safest place for the medical unit would be in the center of the base, where the bunkers and the perimeter could protect it from ground attacks. No one had thought about the mortars. Though mortars were hard to aim, the VC and NVA tried to hit the center of the combat base, figuring that short or long rounds would still land in the camp, hitting something. Charlie Med became the aiming stake.

As the rounds detonated, Dobson picked up the binoculars and searched the hills around the base. He spotted the flash as several rockets ignited.

"Rockets," he announced to Conica, his voice calm. After nearly two weeks of daily mortar and rocket attacks, he was no longer frightened by them. He kept his head down and listened to them roar overhead, exploding in the camp. Dobson had learned that Charlie wasn't trying to blow up bunkers with his artillery; he was trying to destroy the camp.

"Shit!" Conica said. "I wish they'd leave us alone for a while."

Dobson turned the binoculars on the perimeter wire, searching the open ground carefully, but there were no indications that Charlie was moving around out there. No movement toward the wire, no movement on the open ground of the killing fields and no movement in the trees several hundred yards away. There were mortars and rockets, but no ground assault.

Dobson finally put down the binoculars. "It's your turn to watch. I want to catch some sleep."

"You can sleep through this?"

Dobson laughed. "If I couldn't sleep through it, I'd never get any sleep."

Conica shrugged. "I guess that's right."

"If anything important happens, wake me."

FOR A FEW MINUTES Maxwell remained sitting on the floor in the hall, listening to the sounds of the rocket attack above him. The guard, too, sat there calmly, glancing upward as the booming continued. Then there was a single, loud crash, and the walls seemed to vibrate.

"Close one," the guard said.

"Too close," Maxwell said. "Way too close."

The guard bent over and scooped up the two bandoliers from the floor. "I think maybe I should head upstairs in case they need some help."

"Wait." Maxwell scrambled to his feet. "Wait right there." He ran back to his office, looked around and saw stacks of paper everywhere. None of it was classified, so he left everything where it was. He slammed the drawer on the safe and spun the combination lock, then opened his desk drawer where his Swenson .45 Auto Custom rested. Jerking it from the holster, he pulled out extra magazines and dropped them into his coat pocket.

After taking one last look around his office, he ran down the hall, catching up with the guard at the gate. As the man locked the gate again, Maxwell asked, "Aren't you deserting your post?"

"Hell, no! I'm just moving it to a more advantageous position. We keep the slopes out of here and everything will be fine. I get picked off, and it won't make no fucking difference to me anyway."

"Then let's go."

The two of them raced upstairs. Now they could hear the rattle of small arms along with the crump of mortars. Maxwell didn't know if the sound was fighting or just the Vietnamese celebrating the Tet holidays.

Upstairs they found that most of the lights had been extinguished. Near the front door a desk had been overturned and two MPs crouched behind it, both armed with M-16s and wearing flak jackets and steel pots. An M-79 lay on the floor between them.

Maxwell turned down a corridor and headed for one of the lounges. Inside, a man with red hair crouched by the window, watching the show outside.

"Christ, you'd think World War III had broken out!" he said to Maxwell.

The CIA man took up a position at the other window. The sky was alive with tracers, thousands of them. There were bright flashes as fireworks detonated, and Maxwell wondered whose bright idea that was. The city was in a war zone where sudden detonations meant sudden death, and some asshole was shooting off fireworks.

There were also flares hanging over Saigon. A dozen of them, dropped from airplanes, were floating low, turning the night a sickening green. Ruby-colored tracers streaked toward a few of the flares as if the Vietnamese were trying to shoot them down.

Underneath all that, in the blackness that shrouded the buildings were flashes of red-orange, either rockets and mortars exploding or more Vietnamese celebrating. Maxwell filed away the thought: if he ever wanted to attack a city, he'd time it so that the entire population was in the streets to mask the assault.

"Can't tell what's going on," the man told him. "Little bastards have been shooting up the sky for an hour."

Maxwell didn't respond; he just watched the street near MACV. Suddenly he realized he had been right; his judgment had been vindicated. He wasn't sure if he was happy about that. Maybe it would have been better if the enemy had called off the attack.

Out by the gate there was a wall of sandbags that hadn't been there that afternoon. Parked behind it was a jeep with an M-60 mounted in it. Five MPs crouched by the wall. A sixth stood near the jeep, binoculars to his eyes as he searched for the attackers who had to be coming.

"I got movement," said Maxwell's companion in the lounge. He lifted his M-16 to his shoulder. "I got movement."

Maxwell looked to the left. He could see the fence that surrounded the MACV compound and the ground just outside it. Floodlights illuminated part of the area. On top of the chain link were huge loops of barbed wire. As Maxwell watched, a man reached up; it looked as if he was trying to cut a hole in the fence.

"That's right, you asshole," said the red-haired man. "Give me a target." He aimed and then shot. The shot sounded as if an artillery piece had been fired. The window shattered with the first round. The man squeezed off another three shots and then grinned at Maxwell. "Never could understand why those assholes in the movies break the windows. The first shot takes care of it."

Maxwell kept his eyes on that section of the fence, but the VC didn't reappear. Then he watched one of the MPs climb into the rear of the jeep, work the bolt of the M-60 and open fire in a short burst. The muzzle-flash stabbed out over the hood of the jeep, illuminating it in yellow.

A green tracer flashed by the man at the machine gun, and he swung around, holding down the trigger. Ruby-colored tracers floated toward the city, some of them bouncing. There was an explosion far short of the sandbags in front of the jeep, and the men there opened fire. They popped up, shot and dropped, moving around, keeping a steady stream of lead pouring out.

Maxwell searched for a target, but had no luck. He could see nothing moving in the partially lit streets or over the grassy slopes that led up to the headquarters building. He shifted right and left, his pistol clutched in his hand. He wanted to smash the window, but the other man's comment about the movies kept him from doing it.

In the distance around him a battle seemed to rage: dueling M-16s and AKs and explosions from mortar shells and rockets. But nothing came close to him. Some of the tracers coming down now were from helicopters or gunships over Saigon. But nothing was happening near Maxwell.

He thought about leaving the window and looking for a post on the second floor. From there he'd be able to see farther, see more. But he would feel as if he was deserting his post—a post that no one had assigned him, but that he had taken.

"Yeah!" said the red-haired man. He fired again. "Got you, you little bastard."

Maxwell turned in time to see the Vietnamese in black fall from the fence to the right.

There was a popping, and the window near Maxwell shattered in an explosion of glass. He dived to the right. The other man turned and quickly opened fire. The sound reverberated in the tiny room, which was filled with the smell of cordite.

Maxwell scrambled to his feet and flattened himself against the wall so that he could peek out the window. The shadows shifted and swayed as the flares swung beneath their parachutes. The MPs at the front were pouring fire into some buildings fifty yards away, but now there was nothing happening in close.

Then a shadow seemed to jump up, hesitate and finally run. Maxwell stepped away from the wall and turned, holding his pistol at arm's length. He fired once, and what little glass was left in the window disintegrated. He aimed at the shadow as it loped across the lawn. The pistol bucked in his hand, but he kept shooting until the shadow sprawled.

"Yeah!" said the red-haired man again. "Nice shooting with a handgun. Nice shooting."

Maxwell dropped to one knee, well back from the window, but still watching everything that was going on outside. The firing around him had tapered off, but not in the rest of Saigon. There were constant explosions from rockets and mortar shells and the boom of the American artillery that ringed the city.

Finally Maxwell sat down, his back against the wall. He wiped the sweat from his face and hands and looked at his watch. Two hours had passed since he and the guard had run upstairs. Two hours that seemed like ten, fifteen minutes. So much had been done. And so little. He had watched the city catch fire as parts of it exploded. He'd watched the MPs take the machine gun out of the jeep and set it up in the center of the sandbagged wall to give the gunner some protection. They had fired a couple of times, but Maxwell hadn't seen the target. Occasionally he had looked at the lawn where the shadow had fallen. It hadn't moved since he'd shot it.

"I think that's about done it," said the red-haired man. "Be light in a little while."

Again Maxwell wiped the sweat off his forehead with the sleeve of his suit coat. He noticed his clothes were smudged with grease, but he didn't really care. "What's your name?" he asked the red-haired man.

The man turned and looked at Maxwell. The CIA man saw for the first time that he was very young—under twenty. He was dressed for war, but didn't have the look of a warrior.

"James Mercher," he said.

"Well, James, where do you work?"

"Clerk typist in the MACV pool. I circulate around the building and help out wherever."

"You did a good job tonight."

"Yes, sir. Knew something was going to happen, so I hung around here and waited."

Maxwell turned to face the window. The sky was beginning to pale and there were black clouds blowing on the morning breeze—smoke from the dozens of fires that had been started during the night. The skyline of Saigon was partially obscured by the smoke. Firing was still coming from there.

Maxwell stood and looked out the window. What had been a shadow on the lawn was now obviously a body, and as he watched it took on detail. Black shorts and a black shirt. A khaki bag that probably contained explosives. It hadn't been much of a sapper attack, but then he should never have gotten inside the wire.

Maxwell looked at his pistol, then put it into his coat pocket. It tugged at that side, pulling the garment out of shape, but the CIA man didn't care. "I'm heading back down to my office, Mercher. I think we've weathered the storm for the night. Charlie's going to be pulling back now. He won't want to be caught in the open during the day."

"Yes, sir. I think I'll just hang on here."

"Fine," said Maxwell. He left the room and walked down the hall. The only damage he could see was minor—a few bullet holes from stray rounds. No rockets or mortars had landed close enough to destroy anything.

The iron gate in the basement was again guarded, but Maxwell didn't recognize the man who checked the access list and Maxwell's ID. In his office the CIA man dropped into his chair, pulled the pistol from his pocket and put it on top of the papers stacked in front of him.

"What a night," he said out loud. He hadn't liked crouching in a dark room waiting for the enemy to come at him. But there had also been a certain exhilaration about it—a dangerous situation that wasn't all that dangerous, a chance of dying without the chance being all that great.

He leaned back, rested his head against the wall and closed his eyes. The situation had been hairy and frightening, but it was what the war was all about. That and career advancement. In a few hours he'd have the chance to advance his career again—just as soon as he saw Gerber and Fetterman.

But that would be later in the day, after he caught a little sleep.

11

Captain Mack Gerber sat in the small below-ground-level office that belonged to Jerry Maxwell. It was a cinder-block structure with a dirty green tile floor and fluorescent lights. Maxwell's desk was shoved into a corner, the edge against the wall lined with Coke cans. There was a visitor's chair next to the desk and opposite the desk and chair was a bank of filing cabinets, the one on the end a massive thing with a combination lock on the second drawer. Papers littered the tops of the filing cabinets and desk. On the wall was a single framed print of American Cavalrymen fighting the Sioux at the Wagon Box Fight.

Maxwell, his rumpled suit stained with sweat and dirt, was sitting at his desk. Black circles under his eyes showed he'd had no sleep the night before, when the Communists had suddenly appeared in the streets of Saigon. His pistol, a Swenson Auto Custom .45 with ambidextrous safeties and slide releases, sat on top of the papers.

For a few moments he just sat with his head down, as if recharging his batteries. Finally he looked up. "Christ, what a night!"

Gerber glanced at Fetterman, who stood leaning against the filing cabinets. The diminutive sergeant's jungle fatigues were stained and dirty, the result of the brief but deadly fight at the U.S. embassy a few hours before. Sappers from the C-10 battalion had blown a hole in the wall around the embassy grounds and tried to get into the buildings. All had been killed, along with a couple of American MPs.

"Jerry," said Gerber, ignoring the normal byplay, "you didn't call us here to talk about last night."

"The funny thing," said Maxwell, "is that we knew it was coming. Knew all about the attack." He turned and stared at Gerber. "General Westmoreland, briefing the press a few minutes ago, told them we know the whole of the Vietcong and NVA plan, but they didn't believe him. Didn't believe a word of it."

"And *do* we?" asked Fetterman.

Maxwell shook his head slowly, like a dog about to attack. "We've got it all," he said. "A captured soldier laid it all out, and he's been right all along. A couple of deviations, but that's understandable. Hell, you two were out there looking around. What didn't we know?"

"The attack on the embassy," Gerber said.

"So what? They sent in a suicide squad and it was wiped out. You wouldn't usually expect the embassy to be a target."

"So how are we doing?" asked Gerber.

"Everything's going fine. Enemy casualties are really high. Ours are heavy compared to the past, but only a tenth, if that, of the enemy's. They're getting hurt badly."

"What's all this got to do with us?" asked Fetterman.

Maxwell leaned back in his chair and tried to smile, but it didn't work. He was too tired. "Intelligence has placed General Giap in this battle. The North Vietnamese hero of World War II and Dien Bien Phu is commanding the troops on one of the battlefields."

"Oh-oh," Gerber said. "I don't like the direction this is taking."

"Now hear me out," said Maxwell, holding up a hand. "We think we've got his headquarters pinpointed and we think we could put a team into the field."

"To do what?" Gerber asked.

"To take him out, of course. Think of the blow to enemy morale if their military hero is cut down. Their plans would be thrown to the four winds, and we might be able to relieve the siege building up at Khe Sanh."

"Hold it a minute," said Gerber. "What's all this crap about Khe Sanh?"

"That's where Giap is. In that area."

"And we're just supposed to figure out where he's hiding and go in and shoot him?" asked Fetterman.

"Well, as you can imagine, the area around Khe Sanh is some of the roughest territory. Mountains, jungles, and they've got artillery in Laos that can lob shells into the Marine combat base there."

"Which means we have about two chances of finding Giap," said Gerber. "Zero and none."

Maxwell pawed through the blizzard of paper that had drifted over his desk. "No, it's not that bad at all. I've got—" he continued to dig and came up with a map "—I've got good information for this one."

"Jesus!" Gerber looked at Fetterman.

"Wait until you hear what we've got," Maxwell said. "Just wait." He spread out the map and then opened a desk drawer and took out a file folder stamped Unclassified in big red letters. From it he extracted a photograph and set it on the map.

"This is Vo Nguyen Giap." Maxwell tapped the picture with a fingernail.

The photo showed a round-faced Oriental man in a military uniform. He didn't look particularly distinguished. He didn't look like someone who could command armies, but then some of the greatest military leaders blended right in with common soldiers.

Gerber picked up the photo, studied it, then handed it to Fetterman, who had moved closer. Fetterman examined the picture for thirty seconds and handed it back.

Maxwell turned his attention to the map. "I don't suppose I have to caution you that anything said from here on in is classified. Highly classified."

"No, Jerry," said Gerber. "You don't have to remind us."

"Fine. Now, as you know, we have a half-dozen small bases monitoring the radio signals out of the North. We also have bases that try to pick up enemy broadcasts in the South and in Laos and Cambodia. We're always on the lookout for enemy radio stations."

"Yes, Jerry," Gerber said. "We're well aware of all that. We helped you out on one of those, remember?"

"Okay," said Maxwell. He bent over the map, examining it closely. He pointed to a place in Laos. "Our monitoring has begun to pay off. We've detected a radio station in this area that could easily be in a cave complex, given the nature of the terrain."

"Yes," said Gerber.

"There's a lot of message traffic out of the radio site, a constant flow of messages directed toward North Vietnam with enough of it in codes that we've broken to know that it's probably some kind of command complex. It's quite possible the whole battle from the Khe Sanh area is directed from there.

"There a point to this?" Gerber asked impatiently.

"That's where you'll find Giap. Little more than a grid square to search with enough enemy troops around to lead you to Giap. What more could you ask for?"

"Orders to the World," Fetterman said. "Orders to the World."

THE PRESIDENT RAGED around the room, his anger obvious in the way he moved and spoke. He stopped, stared at the model of Khe Sanh and raised a hand as if he was going to smash it. Instead, he whirled and moved to the situation map of Vietnam that had been tacked to the wall. He slammed his fist into it and nearly screamed, "How?"

Lockhart sat at the far end of the room, lost in the shadows. Only three lights were on—one over the Khe Sanh mock-up, one by the situation map and the last over the aerial chart of Quang Tri Province. Other men sat along the table, colonels and generals from each of the services and a number of civilians, several of them from the CIA.

The President whirled and pointed at Lockhart. "You told me nothing about this. You said nothing."

Lockhart got to his feet and realized he was trembling. He felt like the boy called from class to be punished by the principal. "Mr. President, my task was to monitor the activity at Khe Sanh, to the exclusion of the rest of South Vietnam."

"Okay," said Johnson. "Okay. Jesus Christ! First the damn South Koreans talk about pulling their troops out, then we lose the *Pueblo* to the North Vietnamese and now this Tet crap."

One of the generals got to his feet. "Sir, I think we should look at Tet as a blessing, as an opportunity to meet the North Vietnamese in open battle where our superior firepower, training and capabilities will destroy them."

"General," the President snapped, "the news media are talking about some kind of rout, and they're not talking about the Vietnamese. They're talking about the Americans."

"Sir, we're holding our own and, in fact, destroying some of the enemy units—"

Johnson nearly leaped onto the table. He slammed his hand against the top. "I don't care what's happening in the field. I'm talking about what's happening on the six o'clock news."

"That doesn't accurately reflect the current situation in Vietnam."

"General," the President said quietly, "the situation that exists on the six o'clock news is the situation that exists in the mind of the American people. Everything else is bullshit."

"Mr. President," Lockhart said, realizing he was courting disaster, "General Westmoreland said this morning that he believes the assaults last night were diversionary attacks carried out to draw our attention away from Khe Sanh."

"Diversionary attacks," said Johnson. "Diversionary attacks all over South Vietnam. Diversionary attacks on our embassy. Is that what General Westmoreland thinks?"

The general who had called Tet "a blessing" had been staring quietly at the tabletop. Now he said, "Most of the enemy's initial gains have already been reversed. There's some
tough fighting in Hue and there are still small firefights raging in Saigon, but in other areas the enemy has been forced to
withdraw, leaving hundreds of dead behind."

"Khe Sanh," said the President. "What the hell's going on
at Khe Sanh?"

"Mr. President," Lockhart said, "indications are that the
night passed fairly quietly at Khe Sanh."

KORSKI AND GODDARD sat in the communications center at
Khe Sanh and listened to the reports of fighting going on all
over South Vietnam. Hundreds of soldiers, thousands of
them, were seeing the elusive Vietcong for the first time. Tens
of thousands of enemy soldiers had swarmed out of the jungles, rice paddies and hamlets to attack the provincial capitals, the American bases and even Saigon. Fighting was heavy
all over South Vietnam as the enemy waited for the uprising
of popular support that the leaders in Hanoi had promised.

"Looks like old La Than Tonc was right about everything," said Goddard.

Korski grinned. "And the assholes wouldn't believe him.
Thought he knew too much for a lowly lieutenant."

"I seem to remember, sir, that you thought the same way,"
said Goddard.

"You know, Sergeant, it isn't a good idea to remind officers
of their mistakes."

"No, sir, even though it's true."

Korski got up and walked toward one bank of radios, listening in for a moment as the Army specialist tuned in the
command frequencies of various units. He looked back at
Goddard. "You know, we've been sitting on our asses, listening to everything Tonc tells us, but it seems to me his information is now all out of date. He's no longer a fresh source."

"Yes, sir," said Goddard. "What does that mean?"

"We've had our moment in the sun, but now we're back in the shadows. We've got to do something to get back out into the limelight, to look good for promotions for both of us."

"Not to mention the fact that Tonc came to us. We kind of fell into that deal."

Korski moved away from the radios and sat down close to the sergeant. He lowered his voice, though he knew the Army specialists were too busy with the radios to listen to anything he had to say.

"What we don't know, anymore, is what's going on just outside the wire," he said, pointing at one wall of the bunker.

"Not since the colonel stopped the recon patrols into the jungle."

"So we've got to get with the recon boys and see if we can get someone into the hills around here."

"Excuse me, sir, but with all the bombs falling and all the artillery being fired isn't that a real danger to our people? They're as liable to be hit by the bombs as Charlie, and Charlie at least knows where to hide. Our guys won't have that advantage."

Korski thought about that. "But if the enemy is massing for the big push, then we have to know it. If we could tell the colonel when and where that push will be, it would be quite a coup for us."

"Yes, sir," said Goddard. He could see the light dancing in the lieutenant's eyes and knew there would be no talking him out of it. After ten days of nearly constant rocket and mortar attacks, the men, all the men, were beginning to get squirrelly, trying to figure out a way to end the constant terror.

Goddard had seen it before. He'd seen it in Korea when the Chinese surrounded huge pockets of Marines and sat back, saturating the hillsides with thousands of artillery rounds, a pounding they kept up until the Americans could stand it no longer. The lack of sleep, the constant fear, the waiting for the shell to fall and end it all had been a strain on even the toughest of men.

At Khe Sanh the shelling had been going on for ten days. The supplies that were supposed to come by air usually failed to arrive. Those that did were insufficient. Aerial drops sometimes went astray so that Marine gunners had to destroy them with artillery to keep the enemy from recovering them. The water supply was adequate, but it came from a single stream that the enemy could easily dam, or poison, which would mean all the water would have to be flown in along with the food and ammo.

Although the majority of Marines didn't know that, they still had to sit in bunkers riddled by shrapnel and wait for the final shell that would kill them. Out of that fear a desperation was born, one that demanded they get out of their holes and do something, anything. Such desperation was what enabled the Japanese to talk soldiers into suicide charges in the Pacific. It caused men to surge out of hiding, to attack anything in a blood lust that was more destructive to the human mind than to the enemy.

Now the lieutenant was beginning to manifest the symptoms. He wanted to go out on patrol to search for the enemy. That wasn't necessary. It was obvious the enemy was all around them. Thousands of them in the hills and jungle around Khe Sanh, waiting for patrols to come out so they could chop them into pieces. And when the rescue parties came out, they, too, would be attacked.

But Goddard knew he could say none of this to the lieutenant. He could only go along with the idea and hope cooler heads would prevail. He had to hope the colonel would see such a mission for what it was and forbid it, because if the colonel thought it was a good idea, a bunch of Marines might die for no reason.

"Let's head over to our bunker and get this thing organized."

"Yes, sir," Goddard said. He buckled the strap on his steel pot, zipped up his flak jacket and picked up his rifle. Although there hadn't been a mortar or rocket explosion for thirty minutes, that only meant the next one was that much closer.

Together they moved to the mouth of the bunker. Outside, the camp was in ruins. Every structure was filled with shrapnel holes. There were craters everywhere. Debris, paper, shell casings, bits of metal and broken equipment were scattered all around.

Goddard didn't want to leave the commo bunker, or even plan a mission outside the wire, but he had no choice. The lieutenant had given an order, and until someone else countered that order, he would have to obey.

Korski slapped his arm. "Let's go."

Reluctantly Goddard got to his feet and began the sprint to the protection of the next bunker.

NEITHER GERBER nor Fetterman spoke as Maxwell outlined the whole plan. They would be flown into the Khe Sanh combat base, would get their sniper rifle from the Marines and then sortie out of the base, avoiding Route 9, the remains of the town of Khe Sanh—now nothing more than a deserted ruin—both the town of Lang Vei and the Special Forces camp there. Then they would walk into Laos.

Fetterman studied the map and shook his head. "That's stupid," he said.

"What's stupid about it?" Maxwell asked.

Before Fetterman could answer, Gerber said, "First, we should take our own sniper weapon. Sergeant Fetterman has a better rifle than most of the weapons the Marines have. Second, there's no reason for us to walk in. You yourself told us about the tens of thousands of enemy soldiers in the region. There's no way we'd be able to avoid them all. We can stage out of Khe Sanh."

"Not to mention," Fetterman added, "that there's a Special Forces compound at Khe Sanh. We could draw a security team from there—people who know the countryside. That would be a help."

"No, it's just going to be the two of you," said Maxwell. He sat down and leaned the back of his chair against the wall.

"There's no way I'd take this assignment without a security team," said Fetterman.

"You went after the Chinese officer without a security team," Maxwell pointed out.

"Different circumstances," Fetterman said. "We weren't walking into a battle zone that time. No one expected us or was looking for us."

"Besides, there's no airlift," said Maxwell. "You can't expect to be flown into Laos."

"Why not?" Gerber asked. He pointed to the map. "Even if we flew over the target area and walked in from the west, it would be better. We'd be avoiding the majority of enemy troops. They wouldn't expect us from the west."

"And one other thing," said Fetterman. "I think we should be armed with those new sound suppressors. Only noise from the M-16 is a quiet pop lost in the jungle."

"You can't snipe with that," said Maxwell.

"Of course not," said Fetterman, "but it gives our security team an advantage. They can shoot it out with the bad guys without a lot of noise from our side."

"This is ridiculous," Maxwell said. He picked up one of the Coke cans, and shook it. When he determined it was empty, he tried the next one. Finally he gave that up and faced Gerber and Fetterman again. "You can't go giving us instructions."

"Jerry," said Gerber, "how many times do we have to go through this? If you expect us to go on the mission, you've got to expect us to tell you what we need. Now if we leave from the Khe Sanh base on foot, we're not going to get far. We fly out, and we're going to be able to get into position."

"If that's the case," said Maxwell, "why don't you just leave from Da Nang, or Nha Trang, for that matter?"

"A good question," Gerber said. "It was you who said we had to land at Khe Sanh."

"That was when you were going to walk out."

Fetterman looked at the map again. "I think Khe Sanh is still the best staging area. Provides us with some protective coloration. A flight out at dusk, winging around toward Da Nang and then breaking for Laos, would certainly confuse the enemy. Everything we need is at Khe Sanh. I imagine the Marines could tell us everything we need to know about the territory. We wouldn't have that advantage at Nha Trang."

"Is there a problem getting into or out of Khe Sanh?" asked Gerber.

"The base is still under the eye of enemy gunners, but the resupply aircraft and helicopters are landing there daily." Maxwell laughed. "Men scheduled for R and R are getting out for their leaves. Wounded are evacuated all the time. There are a dozen, two dozen flights in and out."

"Then it seems to be the thing to do. You arrange for us to get on a plane to Da Nang, or whatever staging area is being used for the airlift into Khe Sanh, and we'll set everything up there."

"I'll have to clear the changes with my higher-ups," said Maxwell.

"Why? They don't need to know our plan. Let them think we're doing it their way. In fact, once we get there, we might make other changes."

Maxwell nodded, conceding the argument. "When can you be ready to leave?"

Gerber glanced at Fetterman and thought about the long night they had just spent fighting in the streets of Saigon. Flight time to Da Nang was something less than two hours. Not enough time to get rested. But then it would take a couple of days to get ready for the trip into the field, if they were going to do it right. Plenty of time to get some sleep.

"This afternoon. Let us get cleaned up, grab our weapons and we'll be back here."

"No," Maxwell said. "From the SOG compound at Tan Son Nhut."

"Tan Son Nhut then," said Gerber. "See you then."

12

KHE SANH COMBAT BASE

Dobson was huddled in the remains of his bunker, trying not to think about another night of enemy shelling, of enemy probing. His body stank, but he was unable to do anything about it. Water was precious at the combat base and was used only for drinking. There was none for showers and little for shaving.

Conica was at the firing port, watching as the rain fell, turning the grass bright green, but also turning the scarred plateau into a sea of thick, choking mud that made life that much more miserable. The constant damp soaked through everything, into everything, so that nothing dried. When the sun was out, baking the ground, the humidity was almost visible.

Dobson tossed the can from his C-ration meal out the door at the rear of the bunker and into the pile of others like it that sat there in a rotting, festering dump that grew each day and would have drawn a colony of rats if it hadn't been for some of the other trash heaps. The rats that had survived the enemy shelling were attracted to the huge piles of garbage around the mess halls that still operated, to the Vietnamese parts of the perimeter, and to Charlie Med in the center of the base where medics worked to save lives and patch wounds. Rats were becoming a serious problem there. Near Dobson's end of the perimeter they weren't a problem because the men there shot at everything that moved, even if the movement was inside their own bunker. Dobson had killed two rats that morning with his pistol and had chucked the bodies into his miniature garbage heap. It seemed to work like a talisman to keep the rats away.

Conica finally turned from the firing port. "Your turn."

"What's the point?" asked Dobson. But even as he spoke, he crawled forward so he could look out onto the open field where Charlie never appeared. Once or twice he saw flashes in the distance and knew that enemy rockets had been ignited, but he couldn't shoot at them and couldn't stop them.

Dobson and Conica had been sitting there for days, going out only long enough to piss or to run to the shitter at the rear of the line. The stench was almost as overpowering as a gas attack, when the wind blew from the wrong direction.

"A cold beer," said Dobson.

"What about it?" Conica asked.

"I wish I had one. A cold beer and a shower, even a cold shower. And hot water to shave with."

"Don't want much, do you? While you're at it, how about a woman? There's plenty of them with the USO shows touring the country."

"But we'll never see one in here," said Dobson. "There'd be hell to pay if one of the dollies got herself greased while entertaining the troops."

"Besides," Conica added, "there's no generals around here to impress. Best we can do is scare up some colonels, and they don't have enough pull."

"A long-haired woman in a short skirt. No, better yet, a bikini. A stripper. That's what we need in here. A stripper."

"Christ on a stick!" said Conica. "I think you've flipped out." He glanced down at the mud bubbling up through the slats of the bunker's wooden flooring. Dirt was spilling from the sandbags, and cans from C-ration meals were heaped in the corner. A heavy odor of unwashed bodies hung in the air. "A stripper would take one look at you and run for her life."

"What's your favorite position?" asked Dobson.

"My favorite position? For what?"

"Fucking, you asshole. What'd you think? Mine's with the girl on top, leaning forward so her tits hang in your face and you can lick them. Let her move her hips back and forth slightly, sort of rubbing herself on you, know what I mean?"

Conica grabbed at his crotch and tugged at his pants until he was comfortable. "This isn't doing us any good," he snapped. "Talking about it makes it worse."

"How can things be worse?" Dobson asked. His feet were wet, his clothes were wet, and the coming night didn't seem to offer any relief. He was sick of eating cold C-rations, but it was nearly impossible to build a fire now that the monsoons had arrived. Rain soaked through everything, and the humidity stayed at one hundred percent. Nothing dried. Besides, hot C-rations weren't really any better than cold.

"Well, we ain't going to get a USO show or anything else. We're lucky to get enough ammo."

"She'd be tall," Dobson said. "Tall and naked with just a hint of hair between her legs."

"Shut up! Shut up! I don't want to think about it anymore."

There was a distant pop. Dobson leaned forward, searching for the enemy mortar tube. He glanced back in the gloom of the bunker. "Incoming."

"Who the fuck cares," Conica snarled. "If they'd hit us, we could get the fuck out of here."

FETTERMAN CAME AWAKE as the plane touched down at Da Nang. It bounced once and settled onto the runway. The engines roared as they slowed suddenly. The back of the plane filled with the odor of hot oil and grease. Then the roar died and the plane slowed, turning and taxiing to the ramp at the bottom of the tower. As it lurched to a halt, the loadmaster, trailing a long, black cord, moved to the front and opened the hatch.

Gerber was on his feet, pulling his rucksack from under the troop seat. It hadn't taken Maxwell long to get everything arranged for them. Almost as he'd said it, they'd found themselves on their way to the airport with only enough time to grab the equipment they would need. Fetterman had retrieved his sniper rifle, which was now enclosed in a solid case that could take a real beating. They had changed uniforms and run right back out. The jeep took them through the streets of Saigon, which were strewn with rubble from the fighting the night before. Smoke drifted on the light breeze. There weren't the crowds on the street they would have expected, but given the activity of the night before, that wasn't surprising.

The gate at Tan Son Nhut was guarded by a tank and a dozen military policemen. No Vietnamese, man or woman, was being allowed on the base. Too much had happened in the early-morning hours. All around was the destruction from the attacks launched against the Air Force. Rubble, bits of wood, equipment, paper, garbage littered the area. One building had burned to the ground and was little more than a smoking ruin. Only a few men were visible and all were armed. The casual civilian air of the base had been replaced by the air of men waiting for a war to start.

They had to wait on a ramp, and then the airplane, its engines running already, was brought out. They rushed into the rear, up the ramp, and almost before they could get seated, the aircraft was rolling again. No one was giving Charlie the chance to destroy a C-130.

The flight itself, at twenty-five thousand feet, was relaxing. The enemy had no weapons in South Vietnam that could reach that altitude, but just in case, the flight route was over the South China Sea out of sight of Vietnam.

Now, with the C-130 safely on the ground, it was time to get out. Gerber, holding his M-16 in his left hand, stepped back, waiting for Fetterman to stand up. "Let's go."

"What's the big rush?" asked Fetterman.

Gerber grinned. "I don't like standing around in this big, fat target."

Fetterman picked up the case that held his sniper rifle. He checked it over and found that it was as clean and sound as it had been when he'd stored it.

As they climbed from the plane, two of the propellers were still spinning. They dodged toward the nose and saw a jeep at the base of the tower.

"A ride for us?" Fetterman asked.

Gerber angled toward the jeep. "I wouldn't be surprised. Maxwell's good at that sort of thing."

As they approached the jeep, the driver hopped out and came forward, saluting. He was an Air Force NCO, the huge black stripes of his rank covering both arms of the short-sleeved shirt of his tailored fatigues. "Welcome to Da Nang. Are you Captain Gerber?"

Gerber returned the salute. "With Sergeant Fetterman."

"Yes, sir. We've got you scheduled out of here on the first flight tomorrow. I've arranged for quarters for both of you, and dinner."

Fetterman threw his rucksack into the back of the jeep and crawled in after it. He sat there, looking pleased with himself. Gerber handed him his rucksack, then climbed into the passenger seat.

"I'll take you by the billeting office so you can store your weapons," the Air Force sergeant said.

"Wait a minute," Gerber said. "We'll just hang on to the weapons, if you don't mind."

"Sir, policy here is that all transients and nonessential personnel store their weapons when not actually assigned to duties that would require a weapon."

Fetterman laughed, but not because he found anything funny about the situation.

"Sergeant," said Gerber, "I'll hang on to my weapon. After what happened last night, all over South Vietnam, I'm not about to give up my weapon for some stupid, local regulation."

"Yes, sir. Then we'll head over to get you settled in for the night."

They wound their way off the airfield and passed the smoking ruins of a building, the embers still glowing, despite the dampness of the monsoon season.

"Rocket attack," said the sergeant. "Charlie hit us with a lot of rockets last night, probably hoping to destroy a lot of airplanes."

"Anyone hit the wire?" asked Fetterman.

The driver shot a glance over his shoulder. "I guess there was a probe or something. I don't know. This morning we went over to one side and looked at the VC hanging in the wire. Not too many of them."

As they got away from the airfield, there were more lights. Not just small lights so the men could see to go about their business, but larger lights that marked the locations of the clubs and night spots. A number of soldiers were dressed in flak jackets and steel pots, but there were quite a few men without them, as if the war was directed at only some of the men.

They pulled up in front of a long, low building made of plywood and screen. On top of the tin roof green rubberized sandbags had been laid in rows with a military precision. There were a couple of large shrapnel holes in the roof.

"A little damage done here last night," said the sergeant. "A couple of men were wounded before they could get to the bunker."

"And where might that be?" Gerber asked.

The sergeant got out and pointed at the side of the building where a sandbagged structure stood. There were fifty-five-gallon drums on top of it, covered with PSP, with another couple of layers of sandbags on top of that. It was designed to detonate mortar shells and rockets and throw the shrapnel down into the lower levels of sandbags. That kept the destructive power of the rocket or mortar shell away from the bunker itself.

"The bunker should be on a straight line from the doorway," observed Fetterman.

"But then it would have to sit in the parking lot and wouldn't look good."

"Heaven forbid that it not look good," Gerber said.

They went inside. Gerber had half expected to see red lights in the hallways, but that wasn't the case; bright white light burst from the door when it was opened. They hurried inside to a clerk's window. The man there was wearing civilian clothes and didn't look happy about his job.

"Guys from Saigon," the driver said to him. Then he turned to Gerber and Fetterman. "I'll leave you here."

"Whoa," Gerber said. "Before you run off, there are some things I need to know."

"Yes, sir."

"First, we're supposed to be getting to Khe Sanh."

"Yes, sir," said the driver. "That's no problem. You're manifested through on the first flight in the morning."

"Will you pick us up?" asked Fetterman.

"No, but someone will be here. The flight's scheduled to take off at seven, but I doubt it'll go. The weather's been taking a real toll. Low-hanging clouds both here and at Khe Sanh have kept us from getting off on time. Late morning at the earliest. And the enemy's screwed things up."

"But someone will be here?" Gerber repeated.

"Yes, sir, by six-thirty. Anything else?"

"That covers it," said Gerber.

As the driver left, the clerk pushed a couple of keys across the desk. "Sir, you'll be in the right wing with the other officers. Sergeant, you'll be in the left."

"I'd prefer it if we could stick closer together," said Gerber.

The clerk shrugged and turned to the board behind him where the keys hung. He snagged another one and said, "You'll both be in the right wing then." He turned to his left where a white board covered with acetate hung. Wiping Fetterman's name off one place, he wrote it over the new room number.

"You get many Vietnamese in here?" asked Gerber.

"No, sir. This is an American-only billet."

"Yes, but do you have Vietnamese workers who come in here? To clean or paint or whatever."

"Yes, sir. They didn't make it in this morning, of course, but normally we have Vietnamese staff."

"So they know the names of everyone in residence in this billet, and can track their movements."

The clerk looked at the information board, then looked back at Gerber. "Nothing there to tell anyone anything."

"Right," said Gerber. "Just the names of every officer and NCO in the place. With a little research, the enemy could be getting a great deal of important intelligence about troop movements. We make no secret of who commands what divisions, who their aides are and so on."

The clerk stared at Gerber for a moment, then sat down. "That's not my problem. I just do what I'm told."

Gerber picked up the keys and flipped one to Fetterman. They left the man sitting behind his desk, and walked down the hallway. Plywood walls, a plywood floor covered with a cheap carpet and a ceiling that opened to the roof. There were fans set up there to circulate the air, helping to cool the interior of the structure.

Gerber found his door and opened it, reaching inside to turn on the light. "You want a drink of Beam's before you sack out?"

"Of course," Fetterman said.

They entered. There was a cot with a blanket and pillow, a dresser that had seen better days, a single chair and a shelf near the bed that held a towel, washcloth and glass.

"Not quite as comfortable as the hotel in Saigon."

"No, sir, but it's better than a hammock in the jungle or a bunker at Khe Sanh."

Gerber dropped his rucksack onto the bed and opened it, extracting a bottle of Beam's.

"I'm a little surprised that you'd want to hump that," said Fetterman.

"Oh, no," said Gerber. "I have no intention of taking it into the field, but I knew we'd need something before we got into Khe Sanh. Once there, I can trade it for anything we need."

Now Fetterman grinned. "Then I won't drink too much of it tonight."

"That would be appreciated, Master Sergeant."

Fetterman took the glass from the shelf and held it out. Gerber poured two fingers into it, then held up the bottle. Fetterman touched the rim of the glass to the bottle and swallowed the liquor. "It's still smooth."

Gerber sat down on the bed and drank from the bottle, then set it on the floor. "You been thinking about this mission?"

"Yes, sir."

"Seems to me," said Gerber, "we'll want to get the parachutes here. The Air Force probably has something we can use. Marines at Khe Sanh might not have what we need."

"I don't like letting someone else rig the chutes. Never have."

"That's the only problem I see, until we get to Khe Sanh. Once there, you might even have the opportunity to rerig the chutes."

Fetterman didn't respond.

"You've got to hand it to Maxwell," said Gerber. "He decides on something and he gets it organized to the last detail. Manifests us through to Khe Sanh. Everything ready for us."

"Except the chutes."

"Only because that's a detail we added ourselves. I wouldn't be surprised if we find ten, twelve chutes on the plane tomorrow, or find them waiting at Khe Sanh. We'll just take care of that detail, too, in case something fell through the crack."

"Yes, sir," Fetterman said, finishing his drink. He sat back, closed his eyes for a minute, then opened them. "Quite a day."

"And night." For a moment the visions of the fight at the American embassy swirled through Gerber's mind. Crouching outside the wall, waiting for daylight so they could attack the Vietcong who'd breached the wall. The fighting in the street. The dead and wounded MPs caught by the savagery of the assault.

He shook his head, driving the thoughts from it. After the mission out of Khe Sanh there would be time to think about everything that had happened just before Tet and during the hectic time last night. Now he had to concentrate on the upcoming mission.

Fetterman got to his feet and went to the door. "See you for breakfast tomorrow?"

"Sure," said Gerber. "Breakfast."

"Night, Captain."

"Good night, Tony."

WHITMIRE DIDN'T EVEN bother going to the club. The USO show for the night had been canceled because of the enemy attacks the night before. The performers had been held at Da Nang, where it was felt they would be safer. The base there was so large and well protected that the odds of anything happening to performers was considered remote. Orders for their evacuation had been canceled when the plane warming up on the ramp had been bracketed by mortars.

Whitmire lay on his cot, a cold beer near his hand on the tiny nightstand some grunt had cobbled together from an old ammo crate and sold to him for a couple of bucks. A single lamp burned, the glow dimmed by the OD green towel thrown over it.

Standing near the lamp was Marie, her long hair hanging down her back. She hadn't been in her clothes for more than a few minutes since the two of them had heard the news that the USO show was canceled. Her clothes lay on the footlocker where they had been thrown. She turned, a hand on her naked hip, and asked, "Can't we do something?"

Whitmire couldn't let that comment pass. He tossed the sheet off his body. "Sure. Come here."

"No, something other than that. I want to go out."

Whitmire reached for the beer and took a deep swallow. "You know, you're becoming a real bitch. This is a combat zone. It's not like the World where there are nightclubs on every corner downtown. What the fuck do you expect us to do?''

"How about a movie? They show movies here, don't they?"

"They've been canceled for the duration of the crisis. Nothing I can do about it." Whitmire sat up and swung his feet onto the floor.

She stood there, her body highlighted by the lamp's glow. A slight sheen of perspiration coated her skin. "Well, I want to do something."

Whitmire shook his head slowly, and wondered why women always had to talk afterward. Why couldn't they just lie there quietly, basking in the afterglow, and keep their stupid mouths shut? They always wanted to talk, to be told they were wonderful and beautiful and that it had never been so good, as if that would absolve them from the guilt they all seemed to feel.

Marie came closer and sat on the bed beside him. She put a hand on his naked thigh. "I don't mean to be difficult, but this is boring."

"Thank you very much."

"No, silly, not that. This. Nothing to do. You have missions to plan and fly, but I'm left here without even the show to break up the monotony. It's just no fun."

"Listen," he began sharply, then realized it wasn't her fault she was stupid. "Okay. I'll get into a flight suit and see if I can borrow a TV. Maybe AFVN is on the air and we can watch a little television."

"Oh, would you? That would be nice."

Whitmire stood up, just to get away from her touch. It wasn't that he was being nice; the television would shut her up for a while, give him some peace and quiet. That had been the nice thing about the USO show; it had gotten her out of the hootch for a few hours, and if he didn't feel like seeing the show, he could stay where he was.

He slipped into the flight suit and stuck his feet into his shower shoes. "You wait right here and don't get dressed. Understand?"

"Sure, sweetie. I'll wait right here."

Whitmire headed out and turned to the right. Davis had a small black-and-white television he should be able to borrow. Davis was on R and R and had locked the TV into his wall locker. Fortunately Whitmire had the key.

As he stepped into Davis's hootch, he mumbled again, "War is hell."

13

DA NANG

The C-130 Hercules sat on the ramp, but the engines weren't turning and the red flags that had to be removed before flight were still attached to it. There didn't seem to be anyone around to make the preflight inspection. Gerber stood at the side of the control tower in the moisture-laden air and looked at the water standing on the ramp and runway. Heavy monsoon rains had battered the base the night before, and now in the daylight, the sky seemed to be coming down out of the hills to attack, just as the enemy did—roiling, boiling blacks and grays that didn't look to be more than one or two hundred feet above the ground.

A single ray of sunlight burst through like a spotlight on the featured act. Gerber stared up into the sky, but the clouds closed over again, and there didn't seem to be any other holes.

"Doesn't look like anyone plans to take off soon," said Fetterman.

"Sure doesn't." Gerber moved to the right and through the open door of the terminal. A bored-looking clerk dressed in Army fatigues sat with his feet propped on a flimsy wooden desk. His uniform was a faded gray and his boots hadn't seen polish in months.

When the man saw Gerber, he asked, "Can I help you?"

Gerber shook his head, wondering what had happened to discipline. Then he remembered that they weren't at a forward base where the discipline had to be tough. Here at Da Nang it didn't make that much difference. The majority of the soldiers were draftees, who were just marking time until they could DEROS and then ETS. "Flight schedules?"

The man grinned and closed his comic book. "Fucked up beyond all recognition. Weather's so bad that nothing's taking off for an hour, maybe more."

"We were scheduled to fly to Khe Sanh," said Fetterman.

"Shit, why do you want to go there? A real mess. People shooting at one another."

"Yes," said Fetterman with a sinister smile. "Just the thing we're interested in."

The man twisted around and looked at the board behind him. Aircraft numbers, aircrews, destinations and cargos were written there for all to see. If enemy intelligence could get an agent into the terminal with any regularity, they would have no trouble preparing for American attacks. Everything was telegraphed as surely as if the enemy command structure was on the distribution lists for the orders and the battle plans.

"Maybe an hour," said the clerk, "if the ceiling raises some. I understand the weather at Khe Sanh is even worse."

"Thanks," Gerber said. He and Fetterman retreated to the ramp. He rubbed a hand over his face and wiped the sweat on his jungle shirt.

"Now what, sir?" Fetterman asked.

"Well, we've plenty of time to scare up the parachutes, eat breakfast and then just come back here to wait for a plane to take off."

"Weather's sure tearing up the schedules."

"Think of how the Marines must feel. Their lifeline is the Air Force flying in supplies, and the Air Force isn't flying anything, anywhere."

HOBBS STOOD OUTSIDE the bunker of the Special Forces compound on the southwestern corner of the Khe Sanh base, about as far from the runway as he could get, and stared into the fog-choked jungle. There seemed to be a cool breeze blowing in from Laos.

With a pair of binoculars borrowed from the Marines, he tried to see down Route 9 toward Lang Vei. For several days he'd been telling the Marines that he wanted to get to Lang Vei, and for several days the marines had been telling him to hang loose, something would be worked out. Now there were orders from Nha Trang, holding him at Khe Sanh when he wanted to be at Lang Vei.

With the Marines, he'd endured thousands of mortar rounds and rockets, he'd helped turn back one probe of the wire and he'd listened to the fighting taking place on the hills around the combat base. Unlike the Marines, he felt left out. Somehow, he felt, he should be out there in the thick of it, not hiding behind the wire and bunkers at Khe Sanh.

Quinn, holding a can of C-rations, walked up beside him. "Communications tells us that some hotshots are inbound from Saigon. We're to wait for them."

"Wonderful," Hobbs said. "They tell you anything else?"

"Just that we're supposed to be at the airfield in about three hours to meet the people. They'll have orders for us."

"But nothing about them?"

"Not really, no."

"Okay," said Hobbs. "Alert the others so we can all be there. The only thing we can do is play it by ear."

BY LATE MORNING, the plane was ready for takeoff. Gerber and Fetterman were stuck up front near the cockpit, while the majority of the space was taken up by huge pallets that held a ton of material, held in place by giant cargo nets and thick straps. They were set up on rails on the deck of the aircraft so they could be pushed from the rear of the plane by one man, or dragged out by parachutes at low altitude.

Gerber wasn't happy about being crammed in there with tons of ammunition and supplies. He was thinking about a bumpy ride where the loads broke loose, crushing him. Fetterman, however, didn't seem to be all that concerned.

For nearly thirty minutes they sat strapped into their seats, waiting for something to happen. There was no cooling system, and with the sun now peeking through the clouds, the metal was beginning to bake. The smell of fuel filled the plane making it hard to breathe.

"Any time," Gerber said.

"You have to relax, Captain," Fetterman told him. "Nothing you can do about it."

"They didn't have to put us in here so early. We could have waited in the terminal building."

"This way we don't miss the plane."

"No, this way they fly our bodies to Khe Sanh," Gerber said. He wiped sweat from his face and shifted around in his seat. Heat radiated from the fuselage, and the temperature in the plane climbed. Finally there was a roar, and the Hercules began to shake as its first engine started.

The loadmaster worked his way forward and bent over them. "I have to make sure your seat belts are buckled," he shouted over the sound of the engine. "Now, when we land at Khe Sanh, we'll open the passenger and crew access door there. Get out and run for the front of the plane. There should be someone on the ramp to direct you to safety."

"It's that bad?" Gerber yelled.

"Sir, they're in the hills around the base, waiting for planes to land. They'll start shooting the moment we appear, trying to put holes in the runway in front of us. We have thirty seconds to a minute and a half to unload and get out. We put you out the front so that we can shove everything down the ramp. We hardly stop taxiing."

"Okay," said Gerber. "How long is the flight to Khe Sanh?"

"Thirty minutes, more or less," said the loadmaster. "But we might have to orbit for a while, depending on the weather and the situation on the ground."

"Thanks."

The pilots started the other engines and then the plane just sat there, waiting to join the line of aircraft scheduled for takeoff. The noise prevented conversation, and both Gerber and Fetterman had been given earplugs.

The plane rolled forward finally, stopped, then continued out. After a few minutes, it began to coast down the runway, picking up speed. The sound of the engines filled the cargo bay along with the odor of hot oil. With a sudden bounce the plane was airborne, climbing steeply.

After several minutes the level of noise diminished, and the angle of the climb smoothed out. They were at altitude, above the clouds that had shaded Da Nang. Gerber unbuckled his belt and moved around the huge pallets of cargo, working his way to the rear of the plane where he could stand and look out. But there was nothing for him to see, just the endless green of the jungles and the fields, some rice paddies, rubber plantations and a few coffee plantations. Gerber had been surprised to learn that there were areas of Vietnam where coffee was grown. But then, he'd also been surprised to see fields of corn. To him, Vietnam meant jungle and rice paddies.

He stood there, looking out, until the loadmaster touched his shoulder. "Sir, you'll have to return to your seat. We're about five minutes away now."

"We going straight in?"

"That's the plan right now."

"Thanks." Gerber worked his way to the front and dropped into the seat next to Fetterman. The master sergeant had pulled their equipment out from under the troop seat and was holding on to his, his weapon in his right hand and his rucksack in his left. Gerber's equipment was stacked there waiting. The parachutes they had wanted were stacked on the last pallet and strapped down. They wouldn't have to worry about them until after they were on the ground.

The noise of the engines changed, becoming louder and higher, as if the engines were straining. The plane vibrated and the angle became steeper, as if they were plunging out of the sky. The loadmaster, using the cargo nets and the fuselage for hand holds, worked his way toward them. "Couple of minutes. Get ready."

Fetterman nodded and Gerber held up a thumb.

Moments later they seemed to hit the ground. The plane bounced sharply, shaking violently, and then the engines began to shriek. Gerber and Fetterman were thrown forward as the pilots fought to slow the aircraft. The plane turned sharply, and as it did, the loadmaster was up, and moving to the hatch. As the Hercules jerked to a stop, he opened the door, lifting in and then up.

At the same time Gerber jerked at the catch of his seat belt. It fell away, and he headed for the door. Dropping to the PSP of the ramp, he moved toward the nose of the airplane. As he did so, he saw a dozen men run from the terminal building. They were dressed in dirty fatigues, carried weapons, duffel bags and rucksacks and were holding their helmets on their heads.

As the Marines who were boarding to leave Khe Sanh ran past him, Gerber hurried toward the building. Scattered piles of sandbags littered the ramp, looking like bunkers that had collapsed. At one side were twisted strips of PSP, torn from the runway and replaced by new pieces. As he approached the low sandbagged building, he saw a sign that welcomed him to Khe Sanh, courtesy of the Air Force's Fifteenth Aerial Port Squadron.

Fetterman joined him as the C-130's engines roared again and the prop wash hit them like a brick wall. Gerber crouched, his back to the plane. There was an explosion at the far end of the ramp and then another closer to them.

Gerber leaped up and over a low wall of sandbags, flattening himself against the ground. Fetterman joined him as another round detonated nearer. The roar of the plane nearly drowned out the sound of the enemy mortars. There was a shower of dirt and debris as a mortar round dropped closer. Then came the sudden, flat bang of a rocket.

Gerber peeked over the wall and saw the plane on the runway. Sunlight flashed from its windshield and a plume of smoke and dirt sprouted behind it. Then the plane leaped into the air, almost as if it had been kicked in the ass. It struggled in a steep climb. From the hills around Khe Sanh, the enemy opened fire with small arms and machine guns. Tracers flashed dimly and then the Hercules was through the clouds.

The barrage didn't stop. Enemy gunners kept shooting, trying to hit the supplies now unprotected on the ramp. Puffs of smoke rose, and dirt and bits of metal from the PSP flew about. Marines were hiding behind whatever protection they could find, waiting for a chance to get at the supplies and get them under cover.

Then the artillery, the 155 mm battery on the west side of the camp, opened fire. There were six loud crashes, a moment of silence and then six more. On the hills to the north and west, the artillery rounds exploded. Gerber was up then. He moved to the right, along the short wall.

A man came from the terminal building. His green beret was molded to his head, his uniform dirty. "You Captain Gerber?"

"That's right."

"Sergeant Hobbs. I was ordered to meet you here, sir. Welcome to Khe Sanh."

"Are the landings always like that?"

Hobbs grinned and reached out to take Gerber's rucksack. "No, sir. That was a relatively safe one. Charlie sometimes launches twenty or thirty rockets."

"Great." Gerber jerked a thumb over his shoulder. "That's Sergeant Fetterman."

Hobbs looked and held out a hand. "Welcome, Sergeant. I suggest we get the hell out of the open."

"I'm right behind you, Sergeant," said Gerber.

WHITMIRE SAT STIFFLY, his hands near the controls as the plane plunged out of the sky, the runway into Khe Sanh spread out in front of him. He was bathed in sweat and his muscles were tight. He knew the hills and fields around Khe Sanh were alive with enemy soldiers who would love nothing more than to down one of the C-130s.

He tried to concentrate on the instruments and then the runway, but found himself searching the green valleys and hills for a sign of the enemy. He watched for the telltale muzzle-flashes of the big antiaircraft guns and waited for the thud of rounds slamming into the thin skin of his aircraft.

The intelligence briefing hadn't changed much in the past week. Ten thousand, twenty thousand NVA and Vietcong armed with AKs and 12.7 mm machine guns. Heavy firing could be expected.

Whitmire hadn't bothered listening to that because there was nothing he could do about it. He didn't have a weapon with which to shoot back; he had no bombs to drop and no missiles to fire. He could only sit in his world of Plexiglas and metal and wait for an enemy bullet to find him.

On the flight to Khe Sanh he had tried to concentrate on Marie. She'd been so grateful after he'd found the little TV that she had ignored it and tried to please him. She had laid her head on his bare belly and first used her hands and then her mouth. Whitmire had appreciated it and done absolutely nothing for her. He had let her work on him but kept his hands to himself, as she'd sucked him to the very edge of oblivion.

But even the memory of that pleasure wasn't enough to keep his mind off the gauntlet of Khe Sanh. The closer they had gotten, the more scared he'd become. He knew, just knew, that he was going to die on the run in, and he felt himself grow cold at the prospect.

He tried to divert his mind by listening to the men on the intercom, but that didn't work. He could feel the bullet smashing into him. He could see it shatter the windshield in front of him.

And then they were on the radio with the control tower, getting the instructions on the landing. They were cleared straight in, the winds out of the west at ten knots and visibility unrestricted. Not the way he would have liked it, but there was nothing he could do about it.

Carson flew the plane, shooting the approach to avoid the first third of the runway because of recent combat damage. That was no problem for the C-130, which had been designed for short-field landings.

Whitmire reached out and touched the controls, although Carson still flew. He helped with the radios and throttles and the flaps and wheels. He took the orders as they were given to him, trying to focus his attention on what was happening now. There was a flash of Marie bent over his crotch and then another of an imagined bullet smashing the windshield, and then he was busy flying the aircraft.

As they touched down on the runway, they hit the brakes and reversed the props. There were changing forces and a sudden turn to the left until they were on the ramp in front of the terminal area.

"Down," said the AC.

Whitmire relaxed for a moment, the sweat dripping from his face and down his sides. Sunlight poured through the cockpit windows, baking him. He held up a hand to shade his eyes and then turned to look toward the rear.

Although he couldn't hear the enemy gunners firing at him, he could see the results. The first puff of smoke and dirt caught him by surprise. He jumped slightly and stared. Then there was a second, closer to him, and he wanted to scream. He wanted to order everyone away from the plane so he could get the hell out. The fuselage offered no protection from the white-hot shrapnel of mortar shells and rockets.

"Let's go," he whispered to himself. "Let's go."

He glanced to the left and rear where he could just see the open hatch. One man disappeared out it and then a dozen others burst in. There was an explosion in front of the plane, and Whitmire knew the next one would drop right on him.

"Let's go," he shouted, but no one could hear him over the roar of the engines.

Finally, after what seemed to be an eternity, the loadmaster reported they were ready. The AC released the brakes and hit the throttles, turning the plane a little, and then a little more.

They picked up speed and headed toward the runway. Now, with the tons of supplies dumped onto the ramp behind them and with only a dozen or so men on the plane, they didn't worry about taking off into the wind. Taxiing out to the far end of the runway was more dangerous.

They pulled onto the runway, facing east, as the AC ran the engines up to full operating rpm. They sat there as the artillery on the combat base fired countermortars, the rounds arcing over the west end of the runway.

Carson released the brakes and they lurched forward. The AC held the wheel forward, forcing the airplane to stay on the ground as the markers and bunkers raced by. Everything became a blur as they passed through normal takeoff speed. They reached the end of the perimeter wire, and then just short of the first of the new holes in the runway, the AC jerked back on the wheel. The plane leaped into the air, almost like a fighter. But then, to prevent a stall, he had to ease the angle of attack. They climbed out rapidly.

Whitmire, now clammy with a cold sweat, glanced out the window to the right. There was a burst of fire, barely visible to him. A single string of green tracers was soaring toward them, then arcing away as they banked to the left, still climbing.

"Yeah!" Whitmire screamed, suddenly elated. "Yeah!"

And then they were through the clouds, still climbing higher, away from the enemy and the fields around Khe Sanh. They had made it in and out without taking a hit.

"Everyone okay?" asked the aircraft commander.

One by one the men reported in. No hits to the rear of the aircraft. Everything in the green and nothing to worry about until they got back to Da Nang.

"You've got it," the AC said.

Whitmire hadn't wanted to fly, but he knew there was no getting out of it now. He'd dogged it on the way in, sitting there watching the world around him.

"I've got it," he said as he put his hands and feet on the controls. With his left hand, he wiped his face and then grinned. The feeling that he was going to die hadn't gone away, but he was no longer worried about it. They had gotten into and out of Khe Sanh, and no one had died.

Tonight he would be ready for Marie. He'd even buy her dinner in the officers' club, after he took a long, hot shower. She'd have to rub his back, too. But tonight things would be a little different.

Yeah, he said to himself. Tonight would be a little different, but not all that much.

14

BASEMENT OF THE
WHITE HOUSE

Lockhart picked up the report and read it through again. During the fighting, first to establish the base at Khe Sanh and later to hold it, the bodies of Marines had been found with their weapons broken down for field cleaning and the cleaning rods and equipment out. Not just on one occasion but on several. In more than one instance it seemed that every Marine who died had been trying to clear his jammed weapon.

There had been congressional investigations, and the firearms manufacturers were blaming the Marines. In tests conducted to simulate field conditions, they said, the weapons always worked just fine. They claimed the Marines didn't properly maintain the weapons, and that if they had done so, they wouldn't have had the jamming problem.

"Bullshit," said Lockhart, but kept reading anyway. When he finished the report, which ran to nearly five hundred pages, he thought he knew the problem inside out. It had nothing to do with the Marines not cleaning the weapons.

He stood up and slipped from behind his desk and around the safe so he could open the door. He needed to move, needed to pace up and down the hallway.

In the past week he'd read reports from Khe Sanh and learned that the Marines were being hammered by an enemy force of several thousand. He'd read the results of Operation Niagara, where the Air Force counted the enemy killed by some weird method that had pilots flying over the battlefield at several knots at an altitude of several hundred feet, telling the people at the various bases how many enemy soldiers were killed. He'd briefed the President on the battle at Khe Sanh, touched on Tet and kept up on everything that was happening in Vietnam without resorting to network news, which was going off on tangents that had nothing to do with the war in Vietnam. Reporters in Saigon who never left their hotels were telling the people how the war was being lost.

And now he held a report on the investigation into the jamming of the M-16, written by the manufacturer of the weapon, who had found nothing wrong with it. It was such a crock that he couldn't believe it, yet he knew Congress would be appeased by the report. They'd been told of the problem and they had investigated. Here was a two-inch-thick document that proved they were interested.

"What a crock," he said to a startled Marine guard, who didn't respond.

The funny thing was that Lockhart remembered reading an account of the Battle of the Little Bighorn, describing the bodies of the cavalrymen killed there. A large number of them had been found with broken knives in their hands or near their bodies. The problem was that the carbine they had been issued fired a cartridge that had a copper jacket. After three or four rounds were fired, the copper expanded so that the weapon jammed, forcing the soldier to use a knife to extract the empty shell—not a desirable exercise with thousands of Indians riding down on their positions.

Now, almost a hundred years later, dead Marines were being found with their weapons broken open, killed while they tried, probably frantically, to clear the jamming.

"Christ!" he said. He wondered if he should say anything to the President. Men were dying because of some foul-up that had nothing to do with them.

Lockhart returned to his cubicle and squeezed in behind the desk. He flipped the report closed and initialed it, so he could prove he'd seen it.

The report directly under it was another explanation of the problem with the M-16. It wasn't the fault of the weapon, but of the powder used to manufacture the bullets. The powder was being replaced, and shipments of the new ammo stocks were on their way to Vietnam.

"Christ!" Lockhart said again. The soldiers in the field couldn't get anything that worked right. He remembered the President raging because even though the enemy's plans had been known prior to the attacks, it had been a close fight on some of the major fronts. The Marines had almost lost one of the hilltop bases, but that was no wonder. Weapons that didn't work and powder that burned dirty added to all the other problems. The wonder was that the Marines had been able to hold the hilltops at all.

Lockhart opened the middle of his desk, took out a pad of paper and picked up a pen. He was going to draft a report to the President to let him know exactly how the American corporations were letting down the fighting men, supplying inferior equipment that couldn't be counted on. No wonder the Marines were throwing away the M-16 for the AK-47. At least it didn't jam.

JERRY MAXWELL, having received word that Gerber and Fetterman had arrived in Khe Sanh, left his office and headed upstairs. It was time to let General Howard know that the operation to eliminate Giap was under way.

Maxwell signed out at the iron gate that protected his office and a dozen other secret operations. He walked up the stairs into the headquarters proper with its long hallways and hundreds of doors. The floor was covered with green tile and the walls were painted a dark green halfway up and finished with a lighter green. On the walls hung photos of the American chain of command from President Johnson right down to General Westmoreland. There were bulletin boards that held orders, regulations and notices. There were posters on the proper wearing of the uniform, on the wearing of ribbons, on protecting COMSEC and on the privilege of serving to preserve the freedom of South Vietnam. Maxwell ignored it all.

He made his way to General Howard's office on the second floor. The door that led to his office was a dark mahogany. If the enemy ever penetrated headquarters, they could find the important offices, not by reading the signs but by crashing through the fanciest doors.

The interior was no less magnificent. There was a carpet on the floor that had to be a bear to keep clean—a thick, light green. There were two desks, one for the civilian secretary who was absent, probably held at Tan Son Nhut in case the enemy tried another assault. At the other desk sat a sergeant, who didn't look as if he would be much of an aide. A burly man whose nose had been broken sometime in the past, he hadn't shaved recently and wore jungle fatigues that might never have been starched. On his desk sat his steel pot, and hanging on the back of his chair was a flak jacket. An M-14 was in the corner, within easy reach.

"Can I help you?" he asked when he saw Maxwell.

"Need to see General Howard for a few minutes."

"May I tell him in what it is reference to?" He stopped, screwed his face up as if thinking hard, then tried again. "*In* reference to?"

"Khe Sanh. Tell him Jerry Maxwell needs a minute or two of his time."

The sergeant stood. He was a tall man, probably six and a half feet. At his side he wore a pistol, and two hand grenades were attached to his belt. Moving to the door, he tapped on it, then looked in. A moment later he motioned Maxwell forward.

Howard stood behind his desk, which was bigger and fancier than the two in his outer offices. The carpeting was thicker, the walls paneled and the blinds pulled to keep out the late-morning sunshine. The room was comfortably cool.

Howard was a heavy-set man with a receding hairline and a belly that hung over his belt. He wore jungle fatigues that had been starched and that held their crease because of the air-conditioning in his office.

"Come in, Jerry, and have a seat."

Maxwell sat down in one of the high-backed leather chairs. He felt tired, suddenly, so very tired. He was stuck in a basement office with a concrete floor, water that dripped and mildew that threatened his files. Two floors above him there was carpeting and paneling and air-conditioning. A waste of money so that a general could spend his year in Vietnam in relative comfort.

Howard rocked back in his chair and laced his fingers behind his head. He stared at the ceiling. "What can I do for you?"

"Thought I'd let you know we've got Operation Quick Kill in motion."

Howard leaned forward and dropped his arms so that his elbows rested on his desk. "Refresh my memory on this one. Operation Quick Kill."

"Yes, sir. As you probably know, we picked up radio traffic, originating in Laos, that suggested the North Vietnamese Army had a headquarters in a limestone cave area just on the Laotian side of the border. Intelligence has placed Giap at that headquarters. Operation Quick Kill was designed to eliminate Giap."

The color drained from Howard's face. "Christ, you went on with that? We put bombers over the target three days ago. The signals have stopped. Where's your team?"

"Staging in Khe Sanh. You want me to stop them?"

Howard held up a hand. "Let's think this thing through. Slowly."

"We can just cancel the mission," said Maxwell, moving to stand up.

"No," Howard said. "Too many decisions are made on the spur of the moment. We've time to think this through."

"But, General. I hesitated in sending them in the first place. Operation Niagara is as much of a danger to them as it is to the enemy. Those B-52 strikes give no one a chance to hide. Five-hundred-pound bombs falling out of the sky."

Howard opened a drawer, pulled out a report and glanced at it. "I'm not convinced our bombing is that big a problem. Odds are our boys won't be hit by the 52s. They've more of a chance of walking into an ambush."

"Not these men," said Maxwell. "They won't walk into an ambush."

"Doesn't matter. What we have to decide is whether or not it makes sense to let the mission continue."

"General, hundreds of fighter aircraft are participating in Operation Niagara. There's artillery from a dozen American bases falling on those jungles."

"Doesn't matter," repeated Howard. He turned his attention to the report he held, reading it slowly.

Maxwell sat quietly, at first watching the general read, then studying the watercolors hanging on the walls. Paintings of scenes in South Vietnam, but none of them on a combat theme. Rice farmers in their fields, water buffalo pulling plows, street scenes in downtown Saigon, and in Nui Ba Den with no Americans, no one in uniform to be seen.

"Mr. Maxwell," said the general, setting his report aside, "we have a couple of problems. One of them is that we don't have any idea how effective our air strike against that suspected headquarters was. It would be nice to have someone on the ground check it out. As a side benefit of the mission, your boys could do that."

"But the main purpose, to assassinate Giap, is out the window."

"Now we don't know that," said Howard. "Don't know that at all. What we know is that the radio messages have ceased from that specific site. Once your boys are on the scene, they just might find a clue about where Giap and the headquarters moved."

"It's just not worth it," said Maxwell. "When we had a specific site, a specific target, it made sense to deploy the assets, but not now."

"Give me the details of the mission," said Howard. He rocked back and closed his eyes.

Maxwell went through the details, including the changes that put Gerber and Fetterman into Laos and their orders to shoot Giap if they got a crack at him.

"Okay," said Howard. "I see no reason to pull the team. First, for at least part of the mission, they'll be outside the main target areas of Operation Niagara. Danger to them from friendly fire is minimal. I can't see any reason to scrub this mission. It could provide us with valuable intelligence as to enemy troop movements and locations."

Maxwell sat there quietly, trying to come up with a reply. With the main target already eliminated, it made sense to him to cancel before someone got killed unnecessarily. He said as much to Howard, and got nowhere. Howard just repeated what he'd already said.

"First, we don't know if the target was destroyed. We only know the radio transmissions from that site ceased. Second, we need a recon of the area, which your team can provide. Third, they may still have a chance to kill Giap, which would be of great propaganda value for us as well as demoralizing the enemy. No, leave the team alone and let them go."

"Yes, sir." Maxwell shrugged, got up and went back to his office.

ONCE THEY GOT OFF the airfield, Hobbs escorted Gerber and Fetterman through the Khe Sanh combat base to the Special Forces compound on the opposite side of the perimeter. As they drove around, Gerber was appalled at what he saw. No longer was this an American military installation; it was a trash dump. Few of the structures stood without combat damage. Sides were riddled by shrapnel and rifle fire. Many had burned, the charred rubble left where it had fallen. There were piles of sandbags, the ruins of bunkers that had been hit and destroyed. Shell casings were scattered everywhere. Paper blew in the breeze. Broken lumber lay everywhere. Twisted hunks of tin from the roofs of hootches littered the ground.

"Christ, what a mess!" Gerber said.

"The Marines aren't interested in rebuilding anything or cleaning up," said Hobbs. "They stay in their bunkers and trenches, shooting when they have a target. A real siege mentality has developed."

"Patrols?" asked Fetterman.

"None. Or rather nothing much. They get out of sight of the base and they get ambushed immediately. Everyone wants a fight, but they want Charlie to attack them here."

As they approached the Special Forces compound, there was an explosion in the distance, then a second and a third.

"Mortars," said Fetterman, looking back toward the runway and the center of the base. "Not coming toward us."

They passed several howitzers partially protected by revetments of sandbags. Around the revetments were piles of shell casings, bags that had held powder, paper and other trash. There were no Marines around the weapons.

"We'll need a bunker or something for planning purposes," said Gerber. "I'd like to have an isolation compound, but I doubt that can be arranged."

"Not here," said Hobbs, pulling up near a large bunker. "There are some long tables inside. Light comes from the camp generators, and if they get knocked out, then we've got lanterns and flashlights."

"Shit!" said Gerber. "We should have staged from Quang Tri or Da Nang."

Fetterman hopped out of the rear of the jeep. "Then we'd never have gotten the feel for the war here."

They moved to the bunker entrance and stopped. Gerber looked south, down from the plateau, and into the coffee plantations that had surrounded the town of Khe Sanh. Smoke and dust hung in the air in that direction, countermortar being fired by the weapons on the other side of Khe Sanh. There was the rattle of small arms, but that was probably Marines, frustrated with their new underground life, firing into the trees for something to do.

"I don't like this," said Gerber.

Fetterman didn't say anything. He slipped past the captain and descended into the bunker. Gerber followed. The interior was brightly lit with naked light bulbs hanging from wire tacked to the thick beams that supported the PSP-and-sandbag ceiling. The floor was made from planks that still bled sap. The walls were sandbags, but someone had fastened a plywood board to one, with a battle map mounted on it.

In the center were a couple of long, thin tables, ringed by metal folding chairs. The floor along the walls was lined with sleeping bags. There were weapons lying on some, men lying on others. None of the men wore a complete uniform. They were dirty and unshaved. The place smelled like a locker room that had been sealed for a long time.

"These men Special Forces?" Gerber asked. He didn't care that the Marine officers had let the men under their command slide during the siege, but he wouldn't stand for the Special Forces to become a ragtag unit.

"Some of them," said Hobbs.

"Who's in charge?" asked Gerber.

Hobbs pointed to a tall, stocky man. "Sergeant Fitzsimmons is the ranking NCO."

Gerber looked at the sergeant. He had a round face, bright blue eyes and black hair. Like the others, he hadn't bathed recently, and that made sense, given the water shortage at Khe Sanh. But he had shaved and his uniform was neat, though stained and torn in a few places. He seemed to be trying to do the best he could under the present conditions. On his shoulder, Fitzsimmons wore the Special Forces patch.

"I'm appalled by the living conditions in here," Gerber said bluntly.

"We have a war here, Captain," Fitzsimmons replied.

"That's no excuse and you know it. Soldiers who get sloppy in their personal habits aren't good soldiers."

"Sir, the conditions here haven't been all that great. Besides, the Marines control everything, and they've been fairly tight-fisted."

"Sergeant," said Gerber, "I don't mean to criticize, but this place—" he waved a hand around the bunker "—Khe Sanh itself is no longer a military base."

"Yes, sir."

Gerber was going to say more, but the men had been under the gun for nearly two weeks of constant shelling. A certain amount of sloppiness was understandable, but they had to maintain discipline. They had to instill pride in the soldiers, because if they didn't, when the enemy hit the wires, there wouldn't be a military force to oppose them—just a mob that was heavily armed but not well coordinated.

"Sergeant Hobbs, you and your men will form up here, and we'll see if we can't figure out something before our deployment."

"Yes, sir," said Hobbs. "I take it we're getting out of here."

"We'll discuss it later, Sergeant."

"Yes, sir."

"Sergeant Fitzsimmons, I'll need to make use of this bunker for a briefing in the near future. Is there a place where your men can be sent for a couple of hours?"

"These are our quarters, sir."

"I understand that. I just need to use it for a couple of hours and then your men can return. I wouldn't want to put you out of your home."

"When would you like to hold your briefing?"

Gerber looked at his watch. "Sometime in the next hour or so. And we'll need a place to stay tonight."

Now Fitzsimmons grinned. "Not exactly the best accommodations, but you're welcome to stay here. It's a roof over your head."

"Thank you, Sergeant."

Fitzsimmons turned and started getting the men moving. As they began to straggle out of the bunker, Fetterman said to Gerber, "Kind of hard on him, weren't you?"

"Tony, I would have thought you'd say I was too soft. Hardship is no excuse for letting discipline go. You make allowances for the conditions, but you don't throw the rule book away. That's not the way to fight a war."

"I know that, sir. I was just checking." He moved forward and set his rucksack on the table. "How long we going to be here?"

"If I have my way about it," said Gerber, "we'll be out of here tomorrow. At the latest."

"Good," said Fetterman. "The sooner the better."

15

KHE SANH COMBAT BASE

Korski stood at the edge of the perimeter, the thirty-man patrol spread out behind him, crouching among the sandbagged bunkers and short walls. Thirty men wearing steel pots, flak jackets, pistol belts with two canteens and six hand grenades. There were three M-60 teams of three men each: a machine gunner, his assistant and a third man to carry extra ammo for the weapons. With Sergeant Goddard, Korski checked the men, making sure they each had all the ammo they could carry, plus a combat knife, and were prepared to engage the enemy, if it came to that.

Around them the artillery began to fire in random patterns, aiming at preregistered targets in an attempt to keep the enemy's head down. The first of the rounds rocketed out, dropping into the remains of Felix Poilane's coffee plantation, and the next volley blew up among the ruins of the town of Khe Sanh.

With that, Korski was waving the men forward. A corporal ran out over the fields of burned-off grass and across the road that led south into the town. He stopped at the trees, still in sight of the men at the combat base, and waited.

The remainder of the patrol snaked out, moving cautiously, each man with his finger on the trigger, waiting for the enemy to open fire. After weeks of continual bombardment, they all knew the enemy was close to them, probably watching them. Korski wanted to confirm that.

As the men crossed the road, the point man stepped into the trees, disappearing for an instant. The patrol caught up to him and they entered the trees. The jungle was fairly open that close to the combat base. Seabees had cut and burned away much of the underbrush in the weeks when the Marines were preparing for the coming of the enemy. Overhead, the thick leaves of the trees protected the men from the sun, though clouds were blowing in and the air held a hint of rain. The pace was slow as the men searched the ground around them for signs of booby traps and indications of an ambush.

Korski took his place near the center of the patrol, next to the radio operator. He carried his M-16 with the safety on, because he didn't trust his shaking hands. He was bathed in sweat from the afternoon heat and from the danger he now felt himself in. He suddenly wished he'd listened to Sergeant Goddard, but he'd been sure he'd known what he was doing. This wasn't like the other patrols he'd been on in late November and early December, when the enemy was known to be around somewhere, but probably not near the patrol. Then, the enemy would have run from the Marines. But that was in November and December. The situation had changed radically.

As they walked downhill, paralleling the road that was now a hundred yards to the left, Korski wondered just how long he would have to let the men patrol. His orders had been clear on only one point. He was to return before dark. Although he hadn't been given orders about the range of the patrol, he didn't want to go much farther than a mile or two from the combat base, a distance that would make a tiring run, but one that could be made, if the situation dictated it.

Korski noticed that the men were tense. It was obvious in the way they moved and the posture they held. Fingers close to the triggers, heads pulled down as if to protect them and eyes shifting continuously, looking for the enemy. Korski also noticed that the afternoon was unnaturally quiet. The animals and insects that were usually around had been chased from the area by fighting. The air seemed to be electric, and not because of the imminent rain.

All at once the men in front of Korski dived for cover. He stood for a second, watching, and then fell to the ground. He waited. No one said anything, no one called to him. Finally, wondering what was going on, he began to crawl forward, using his elbows, knees and feet. He hadn't done that since OCS.

He reached the front of the patrol and saw that the point man was lying on his belly, his weapon stretched out in front of him. He was watching something in the coffee plantation at the edge of the jungle.

"What you got?" asked Korski when he'd crawled close.

The point man turned his head and looked at the Marine officer. Quietly he said, "Two guys, sitting out there. Backs against one of the trees. See 'em?"

Korski slowly scanned the field in front of him and then saw the men dressed in black pajamas and Ho Chi Minh sandals. There was nothing about them to suggest that they were enemy soldiers, but then they were young men who would either have been drafted by the Saigon government or dragged away by the Vietcong. There was no way that they could be innocent.

"Let's take them," said Korski.

"I don't know about that," whispered the point man. "I don't like this setup."

"Look, Corporal, we're going to have to stay out here all afternoon unless we grab a couple of prisoners early on. Now, if they turn out to be civilians, we can't help that because we can't interrogate them in the field, but even if they're civilians, they can probably give me some information on enemy troop movements, which is all I want anyway."

"Yes, sir."

Korski rolled onto his right side and looked to the rear. He could see a half-dozen Marines crouched in the grass, using the bushes and trees for cover. Hot, tense men who looked fierce.

Korski waved them forward. The men came from their cover, moving slowly and silently. They were spread out along the edge of the jungle, watching the Vietnamese. Korski waited until each man was in position. During the ten minutes it took to move, the Vietnamese never even looked up. They sat there, talking to each other as if they were the only two men in that part of Vietnam.

Korski pointed to ten men and waved them forward. He got to his feet and stepped out of the jungle and among the trees of the coffee plantation. He walked slowly, his weapon pointed in the direction of the men, but not directly at them.

As the Americans appeared, the two men looked up. One of them shouted something, as if surprised by the appearance of the Marines. The other got to his feet and slipped behind the skinny trunk of the tree to use it for protection. When that happened, the Marines stopped moving. Two dropped to their knees, their weapons pointed at the Vietnamese.

"You will have to come with us," Korski shouted. He spoke in English, expecting the Vietnamese to understand. Then, waving an arm, he signaled his men forward.

Half the marines started to move toward the Vietnamese. The man who hadn't sought shelter behind a tree dropped to his belly as if he had been shot. There was a moment's pause, and then a ripping burst from a machine gun. Two of the Marines dropped, hit by the volley.

Korski fell to the ground and began crawling forward to the trunk of a tree. Bullets from the hidden machine gun, joined by AKs, slammed into the trunk and into the ground around him. There were two small explosions as grenades detonated, throwing dirt into the air.

Firing from the Marines who were still in the jungle joined the noise. Korski looked to the left. Two Marines were on their backs, blood staining their flak jackets. One of them had part of his head missing, and his legs were kicking spasmodically.

He turned toward the front and saw both Vietnamese decoys lying on the ground. He couldn't tell if they had been hit or not, so he aimed at one and pulled the trigger. The round struck the man in the side, lifting him slightly. Blood poured from the wound.

Calmly he shot the other one, making sure he was dead. As he did so, more enemy fire was directed at him. He dropped, trying to push his face into the ground. Bullets from the RPD and the AKs were smashing into the coffee tree, shaking it. Leaves, bark and coffee beans fell on his back and the earth around him. The only sound he could hear was the hammering of the enemy machine gun and his own breath rasping in his throat.

"Fall back!" yelled Goddard as the enemy began to fire. He opened up, aiming into the shadows on the other side of the field where there were bunkers. He thought he could see the muzzle-flashes of the enemy weapons.

To his right, one of the men got to his knees and tried to throw a grenade. He let the motion carry him forward so that he was under cover, but the grenade didn't make it halfway across the field. It fell short, exploding in a geyser of black dirt and shrapnel that did no damage.

All around, the Marines began to fire, trying to pin down the enemy soldiers so that the men in the coffee grove could get out. But the enemy had better protection. Their firing didn't let up, but continued to build until it was a single, long, loud detonation and the bullets slammed into the jungle like the rains of the monsoons.

Goddard crawled to the rear, using the bushes and the trees for cover. The men had deployed in a skirmish line, facing into the grove. They were putting out rounds, some firing on full-auto, trying to pin down the enemy. Others were shooting single-shot, but there were no targets in the open, only the flashes from enemy weapons, hard to see in the afternoon sunlight. Shadows crossed the grove as the clouds built toward a storm.

The Marine machine gunners had set up their nests, one at each end of the line to anchor it and the third in the center, firing at the enemy machine gun nest.

Goddard stopped moving and ducked. He wiped the sweat from his forehead with the sleeve of his fatigues, then moved forward and peeked through the gaps in the vegetation. Most of the Marines in the coffee grove were pinned down, unable to move, unable to retreat.

Then, from the other end of the grove, came a shout in Vietnamese. A bugle sounded and a dozen enemy soldiers swarmed into the grove. Goddard fired at them, saw one drop, then switched to full-auto. He knew the enemy was trying to kill the Marines trapped there.

The first few Vietnamese fell as they appeared. But then more of them leaped into the grove, running and firing. Goddard got up onto his knees where he could see to aim. He pulled the trigger and held it down, burning through the whole magazine. Dropping it from his weapon, he reloaded, doing the same thing again. Around him the Marines were all putting out rounds, trying to stop the enemy assault.

But the Vietcong and NVA weren't to be denied. They came on, even though men fell from their ranks. They never wavered or hesitated. They fired from the hip, putting rounds into the jungle. They shrieked with hate, screaming their rage as they crossed the open ground, dodging through the trees.

The Marines trapped in the open shot back. The corporal who had been the point man jumped to his feet to meet the onslaught. He swung his rifle around, firing from the hip just as the enemy was doing. One man ran straight for him and he shot him once, twice. The enemy soldier fell, tumbling forward.

Then the Vietnamese were among the Marines in the coffee grove. It became a hand-to-hand fight—men using their weapons, their knives, their fists. The firing tapered off for a moment, and in the lull, there were grunts of pain, shouts of anger.

One Marine was fighting with an NVA when a second Vietnamese leaped onto his back. The Marine ducked, flipping the enemy onto the one in front of him. He dropped to his knees and grabbed an AK from the ground, firing it as his hands touched it. Both enemy soldiers were killed by the burst.

But then three other NVA jumped him. There was a burst and the Marine got to his feet. He slammed a fist into a soldier's face, kicked him, then took two rounds in the chest. The flak jacket hadn't been designed to withstand rifle fire at point-blank range. The Marine fell, wounded but not dead.

Korski was up and running to the right. He leaped into the air and kicked one of the Vietnamese to the ground. He stomped on the man's throat, crushing it. As the Vietnamese jerked in pain, trying to breathe, Korski shot another one, four rounds that blew his head apart, spraying blood and scattering bone.

Goddard was up then, moving to the very edge of the jungle. He dropped his weapon to his side and shouted, "Get out, Lieutenant! Get out!"

But Korski couldn't get out. He'd led the men into the field when good sense had dictated otherwise. He'd gone after the easy marks, hoping to get out of the patrol without a serious fight, and now he was stuck in the middle of one.

He slipped to his knee, aiming over the body of the wounded Marine. As the enemy came at him, he calmly fired, shooting the VC as quickly as he could. Two of them fell. Then three. Then four. The bolt locked back and he dropped the magazine from the weapon. Reloaded, he opened fire again, trying to protect the wounded man.

Around him the others died quickly. The enemy overran them and the fighting degenerated almost entirely into hand-to-hand—Marines with knives and pistols against the NVA with machetes and bayonets. One Marine was standing in the center of four bodies, shooting and stabbing. Two men rushed him and the Marine shot one in the face, spun and kicked the other in the crotch. As that man fell, the Marine cut his throat, but then he was hit in the back by a burst from an RPD. He fell on the dying soldier, jamming his knife into the man's chest in a final defiant act.

One Marine, his back to a coffee tree, fought to unjam his weapon. He'd broken it in half, working to extract the cartridge that was fouling it. A Vietcong, his head down, ran at the Marine, screaming. Almost without looking the Marine swung his weapon by the barrel, the lightweight M-16 smashing into the enemy's stomach. That was enough to throw off the attacker, and the Marine then used his knife. He grabbed the enemy's AK and flipped it around, but as he did, another NVA soldier shot him. The Marine collapsed.

Now only Korski and the wounded Marine were left alive. A Chicom grenade exploded near them. It knocked Korski onto his back, but he was right up again, bleeding from minor wounds to the face and neck. He kept shooting and shooting.

"Get out! Sir!" shouted Goddard, but it was as if the lieutenant didn't hear him.

When his weapon was empty, Korski threw it aside and grabbed the collar of the flak jacket the wounded man wore. He dragged him away from the fight as the Marines in the jungle tried to cover him. Firing intensified, M-16s and M-14s on full-auto, pouring out rounds, the unbroken hammering of the M-60s. The coffee trees shook, and the air was filled with bits of bark and leaf.

Overhead lightning flashed, and rain fell suddenly, as if someone had shot the clouds full of holes. A thick gray curtain dropped over the field, obscuring the adversaries.

Korski staggered and slipped in the mud. He fell to his knees, and as he did, the wounded man reached up to grab his flak jacket. Korski leaned close as the man coughed once, blood pouring from his mouth. He died then, his face covered in rain and blood.

"Run! Run!" Goddard screamed.

Korski got to his feet, but as he did, he slipped again. A bullet struck him in the back, knocking him down. Again he struggled to his feet, but the enemy had found the range. The burst caught him low, lifted him and threw him toward the waiting Marines. He landed facedown in the mud, slid a few feet, then was still. Blood poured from under his flak jacket, staining the ground and turning the growing puddles crimson.

"Shit!" screamed Goddard. "Shit! Shit! *Shit!*" He dropped onto his belly and cut loose with everything he had, holding the trigger down until his weapon was empty. Then he turned, and crawled toward the RTO, who had stayed near the center of the skirmish line.

The rain was heavier now, coming down in sheets. They couldn't see five feet in front of them. The firing from the enemy bunkers on the other side of the grove slowed but never stopped. Thunder masked the sounds of artillery firing in the distance, and the storm meant there would be no air support.

Goddard got to the radio and took the handset from the RTO. He keyed the mike and said, "I've got a fire mission, over."

The artillery officer at the combat base was on the horn immediately, asking for specifics. Goddard gave him the information and was asked, "Can you spot?"

"I'll do the best I can. It's raining hard here. Over."

"Roger. Rounds on the way."

There was a distant booming that Goddard thought might be thunder, or the artillery at Khe Sanh. Overhead was the sudden rush of air that signaled the artillery round. In the coffee grove there was an explosion, but Goddard couldn't tell where it had landed. He stared into the gray mist of the rain, the trees closest to him just ghostly shapes.

"Add one hundred," he said. "Fire for effect."

As the artillery opened fire, the RTO asked, "Shouldn't we get the hell out of here?"

"We should," said Goddard, "but we've got to get the bodies of the dead."

"No, we don't."

"Look," said Goddard. "We've got artillery coming in and we've got this rain. We can get the dead out of there so that the enemy can't mutilate them."

The RTO said nothing. Goddard moved toward the center of the line. "Let's go," he said, and began crawling forward. He looked back once and saw there were three men following. As he left the protection of the jungle, more of the survivors joined him. The artillery and the rain covered the sound they made. At both ends of the line, the M-60s continued to fire. The NVA was only shooting sporadically. The artillery was either making them keep their heads down, or they were getting out.

Goddard reached the body of Korski. The rain had washed the blood and much from his face. There was a neat little hole in his cheek, blackened around the edges, that didn't look as if it could have been fatal. The other wounds, in his back and side, had killed him.

Goddard dragged him toward the rear then, working toward the jungle. He reached it and pulled Korski to safety, then collapsed, waiting there for a moment, the rain filling his ears with a sound like frying bacon. Rolling onto his back, he stared at the boiling mass of black clouds, and felt tears burn his eyes. He didn't care; the others wouldn't know, not in the rain.

"Why didn't you listen?" he asked the dead man, but didn't need the answer. He knew it. Korski had led them into the ambush, and he wouldn't run for safety until all his men were out of danger or dead. He wouldn't leave them lying in the field.

Goddard rubbed at his eyes with the heel of his hand. He rolled onto his stomach and stared into the gray fog of the rain, knowing he should be organizing the men for the withdrawal to the combat base, and knowing that the men knew what to do without his giving them the orders.

He checked the body of his dead friend again, just in case there was a spark of life, but the open eyes were dull. Raindrops spattered on them and there was no indication that it was felt. They were as dead and unfeeling as a desert. No spark at all.

The firing on the right tapered and stopped. One of the men ran over. "We're almost out of ammo for the M-60."

"Okay, let's start collapsing the line." He pointed at a corporal. "Get a head count."

The man disappeared into the mist, then reappeared a moment later. "I think we've got everyone."

"You sure?"

He shook his head then, but said, "We've got everyone who's still alive."

"I'll settle for that," said Goddard. "Let's start a withdrawal. I want to fall back about a hundred meters, then turn east and cross the road. We'll follow it back to the combat base."

"Aren't you worried the men on the perimeter will open up on us before we get there?"

"Shit, we'll use the radio to alert them. That's no problem."

The man shrugged. Rain dripped from the rim of his steel pot and the end of his nose. He held his weapon with the barrel pointed down in an attempt to keep the water out of it.

"Take the point. Only about ten, twelve meters in front of us," said Goddard.

"Sure, Sarge. You got it."

As he took off, Goddard bent and picked up the body of Lieutenant Korski. He threw it over his shoulder in a fireman's carry, then retrieved his weapon.

The others were picking up the bodies they had dragged from the coffee grove. Two were so badly shot up that they couldn't be carried. They were wrapped in poncho liners, the ends tied, one man cradling the remains in his arms.

Two men dropped off as the rear guard, though they expected no trouble. The artillery continued to roar overhead, and each time the artillery officer asked if that had taken care of the problem, the RTO told him to keep it coming. He wasn't going to let him stop firing until he was well inside the wire at the combat base.

Quickly they made it to the road and then across it. It had turned into a river of mud, flowing downhill toward the town of Khe Sanh. They struggled up the hillside with their dead, and when they were close to the base, Goddard alerted them that they were coming in. They had taken casualties. They had a dozen dead and two wounded, but the wounded weren't badly hurt.

At the gate they were stopped by a major, who wanted to know what had happened. Goddard stood there, staring at the officer, Korski's body still on his shoulder. "We learned the enemy is out there, and we got shot to fuck."

The major shook his head. "I'm sorry." That was all he could say.

Goddard began the slow trek to Charlie Med, where they stacked the bodies of those killed so that they could be shipped home. It seemed as if the journey would never end.

16

**SPECIAL FORCES
COMPOUND KHE SANH
COMBAT BASE**

Gerber sat at the head of the table, the map of the area spread out in front of him. Around the table were the members of the team: Fetterman, who would be second in command, and Hobbs, Quinn, Lawrence and Rogers, who were the security team. Everyone who would be going and everyone who had to know the mission.

Gerber laid it out for them quickly, giving them only the information they would need to complete the mission. It wasn't necessary for Hobbs and the security team to know about the radio monitoring facilities that had intercepted the message traffic and understood its significance. They didn't have to know about the intelligence reports that put Giap in the area, although he wasn't sure about them himself. All they had to know was that the target was Giap and that there was good reason to suspect he was in Laos, near Co Roc Mountain.

And all they had to know was that Sergeant Fetterman would be the shooter, with Gerber acting as the spotter. If something happened to Fetterman, then Gerber became the shooter and Hobbs would be the spotter. The security team would be placed behind the shooters, and it was their job to make sure no one stumbled on them.

"We have special equipment," said Gerber. "Rifles, scopes, silencers, everything we need. We'll jump into Laos tomorrow about dusk and use the night to get into position."

"About dusk?" questioned Hobbs. "Before or after?"

"After, naturally," said Gerber. "We don't want everyone in Laos to see us bail out. We'll move off the DZ and into the jungle. Get organized, oriented and head for the mountain."

"Do you have a DZ spotted?" asked Hobbs.

Gerber grinned. "Not yet. That's why we're here. Figured you'd have something to say about that, given that you work this AO."

Now it was Hobbs's turn to smile. "Well, Captain, as you know, it's illegal for soldiers of the United States to operate across the border in Laos."

"Of course." Gerber spun the map around so Hobbs could get a better look at it. "Now, I'd like to hold the hike down to something around ten, twelve klicks if possible, but I don't want to drop into the lap of the NVA, either."

Hobbs stood up and bent over the map, his elbows on the table. He smoothed out the map and pointed to the border near Lang Vei. Then he touched Co Roc in Laos. "Now if we'd just had a mission in that area, we'd know where the enemy was massing, where the routes of march were and what to avoid."

"If you'd just been there," echoed Fetterman.

Hobbs looked up and nodded. He then gave Gerber a complete briefing on everything he'd seen and everything he'd suspected, describing the trip from Laos into Vietnam and his eventual arrival at the gate of the combat base.

"All right," said Gerber when Hobbs finished. "First order of business is to pick a drop zone. It doesn't have to be all that large."

Hobbs said to Quinn, "I seem to remember this area has a dozen or more clearings that would be suitable—none of them more than fifteen klicks from Co Roc."

Quinn moved so that he was next to Hobbs. "Yeah. At least a dozen. The map doesn't really show them, but they're there."

"I don't suppose you've got coordinates for them," said Gerber.

"No, sir, but I'll bet the artillery has maps with everything on them that we need."

"Okay," said Gerber. "That'll be your first job. A map with the DZ marked on it so that we can give it to the Air Force and so that we'll have a good idea of the direction and distance to the target."

Again they went over the plan, such as it was. Get in, shoot Giap and get out. "We'll make our way to the camp at Lang Vei," said Gerber. "From there we can get out by helicopter if we decide that's necessary. Questions?"

"This a sterile mission?"

Gerber shook his head. "Given the situation here, no. If some of our people are caught on the other side of the border, it's not going to be that big a deal. With the Tet attacks, no one is going to worry about half a dozen men on the wrong side of the border."

"How long are we going to be in the field?"

"Five days," said Gerber. "One to get into position, three at the target and one to get out. With luck, we'll be out before that."

"Radio codes?"

"We're not going to be using anything special. Normal radio security, though once we're into Laos, we'll be on radio silence. No reason to contact Net Control until after we're out. This is a real quick, dirty mission."

It went on like that for almost an hour. They went over the mission a dozen times, each man talking his way through it so that everyone knew exactly what had to be done. They talked about the weapons again and the escape-and-evasion plan in case things went to hell quickly.

That finished Gerber said, "Hobbs, I want to pick up those maps as quickly as possible."

Fetterman sat down. "I want to go back to the Aerial Port Squadron and check out our gear."

"Okay," Gerber said. "See if you can get it back here where we can keep an eye on it."

"Yes, sir."

Gerber folded up his map and stuffed it into the side pocket of his jungle jacket. "If there's nothing else, let's hit it. I'll expect you all back here by 1800 hours."

"Yes, sir."

AFTER THEY LANDED, Whitmire went over to the intelligence office for the debriefing, a routine he couldn't understand and a waste of time he couldn't stomach. A man who never flew sat behind a desk asking a bunch of stupid questions about enemy troop locations and movements, as if anyone had time on the run into Khe Sanh to look for the enemy.

Whitmire sat on a metal chair in the depths of a bunker that smelled of dirt and sweat, and tried to concentrate on the flight. Around him were dozens of charts and posters showing a variety of enemy equipment, from the twin-barreled ZSU-23 that they might run into to the long-barreled S-60 that they wouldn't. There were pictures of Soviet-designed and -manufactured fighters that hadn't ventured south of the DMZ in two years. And there were pictures of the small arms, the AK-47 and the RPD, as if there would be an opportunity for Whitmire and the flight crew to see something like that hidden in the jungle.

The intel officer, a young man with dark circles under his eyes and pale skin, sat behind the beat-up gray desk, hunched over the form he was required to fill out. He went through the questions slowly, writing down the negative responses. Finally he asked, "You see anything that might adversely affect the follow-up missions?"

"You mean like craters in the runway?"

"Are there craters on the runway?"

"The first third was unusable, but there were crews out to repair it. As we took off, mortar rounds landed around us, so the runway could be in worse shape now."

The officer made a note. "Anything else?"

Whitmire shrugged, trying to think of something to say. He knew that everything he had observed, what little there was, had been reported time and again. They were just going through the motions, filling in the blanks, to please the paper pushers in Saigon and Washington, who liked to see piles of paper moved around. "Nothing else," he finally said.

"Fine. Thanks for your help."

Whitmire pushed back his chair and retreated rapidly up the four steps and outside. A jeep was sitting in front of the bunker, and Whitmire thought about driving away in it, but he wasn't that far from his hootch.

As he walked through the squadron area, his rage welled up again, a rage born from the heat and humidity that never diminished even during the rainstorms. In the World a summer rain usually meant the heat was breaking and the evening would be cooler, but in Vietnam it only meant the day was going to be hotter and more humid.

He stopped at the road, the red dirt turned into a thick gruel by the heavy trucks and the monsoon rains. It just wasn't fair, he thought. His friends from college had successfully dodged the draft. They had gotten student deferments and doctors' statements and continued their schooling. Whitmire, attracted by the promise of fifty dollars a month and a scholarship that paid tuition and books, had joined the Air Force ROTC unit, figuring the trouble in Vietnam would be over before he could get there. Then the year-long pilot's training had offered another opportunity for the war to end, but that hadn't happened. While his friends had moved into corporate America, Whitmire had received orders for Vietnam.

It just wasn't fair.

He opened the door to his hootch and saw that Marie hadn't moved from the cot where she'd been when he'd left. She was dressed only in a jungle fatigue jacket and was watching the little black-and-white television.

He entered and dropped his flight bag onto the floor. Sitting down, he began to take off his boots. "That all you had to do today? Lie around and watch the damned TV?"

"Thank you," she said. "Hello to you, too."

Whitmire's head snapped up and he glared at her. He wanted to slap her face and started to lean forward to do it. Suddenly he stopped. The rage drained out of him all at once. He leaned back against the rough wood of the wall and studied her, from her bare legs to her blond hair. "Sorry. It was a rough day, and I have no right to take it out on you. It's not your fault."

She swung around, giving him a view that proved she was wearing nothing besides the jungle jacket. She grinned and leaned forward, reaching for him.

Whitmire kicked off his boots and stood up to unzip his flight suit. He shrugged out of it, then lifted her to her feet, pressing himself to her. Slipping a hand between them he unbuttoned the fatigue jacket and pushed it off her shoulders. Her skin was hot to the touch, covered with a light coating of perspiration, but that only enhanced the sensuality.

She stepped back and sat down on the cot as Whitmire stripped off his underwear. She lay back and Whitmire lay beside her. For a moment neither of them moved, and then Whitmire slipped his arms around her.

She grabbed the rail of the cot behind her and held on as her emotions bubbled through her. She moved to meet him and together they lost all thought of where they were. She bit his shoulder to keep from crying out as the feeling soared and then peaked.

Moments later Whitmire shuddered and then was still, his weight supported on his elbows as he kissed her deeply. When he rolled to the side, he was suddenly filled with calm. The anger that had boiled through him almost from the moment he'd set foot in Vietnam was gone.

He closed his eyes, breathed deeply and wondered what had happened to him. He felt good. There wasn't that much time left on his tour, less than nine months. Not that much time at all.

"Can we do something tonight?" she asked.

"There's still not that much to do," said Whitmire. "We can go to the club for a steak and a baked potato, but you're going to have to put up with everybody and his brother stopping by to talk to us."

She sat up and moved to the rear so that she was leaning against the rail of the cot. With one hand she pushed her hair back out of the way. She smiled broadly. "That's the first time you've agreed to anything I wanted to do. The very first time."

Whitmire rolled onto his side and reached up to rub the inside of her thigh. "Well, I'll make sure all that changes then."

"We're scheduled out of here, out of Da Nang, in about a week now. We've got USO shows to do all over South Vietnam."

"What does that mean for us?"

She smiled and touched the top of his head, feeling his hair. "I didn't know there was an us. I thought there was just a you and sometimes a me that was allowed to provide some recreation."

"Okay," said Whitmire, "so I was an asshole."

"Well, I can give you a schedule so that you'll know where I'll be and maybe you can get down to some of the other shows."

"That's very possible," he said, "but would it be worth it?"

"Haven't I been worth it up to this point?" she asked.

"Oh, yes, you've been worth it. More than worth it."

"So there's no reason to believe I'll suddenly not be worth it anymore, is there?"

Whitmire didn't care for the conversation. He changed the direction of it by asking, "Isn't there a way you could stay here?"

"Nope. The USO is careful to prevent that from happening. We have to move on with the show or return to the States immediately. Besides, there's nothing for me to do here other than entertain."

"Well, you've been very entertaining up to this point," said Whitmire, letting his fingers climb higher on her thigh.

"Do you have to fly tomorrow?" she asked, suddenly serious.

"Nothing's scheduled at the moment, but I'm sure something will come up. It always does."

"You be careful tomorrow."

"I always am," he said, unhappy with the sound of her voice and the tone of the warning.

HANRATTY STOOD at the crest of Hill 861 and wondered why he was being transferred to 861A. In the past few days the Marines had moved men all around, taking them from one base to another as if by whim. It seemed that men should be on 881 North and then they were moved to 861 and now they were being taken to 861A, which was not that far from where he stood. The only good thing was that it wasn't going to be a hike. A chopper was inbound to take him and twenty-three other men to the new location.

A sergeant ran from a bunker and tossed a smoke grenade onto the middle of the helipad. It was separated from the crest of the hill by a line of bunkers and some low bushes that hadn't been cut away.

As the sergeant tossed the smoke, Hanratty and the others started down the hill, following the rutted road. They passed between the two clusters of bushes and then stopped among the bunkers, crouching there as the twin-rotor chopper came from the east out of the clouds.

The aircraft came to a hover with the nose over the smoke grenade, the rotor wash swirling around and grabbing at the smoke, dirt and debris. As the wheels touched down, the ramp at the rear lowered and three men darted out, running for the cover of the bunkers in front of them.

Hanratty and the others were up and moving as the sergeant who had thrown the grenade shouted, "Go! Go! Go!"

Hanratty hit the ramp, slipped on the metal, but kept his balance. He rushed into the open interior of the helicopter. Door gunners leaned over the M-60s at the front, just behind the cockpit. Another crewman stood at the rear, wearing a flight helmet, a long black cord running from his helmet into the intercom system.

As the last of the men ran up the ramp, it began to close and the chopper lifted. The dirt whirled around, giving definition to the swirling eddies of wind. They blew into the rear of the aircraft and hung in the air.

The chopper leaped straight up and then the nose pitched forward. Hanratty lost his balance and fell to the deck as the helicopter began a spiraling climb over the camp, trying to avoid the enemy, who were believed to be on the slopes of the hill. When the chopper burst through the clouds, it seemed that all the power went out of it. The nose leveled and the pressure of the steep climb was reduced.

Hanratty and the others moved to the troop seats and sat down, but none of them bothered with the seat belts. When they landed in a few minutes, no one wanted to hang around there, a big fat OD green target, while some PFC tried to un-buckle his seat belt.

They orbited for a moment in the bright blue of the late afternoon, above the clouds that hid the landscape from them. They stayed up there in the cool air as if resting before the next landing, as if the coolness somehow sapped the strength of the crew and the aircraft.

The door gunners had moved away from their weapons and were sitting on the troop seats. One of them was smoking a cigarette and another was eating peaches from a C-ration can. Hanratty hadn't seen fruit in two weeks, and the cigarettes they got were old stale ones that had probably been sitting in a warehouse for a couple of years, though the Marines at Khe Sanh and the outposts never complained about it. Getting them at all was half the battle.

"What's the deal?" Hanratty shouted over the roar of the turbine engines and the pop of the rotor blades. "What's taking so long?"

The cigarette smoker grinned and leaned closer. "Hey, these combat assaults aren't all that simple. We're taking a break here for a blow."

Hanratty shrugged and sat back. He didn't care if they stayed airborne all night. In fact, he would prefer it. Hidden by the clouds, where the air was cool and fresh. Why should he complain about that?

But then the door gunner threw his cigarette onto the floor and crushed it under the toe of a polished, spit-shined boot. Hanratty knew that if he had free time, if there was an opportunity to sit around without the danger of enemy mortars or rockets, the last thing he would be doing would be spit-shining boots. He would be drinking or chasing the local women or sleeping, but not spit-shining boots, no matter how good a pair of spit-shined boots looked.

As the door gunner stepped behind his weapon, the crew chief stopped in front of the grunts. "We'll be landing in about three minutes," he shouted. "The instant, and I mean the very second that ramp is opened, you get out. Don't fuck around. Just run out and get clear of the rotors. Everyone understand?"

Hanratty nodded, as did the others. He fingered the safety of his weapon and wondered if he should chamber a round now. Normal rules dictated that the chamber be empty when flying into a camp, but the situation at Khe Sanh was different. Most of the regulations, designed to prevent a peacetime Marine from shooting himself, had been canned.

Then the nose dropped and the door gunners were hanging on to their weapons. The roar of the engines increased, and Hanratty left his stomach behind, floating somewhere above the clouds as they plunged into the grayness.

There was a single burst of fire, and Hanratty wondered how the door gunners could see anything to shoot at as the floor suddenly exploded in front of him. Holes the size of his fist opened up. The metal peeled back like the petals of a flower. One of the Marines screamed, blood splattering from the top of his boot. He fell forward, his hands wrapped around his foot. Blood poured from between his fingers.

They were out of the clouds then and the door guns on each side of the aircraft began to hammer. Hot brass ejected to the left and bounced on the deck. There was more shooting, some of it distant, and one of the windows on the side of the fuselage disintegrated.

The door gunners never stopped shooting. They reached down, pulling the linked M-60 ammo from the cans at their feet, feeding it into the weapons as they held the butterfly triggers down. There was a crash under them as a rocket landed, exploded, but the approach never wavered. They continued on in.

The ramp began to lower, even before they were near the ground, and as it did, the crew chief shouted, his voice barely carrying over the shooting and the turbine whine, "Get ready. Get ready."

They bounced then, a jarring landing that knocked one of the door gunners off his feet. He scrambled up again, but didn't fire. There was a second explosion outside. Shrapnel rattled against the fuselage.

"Go! Go! Go!"

Hanratty leaped for the ramp and dropped to the ground. He crouched there for a moment, then sprang forward, running toward a bunker and diving onto his belly behind it. Then he crawled up so that he was next to the sandbags as the rockets behind crashed around him.

The other Marines fled from the chopper, scattering. As the last of them cleared the ramp, the chopper leaped straight up nearly a hundred feet. The rotors seemed to stir the base of the clouds. A stream of green tracers chased the chopper, but they were wide. Red tracers flashed downward toward the jungle on the slopes of Hill 861A.

Firing from the bunker line erupted as the helicopter's nose dropped, and then the aircraft disappeared into the clouds. Tracers from the door guns poured out still, and then finally stopped.

Hanratty pressed his face against the sandbags, trying to crawl through them as the last of the rockets exploded in loud, flat bangs. Shrapnel cut through the air, slashing into the bunkers. Then it was quiet, as if everyone and everything had to take a few moments to regroup.

Hanratty sat up and looked around. One man stood on the other side of the helipad. He had a steel pot on his head and wore dirty fatigue pants with an open flak jacket. In his left hand he held an M-16, which he used to wave the men forward.

Hanratty got up and crouched by the side of the bunker. He hesitated, then sprinted across the open ground, sliding to a halt near the standing Marine. Hanratty dropped to one knee, his ears cocked, listening for the sound of incoming.

As the others from the chopper joined him, the man with the M-16 said, "Welcome to Hill 861A, home of E Company. You men are just in time for the party."

17

SPECIAL FORCES
COMPOUND KHE SANH
COMBAT BASE

Gerber sat at the far end of the bunker where he could watch everyone as he entered. Fetterman, of course, had been the first, returning with the equipment that had been off-loaded by the C-130 as it shed its pallets in the rush to get off the ground before a rocket destroyed it. Then Hobbs had arrived with the jeep, and there had been no opportunity to check the gear.

Three men helped Fetterman carry it into the bunker. They set everything down near the door, but against the wall so that it wasn't in the way. Without a word they retreated.

"What's with them?" asked Gerber.

"Marines don't like associating with us Army types. They're afraid something might rub off on them."

"You get a chance to look at the equipment?"

Fetterman stooped, examining the piles of equipment. "Not really. The Marines weren't too keen on standing around outside on the exposed ramp while I checked it all over. We grabbed everything and got the hell out."

Gerber came over. "Can't say I blame them for that."

Fetterman moved to the right and examined one of the parachutes. "Looks like everything is all right, but it'll take me about an hour to be sure."

Gerber grabbed the long package that held the M-16 and the sound suppressor that went on it. He opened it, checked the weapon, then examined the silencer. Satisfied that no damage had been done, he closed it all up. "Reporters would have a field day if they got a look at some of the stuff we have here."

Fetterman nodded. "They'd have a field day if they knew some of the things that were going on here at Khe Sanh."

Gerber laughed. "You're out of sight for an hour, and you've already stumbled onto something."

"No, sir," said Fetterman, putting one of the parachutes back. "I kept my eyes open as we were rushing around on the ramp there. Saw some radio equipment I couldn't identify, and there was some talk about sensor readings."

Gerber kept digging at the equipment. "Looks like someone raided our C-rations."

"Yeah, that's a real problem here. These guys haven't had anything good in a couple of weeks. I can't blame them for stealing the good stuff. The majority of the supplies brought in is ammunition and the like."

Gerber stood up and moved to the table where he sat down on a metal folding chair. "This whole thing is a mess. I don't understand what they're trying to prove here."

"Maybe it's just that we don't have the big picture," said Fetterman. "Maybe there's something so special about this place that we, meaning the U.S. Army and Marine Corps, have to sacrifice ourselves to hold it."

Gerber laughed again. "You believe that?"

"Hell, no, sir, but it sounds real good, doesn't it?"

"Sounds absolutely marvelous."

THE WORKING BREAKFAST, ordered by the President and arranged by one of his staff, had been scheduled for the situation room. The model of Khe Sanh had been moved to one side where everyone could see it. One wall was covered by an aerial display of the Khe Sanh area, including all the outposts that controlled the high ground. Spotlights had been set to highlight both the model and the aerial map.

Lockhart was sitting at the far end of the table, the lowest-ranking man in the room. The four-star generals and the top civilian leaders sat nearer to the President. Lockhart didn't mind the arrangement, because it kept him out of the direct line of fire.

Several men and women wearing red-and-white uniforms were serving the breakfast: eggs cooked four ways, ham, steak, sausage, half a dozen different juices, potatoes, bacon, toast and a dozen jams and jellies. There was coffee and tea and even a few Cokes for those who insisted on having their caffeine in something cold.

The food was served on fine bone china. There were teacups and coffee cups and crystal for the juices. The silverware was sterling and the napkins linen. The opulence in the air would have sickened the taxpayers if they had been allowed to see it.

When everyone had been served and had had a chance to eat some food, the President said, "I think it's time to get started. What's the latest on the Tet situation?"

The Army chief of staff wiped his mouth and stood up. He moved to the map of Khe Sanh and then turned his back on it. He seemed to have moved so that he could stand in the spotlight. Without consulting notes, he said, "Most of the ground we lost during the initial assaults has been retaken. Casualties have been light, considering that—"

"Light?" snapped the President. "We lost more men in the past week than we lost in a month last year."

"Yes, Mr. President," said the general, "but then compared to the damage done to the enemy, our losses and the losses of our allies are very light."

Lockhart didn't want to hear it. He'd read the intelligence reports and the after-action reports and knew what was going on. From the enemy point of view the Tet offensive had collapsed. They had lost tens of thousands of soldiers; there had been no uprising in the cities to support the Vietcong. There had been an utter lack of interest shown by the Vietnamese people, except for those caught in the fighting. Their reaction had been to flee just as quickly as they could.

The President slammed a hand against the table. It sounded as if a shot had been fired. "Damn it, General, I'm getting sick of this. Walter Cronkite is suggesting that all is not as it should be in Vietnam. The media people are running around calling us liars. They don't believe anything we say. And now you're trying to soft-pedal this fight and our casualties."

"Yes, Mr. President."

"Damn it, man, I don't want to hear what you think I want to hear. I want the goddamned truth as to what's going on." He leaned forward and pointed at Lockhart, snapping his fingers. "You tell us what's happening at Khe Sanh."

Lockhart pushed himself away from the table and stood up. He swallowed the steak he had been chewing and wished he could wash it down with some juice. Wiping his mouth, he dropped his napkin onto the table beside his plate. "The situation there has stabilized somewhat."

"Now what in hell does that mean?"

"It means, Mr. President, that the expected push from the Communists hasn't materialized, but that sensor readings—"

"What are you talking about? What goddamned sensors?"

"Prior to the first enemy assault on Khe Sanh," the Air Force chief of staff responded, "we sowed the hills and approaches to Khe Sanh with a sound tremor detector, a sophisticated device that picks up enemy troop movements and broadcasts a signal to a listening post inside Khe Sanh. Major shifts in the enemy forces, even minor shifts, can be detected. Artillery can be called in on those locations, bombing runs can be planned, so that the troop concentrations can be broken up."

"Thank you, General," said the President. "Continue, Colonel."

"Sensor readings have indicated that the majority of the enemy forces have remained around Khe Sanh. As happened at Dien Bien Phu, the enemy is apparently tunneling, trying to breach the Marine lines by digging under them."

"There you go again," the President growled. "Dien Bien Phu."

"Sir," said the Army chief of staff, "the parallels between the two battles can't be ignored. To do so would be to court disaster at Khe Sanh. The difference is we know what happened at Dien Bien Phu and can move to prevent it."

"Do you know what the loss of that base would do to this Administration, General?"

"Yes, sir, and I can assure you that Khe Sanh isn't going to fall."

The President pointed at Lockhart, who still stood in front of his rapidly cooling breakfast. "What do the goddamned sensors have to say?"

"That the enemy is still out there, but they're not massing for an attack. There are thousands of them in the hills around Khe Sanh, but nothing to suggest an assault."

As LOCKHART WAS ASSURING the President that the sensors around Khe Sanh had yet to reveal movement of a mass of enemy soldiers, they began to broadcast that movement of troops. A large body of men was heading toward Hill 881 South.

The Air Force seeding of the sensors had been rapid and not fully documented. That meant that the operators at the Khe Sanh combat base weren't exactly sure where the enemy's large force was. They made their best guess and passed it along to the artillery men so that they could open fire.

On Hill 861A Hanratty knelt in a bunker and watched the artillery display as it played across the slopes of Hill 881 South—flashes of orange and yellow fire, a burst of bright white as willie pete was used to mark the location. Fires flared and died in minutes, the wet vegetation and soggy ground stopping the spread.

The ground underfoot trembled with the artillery barrage. The air was heavy with the booming, which sounded like a distant summer storm, complete with lightning. Except that the lightning was more deadly than that from the heavens, and the thunder more ominous.

Hanratty was fascinated by the distant fireworks. After a couple of weeks on Hill 861, living with the constant barrages of enemy mortar shells and rockets, living underground and coming to the surface rarely, it was good to see the enemy catching hell.

The man who shared the bunker with him, a gigantic black Marine named Stubbs, hadn't said much since they'd been put together. He'd grunted a welcome and then resumed eating his cold C-rations. After drinking some water from his canteen, he'd moved to the firing port to look out.

That didn't bother Hanratty. He was happier not having to make conversation with a man he didn't know. The Marine seemed to know what he was doing and the bunker had been organized for a fight. Grenades off to one side, but within easy reach. Spare magazines for his weapon where they could be grabbed without having to search for them. A number of star-cluster flares in case more illumination was needed.

The structure itself seemed solid enough. It was dug into the side of the hill, the walls lined with sandbags. There were huge beams across the top and then more sandbags. A mortar round wouldn't penetrate it, though the men inside might not be able to hear well for a week and would probably have a headache. A rocket could destroy it. Depending on the angle of the hit, the bunker might absorb the force of the explosion, or it might not.

As the sun set, Hanratty had retreated to the far end of the bunker so that he could eat his evening meal of boned chicken, canned bread and soupy jelly. Not much of a meal, but it beat starving. At least that was what Hanratty told himself.

When he moved back to the firing port, he again watched the artillery show on the slopes opposite him. It was a long barrage that slowly shifted from the valley, up the hill, until it was blasting into the jungle only half a klick from the Marine camp there.

"You know what's going on?" Hanratty asked Stubbs.

"Sarge said they heard the VC were on the move. Preemptive strikes."

"Yeah," said Hanratty. "Preemptive."

The fire shifted again, back down the valley and onto the hillsides of 861A. Hanratty couldn't see all of it now because of the terrain, but he could hear it—a pounding, like a giant with a bass drum, hammering away in the distance. He couldn't understand how an enemy force would be able to survive the firing, but knew that it could. The enemy always found a way to survive.

The artillery finally fell silent. They fired an occasional illumination round, a flare with a parachute that hung over the approaches to 861A. The swirling clouds of the monsoons hid some of the flares, but others burst through, swinging under their chutes and giving the dark jungle a swaying, dancing motion.

After an hour, Hanratty wasn't sure what he was looking at anymore. The shadows fluttered and flickered and the bushes seemed to gyrate. But the motion was caused by the flares overhead.

He looked at his watch. The night had slipped away during the artillery barrage. It was now after three in the morning, and he began to relax. Charlie didn't attack much after 2:00 a.m. He needed the dark to escape in case the fight went against him.

Hanratty saw that Stubbs was still awake. "I'm going to catch a little sleep."

"Go ahead."

Just as he stretched out in the rear of the bunker, he heard a series of pops in the distance. Moments later mortar rounds began to fall inside the wire. Hanratty rolled onto his belly and scrambled closer to the sandbags.

The shells exploded in the center of the camp. Then rockets began to hit, their detonations scattered all over the hilltop. Hanratty crawled forward, toward the firing pit.

"Anything going on out there?" he asked.

"Nothing. Nothing at all."

They took turns searching the hillside for enemy soldiers. Hanratty was sure they would be attacking, that the big push was coming. He could see explosions in the camps to the west of them and figured that mortar rounds and rockets were landing at Khe Sanh.

For an hour the rockets and mortar shells exploded inside the camp, random detonations all over the hilltop. There had been cries for medics during the first few minutes and the mortarmen were working to return the fire. The heavy machine guns, the .50 calibers, were hammering away, their softball-sized tracers bouncing down the hillside.

The men in the other camps were firing, too. Mortars and machine guns. Ruby-colored tracers flashing into the night. Streaks of fire into the valleys and the jungle around the camps.

Hanratty was no longer frightened by the mortar shells and rockets. He'd lived through so many attacks in the past few days that his fear of them had evaporated. He'd been close to several when they'd exploded. There had been a blast of heat and a taste of dirt and gunpowder. He'd heard shrapnel snap overhead and slash into the sandbags or the wood of the bunkers. Once or twice he'd been clipped by the white-hot metal, enough to draw blood and earn a Purple Heart if he had told anyone about it, but nothing bad enough to require medical attention.

The constant mortar rounds and rockets were nothing now, just loud noises that didn't frighten him as they had during the first attack. After a glance out the firing port to make sure the enemy wasn't advancing on his position, he stayed down and waited for the barrage to end.

And end it did, just as it always did. There were two or three final explosions, then silence. He took a deep breath, happy to have survived another rocket attack, and then he heard the first of the bangalore torpedoes explode in the perimeter wire.

"Oh, shit!" Hanratty yelled.

"What!"

"We got gooks in the wire." Hanratty stuck the barrel of his M-16 out the firing port and opened up. He aimed at the shadows moving toward the outside wire. Red tracers from the machine guns crisscrossed over them, or hit the ground near them, bouncing upward, tumbling.

Another section of the wire exploded and then another, and the enemy seemed to rise from the ground, rushing toward the bunker line, sounding bugles and whistles, and shouting. RPD raked the bunkers, trying to protect the attacking troops. AKs fired, their green tracers tearing through the night.

"Oh, shit," said Hanratty again, remembering the NVA assault on the last camp he was in. He flipped the selector switch to full-auto, firing five- and six-round bursts.

RPGs fired by the attacking soldiers slammed into the corner bunkers. The heavy machine guns went silent, as the Marines manning them fell back toward the center of the camp, their bunkers ruined, their weapons destroyed.

Hanratty slipped from the firing port to the entrance of the bunker, watching the fight to the south of him. Three men came stumbling out of a bunker. One of them fell to his knees and the other two grabbed him, dragging him up the hill.

Then two men appeared out of the darkness, small men holding AKs. Hanratty opened fire, trying to cut them down. One fell to his side, pulling the trigger as he dropped. The other dived for cover as a grenade exploded near them. He flipped up into the air and then dropped to the ground.

Another of the bunkers blew up then—a flash of fire and smoke as the sandbags seemed to lift and then collapse. One of the attacking soldiers stuck the barrel of his weapon into the firing port and emptied a full magazine into the interior.

The enemy seemed to channel themselves toward smoking bunkers. One of them turned suddenly, and raised an RPG to his shoulder. He aimed at a bunker and fired. An instant later the bunker was gone.

Hanratty fired at those men. One fell but the others shot back. The bullets slammed into the sandbags and the beam near Hanratty. He fell to the floor, a hand over his head. Splinters from the beam and sand from the bags showered over him.

"We're about to be flanked!" yelled Hanratty.

"Got it." Stubbs backed away from the firing port, his weapon at his hip. He was firing out into the night. "Go. Get out!"

Hanratty leaped out and landed on his belly. Around him, through the smoke of a dozen fires and through the clouds of dirt, he could see the enemy advancing on them. He aimed and fired. There was a single scream, and then the flashing of enemy weapons as the VC turned on him.

Stubbs jumped clear of the bunker and threw a grenade. "Go," he ordered again, and then tossed another grenade.

A stream of men retreated toward the crest of the hill, big men with M-16s and M-14s firing into the darkness. There were explosions from grenades, firing from machine guns, shouts and screams and grunts.

"Gas masks!" yelled someone. "Put on your gas masks."

The order was repeated again and again, but Hanratty could do nothing about it. His mask was inside the bunker with his extra canteens and his entrenching tool. He could do nothing but ignore the order as he ran from bunker to bunker, trying not to get killed.

Stubbs was right behind him. The big man turned once and fired a burst from his weapon. Then he threw his last grenade and whirled to run.

Gas grenades arced over their heads, gray tin-can-sized weapons that landed and burst and began to spew CS gas. White clouds of choking gas, more potent than tear gas. Hanratty ran through a cloud of it and felt it sting his face and hands. His eyes burned and tears rolled down his cheeks.

There was nothing he could do about it now. The enemy was coming.

And the enemy, without masks, kept coming. They charged into the gas, firing from the hip, falling to the ground and continuing to fire. The muzzle-flashes popped like flashbulbs at a sporting event. Green tracers danced through the clouds of gray CS gas.

Hanratty reached the crest of the hill. From the inside of a bunker he heard the frantic voice of the company commander as he tried to get artillery support for his camp. He called for anything, demanding that it land in the wire and at the rally points for the enemy soldiers.

"Our men clear?" someone shouted. "Our men off the perimeter?"

"Yeah! We're out."

"Get them!" yelled the voice.

Behind him the mortarmen tilted their tubes, trying to drop the rounds on the perimeter and in the wire just beyond it. They wasted their precious water, pouring it on the tubes to cool them, and when the water was gone they used beer and juice, and finally men began to piss on them. And still the enemy came through the rain of mortar rounds and artillery and through the CS gas.

The Marines in the contracted perimeter poured out a sheet of lead. The firing from their weapons blended into one long detonation. The sound of voices, orders, commands and demands for medics were lost in the firing.

The platoon leader leaped from a bunker and ordered three men to the right, three to the left, fire teams to flank the enemy. When the cross fire was set up, he ordered the men to throw grenades. All the grenades they had.

The weapons detonated into a wall of swirling dust and smoke. The Marines, roaring, attacked then, bayonets fixed. They ran from the crest into the enemy lines. Fighting was suddenly hand-to-hand. The first few enemy positions were overrun quickly, the VC and NVA killed.

The charge carried downhill to the trenches that ringed the inside of the perimeter. Marines leaped in to fight the NVA with fists, knives and rifle butts. Firing tapered off and the artillery moved away, down the slope in case the NVA planned a counterattack of its own.

Hanratty used the butt of his rifle to knock a VC from his feet. As the man rolled onto his back, Hanratty fell on him, hitting him in the face. He felt the bones crack and the man groaned. Hanratty flipped his weapon around, the barrel next to the enemy soldier's chest and pulled the trigger.

As Hanratty jumped from the body of the dead man, he saw a grenade land in the bottom of the trench. He rolled away as the weapon detonated. He was up then, running along the trench.

He came to the body of a dead NVA soldier holding a magazine. His weapon was lying near him. As Hanratty bent to pick up the weapon, another of the enemy jumped on his back. Hanratty shrugged and the soldier fell to the bottom of the trench. Hanratty kicked out, catching the man in the side, and then shot him.

With that, Hanratty turned and leaned against the front of the trench. He dropped the magazine from the rifle and replaced it. He worked the bolt and opened fire, a few rounds directed at the fleeing enemy soldiers.

Hanratty turned and glanced east. The sky there was gray as the sun came up. In the half-light he could see the bodies of the NVA and VC killed in the attack littering the ground. Weapons were scattered among them. Equipment was strewn everywhere. Smoke from the fires and lingering clouds of gas drifted down the hillside.

Around him the firing tapered off until it stopped. Only the heavy weapons, the mortars and the machine guns that hadn't been destroyed, continued to fire. The incoming stopped falling, and then the American weapons fell silent.

Hanratty looked up and saw Stubbs standing over the body of a dead NVA. He held a captured AK in one hand and the helmet the man had worn in the other. He was grinning broadly. "Little assholes gave us quite a fight."

Hanratty laughed out loud. "One hell of a fight," he agreed.

18

MARINE CAMP ON THE
SUMMIT OF HILL 861A

With the sun up, Hanratty could see the damage done to the camp during the attack. The wire around it had been destroyed by the bangalore torpedoes. Bunkers that had housed the crew-served weapons had been blown up. Many of them were little more than smoking piles of sandbags and broken lumber. Bodies of Vietnamese were scattered in the wire, lying where they had died.

Around the camp the jungle had been shredded by the artillery barrage that had destroyed the reserves of the NVA and VC and that had tried to kill the enemy soldiers fleeing the hilltop. Wisps of white smoke, some of it fog, some of it the remnants of the CS, and some of it from small fires, drifted on the morning breeze.

Hanratty looked down the trench. The bodies of the Vietnamese were still there. Their weapons and military equipment had already been stripped from them. Their blood soaked into the already muddy bottom of the trench. There was a heavy smell of copper in the air that sometimes overwhelmed what was left of the CS.

A dozen Marines, armed with pistols, moved through the trenches, checking the dead Vietnamese to make sure none of them was playing possum. No one wanted to be killed by a suicidal wounded NVA or VC. There were occasional shots.

Stubbs moved closer to Hanratty. "More than a hundred."

"What?"

"There's more than a hundred dead enemy left behind. We kicked their asses good."

"Right," said Hanratty, looking at the destruction in the camp. Everything was full of bullet holes or had been knocked down or burned. Debris from mortar rounds and rockets lay all around. Chunks of lumber were scattered. Equipment, shell casings, weapons were everywhere.

"Only seven Marines were killed," said Stubbs.

The sergeant who had met Hanratty at the helipad the day before suddenly loomed up, almost out of the ground. He stood over them, his hands on his hips, his weapon slung over his shoulder. His uniform was torn and bloodstained, but it didn't look as if he'd been injured. "If you gentlemen would care to join us, we have a lot of work to do this morning."

"No rest for the weary?" asked Hanratty.

"You can rest when you get back to the World," said the sergeant. "Right now we've got to get these bodies out of here before they start to stink."

"What are we going to do with them?" Hanratty asked.

"Drag them down the hillside about a hundred meters or so and dump them in a ravine. Couple of guys have been detailed to throw some dirt over them."

"Sounds like a job for graves registration," said Stubbs.

"Well, then, you both have just been reassigned to graves registration. Let's get at it."

Hanratty climbed out of the trench and straightened. He started to take a deep breath, caught a whiff of CS, coughed, then wiped his nose.

"Shit hangs on forever," said the sergeant. "It's not a gas, you know. It's powder. Settles to the ground and then someone walks by, stirring it up."

"Great," said Hanratty. He wiped the tears from his eyes. "First we have to put up with the heat and the humidity and now we've found another way to make life miserable."

"Let's get a move on," said the sergeant. "If Charlie comes back, we want to be ready for him, and there's a lot of work to be done in the next few hours."

Hanratty glanced at Stubbs, then slung his weapon and moved down into the wire and through it. The body of a Vietnamese lay tangled in it, his arm shot away. There didn't seem to be another wound on him. Hanratty grabbed a foot and began to drag him. Stubbs was there suddenly, helping. They started down the hill with the dead man.

GERBER, FETTERMAN and the members of their new team spent the night in the bunker, listening to the artillery duel taking place outside. Dozens of mortar rounds and rockets fell on the Khe Sanh combat base. Then artillery, every tube in every battery, opened fire, and that continued through the night. Loud, long crashes as the pieces fired in support of the small camps around the major base. Outgoing and incoming. Loud enough to wake the dead, to wake all the soldiers who had died in Vietnam during its whole long bloody history.

But like everything else, men got used to the noise. It slipped into the background where they were barely aware of it. They went to sleep with their minds tuned to the noise, so that when it stopped, they woke, wondering what they had heard.

It wasn't until nearly seven in the morning when the tubes finally fell silent. Gerber was sitting on his sleeping bag then, looking like a man in meditation. His eyes were closed and he was walking himself through the mission, trying to spot a flaw in what little planning had been done. A jump into Laos and a walk to a specific point. Nothing in there to go wrong, nothing to plan. Five days in the jungle and then a hike to Lang Vei, the closest American camp.

When the last of the artillery rounds was fired, Gerber opened his eyes. The interior of the bunker was still dim, a single light burning in the far corner. There was enough light for a man to see to get out, if it came to that.

Fetterman sat up. "Breakfast."

"I'd like to get something hot into the men before we take off," Gerber said. "A good substantial meal, because we won't have the chance for the next week."

"No hot food," said Hobbs. "The mess halls have been shut down—some of them destroyed by the enemy, some of them closed because the cooks don't like standing around the stoves, exposed to enemy gunners."

"I can understand that," said Gerber. "Especially with the number of mortar shells and rockets dropping on this place."

Fetterman moved to the supplies and pulled out one of the cartons of C-rations. He yanked it open. "We can make a fairly big meal out of this. A little fire in the bottom of a butt can and we can heat it up."

"Only thing we need is juice," said Gerber.

"That I can arrange," said Hobbs. "It's powdered, but hell, there's tons of it."

Gerber got to his feet and looked out the bunker's entrance. A gray light filtered in. He climbed a couple of steps and looked up into the sky at black low-hanging clouds that seemed to be filled with rain. He didn't think the flight would be able to get in very early, which didn't matter that much. He didn't want to hit the DZ until after dark. "Let's get this feast organized," he said. "Then I've got to get over to the airfield and coordinate our ride with the Air Force."

He moved back to the table as Quinn ran up the steps. Fetterman was opening C-ration boxes, taking out the cans of good food and pushing the rest to the side. Ham and lima beans, tins of crackers and boxes of cigarettes joined the unusable food.

"Cigarettes make good trading material," said Lawrence.

"You're welcome to them, but I'd leave them here when we hit the field."

"Just thought we could trade them to the locals."

"Whatever," said Fetterman. He picked a steel pot off the floor and pulled the helmet liner from it. Peering into the helmet, he felt inside. It seemed to be clean enough. He propped the helmet on the table and began working with a P-38 can opener. Then, dumping the contents of a dozen cans into the helmet, he mixed everything quickly.

"Just what in hell are you doing?" asked Gerber.

"Making a stew. A thick stew that will fill you up and give you energy."

Gerber stared at the contents. Some of them made sense: the boned chicken and turkey and even the scrambled eggs. But the beans and franks bothered him. The eggs and beans just didn't seem to go together. The only thing to be thankful for was that Fetterman hadn't dumped in the spaghetti and meatballs.

The master sergeant stirred the mess, opened packets of salt and poured them in. "Makes an interesting stew. A barbecue flavor. It really is quite good."

"How come you've never made this conglomeration before?" Gerber asked.

"We've always been able to get real food. Even at the old Triple Nickel we got good supplies of food. This is the first time we've been forced to eat C-rations at a camp."

Gerber looked down into the helmet. "You sure we can eat this?"

"It's an old Army recipe. Trust me. It'll be very good."

"How come I'm not reassured?" asked Gerber.

"Wait until we get it heated up. Then you'll see how good it is."

Quinn returned with a box that held powdered orange juice. Lawrence filled another of the steel pots with water, then began to mix the juice.

"Afraid we couldn't get any ice," said Quinn. "There's none to be had in the camp."

"You're doing fine." Fetterman picked up his steel pot and carried it to the entrance of the bunker.

"Going to throw it out?" asked Gerber.

"No, sir, I'm going to heat it. Don't want to start a fire in the bunker."

Gerber sat there and watched the preparations for breakfast. The men were opening the tins that held bread and jelly and then the ones that held fruit. Again they mixed it all together, creating a super fruit cocktail of chunks of peach and pear. They didn't dump the applesauce into the mess. That would have made it too sweet.

Fifteen minutes later Fetterman returned with the steel pot, using an OD towel to hold on to it. "This fucker's hot now," he announced. He set it on the table, then said, "Let's eat."

The men moved forward, their mess kits in hand. Gerber was the first in line. He dished some of the stew onto his plate, tasted it and said, "You win again, Master Sergeant. This is quite good."

"Told you I knew what I was doing."

Gerber sat down and ate in silence. He drank some of the juice that the others had made. It tasted just like what it was—powdered orange juice. There was a cardboard aftertaste to it, but it was wet and Gerber drank a lot of it, knowing that later he'd need the moisture. When they finally finished, he said, "Let's get the equipment split up and figure out who's going to carry what."

They pushed the dishes aside for the moment, knowing they would have to clean everything later. Gerber pulled out the map and went over everything with them again. After an hour he was satisfied. Now it was all up to the Air Force and the weather. He could do nothing but wait.

USUALLY BRIEFINGS for the flights into Khe Sanh were held early in the day, but the last of the monsoons were closing off the base until late morning. Takeoff times were delayed several times and then, when the enemy activity was the heaviest, they were delayed even more. But even with all that, briefing and preflight were normally accomplished by noon. Then it was a matter of waiting until the weather broke so that they could get off the ground.

The operations officer told Whitmire he would have a special briefing right after lunch and that the takeoff time had been delayed so that they would be landing at Khe Sanh about dusk.

"Won't that give Charlie the perfect chance to shoot at us?" asked Whitmire.

The operations officer laughed. "At Khe Sanh it no longer matters what time you land, because Charlie will probably shoot at you every chance he gets."

"What's this all about?"

"You'll find out later." The operations officer turned and disappeared.

Whitmire returned to his hootch and Marie lying on his cot naked. When she heard him, she rolled onto her back and laughed out loud. "Just like Pavlov's dog, but instead of the dinner making my mouth water, it's you appearing making...well, never mind."

Whitmire stared at her for a moment. "Won't do you any good now. I've got a briefing to go to."

Marie sat up and crossed her legs, almost as if she was trying, suddenly, to keep him from seeing anything. "That seems to be all you people do. Briefings, preflights, debriefings. Hours and hours wasted in talk, talk, talk."

"Sometimes I think you're right. We have a saying in the Air Force: when the weight of the paperwork is equal to the gross takeoff weight of the aircraft, you're finally ready for the mission."

She stood up and moved to him, molding herself to him, and brushed his cheek with a kiss. "Isn't there some way I could talk you out of this?"

"Oh, yes," he said breathlessly. "There certainly is, but I really have to go."

"Then, when you come back, you'll find me fully dressed in layers and layers of clothes." She grinned.

"That I don't believe." He grabbed his notebook and escaped. Outside, with no one else in sight, he adjusted his clothes so that he could stand up without physical pain.

He hurried along the boardwalk, crossed an open field and entered the intel bunker. He blinked in the dimness of the interior, waiting for his eyes to adjust, then walked to the briefing room. He found Major Carson inside already. The AC had his notepad out and was waiting for the briefing to begin.

When he saw Whitmire, he said, "Nice that you could join us. I have nothing else to do with my time."

Whitmire slipped into the chair next to the aircraft commander. "Sorry, sir, but I was only just told about this."

The intelligence officer pushed a map across the table at them. "We've been requested to fly a follow-up mission after the supply drop at Khe Sanh, adding no more than thirty or forty minutes to the flight time."

"What is this?" asked Carson.

"Okay, from this point the briefing is classified secret." The intel officer glanced at the wooden door and saw that it was closed. A sergeant stood near it, as if guarding it.

"Understood," said Carson.

"We're going to drop a Special Forces unit into Laos. Just on the other side of the border, no more than twenty klicks deep. Drop is to be made at night into one of the DZs marked on this map.

"This looks like a job for the Army. A chopper into Khe Sanh to pick them up and then drop them off," Carson said.

"I would agree, except that an Army chopper landing at Khe Sanh like that might give Charlie something to think about. We've got C-130s landing there all day long. Nothing that unusual about it."

"Shit," said Carson. "It just tacks on a little flight time. I guess it's no big deal."

"Okay," said the intelligence officer. He turned, grabbed another map covered with acetate and laid it on the table. There were red marks from a grease pencil all over it. Pointing, he said, "This is the current situation chart. Enemy units marked in red, of course. Elements of three divisions have been identified around Khe Sanh, and support for them stretches back into Laos."

"We got all that at the serial lead brief this morning," Carson said.

"Of course," said the intel man, "but I want to make sure you were paying attention. Going into Khe Sanh, you can expect small-arms fire. While on the ground, you might get hit with mortar shells, rockets and small-arms fire. Coming out, more small arms and some 12.7 mm stuff."

"As you said earlier."

"Right. Now you may want to turn north after takeoff, flying up the road here. Marines were in heavy contact there last night, but there's nothing new today. Charlie might be lying low. Turn back to the west before you reach the DMZ, and be careful when penetrating the Laotian border."

Carson studied the map, then pushed it aside so Whitmire could take a look at it. "Anything been spotted on the border? Anything heavier than the 12.7s?"

"No antiaircraft in the area. I would expect some ZSU-23s or maybe some 37 mm guns, but none of that has been reported by anyone yet."

"How are we going to know which drop zone the Green Beanies want to hit?" asked Whitmire.

"Their leader will give it to you once you're airborne. It'll be somewhere in this area, because it's about the only area that has clearings available for drop zones."

"Then won't the enemy know that?" asked Whitmire.

"According to their people, that doesn't matter."

"After we drop them?" asked Carson.

"Fly straight and level, or rather just more or less continue on your heading for five, ten minutes, then turn and return here the quickest way possible."

"Christ," said Carson, studying the battle map. There were so many red marks on it indicating enemy units that it looked as if someone had been fatally wounded on it. Everything around the combat base was colored red.

"Most of that won't affect you. They're units equipped with small arms, AKs and RPDs, nothing too heavy. When you cross into Laos, that could change, and I would suggest you climb to twenty or twenty-five thousand feet after the troops have jumped.''

''Fighter escort?'' Whitmire asked.

''Again we don't want to call attention to this. Fighters will be on-station within minutes of you, in case they're needed, but remember, we haven't seen any MiGs south of the DMZ in a couple of years.''

Carson looked at Whitmire. ''You have any questions?''

Whitmire shook his head. ''Seems to be fairly straightforward. Just a little jaunt tacked on to the end of the resupply mission.''

''It's the reason your takeoff time has been delayed by forty minutes,'' said the intelligence officer. ''The rest of the mission is going in as planned, with only a slight delay to cover this.''

Carson stood. ''Okay. Got it.''

''And don't mark the DZs on the maps you take into the aircraft.''

''You say that every time.''

''And the first time that I don't, one of you people will decide it's all right. The VC could end up with all the battle plans that way.''

''I doubt it,'' said Carson.

Whitmire and Carson left the intelligence bunker together. They stopped just outside the entrance, where Carson stared at the western sky. Earlier it had been nearly cloudless, as the monsoons had blown away, but now clouds were starting to build again. To the north and west there could easily be bigger clouds and more monsoons.

''I don't like these tacked-on missions, especially ones the Army should be running,'' said Carson.

''Why's that?''

''Shit, don't you ever watch war movies? Every time you do something out of the ordinary, you get your ass shot off. Fly in someone else's place because he's sick or drunk or whatever, and it's like signing your own death warrant.''

"But this is only a little diversion," said Whitmire.

"I know. That's what scares me shitless."

19

**SPECIAL FORCES
COMPOUND KHE SANH
COMBAT BASE**

After the meal, the men spent the day resting. Gerber and Fetterman checked the equipment, and then Fetterman wrapped up the silencers so that they could move them across Khe Sanh without anyone seeing them. Reporters, holed up in a spacious, well-lit concrete bunker known as the Alamo Hilton, would have had a hundred embarrassing questions if they had seen the two-foot-long silencers. Once the team was on the plane, out of sight of the reporters, they would be able to equip their weapons with the silencers.

Gerber didn't want the men to get too far from the bunker. Normally, before a mission, they would have gone into isolation, but there was no way to manage that at Khe Sanh. All he could do was keep them in the bunker during the day, eating and resting, preparing for the mission that night.

Late in the afternoon they moved from the bunker to the control tower near the airfield and sat behind the structure, watching the wind indicator spin atop the glass-lined tower. The C-130s, spaced out, came in, landed then pulled out as quickly as possible. The enemy fired at some of them, but ignored the others.

An hour before dusk one of the men from the MATCU 62 came down from the tower, searched for Gerber and told him, "This is yours, sir. Be ready."

"They bringing in any cargo?"

"Yes, sir. Can't have airplanes landing here without something on board. As soon as the pallets are out, you'll need to run right up the ramp. Find a seat and strap in until takeoff has been made."

Gerber nodded and looked at the tight knot of men around him. "You all got that?"

When they had answered, the man added, "But let us get those pallets off first."

"Got it."

"Watch for one of us in the tower. We'll let you know when it's on final. You can line up at the edge of the ramp."

"Okay."

The man returned to the tower. As he did, Gerber said, "Let's have a final equipment check. You forget anything now, and you're going to be without it for the next week."

Fetterman checked each man a final time, making sure he had his three canteens, his weapons and the ammo for them, his share of the squad equipment and his food. None of the men were carrying anything extra. No books to read, no paper to write home on, no pens and no cameras. Everything they had was related to the mission and the mission only. When the check was complete, he examined Gerber's rucksack and then the captain did the same for him.

They were quiet for a moment, but no one sat down. They knelt in the dirt behind the tower area, watching the glass cage where the Air Force people worked. Gerber felt a light breeze blowing from the west, cooling him. Sweat had soaked his uniform under the arms and down the back. It had beaded on his forehead and dripped. The humidity was so high that the dampness wouldn't dry. He rubbed at his face, wishing they were off Khe Sanh.

It wasn't that there was anything wrong with the base, though to his way of thinking, the Marines had let things de-

teriorate more than they should have. No, it was sitting at the
center of a giant target. The enemy held the high points around
the camp, and the camp was sitting on a bull's-eye. There were
rings near the perimeter for the near misses, but the majority
of the rockets and mortar rounds were falling right in the center, close to where he crouched, out in the open, with his team.

When they reached the jungle, even the jungle in Laos
where the VC and NVA operated without much fear of the
American Air Force, Gerber would feel better. Once there, he
would be able to do something to protect himself. He would
have control of his destiny. At Khe Sanh the falling rockets and
mortar rounds were entirely random. To get out unhurt was
the luck of the draw. Men who'd done nothing wrong, other
than leap into the wrong bunker, had been killed or injured.
He would be glad to get out.

The man appeared in the window and waved at them once.
Gerber got to his feet and looked east. In the far distance, just
over the green hills, he could see the four smoke trails of a C-
130. The landing lights flashed once, as if the pilot was trying
to draw attention to himself.

"Let's go," said Gerber. He moved forward, around the
sandbagged bunkers that housed the radar and communications equipment, so that he was at the edge of the ramp. He
crouched and waited as the men spread out around him.

The C-130 looked larger now, coming straight in, resembling a giant bug. It descended rapidly, then held at about a
hundred feet over the terrain, lined up on the runway. For
thirty seconds nothing seemed to happen, then the plane
dropped from the sky, hitting the far end of the runway. It
didn't bounce and there was no dust or smoke as it touched
down.

The C-130 rushed forward, engines roaring. As it neared the
ramp, it turned so that the ramp was pointing toward the
tower. As that was happening, the first of the pallets slipped
down the ramp.

Gerber was up and moving then, running across the open ramp. He could smell the exhaust of the four engines, see it as it rolled across the ramp.

He stopped short and saw that the last of the pallets had been off-loaded. The loadmaster, an Air Force NCO in a green flight suit and wearing a flight helmet, stood at the bottom of the ramp, waving them forward.

Again, as if the men didn't understand what they were supposed to do, Gerber yelled, "Let's go."

He ran up the ramp and moved along the fuselage toward the cockpit. Dropping his rucksack onto the floor, he kicked it under the troop seat as he sat down. The rest of the men did the same. As the last of them entered the airplane, the ramp began to close and the loadmaster moved toward the seats.

Before he could sit down, the plane lurched once and the loadmaster stumbled. He grabbed at one of the visible ribs, righted himself, then dropped into a seat. Putting his hands next to his mouth, he screamed, "Buckle up! We're going to take off!"

Taxiing out was nothing at all like Gerber had expected. In the past a plane would maneuver carefully to the runway, wait its turn, then roll down the runway to lift off gently. This time it seemed as if they were in a race to the runway. They bounced around as the plane dashed for its takeoff position. There didn't seem to be any time between pulling onto the runway and the beginning of the takeoff roll. The engines shrieked as they worked to pull the plane through the heavy Khe Sanh atmosphere.

Gerber was thrown forward, slammed back and then tossed up. Before he could catch his breath, the plane leaped into the air, climbing rapidly. He was thrown to the rear, straining at his seat belt. His stomach remained on the ground. To his right, Hobbs looked as if he was going to be sick.

Then, as suddenly as it had started, the turmoil ended and the loadmaster was up, telling them, "We're above the cloud deck. Safe for the moment."

Gerber nodded and unbuckled his seat belt. He walked over to the loadmaster and leaned close to him. "Need to brief the pilots on our destination."

"Yes, sir, we know that. Give them about five more minutes and then you can talk to them."

"Thanks." Gerber moved to the rear of the plane, to one of the troop doors, and looked out. Through breaks in the clouds he could see the deep greens of the jungle and the red scars at the tops of the hills, deepening shadows that hid so much.

Gerber left the window and glanced at the loadmaster, who nodded at him. The captain worked his way to the front of the plane and climbed the ladder into the cockpit. Against the rear bulkhead there was a long benchlike seat that could be turned into a cot. The pilots sat forward, where they could see out the windshield. It seemed almost spacious on the flight deck, more so than in the helicopters where everything was jammed together.

As he reached the top of the ladder, the aircraft commander turned and waved him forward. He peeled off his flight helmet and said, "Welcome aboard, Captain."

"Thank you." Gerber crouched between the seats and hesitated. "You familiar with what we're going to need?"

"Had a briefing before takeoff. All I need is the location of the DZ."

Gerber took a map out of his pocket, unfolded it, then refolded it so that the area of the DZs was on top. He pointed at the map. "Everything's in Laos."

"I know that."

"Okay," said Gerber. "We'd like to fly over this one and this one, but not jump into either of them. We'll jump over here, which is the largest of the DZs within twelve klicks of the target."

"Okay." The AC reached out and took the map, studying it carefully.

"Second problem is that we want to jump in the dark, to make it that much harder for the enemy to locate us."

"That's no problem. We'll just bore holes in the sky until it's completely dark."

"We'd like to jump from no more than a thousand feet AGL. That going to be a problem?"

"Well, the terrain is a little rough, but we should be able to do that. You realize that a thousand feet hangs our butts right out. Well within small-arms range."

Gerber looked up from the map. "I know."

"Okay. Just thought I'd tell you." He glanced at the instruments and then at his watch. "It'll be completely dark in about thirty minutes. We'll turn toward Laos at that time."

Gerber slapped the man on the shoulder. "Thanks. Sorry about the jump altitude."

"No problem. After you're out, we'll just climb to twenty thousand and return to the base for a beer and a steak. We're not in danger that long."

Gerber returned to the rear of the plane. He leaned close to Fetterman. "Be about forty, fifty minutes yet."

"Yes, sir."

With that, Gerber sat down again, but he didn't buckle his seat belt. For a moment he concentrated on the coming mission and then let his mind wander. Everything had been worked out. All he could do now was jump into Laos and take it as it came at him. It was merely a question of patience now.

As soon as the Special Forces captain left the flight deck, Carson, using the intercom, said, "I don't like this at all."

The navigator moved forward with his own map of the area and asked, "Where's the DZ?"

Carson took it and pointed out the DZ. "We'll need the wind directions and speed so that we can put them down on the long axis of the DZ."

"I know that."

"Right. Figure the jump altitude at a thousand feet, then work out the heading for us."

"No problem." The navigator returned to his table to begin to work out the data.

Whitmire eased the wheel to the right, turning back toward the coast of Vietnam, away from Laos and the Marine combat base. He kept the flight straight and level then, heading east. He checked the time and saw that official sunset was only fifteen minutes away. It wouldn't be fully dark until about thirty minutes after that.

"Where you headed?" asked Carson.

"Nowhere in particular," answered Whitmire.

"Okay, I've got it," said Carson. He took the controls, but didn't change the heading.

"I've got the courses worked out," said the navigator. "We need to fly over the top of Khe Sanh in twenty-two minutes. A slow letdown and a final turn to 289 degrees for twelve minutes. That should put us over the DZ in complete darkness."

"How long to Khe Sanh?"

"From our current position, about eight minutes. We fly outbound for another three, then turn to head back. That puts us right on schedule."

Whitmire relaxed slightly. Nothing to worry about for another thirty minutes or more. The crossing of the border might be dangerous, but he doubted it. With the number of fighters and bombers hovering around Khe Sanh, like bees around a hive, anyone foolish enough to shoot at them would be attacked quickly. They could make a single radio call to the flight controller and have a dozen fighters to help them.

He turned in his seat and saw the flight engineer looking up into the cockpit. Over the intercom Whitmire asked, "There any Cokes left, MacIntosh?"

"A couple of warm ones," MacIntosh said.

"Get me one, if you don't mind."

MacIntosh disappeared and soon climbed back into the cockpit with a Coke. He handed it to Whitmire, then asked, "Anyone else?"

"Christ, who can drink those things warm?" cracked the navigator.

As MacIntosh vanished again, Carson said, "I think we're getting close to Khe Sanh again."

"Okay," said the navigator. "Here we go."

Whitmire didn't like the sound of that. He took a deep drink from the Coke, then set the can down on the deck near him. Checking the instruments, he looked out the windshield. The clouds were breaking up and he could see the ground, not that there was anything to see down there. Only the airfield had any lights and they were cut way back so that Charlie didn't have any convenient aiming marks. Nighttime landings had been eliminated with the first of the enemy attacks at Khe Sanh.

They crossed high above the combat base, continued east, then began the gentle letdown. They crossed the border, but no one seemed to care about that. The enemy didn't fire at them, and Whitmire breathed easier. If the enemy had been going to shoot, it seemed most likely that they would do it at the border.

The sky had darkened. Far to the west was a bright band of light as the sun set. Above that was a reddish glow that faded to deep purple and finally to black. Stars blazed and the moon glowed.

Whitmire felt himself tense, the muscles on the back of his neck crawling. He wiped his face and wished he hadn't asked for the Coke. It had seemed to be a good idea at the time. Now his stomach was beginning to act up.

Carson alerted the loadmaster that they were starting the run in, though they were still a long way out. Time to get the Green Berets on their feet and ready to jump.

Carson finished the instructions and turned to glance at Whitmire. As he did, his face suddenly blossomed crimson. He stared at Whitmire for a moment, a smile on his face, then slumped forward.

Whitmire was confused until he looked at the windshield. Holes were appearing there. Alarms started to shrill and the cockpit filled with smoke.

"We're taking fire," shouted a voice on the intercom.

Whitmire grabbed the controls. He checked the instruments and saw that everything was in the green, then checked the heading. Only then did he glance at Carson. The AC hadn't moved. Blood was spattered on the front of his uniform and dripping to the deck, pooling there.

"We have a fire," shouted someone.

Whitmire looked at the instruments, but saw no indication there. Smoke curled around his head as the C-130 continued the descent. Only two minutes to the DZ.

"Someone check Carson," he ordered.

He wanted to pull out now, but they were too close to the DZ. He continued on, fighting the controls, searching for signs of the fire, demanding that the flight engineer and the loadmaster talk to him. The smoke began to clear.

Through the windshield, he could see the dark ground spread out like a lumpy blanket. He searched for the DZ, spotted a clearing and headed in toward it. The only thought in his mind was to get the paratroopers out and then climb to altitude. With luck he could nurse the plane along so that they could get out over Thailand, or very close to it.

The ground began to twinkle, and at first Whitmire didn't understand it. Then he realized it was the enemy turning their AKs and RPDs on the low-flying aircraft. He jerked once, as if to pull the wheel back, but then didn't do it. He remembered reading accounts of Air Force pilots who had tried to save themselves by sacrificing the men in the back. At Normandy the paratroopers had taken a beating because of it. Whitmire was going to make sure the Green Berets he was carrying would have no such complaints.

Three rounds shattered the window to the left. More pierced the floor. Whitmire felt something slam into his seat. Wind whipped through the smashed windshield. There was a howl over the radio. Someone was yelling into the intercom, but he couldn't understand what was being said.

Then they were approaching the DZ. He let the loadmaster know they were coming up on the target, while he kept the altitude level and bled off the airspeed. He tried to hold it all together, watching the distant horizon, watching the instruments and watching the black jungle under him.

There was a sudden pain in his chest, a white-hot burning and he couldn't see very far. Around him he heard noise. Shouting and alarms. Everything was hazy and there was heat near his feet. A wetness slipped down over his stomach to soak his crotch. He wasn't sure what was happening around him anymore. He knew the Green Berets had to jump, but couldn't remember if they had bailed out or not. No longer could he remember much of anything. His mind was a blank.

He glanced to the left, into the vacant seat where the aircraft commander had been sitting, and wondered why Carson hadn't told him he was leaving the flight deck. It was cold there. So very cold.

And then there was a single, searing flash, and Whitmire felt no more.

WHEN THE LOADMASTER told him they were getting close, Gerber got to his feet. Each man had donned his chute as they crossed Khe Sanh, and now they were at the rear of the C-130. There was a buffeting as the plane slipped from the sky. Gerber stood with his feet spread, looking like a sailor on a badly rocking ship.

"Five minutes!" yelled the loadmaster as he opened the door. The sound from the engines increased and wind swirled in the open hatch.

Almost as if someone had given a command, Hobbs and his men pulled the silencers from the pouches that had protected them. They fastened them to the barrels of their weapons, being careful to get them on straight. Gerber glanced at the loadmaster, who was watching them carefully but who didn't say a word.

Gerber then moved closer to the door. Fetterman was in the rear with Hobbs, Quinn, Lawrence and Rogers. They checked each other's equipment. They checked the chutes. It wasn't going to be a static line jump.

The tiny light by the door burned red. The loadmaster signaled Gerber, and he stood in the door, his eyes on the light. The plane rocked from side to side, and there were flashes on the ground. Muzzle-flashes. He doubted that anyone who was shooting at the plane would see them. They looked to be too far away. That didn't mean there weren't enemy soldiers under the flight path who would see them bail out.

Gerber glanced over his shoulder. "Get off the DZ as quickly as possible. Pass it back."

There was a sudden huge bump, and Gerber nearly fell out of the doorway. He caught himself and saw a flash of flame along the wing. The brightness there flickered and then was gone. A line of tracers, a klick or more from the plane, arced upward.

And then the light went green. Gerber didn't hesitate. He launched himself into space, his arms tucked in. He kept his eyes on the horizon rather than on the blackness around him. An instant later he jerked the rip cord and heard the chute spill from the pack. There was a snap and Gerber's descent slowed. He glanced to the right, upward. Dark shapes were there, floating with him.

Beyond them the plane was outlined in flames. It was flying straight and level. Tracers were pouring into the sky, streams of green, white and even red. Thousands of them. Flashing upward like multicolored baseballs. Rain in reverse.

Gerber checked his descent, then looked at the C-130. It seemed to be a flaming ball and then it exploded. A powerful flash of orange-yellow. Flaming debris arced out along the flight path.

"Jesus," Gerber whispered in awe. He was numbed by the scene. Numbed by the sudden, unexpected deaths of the Air Force crew. He'd seen no indication that any of them had managed to get out.

And then he was down. He landed hard, rolled and ran forward, collapsing his chute. He hit the quick-release on his chest and stripped out of the harness. Crouching, he rolled up the chute and headed south toward the rally point.

Around him he was aware of his men landing and gathering their chutes. He saw their shapes as they moved to get off the DZ quickly. As he entered the trees, he turned back toward the west. There was nothing left of the C-130. The wreckage had all fallen out of the sky.

Fetterman appeared beside him and stuck his face close. "Point?"

Gerber touched the master sergeant. "Go."

The team formed silently and began its march into the jungle away from the DZ. For the first few moments Gerber could see the explosion of the plane in his mind, a flaring, burning death trap. Then he forced it from his mind. There wouldn't be time to dwell on it now. He'd drink a toast to the brave men in the plane when he got back to South Vietnam. Now he had to concentrate on getting through the mission so that he could drink that toast.

20

WHITE HOUSE
SITUATION ROOM

"I want to know why the television newscasters are claiming the United States Army suffered a defeat during Tet!" the President shouted. He stood at the head of the table, leaning forward on his fists, glaring at the men assembled in front of him. "I want to know why the American public is being told we're getting our asses kicked, while you all sit here and tell me everything's fine."

"We haven't been defeated," said the Army chief of staff.

"That's not what's being said on television," said the President. "Every night it's the same thing. Pictures of burning villages, dead men lying in the streets and commentators talking about the penetrations of the Vietcong. Stories of their success and our failure."

"That's not the case."

"Then you tell me what's going on!" shouted the President. "Tell me why this was allowed to happen."

The general smiled. "Because we would much rather have the enemy come swarming out of the jungle to hit our base camps with their interlocking fields of fire and their defensive bunkers than chase him through the jungle."

Johnson jerked his chair out and collapsed into it. "And all the while the media rakes us over the coals."

"Only because they don't understand what's happening in Vietnam."

"General," said the President, "in the past month the American people have seen a Navy ship surrendered without a shot being fired by it, they've seen the American embassy breached by Vietcong attackers, and they've seen the American Army reeling under the onslaught of the Vietcong, a third-rate enemy who wasn't supposed to be able to mount any kind of effective military offensive."

The Army chief of staff looked across the table at the Chief of Naval Operations, who shrugged. "Sir, first of all, the American embassy wasn't penetrated by the Vietcong. They got onto the grounds, but that's all. I don't understand the significance of that, anyway. Second, we're not reeling under the Vietcong onslaught. We've repulsed everything they've thrown at us and are making progress in driving them out of Hue."

"What about Khe Sanh?"

The Army man looked at Colonel Lockhart.

The colonel stood and reported. "Latest intelligence from Khe Sanh is that the enemy tried to take another of the hilltop camps and was thrown off with heavy losses."

"What kind of losses?" asked the President.

"The Marines claim to have carried more than a hundred bodies off the camp, which means probably another hundred dead and as many as three or four hundred wounded."

For the first time that morning the President smiled. "That confirmed?"

"We have confirmation of 109 dead carried off the camp."

"What were our casualties like?"

"Seven dead and forty wounded, many of them not hurt too badly."

"I venture to say that none of that appeared on the evening news," said the general.

Johnson stood and moved to where he could study the model of Khe Sanh. "We can't lose it," he said. "We can't even take heavy casualties there."

"Sir," said Lockhart, "the indications are that the siege is shifting over to our favor significantly. Locals report finding stacks of enemy dead in the hills around Khe Sanh. That would mean that the bombing and artillery are hitting the enemy, keeping him off balance."

The President pointed at the Army chief of staff. "This is the kind of thing I wanted to hear."

"Yes, sir. We're cautiously optimistic about Khe Sanh. The tide seems to be shifting completely. Rocket attacks are down, supplies are getting in. A good situation all round."

Lockhart took over. "There have been some patrols out, but they've run into heavy resistance almost within sight of the combat base. That does, however, supply our artillery with targets for their fire missions. Charlie's not being allowed to mass for the big push. The longer we keep him off balance, the better we're going to be."

A civilian now spoke up. "Mr. President, there's something else you should know. Popular support for the Vietcong has eroded. Prior to Tet, there was a feeling that many villagers supported the enemy. After Tet, which was designed to pick up that popular support, the attitude has changed. The enemy is reeling, not our forces."

"Well, we need to get some of this out to the American people," said the President. "We have to let them know the war is going well for us."

"I'd let the situation at Khe Sanh stabilize first," the general said.

"Is there something going on there I don't know about?"

Lockhart was still on his feet, waiting. Everyone turned to look at him.

"I would say, Mr. President, that with an enemy force numbering between ten and twenty thousand, we have to be careful about what we say. We've been very lucky with a couple of those hilltop battles."

"Are you changing your mind, Colonel?" asked the President. "One minute you're telling me how well the Marines did, and the next minute you're telling me it was close."

"Sir, it's just that if Charlie decides he doesn't care how many men he loses, he could overrun one of those camps. The loss would be seen by the media as something substantial, although tactically, it wouldn't be that big a deal. With artillery and air power, we could level the camp and kill the majority of the enemy, but the press would see its loss as the beginning of the end."

"Gentlemen," said the President, "I want one thing understood. We will not lose any of the camps around Khe Sanh. That's something I won't tolerate."

MARINE CORPORAL William Dobson refused to move from his bunker. During the days, he sat on top of it, or on the ground just outside of it. During the nights, he stayed inside, rotating with Conica the duty of sitting at the firing port. They ate C-rations three times a day, shaved every other day with blades that were dull, tried to catch a shower once a week unless it rained. Then they bathed in the open, near the bunker entrance, just in case the VC or the NVA decided to launch an attack.

Dobson had moved from bunker to bunker several times, until now he was on the west side of the Khe Sanh combat base where he could look down from the plateau toward the remains of the village and the Lang Vei Special Forces camp. From the bunker he had watched the flashing of artillery on the summit of Hill 861A, and had listened to the sounds of the battle. Bursts of small-arms fire, the thundering grenades, mortars and 105s, had rolled down the slopes. Everyone at Khe Sanh, when they weren't ducking rockets and mortar shells fired at them, had heard the fight.

Dobson sat on the wood from an ammo crate, leaning forward so he could rest his chin on his hand, which was resting on the sill of the firing port. There had been rain, but it had stopped. The atmosphere seemed to be clearer and fresher than it had been in days. The haze from the stagnant air had been washed out. The temperature seemed cooler. Things appeared to be looking up. There was even talk of a hot meal in the next couple of days.

The artillery on the western side of Khe Sanh had fired a couple of rounds just after 8:00 p.m. Dobson learned that the soldiers at Lang Vei had requested the Marines to test-fire the defensive patterns once again.

Dobson was glad he wasn't at Lang Vei. It was the American outpost closest to Laos, with only a handful of Americans and about five hundred locals to defend the camp of concrete-reinforced bunkers. Two months earlier the marine command at Khe Sanh had ordered a rifle company to rush to Lang Vei without using Route 9 or any of the obvious trails. It had taken just under a full day and night to get there. Even worse, if possible, the day before, an American on a patrol near the camp had been captured. The Special Forces had requested help from the Marines, but there wasn't much anyone could do that close to Laos.

Dobson had left his post by the firing port and was sleeping on his poncho liner when the artillery erupted again. He snapped awake, his heart pounding and his stomach tumbling. As he sat up, he realized it was outgoing. Without a word to Conica he knelt next to the firing port. Flares hung in the air to the west, probably over Lang Vei. There was the distant boom of exploding artillery and the rattle of small arms.

Conica glanced at Dobson. "They've been catching hell for thirty minutes."

Dobson turned his attention to the wire outside the combat base, but there was nothing there to see. No enemy sappers trying to blow up the wire, no enemy soldiers massing for an assault. It looked as if the problems for the Marines were over, and as if they were just beginning for the Green Berets.

"Sounds like they're catching out."

"Watch carefully," said Conica. "You can see muzzle-flashes out there."

Dobson stared as firing increased, and he saw something explode on the ground. Moments later the sound of the detonation reached them.

"Shit! That was a big one."

The volume seemed to increase—more shooting, artillery, rockets and mortars, a mighty roar filtering up from the Special Forces camp.

"I'm just glad I'm not down there," Dobson said.

"You and me both."

SERGEANT GODDARD STOOD in the rear of the command bunker, listening to the radio calls coming in from Lang Vei—desperate pleas for artillery support. As soon as the request was made, the Marines and Army artillery batteries began to fire, pumping out rounds as quickly as possible.

The interior of the bunker was brightly lit. Its walls were covered with maps, showing all the camps around the combat base, each marked with coordinates and codes for the firing of defensive artillery support. Long, narrow tables were heaped with documents and more maps. Along one wall was the bank of radios and field phones that linked the combat base to all its outposts, the Special Forces camp and the outside world.

A cluster of officers stood near one of the radios, listening to the reports from Lang Vei that the enemy was coming at them through the wire. The requests for artillery support hadn't let up. In the background of the transmissions the hammer of heavy machine guns and the crash of mortars could be heard.

At first the reports sounded just like the ones from Hill 861A as the NVA and Vietcong had stormed the wires. The Special Forces camp, more heavily fortified than the Marine hilltop outposts, was doing a better job of holding off the enemy. So far, probes of the wire had been turned back, and although heavy damage had been done to the camp, its defenses were still intact.

One of the Green Berets was on the radio constantly, supplying new coordinates for artillery support so that a curtain of steel kept falling around Lang Vei. His voice was calm, sounding as if he was calling for a chopper to bring them a new movie or resupply. Nothing in his voice conveyed the desperation of the fight at Lang Vei.

That is, nothing until his voice went up an octave and he shouted, "We have tanks in the wire!"

"Say location! Say location!"

There was a pop and crackle of static and a partial answer. ". . . northeastern side, off Route 9."

"Understand northeastern side."

"Roger."

An artillery officer grabbed the handset of a field phone and shouted into it. He waited, then nodded. "Rounds on the way."

Goddard moved forward to where he could see the radio. The operator had a map of Lang Vei on the wooden table in front of him. With a grease pencil he was marking the locations of enemy units as they were fed to him by the men at Lang Vei.

At that moment rockets and mortar rounds began to fall on the Marine combat base, a heavy barrage designed to keep their heads down and to try to stop the artillery from firing in defense of Lang Vei. One of the officers raced from the bunker to see what was going on outside, but had to dive back in when a rocket detonated near him. There were rips in his uniform from the shrapnel, but he wasn't badly injured. He yanked a jagged piece of shrapnel the size of his thumb from his flak jacket.

From the radio came more pleas for assistance. More tanks were rolling over the perimeter now, firing into bunkers, wiping out resistance. The LAW rockets, delivered to Lang Vei after the first reports that there was armor just across the border in Laos, either failed to fire or just bounced off the tanks. The men could do nothing to stop the onslaught.

The reports kept rolling in. Nothing the men did could stop the tanks. They tried hand grenades to blow the tracks off, and that failed. The recoilless rifles had been destroyed or overrun. The defense was collapsing rapidly.

The Marine commander, Colonel Lownds, looked at the one civilian in the command bunker. The reporter, who had been in the Marines during the Second World War and Korea, had been allowed in the bunker because of his background. Now it was time to get him out.

Lownds pointed to him. "It's time for you to leave."

"You sure about that, Colonel?"

The colonel smiled, but there was no humor in it. He pointed at the door. "And if there's a plane in here tomorrow, I advise you to get on it."

For a moment the reporter just stared at the Marine. Then he shrugged and turned away. At the exit he hesitated, then ran for the Alamo Hilton, where the rest of the journalists were hiding.

Over the radio the commander at Lang Vei requested that the emergency rescue plan be activated. The situation was desperate.

Lownds moved away from the radio with his aides and advisers. They stood in a group in a corner, talking quietly. The barrage of rockets and mortar rounds continued to land on Khe Sanh, some hitting so close that dirt drifted down from the ceiling and the lights swayed. They could feel the concussions through the concrete floor.

"We just can't do it," said one of the Marines.

Goddard knew the man was right. The only way to get help to Lang Vei in time was right down Route 9, and that was inviting an ambush. The NVA and Vietcong were famous for that. They would press the attack against Lang Vei until a relief column was sent and then let up at Lang Vei to chop off the rescue party. It made no difference what size the rescue force was. It would be caught in the open on ground of the enemy's choosing, and the enemy had tanks, tanks that could reverse themselves, pull away from Lang Vei and move to slaughter Marines along Route 9.

"We've got to help them," one man shouted. "Westmoreland said he wasn't going to lose a Special Forces camp."

A calmer voice said, "There's nothing we can do to help them except provide artillery support."

Goddard looked at the clock on the wall, surprised that nearly an hour had passed since the first reports had come in. He wasn't worried about the mortar shells and rockets that were still landing outside. He was in one of the few structures that everyone knew could withstand a direct hit from a 122 mm rocket. He'd heard rumors that the enemy now had one that was twice as big, but no one had seen one yet.

"Sergeant," called one of the officers, "please come here a minute."

"Yes, sir?" Goddard said.

"You've been to Lang Vei. You know the capabilities there. If we don't send them assistance, what are the chances they can hang on until morning?"

Goddard rubbed his jaw and stared at the floor. This was the one thing he hated, giving officers an opinion, because most of the time the officers just wanted their own beliefs reinforced.

"Sir, if there are tanks in the wire, then I don't think they've got much of a chance."

"Even with artillery support?"

Goddard glanced at the map behind them. "With Laos so close and by our own count two or three divisions of the North Vietnamese army in the area, I think those boys are in deep shit. Even with our help."

"We've been able to hold two camps with fewer defenders," one of the officers reminded him.

"Yes, sir, barely, but now the enemy's driving up to the wire, hell, through the wire in tanks. At our camps the enemy had to climb the hill to reach our men. This is a different situation."

"Then you don't think they'll be able to hold?"

"No, sir, I don't."

"Thank you."

One of the other officers addressed him. "What do you think would happen to a relief column?"

"Sir, to get them to Lang Vei in time, you'd have to use the most direct route available, and Charlie would be waiting. The ambush would cut them up, and I think, in the end, Lang Vei would still be overrun."

"Thank you, Sergeant."

Goddard retreated to the other side of the bunker. The messages from Lang Vei had become more desperate. They needed help. Portions of the perimeter had been overrun. The tanks were unstoppable by any of the weapons left to the defenders. If help wasn't sent, the camp was lost.

Minutes later a message filtered down the Marine chain of command. The Special Forces request for help had gone all the way to General Westmoreland. Goddard knew that the Army general had fought the Marines in order to take Marine aviation control from them and give it to the Air Force for Operation Niagara. Goddard knew that the Army general, safe in Saigon, would order the Marines to make a useless gesture toward Lang Vei. He just knew it.

But he was wrong. To Goddard's surprise, Westmoreland stated that he wouldn't second-guess the commander on the scene. He wouldn't order a relief force sent.

Minutes later the last message from Lang Vei arrived. The enemy was inside the camp and the defenses were crumbling fast. The request for assistance ended in midtransmission.

Everyone moved toward the radio. All that could be heard was static. Repeated attempts to reestablish contact failed.

"What about the artillery?" asked one of the officers. "We can't keep firing it blind."

"And we can't cut it off," said another. "We don't know what's happened there, but a sudden end to artillery support could be the final straw. We do have permission to use Firecracker."

"We'll continue to fire in support of Lang Vei."

Just after 4:00 a.m., a request came down from Special Forces command in I Corps for a relief column at first light. Again the Marines declined.

Finally one of the officers in the command bunker said, "I guess that's it then. There's nothing more we can do here."

Goddard noticed that the rocket and mortar barrage had ceased outside. To him that could only mean one thing. Lang Vei had fallen. There was no need for the enemy to keep up the barrage—the battle had ended. It would be twelve hours before he found out exactly what had happened at Lang Vei.

21

THE JUNGLES OF LAOS
JUST WEST OF LANG VEI
AND KHE SANH COMBAT
BASE

For the first few minutes after Gerber and his party landed, they ran away from the DZ, trying to put distance between them and any enemy soldiers who might have seen the bailout. The explosion of the C-130 had been so spectacular that all enemy eyes had to have been drawn to it. They wouldn't have been looking into the darkened sky, trying to spot men in parachutes who might have jumped. But there might be search parties in the area. Gerber wanted to get out.

With Fetterman on point, the pace was rapid. The master sergeant seemed to sense the danger and managed to avoid it. Although it was dark in the jungle, it wasn't pitch-black; there were shades of charcoal and gray as well as black. Fetterman dodged the trees, holes and fallen logs, moving the team straight south, away from the drop zone. After thirty minutes they stopped at the bank of a small stream.

Gerber caught up to Fetterman and crouched near him, his lips near the master sergeant's ear. "I make it a klick from the DZ."

"At least," said Fetterman. "You have a chance to check for landmarks?"

"None. Too much happening too quickly. If the Air Force boys hit the right zone, we should be in good shape." Gerber wiped the sweat from his face. He could feel it trickling down his sides and back.

Fetterman nodded. "I'll never say another bad word about those Air Force pilots. Those guys kept right on going, trying to give us cover."

"Yeah. When we get back, I'll see about putting them in for some kind of medal. Won't mean a thing to them, but might make their families feel better."

"You think we've rested enough?" asked Fetterman.

"I don't want to get too far from the DZ before we get ourselves oriented to the map. I'd hate to have to backtrack because we got antsy."

"If the pilots got it right, we need to head south, southeast for twelve klicks. I'd rather walk it at night. Safer for us."

Gerber sat back for a moment and listened to the night sounds around him, animals and insects in the undergrowth, running through the thick carpet of rotting vegetation on the jungle floor, or up the trunks of trees and across their broad leaves. Mosquitoes were out in force. Gerber could hear them buzzing around his face and feel them as they landed. He brushed at some of them leaving dark smears on his skin because there were so many of them. "Let's get going again, but not quite so fast. Easy, with our eyes and ears open."

"Yes, sir. Do we cross the stream here?"

Gerber looked more closely at the brook. Shallow and narrow, probably with a muddy bottom. By daylight any sign they left on the bottom would be washed away. They only had to be careful on the banks. "Straight across. Then wait."

Fetterman got to his feet and slipped through the vegetation like a light breeze. Gerber knew the master sergeant was moving but could hear nothing. Maybe the sounds of the water on the rocks covered the noise that Fetterman made, but somehow Gerber didn't think so. He doubted that Fetterman was making a sound. The man was that comfortable in the jungle.

Gerber waited as the rest of the team caught up, and then sent them on the way. As Lawrence came abreast, he leaned close to Gerber. "There may be someone following us."

"You sure?"

"No, sir, but I heard some noise behind us. Could have been a patrol just wandering around the jungle. They didn't seem to get closer, but then they never went away, either."

"Got it," said Gerber.

As Lawrence passed him, Gerber knelt and listened, but heard nothing behind them, other than the sounds of the jungle and the distant crash of artillery. Gerber wasn't sure, but it sounded as if the combat base was catching hell again. He grinned to himself, glad to be in the safety of the jungle and away from the enemy's mortars and rockets.

He moved forward, a hand out to push a branch aside, then let it slip back into position. He glanced down and stepped into the center of the stream. His boot sank into the muddy bottom and the cold water spilled over the top. He was surprised that the water was so cold, but then they were moving through a mountainous region.

When he got to the other side, he wanted to pour the water from his boot, but didn't take the time. He followed the others, Lawrence no more than a vague shape two or three feet in front of him.

Fetterman had slowed the pace, but it was still hard work. Being quiet, with enemy forces all around, was always hard work. Gerber wasn't worried about ambushes, because it would make no sense for the enemy to set ambushes on the Laotian side of the border. Americans weren't supposed to be there. The enemy could tie up thousands of troops in ambushes that would yield nothing. Twelve miles, twenty miles to the east, it made sense, but not here.

As they advanced, Gerber finally thought he heard something behind them, just as Lawrence had said. A small number of men heading south, just as Gerber and his team were doing. Maybe a coincidence. Maybe not.

He moved forward, touched Lawrence on the shoulder and told him to stop and pass the message on. A minute later the patrol halted and the men spread out in the bush, taking what concealment they could find. Gerber crouched near an outcropping of rock and turned his head in the direction of the sound. He peered out of the corners of his eyes, searching for the tiniest movement, for the smallest thing that didn't belong. He listened carefully.

Just when he thought there was nothing to concern himself with, he heard a single cough, a quiet bark that was stifled immediately. That worried Gerber. If Charlie was operating in his own backyard, unconcerned with an American presence, there was no reason to stifle the cough.

Gerber drew back behind the rock and moved toward the rest of the team. He found Hobbs crouched on the other side of the rock, his weapon in his hand. The M-16 had a bizarre look to it with the thick two-foot-long silencer fitted over the barrel.

Gerber leaned close. "Don't fire unless absolutely necessary, and then make sure you can get everyone in sight."

Hobbs nodded.

Gerber continued on, warning Lawrence, Quinn and Rogers. Then he reached Fetterman.

"What's happening, sir?"

"I think we've got someone moving behind us, but I don't know whether they're on our tail or if they just happen to be going in the same direction."

"So what do we do?"

"I'd like to let them pass us by," said Gerber.

"With the silencers we could take them out and no one would be any wiser."

"Provided the unit is small enough and they don't get a chance to return fire. The smartest thing is to let them walk right by us."

Without saying more, Gerber slipped back toward the rear of the formation. He found a place near the rock outcropping and lay down. He could see the trail, but the enemy wouldn't be able to see him.

Patiently he waited. He knew time was slipping by, but there was no reason to rush now. He had a few hours to waste until it was light enough for him to get a sight on the landmarks and determine where they really were. It was a chance to rest, though after lying around Khe Sanh for a couple of days, he didn't need to rest.

For a moment he laid his head on his arms and closed his eyes. He let the impressions come at him, listening for the enemy soldiers. Again he noticed the artillery in the distance. It hadn't let up for more than an hour. Hundreds of shells landing, probably all over the Marine outposts, with them shooting back with everything they owned. This time, though, the firing seemed to be more urgent, if the sound of artillery could be termed urgent. It was a pitched battle in South Vietnam.

He looked up then, watching the jungle around him. There was nothing he could do about the fighting in South Vietnam, at least not at that moment. He could only take care of the problems at hand. Take care of the enemy force coming at him.

There was no longer a question that the enemy was out there. He'd heard a voice snap a command and then he'd heard another cough. There was a rattle of metal against metal and the brush of cloth against a bush. The enemy's noise discipline left something to be desired.

And then the men were coming out of the trees. Two men walking side by side. Neither carried a weapon in his hands. Both had them slung over their shoulders. Directly behind them were five men, then a gap and three more. Almost a classic patrol structure, though they were bunched too close together.

Gerber watched them walk by, looking neither right nor left. They talked to one another quietly, ignoring the rules that would keep them alive. In Laos they feared nothing. It was a strange attitude that had worked for Gerber more than once. Enemy soldiers, figuring they were safe, walking through the jungle as if they owned it. Under different circumstances,

Gerber would have taken the patrol. Here, he wanted to do nothing that would betray his presence.

It looked as if the whole enemy patrol would walk right by, and then one of them stopped. He turned from the trail and started to drop his pants when he froze. The others hadn't seen anything unusual.

Just as the man began to raise the alarm, there was a quiet pop, like the snapping of a finger, and the man was lifted off his feet. He dropped to the ground, his legs kicking. The others, not sure what had happened, started to gather around him. One of them spoke to him quietly.

The rest of Gerber's team opened fire. There were muzzle-flashes and the working of bolts, but almost no noise from the weapons. Quiet, almost friendly detonations as the M-16s fired and fired.

The enemy soldiers jerked and fell and rolled. Not one of them managed to get a hand on his weapon. Not one of them managed to fire a shot in return. In seconds it was over. A quick, quiet burst of firing, and the enemy soldiers were on the ground, dead.

No, a quiet groan proved at least one was still alive. One of the NVA tried to sit up. He grabbed at his chest, as if wounded there, and then his head disappeared in a splash of crimson. He dropped back and didn't move again.

Gerber got slowly to his feet and crouched at the side of the rock. He raised a hand to his lips, as if to wipe them. Keeping his eyes on the enemy soldiers, he waited for them to spring a surprise, but they appeared to all be dead. Death hung heavy in the air, almost tangible, like the humidity.

Gerber moved from hiding, but waved at the others, telling them to remain hidden. He checked the bodies quickly, dragging the weapons away from them. A couple of the men were obviously dead; one's head was shot away, another had lost an arm. The stink from them told him they had died. One or two of the others looked almost peaceful, as if they had suddenly felt tired or faint and had lain down. But there was no pulse at their throats.

Finished with that, he waved the men from cover, directing them to drag the bodies into concealment behind the rocks. Unless they took time to bury the men, anyone around would find there were dead men close by. But all Gerber's team needed was a day. After that they could get out.

Hobbs appeared and reached down to grab the foot of a dead man. Gerber asked, "What the hell did you open fire for?"

"Man saw me. Looked right at me and was going to call out. I had to shoot him."

As the men cleaned up the field, Fetterman approached. "Now what?"

"We get away from here," Gerber said. "Another klick and then we hole up for the rest of the night."

Fetterman peeled back the camouflage cover on his watch and checked the time. "Two hours to cover that klick and then thirty minutes to find a good place to hole up. That's not going to leave much time until sunup."

"That's fine with me," said Gerber. He turned and saw that Hobbs and Lawrence were crawling over the ground, looking for signs that the battle had taken place. Gerber knew that in the daylight there would be splashes of blood, torn clothing, bits of equipment, things they just couldn't see in the dark. But that couldn't be helped. Besides, anyone finding the field might believe that an NVA unit had been hit by a fighter or the aerial burst of an artillery shell.

When they were ready to move again, Fetterman took the point. He kept the pace steady, somehow avoiding the densest parts of the jungle, finding clearings under the trees that made the going easier. He avoided trails and yet found the path of least resistance. It allowed them to make good time.

Fetterman stopped about thirty minutes before dawn. He sensed rather than saw that the atmosphere in the jungle had suddenly changed. There was something different about it, but he didn't know what it was, just had an impression that something was wrong around him.

Gerber slipped up to his position and found the master sergeant kneeling on the ground, his weapon in one hand and dirt in the other. ''What the hell?''

''Don't know, sir, but I don't want to continue on now. There's something wrong here.''

Gerber looked back the way they had come, then looked at the jungle in front of them. It was less dense now. The trees had strange shapes, and the canopy seemed to have been ripped to shreds. A smell rose from it that wasn't easily identifiable. There was death in it, but also a chemical stink.

Studying the area carefully, Gerber realized it was as if a line had been drawn across the jungle. Everything on one side was green and lush; on the other it was sickly and unreal. The dark prevented any closer observation, but Gerber didn't like it, either. ''Let's fall back about a hundred yards and look for a place to hole up.''

Slowly they retreated and then slid to the right, away from their line of march. If they had left a trail, the straight line would suddenly end, and that might confuse an enemy who was following it. They searched the countryside now, not the relatively flat jungle they were used to, but an up-and-down terrain with intermittent streams, rocky outcroppings and clumps of tall trees. Along some of the rock faces were small caves, and in some places those caves led into larger, more complex caverns. In places like these the enemy would make his home, protected from the American airplanes that crisscrossed the skies looking for hostiles.

Gerber wanted to avoid the enemy. His men moved into a stand of trees, a few teak and mahogany among a variety of others. The ground was covered with ferns, bushes and vines. It was a wet area, but it offered concealment and would protect them from the eyes of the enemy.

They spread out in a loose circle, each man responsible for the man on either side of him. As soon as they were in place, Gerber slipped his canteen from its cover and drank deeply, ignoring the plastic taste. He lowered the canteen, took a deep breath and raised it again. This time he sloshed the water around in his mouth. He didn't spit it out but swallowed it. Water was too precious to waste.

Finally he relaxed slightly, letting his eyes wander over the jungle in front of him, taking it all in. He studied the bushes and trees so he would know where they were, just in case. Satisfied that he was familiar with his surroundings, he let the tension drain out of him. There would be no sleep, he knew that, until much later that day, or possibly the next. Now it was important that he stay awake and be aware of his surroundings.

As he lay there, listening to the sounds of the jungle, he realized the battle in South Vietnam had ended. There was no longer the pounding of artillery and bombers he had heard in the night. It was quieter now, as if a thunderstorm had finally moved on into another country. Gerber wasn't sure if he liked the quiet. The shooting meant that both sides were still engaged in the combat. When the shooting stopped, it meant one side had been defeated. He was uneasy about that.

Then the sounds in the jungle changed. The quiet was broken by a burst of sound as the animals came awake. Monkeys shrieked, shaking the trees and leaping about the canopy. They were joined by birds taking to the air, squawking as they flew. The noise built higher and higher until Gerber could have been involved in a firefight and not been able to hear shooting. He could have stood up and shouted, and no one would have been able to hear him.

Slowly the noise tapered off and an uneasy silence descended. The monkeys, now awake, settled down for the day. The birds landed and called to one another infrequently. Occasionally the quiet was broken by the sounds of insects and animals, or even of jets overhead, but nothing was heard from the enemy.

With the sun up, Gerber could use his map. He moved slowly, carefully, so that he didn't draw attention to himself. He looked at the map and then observed the terrain around him. He checked the DZ and figured they had moved five klicks from it. According to the map, they should be on the southern slope of a small mountain. That was if the Air Force had dropped them at the right location.

Gerber turned around and tried to see through the thick foliage. The ground did drop away as it was supposed to. There should have been another small mountain to the east with a saddle between the two. And below them, in the valley, there should be a river. Not much of one, but a river nonetheless.

The second mountain and the saddle were there as they should have been. The contour lines seemed to be right, and the gross terrain features that he could see indicated they were in the right place. There was no indication that they weren't.

Gerber put the map away, took another drink from his canteen and then put it away, too. They'd rest there for a while and then begin to move again. By evening they should be close to the site and into position long before the next morning. With any luck, they'd be out of Laos in thirty-six hours or less. With any luck at all.

22

The last radio transmission from Lang Vei had been at 3:10 a.m., Vietnam time. Now at four in the afternoon, Washington time, the President already knew there was trouble in South Vietnam. The reports from the message center had been fed to him and coordinated through both the Pentagon and Lockhart's office. When told that communications with the Lang Vei Special Forces camp had been lost, the President demanded some answers.

He sat at the head of the table, a dozen reports in front of him. Next to the reports was a stack of paper from the teletype. He was sifting through it all, and as he did, the rage became apparent.

Lockhart, again the lowest-ranking man in the room, was glad he was sitting at the far end of the table. There were two Army generals in the room, one Marine general and a civilian with the CIA. Lockhart had never met any of them before, though he'd seen the civilian a couple of times.

Each of them was waiting for the President to say something and start the meeting, but he just kept reading the reports over and over. The door opened and a civilian clerk handed another message to the President, then retreated as quickly as possible.

"Jesus Christ!" Johnson shouted. "They're going to do it to us just like they did to the French." He waved the latest message as if it were a banner. "Radio Hanoi is claiming that the American defense line along Route 9 has been breached." He looked pointedly at the Marine general and added, "There are two NVA divisions poised around Khe Sanh, another at the Rockpile and still another at Hue. And there are two other divisions roaming loose in the area. You've done nothing to stop them."

"Sir, we haven't suffered any significant defeats."

Johnson slammed the table with his fist and glared at the Marine. "What about Lang Vei? You're telling me that the loss of that camp isn't significant?"

The Marine general held the President's gaze then dropped his eyes. He rubbed his chin with his hand. "Mr. President, if I might, we don't know that the camp has fallen, but assuming the worst, that it has been overrun, what does that mean in terms of Americans and the perception of the American people?"

"I don't like your train of thought, General."

"Sir, let's look at if from the point of view of the press. They'll see that a Vietnamese camp at Lang Vei was overrun. There were limited American casualties, and if anyone says anything about the location being close to Khe Sanh, that's going to be lost in the translation."

"You've missed the point, General. This isn't a football game where we can minimize the loss by pointing to the statistics to prove we've played a hell of a game." He turned and pointed at Lockhart. "The one thing I was promised wouldn't happen has happened. One of the outposts around Khe Sanh has been overrun."

"Technically, sir, that's not true," the Marine said quickly. "The Marines still hold all the outposts on the hilltops. The Lang Vei camp was a different command structure—"

"You're splitting hairs with me!" the president shouted. "You Marines have done nothing to alleviate the situation in

I Corps. It just keeps getting worse, and now the enemy has had a major victory in the region.''

"Sir, I don't want to minimize the loss, but I don't think it's quite as important as you make it."

"It's what the people are going to see. It's the beginning of Dien Bien Phu again. No one cared about the small gains by the enemy, and the next thing the French were surrendering.''

The Marine general had begun to sweat. Beads of perspiration appeared on his face and dropped onto his starched collar. He squirmed in his chair, uneasy with the sudden hot spot. "If I might—"

"I think you've said quite enough, General. I want a full report as to why the six thousand Marines at Khe Sanh could do nothing for the defenders at Lang Vei."

"Mr. President," said Lockhart, feeling as if he was about to volunteer to run through a mine field, "I think the Marine commander, Colonel Lownds, made a wise decision. The enemy was sure to have been waiting to ambush the relief column, and the disaster would have taken on greater proportions. By the time assistance could have gotten there, the enemy would have destroyed the camp, anyway."

"Then what the hell are we doing spending billions on helicopters?" shouted the President.

"With enemy armor at the camp, we couldn't send in helicopters. They wouldn't have stood a chance."

"And where the hell did those damned tanks come from? No one said anything about tanks in the area."

Now the CIA man spoke. "Well, sir, technically, we've known about the tanks for the past two weeks. A Laotian village was overrun late in January, and there were reports of armor there. I know the Special Forces were given more than a hundred LAW rockets to fight the armor, if it appeared."

"Then what happened?" the President demanded. "Someone tell me what happened!"

The men sat quietly, beside the mock-up of the Khe Sanh area, with its white flag showing where the Lang Vei Special

Forces camp had been. It seemed to shout for attention, and the men tried not to look at it.

The President studied the faces of the men in the situation room, then said, "This situation had better be radically altered in the next few days, or heads are going to roll. This cannot continue."

THE NIGHT HAD BEEN a long one for Marie. Whitmire hadn't returned as she had expected him to, but then, given the state of the aircraft they had to fly, the rigors of the mission and the fluctuating state of the war, it wasn't too surprising. She waited for him in the nude for a while, but as the night lengthened and he didn't return, she put on a robe she found hanging behind the door.

She had slept through the noise of the night. Several mortar shells had fallen, but she had ignored the sound and the shifting patterns of light inside the tiny hootch as the flares overhead descended slowly.

Now she rolled over once and reached out, but Whitmire wasn't there. For a horrifying minute she was concerned about him, but then laughed it off. If anything had happened to him, someone would have let her know. Or someone would have been by and she would have found out.

At dawn she got up and padded to the door. She peeked out at the empty walkways and the squadron area. No one was moving. It was quiet except for the boom of the artillery and the roar of jet aircraft on the flight line. She left the hootch and ran over to the shower. With no one inside, she left the robe hanging on a hook and turned on the faucets, standing to one side, away from the spray. She held out a hand to feel the water, waiting for it to warm up, but it never did. She forced herself to get under the cold water, slowly got used to it and washed herself. Finally she put on the robe without drying and ran back to Whitmire's hootch.

As she entered it, she heard an alarm clock ringing somewhere else. She peeked back out and saw a group of men walking together, talking quietly, but she couldn't hear what they were saying. They looked as if they had just gotten some bad news, but that could mean almost anything.

Ducking back inside, she found a towel and dried herself, then sat on the cot, naked. There seemed to be a slight chill in the air. It was the first time since she had arrived in Vietnam that she had felt a chill.

In the World she would have turned on the television to catch the morning news, but there was no early-morning broadcast in Vietnam. Instead she turned on the radio, kept it low and listened to the music, mostly rock and roll. She took comfort in the music. It was a link to the World, a link to home.

As the sky slowly brightened and morning dawned over Da Nang, Marie went on sitting on the bed, staring at the window. The firing from the artillery stopped and the airfield was momentarily quiet, no more jets and no more helicopters. The rest of the base camp however, seemed to come alive.

Finally she rolled to the right and looked at the clock on the nightstand. Whitmire had been gone for more than twelve hours, and that she didn't understand. She slipped down so that she was lying on the bed, but she didn't pull up the sheet or put on her clothes. When he finally returned, she wanted to surprise him.

She dozed then, waiting for Whitmire, until a noise at the door woke her. She sat up, leaning back on her elbows and bending one knee so that she was stretched out for Whitmire.

But it wasn't Whitmire who entered. It was another man, wearing a flight suit, a short, thick balding man. He glanced at Marie, did a double take as she scrambled to cover herself and then demanded, "What the hell are you doing in here?"

Marie grabbed at the robe as she leaped from the cot. She turned her back, slipped it on and belted it around her waist. "I'm waiting for Lloyd. He was supposed to be back a long time ago."

"Well, you can just get the hell out, because he's not coming back."

Marie felt the blood drain from her face, her knees go weak and her head start to spin. In a flash she knew that he was dumping her, or he had been wounded and evacuated to Japan, or he was dead. With one hand she reached out to steady herself. "What . . . what happened?"

"Get dressed and get out of here. You're not welcome here anymore."

Marie didn't understand the man's hostility. She sat down on the cot. "What happened?"

"No one knows. The plane was lost last night, shot down."

"Is Lloyd dead?"

"He's missing in action. We don't know what happened to him. Now get the fuck out of here."

Marie felt as if she'd been kicked in the stomach. She wrapped her arms around her belly and bent over. Tears stung her eyes. The world turned blurry and gray. She tried to tell herself that it didn't matter because she'd only known him for a few days, a week maybe. But that didn't help.

The man found some of her clothes and tossed them onto the cot. "Hurry up and get dressed."

Marie didn't move. She pressed her eyes to her knees and began to cry. Everything around her had disappeared in a flash of pain.

"Give it a rest," the man said. "Christ, you whores are all alike. You want some money to get out of here? I've got ten bucks if you're out in a minute or less."

Marie didn't hear that, and if she had she wouldn't have cared. Everything that had happened between her and Whitmire had been special. She had felt it the first time he had touched her, and although he wouldn't have admitted it then, she knew that he knew they were special.

She looked up then, breathless. Her body ached. She wiped her nose on the sleeve of her robe and saw her clothes lying on the cot. She snatched them up and then, defiantly, dropped the robe so she could dress.

The man began to search through Whitmire's possessions, packing them into a duffel bag. He tossed clothes, uniforms, flight suits and gaudy civilian clothes onto the cot. As he went through Whitmire's footlocker, he ignored Marie. He kept track of each item, writing it down before he stuffed it into the duffel bag.

"Excuse me," said Marie. When the man didn't look up, she said it again. "Excuse me."

"Yeah. What is it?"

"Well . . ." she started, and then didn't know what to say or what to ask. There seemed to be no delicate way for her to learn about Whitmire.

"Come on, lady. I don't have all fucking day here."

"How do I find out?"

The man laughed and shook his head. "Find out what? Who gets his insurance?"

That struck her almost like a physical blow. Not the insult in the words, but just the word *insurance*. If he wasn't dead, why was there any mention of insurance. Insurance didn't pay unless Whitmire was known to be dead.

She sat down again, a hand to her throat. "I mean, find out about Lloyd," she whispered.

The man sat down on the dirty plywood floor, rested an arm on his knee and looked up at her. "That's a very good question. Well, you could read *Stars and Stripes* and see if his name appears there. You could write to his next of kin and ask them, if you don't mind rubbing salt in the wound. Shit, I'm not the chaplain. You could ask him."

"Please," Marie begged. "What happened?"

The man got to his feet and stared down at her. "The fucking plane disappeared last night. That's all we know. Until wreckage is spotted we don't know shit. There were no emergency transmissions, there was no indication that anything was wrong, so we just don't fucking know."

"Isn't anyone out searching?"

"Lady, it's a fucking combat zone. We have planes in the area, but we can't run a search, for Christ's sake. Now I've wasted enough time on you. Get out of here before someone spots you."

Marie stood up and moved to the door. She looked back into the room, trying to memorize it, because it was where her life had come crashing down around her. There was almost nothing in the room that reminded her of Whitmire. The uniforms could have belonged to any of the four hundred thousand Americans caught in the war. The standard equipment was issued to everyone. There was nothing personal, not even the single painting hanging on the wall; like a hundred others, it had been turned out by the local artists on an assembly line for sale to gullible Americans.

Then, lying on the cot, she spotted one of the Velcro-backed name tags that were worn on flight suits. It showed Whitmire's pilot's wings and gave his name, rank and branch of service. It was the only personal item in the entire room. She reached out, grabbed it, then whirled, running from the hootch.

She expected the man to chase her, but he didn't even shout in protest. She stopped at the road and turned to look back, but no one was after her. No one cared that she had been there, and no one cared that she was leaving.

A jeep slowed and the men in it whistled, then it roared away in a cloud of red dust. The sky was bright blue with only a fringe of white cloud. It was too nice a day to think of death and dying, yet that was the only thing on her mind. Slowly she walked back to the hootches used by the USO people. They didn't seem to be too happy to see her, either.

CORPORAL AMOS HANRATTY sat in his recently repaired bunker and felt the heat of the day begin to build. It had been foggy and overcast earlier, but the fog had cleared soon and the clouds had blown away. The sun beat down on the hilltop, baking it relentlessly. Steam seemed to rise from the pools of standing water and the ground dried quickly. Hanratty felt the sweat soak his uniform, and wiped it from his face.

Up from the valley, where they had dragged the bodies of the NVA who had tried to take the camp, came the unmistakable odor of death. The Marines had thrown a layer of dirt over the common grave, but a hundred bodies rotting in the steaming heat of South Vietnam needed to be buried deeply.

The sickly-sweet odor attacked the gag reflex and made Hanratty want to throw up, but he suppressed the urge.

He glanced at the three AKs in the bunker—one for Stubbs, one for him and one for trading, if he ever got the chance to trade it. The clerks at Da Nang would pay a lot for an AK-47 taken from the body of a dead NVA soldier. The Marines were supposed to turn in the captured weapons, but everyone kept them for souvenirs, even though they couldn't take them home.

Stubbs stirred and rolled over. He, too, was bathed in sweat. He sat up. "Whooee, they're sure stinking today."

"It's gonna get worse, too," said Hanratty.

"Maybe the captain will call in napalm, or we could go down there with some willie pete and burn them."

"I'm not sure that would be much of an improvement," Hanratty said.

Stubbs picked up his canteen, unscrewed the cap and took a deep drink, picked up his towel and wiped himself with it. "Might not be an improvement, but the stink is lifted by the fire and then it blows away. We'd only have to put up with it for a day or so."

Hanratty shrugged and turned back to the firing port. Then another voice joined the conversation.

"Hanratty, get your shit together. All of it."

Hanratty looked at the entrance of the bunker, holding up a hand to shade his eyes from the bright light streaming in. "Why's that, Sarge?"

"You're getting out. Going home."

Hanratty laughed. "Not yet. I've got two weeks left. Fourteen days and a wake-up."

"And they're getting you off this hill now, so you don't get yourself killed."

"How'd *he* get so lucky?" demanded Stubbs.

"Someone took a look at the DEROS rosters and decided to get out all the men with two weeks left on their tours before they get killed. It's bad publicity for us if a bunch of you guys get killed that close to going home."

Calmly, holding his emotions in check, Hanratty asked, "Where am I going?"

"Chopper will be here in an hour to lift you down to the combat base. Then you'll get on the first plane in and be lifted to Da Nang for out-processing, some good chow and a clean uniform. You'll be manifested out from there."

Still Hanratty refused to let himself believe. Like all the other Marines, he'd dreamed of this day for nearly thirteen months. He'd thought of little else in the past few weeks. He'd been preparing for it, and now, suddenly, it was on him and all he could think of was, "I made it."

The sergeant slapped the top of the bunker. "Hurry it up or you'll miss the chopper."

"Oh, no, Sarge, I won't miss the chopper."

The sergeant laughed. "No, I guess maybe you won't at that."

As the sergeant left, Stubbs took a deep breath and said, "Congratulations."

"Thank you," said Hanratty, and then he lost it all. He wanted to leap up and down and dance and scream. He wanted to laugh and cry and run. He deserted his post at the firing port and began to pick up his personal gear. There was very little of it—a couple of uniforms, the equipment issued to him when he'd arrived in-country but considered expendable with the exception of his weapon. There was little that he wanted to take with him. Everything from his shaving kit to his tiny transistor radio was easily replaceable at Da Nang or, better yet, in the World. He realized he had nothing to pack. "Guess that's it."

Stubbs sat and stared, looking as if he wanted to cry. Not because his friend was going home, but because he was going now. Today. In minutes, rather than in days or weeks or months.

Hanratty stuck out a hand. "We made a good team, even if it was for only a week."

Stubbs took the hand and shook it. "That we did."

"Guess I'll head on up to the helipad and wait for my ride."

"Can't say as I blame you. You spent more time here than I would have. I'd have been riding in the sarge's hip pocket."

"Good luck to you then," said Hanratty. Suddenly he felt guilty, as if he was deserting his fellow Marines before the fight was over. For an instant he thought about staying until the battle was over, but that was only a fleeting thought. It was something too ridiculous to consider.

"Best of luck to you, too," said Stubbs.

Hanratty nodded. "Thanks." He picked up his weapon and steel pot and moved to the entrance.

"Hey, aren't you going to take your AK?"

"Don't have a need for it now," said Hanratty. "You keep them all. Maybe you can get yourself something you really need with them."

"Thanks," said Stubbs.

"Well," Hanratty said, "I guess I'll get going." Still he hesitated. In all his dreaming about his last minutes in Vietnam he hadn't thought about what to say to his friends who had to stay behind. It was an awkward, growing silence.

Stubbs laughed. "You know, if it had been me, I'd have been gone already. Out the door and standing at the pad with a smoke grenade in hand to make sure the pilot could find the place."

"You're right," said Hanratty. "Thanks." He turned and crawled into the bright sunshine. Somehow it had never looked brighter, the day had never seemed better. He walked toward the crest of the hill where the chopper was waiting.

23

THE JUNGLES OF LAOS
WEST OF KHE SANH
COMBAT BASE

American fighters kept buzzing through the sky, searching for the enemy that was reported to be filtering down the Ho Chi Minh Trail to join the battle shaping up around Khe Sanh. Gerber sat under the broken canopy of the Laotian jungle, watching them crisscross the sky twenty or thirty thousand feet above him. Flashes of silver that could swoop in to drop bombs or strafe the ground, if they suddenly felt like doing it. An additional danger for his tiny team.

Fetterman had slipped from their cover, moving a hundred yards to the south to scout the territory around them while the rest of the team hid in the shadows, ate a cold breakfast and drank warm water.

When Fetterman returned, Gerber was sure he had them placed on the map. He was sure they were right where they were supposed to be, and that within a couple of hours they would be at the point where the NVA radio transmissions had been intercepted.

Fetterman crossed through the copse to crouch next to Gerber. He whispered, his voice almost lost in the background noise of the jungle. "You're going to have to see it to believe it."

Gerber nodded and then signaled the men to get ready. Quietly, quickly, the patrol formed and slipped from hiding, taking with them everything they had brought except for the remains of their breakfast. Those they buried under the damp, dank vegetation of the jungle floor.

They moved through thick jungle, filled with thorny bushes, ferns dripping water, vines that reached out to grab and trees forty feet in diameter and two hundred feet high. Their broad leaves intertwined to weave a canopy that was only periodically broken.

And then all that changed. They came to a place where it looked as if a giant had drawn a line on the ground. On one side was a thick, rich, green jungle, and on the other was the desolation of the moon, a gray-black area that looked as if the color had been sucked from it. Hundreds of craters dotted the hillside down toward the valley. A silver ribbon of water wound its way along the valley floor. It was flanked by broken, denuded trees and the skeletal remains of bushes. The devastation rivaled or surpassed anything done to Europe in the Second World War.

"Defoliation," Fetterman said.

"And napalm. And five-hundred-pound bombs," added Gerber.

"Christ, what a mess," Hobbs said as he crouched at the edge of the destruction.

"No way to cross that," Gerber said. From where he stood he could have seen anything or anyone moving for miles. The ashes from the fires would create a cloud to mark their route of march. The twisted trees blackened by the bombings, and the brittle remains of those killed by the defoliants, provided no cover. If the Vietcong and the NVA didn't open fire, the American pilots would. It was an effective no-man's-land, one that would give no comfort to enemy soldiers and provide no benefits for friendlies.

"Christ," Hobbs repeated.

Gerber took out his map and noticed they were standing on the rim of a bowl, a huge crater-shaped valley. By moving east they would eventually reach a ridgeline. On the other side of the ridge the jungle could be as full and lush as any they had ever seen.

To move west took them farther away from their target. The gamble was whether the defoliation and the bombing destruction carried all the way into South Vietnam or only a relatively short distance.

"This is what I felt last night," said Fetterman. "We could have moved through it in the dark."

"No, Tony," said Gerber. "Even in the dark we'd have been easy to see. We have to avoid it."

"Maxwell should have told us about this when we were planning the DZs."

"I doubt that he knew about it. Even the CIA isn't told everything that's going on."

"There seems to be a lot Maxwell doesn't know," said Fetterman.

Gerber nodded his acknowledgment but didn't say anything. He studied the map and finally said, "Standing around out here isn't going to get the mission accomplished. Let's skirt the edge of this, staying about fifty or a hundred meters in the trees."

"Direction of travel?"

"East," said Gerber.

Fetterman glanced at his compass, took a reading, then began to move, first angling back, deeper into the jungle, and then due east. The team spread out behind him, each man falling far enough to the rear that he could see only the man in front of him. Gerber was at the end of the column.

They advanced steadily, working their way through the jungle. They kept at it as the sun climbed higher, and then the clouds slipped in from the west. The ceiling dropped, cutting off the rays of the sun, but the heat and humidity remained, turning their uniforms black with sweat.

They came down off one hillside, stayed below the crest of the saddle, then climbed the other hill, winding back and forth along its face to make the task simpler. At noon they reached the top, and Fetterman stopped for the moment.

Gerber was sure the valley on the other side would be the mirror image of the one they had just avoided, but as he caught up to the master sergeant, he saw the same thick foliage that covered the hills. They could now turn south, avoid the moonscape and be back on track in a couple of hours. By evening they would be at the site of the North Vietnamese headquarters.

They formed a defensive ring and ate a quick, cold lunch, then rested, though not for long. The real heat of the day lay in front of them, but now the schedule was thrown off. They had to reach the radio site before dusk, and if they delayed, they wouldn't get there until the next day. There was too much going on for them to worry about the discomfort of hiking through the heat of the afternoon.

Fetterman checked the map, and took a compass reading. They moved out in the same formation as before, heading down the hillside toward the valley floor. It took them an hour to get down and another twenty minutes to get to the stream that cut the valley in half. Fetterman stopped at the bank, then moved away from it.

When Gerber got there, he understood Fetterman's reaction. The stream smelled as if chemicals had been dumped into it. The water wasn't clear, but a milky color, and a few dead fish floated on the surface.

"We've got to cross," Gerber told him.

"Sir, I really don't think it's a good idea to wade through there."

Gerber pulled out his map, then looked at Fetterman. "We can't walk around this one."

"It's not that wide. Let's just bridge it."

Gerber shook his head.

"It'll be easy," said Fetterman. "We just pull a log over and drop it across. No fuss and no muss."

Gerber waved a hand. "Then do it."

Five minutes later they were on the other side of the stream. Fetterman found them a hiding place and they holed up for another rest. Twenty minutes to drink water and gain back some of their strength, and then they would be moving again.

MAXWELL SAT in the conference room at MACV Headquarters, waiting for General Westmoreland, who had returned from his whirlwind tour of Da Nang. In the conference room with Maxwell were a number of generals, colonels and civilians. They all sat in straight-backed chairs, quietly waiting for the commander.

Maxwell pulled a handkerchief from his pocket and mopped his face with it. Like many of the offices in the building, the conference room was air-conditioned. Because it was the one favored by Westmoreland, it had the best of everything. The table was long and highly polished, with leather notebooks in front of each place. The walls were paneled in mahogany. There were bright lights overhead and ceiling fans to stir the air.

But even with all that, Maxwell was sweating, and so were many of the others. Almost everyone was drinking water poured from the silver services on the table. The tension was thick but no one spoke to break it.

Then the door opened. A captain stepped in and said, "Gentlemen, the commander." General Westmoreland entered. He was wearing fresh fatigues, with not a sign of sweat on them. They looked as if he'd just put them on.

Everyone stood and waited until Westmoreland sat down and told them to be seated.

"I've just come from I Corps," the general said, "and the situation there has been remedied." He grinned. "It was necessary to force a few hands, but I think the spirit of cooperation has been achieved. We'll have no repeats of yesterday's trouble."

"Trouble?" asked one of the other generals.

"The problem at Lang Vei and the use of the aviation assets. The logjam has been broken." He nodded slowly but didn't elaborate. Instead, he pointed at one of the colonels. "Colonel Argo, I believe you've reassessed the situation, comparing it to Dien Bien Phu."

Colonel Argo stood up. He was an older officer with short gray hair, a tropical tan and glasses. He wore fatigues, but unlike Westmoreland's, his were wrinkled and stained with sweat. With the knuckle of one hand, he pushed his glasses back up his nose and opened the folder he had brought with him. He was not a happy man.

"General Westmoreland, I've looked at the situation at Khe Sanh and I'm not optimistic at all."

He surveyed the faces of the men around him. The more positive atmosphere that had entered the room with the arrival of Westmoreland suddenly dissipated.

"Looking at the reports from Khe Sanh, I see that the Marines are failing to venture from their camps, whether from the combat base itself, or from the hilltop outposts that guard the roads and approaches. According to the documentation I've seen, orders have been issued by the Marines that there are to be no personal ventures more than two hundred meters, line of sight, from the base. They can't effectively patrol that way, but each time the men have moved any farther from their camps, they've been ambushed."

Argo continued in the same vein, talking about the reports out of Khe Sanh, the lists of men killed in the ambushes and the failure to send a relief column to Lang Vei.

Westmoreland stopped Argo at that point. "Colonel, the consensus was that the relief column would have been ambushed, chopped up, and therefore would not have been able to reach Lang Vei in time to provide meaningful assistance."

"That's the point, General," said Argo. "I note that the enemy hammered the combat base this morning, dropping several hundred shells on it. At the same time the enemy attacked the Marine outpost on Hill 64 near the Rockpile."

"The point?" asked Westmoreland.

"Again the Marines stayed behind their wire while the enemy attacked them in force."

''That was a successful defense,'' a Marine spoke up.

''Granted,'' Argo responded, ''but it highlights the problem. It was a defense. The fatal flaw at Dien Bien Phu was that the French gave up the initiative. They sat behind their wire and let the Vietminh come to them, and come to them the enemy did. At every siege in history the fatal flaw is the same. The defenders wait for the enemy to move.''

''Anything else?'' asked Westmoreland.

As Argo consulted his notes, Maxwell wondered what the solution to the situation would be. The Marines were holed up in their combat base waiting for the enemy to attack and to shatter its divisions against the rock of the combat base. But something had to be introduced to force the issue. The waiting game would go on forever unless some action was taken.

Obviously the destruction of one of the Marine outposts would do it. The destruction of Lang Vei, with only twenty or twenty-five Americans, had not been it. Something was needed to shake one side or the other into action.

Argo finished his presentation and sat down. All eyes in the room were on him. No one wanted to look at Westmoreland, afraid that eye contact would ignite the commander's anger.

Westmoreland got to his feet then. He stood almost at attention, his eyes roaming the room, searching the faces of everyone there. Until that meeting, no one had ever suggested that the Marines wouldn't be able to hold the combat base, regardless of the enemy force surrounding it. Everyone had said that, although there were some parallels between Khe Sanh and Dien Bien Phu, the real situation as it was developing was different. The Americans had too much firepower and too many planes to allow them to lose. Everyone knew that. Everyone except Colonel Argo, who had just told them all exactly what they didn't want to hear.

Westmoreland waited until everyone in the room was looking at him. Slowly, carefully, quietly, he said, ''It's good that we've heard the worst.'' He halted and searched the faces of the men there. ''But we are not, repeat, *not*, going to be defeated at Khe Sanh. I will tolerate no talking, even thinking, to the contrary. Is that clear?''

There was silence in the room. No one spoke. A few nodded in agreement. Westmoreland took that as his answer. He swept out the door, followed by his aide.

The rest of the men sat in stunned silence. One man rubbed the sweat from his face and said quietly, ''That's what he said about the Special Forces. He'd tolerate no loss of a Special Forces camp, but we lost Lang Vei last night.''

''Christ, Jimmy, shut the fuck up!'' said one of the lower-ranking generals.

''We've got to do something to stir up the situation then,'' said Jimmy. ''Otherwise, it's going to continue the way it is for a long time.''

Maxwell opened his mouth to speak and then realized he'd already grabbed the stick and stuck it into the pot. He looked at his watch. When Gerber and Fetterman got into position sometime in the next few hours, and took a shot at Giap, that would stir the pot. Even if they missed Giap but hit someone else, the pot would be stirred. Even if they missed everyone, the pot would be stirred. Giap would know that the attempt had been directed at him. He wouldn't take it lying down. He couldn't.

Of course the Air Force attempt, the bombing of the headquarters, might make it harder on Gerber and Fetterman. But they were still out there and they would certainly stir the pot. At least he hoped they would.

Maxwell grinned, knowing something that everyone else at the table would like to know. He wouldn't tell them, because the United States military didn't sanction assassination, even when it made such good sense.

He pushed his chair back. ''Gentlemen, if you'll excuse me.''

''Just get out, Jerry,'' one of the men said. ''There's nothing you spooks can contribute.''

Maxwell walked to the door and stopped. ''Don't be too sure. The next couple of days should tell the tale.''

GERBER'S LITTLE BAND climbed another hill, worked their way down it, crossed a clear stream that didn't seem to be polluted with chemicals and started up again. Fetterman held the pace down, trying to gauge it so they would arrive at the radio site with no more than an hour's sunlight left. That would give them a chance to find a good place to hide and let them observe the enemy camp throughout the night.

They rested and ate their dinner just after they crossed the stream, then began the tiring climb up the next hill. They still avoided the paths and game trails, working their way slowly to the summit. As they neared it, Fetterman halted them again. He wanted to be careful now, because if the enemy did have some kind of headquarters there, he would have patrols out. The patrols might not be expecting to find anyone, but they would be there, just the same.

Gerber joined him, leaving Hobbs, Lawrence, Quinn and Rogers strung out behind, placed as they would be if they were the sniper's security. It was their job to make sure no one came up on the sniper as he lay in ambush.

Together Gerber and Fetterman worked their way to the crest of the hill, but they couldn't see much from there. The jungle was as thick there as anywhere else. They crept forward and out onto a promontory that overlooked the valley, using the cover available. The vegetation dropped away. They could see the entire valley and up the hillsides opposite them.

They reached the edge of the promontory, a rock face covered with vines and a couple of bushes. Fetterman used his binoculars to survey the area in front of him.

The destruction wasn't quite as bad as it had been in the defoliated valley. It was obvious that American bombers had been here in force. Dotting the hillside were long lines of craters from B-52 runs, some with water in the bottom, hundreds of huge holes that the thousand-pound bombs had torn in the earth, shattering the jungle. Smashed trees—some of them just trunks sticking up or leaning at crazy angles—bushes with no leaves and downed vegetation were scattered everywhere.

Clustered on the face of the hillside opposite them was what was apparently ground zero. Fifty or a hundred craters in a small area, crater dug into crater until it seemed that one small point had been obliterated.

"That the site of the NVA headquarters?" Fetterman asked.

Gerber checked the map and then the landmarks around them. Using his compass, he oriented himself and then nodded. "Looks like someone got here before us."

"Long before us," said Fetterman. "That damage is several days old."

Gerber rubbed his face. He closed his eyes and then opened them again, but the scene spread out in front of him didn't change. Blackened, twisted trees and huge, deep holes. Rows and rows of them, all pointing to one place on the hillside.

"I would guess," said Gerber, "that someone else had the information Maxwell had and did something about it a little faster than he did."

Fetterman kept the binoculars to his eyes and studied the landscape. He focused on the point where the majority of the bombs had landed, searching for something that would indicate the enemy had been there.

"I don't see anything," said Fetterman.

Gerber took the binoculars and studied the terrain. He searched it carefully, but he didn't see anything, either. At that moment he understood what Fetterman meant.

"Maybe they were in a cave or had some kind of underground complex. It wouldn't be the first time," said Gerber.

"No, sir," said Fetterman. "There's nothing there. In Laos, we should be able to see something. That's virgin jungle, or rather, it was virgin jungle. Nobody and nothing down there, never was."

Gerber handed the binoculars back to the master sergeant. "Seems to me that we have two choices. We've done our job. We've gotten to the point where we were sent and found that the target has been eliminated by air power. We can get out now, turn due east, hike through the night and we'll be in South Vietnam."

"But that's not the right site down there."

"That's not necessarily true," Gerber said. "It could be we're too far away to see the signs. It was hit with a fairly big bomb load. It might be that the evidence was all blown to hell and gone."

"It just doesn't look right," said Fetterman.

"Which leads to the second option. We can go down there and search the site in person. Check the ground and see if there's anything to suggest the radio and the headquarters were ever there."

"It would only take an extra day," said Fetterman. "Just a day to do the job right. And if nothing else, we can supply a bomb damage assessment for the Air Force boys."

Gerber took a deep breath. "I'd much rather just go home," he said.

"Yes, sir. So would I."

"Let's get the men and start on down. Nothing else we can do."

"No, sir," said Fetterman. "Nothing else."

24

KHE SANH COMBAT BASE

The crowd began arriving in the middle of the afternoon, at first only a handful, then dozens and finally hundreds. They were the refugees from the fall of Lang Vei, displaced by the NVA and Vietcong. From the ruins of the camp, through the enemy lines they had walked all night, seeking safety. At the Khe Sanh combat base the Marines refused to let them through the wire and into the camp.

Goddard was sitting in front of a bunker, a cup of coffee in his hand, when he first heard about the gathering outside the wire. The bunker was small and the coffee was the first he'd had in several days. The Marines had constructed an awning over the entrance so that it looked like a ramshackle porch in a poorer section of town. Most of the men had taken off their shirts and flak jackets and were sitting on lawn chairs in the sunlight, waiting for the next attack.

"So what's the good word?" Thompson, a big man with shrapnel scars on his face, asked Goddard.

"I don't know," said Goddard.

"Then tell us what's going on outside the wire. No one tells us shit around here."

Goddard took a sip of coffee, then looked out over the combat base. Everything had been damaged and much of it destroyed. Quonset huts were filled with holes from rocket and mortar shrapnel and from rifle fire. There were piles of rubble where a hootch had burned. Debris from the attacks was scattered all over the base, and no one bothered to clear it away. Why clean up when the enemy would be shelling again in a couple of hours at most?

"Outside the wire," said Goddard, "are thousands of bad guys waiting for orders to attack us here."

"Let them come," said Thompson. "I'm ready for the fight."

Goddard finished his coffee and set down the cup on the red dirt of the compound. He glanced at the sky, but the clouds that had been hanging over them had dissipated. For the first time in weeks the sky was completely clear, no clouds, no threat of rain.

"I think Charlie's stepped on his dick," said Goddard suddenly.

"What do you mean?"

Goddard pointed at the sky. "The monsoons are over for the time being. The bad weather that kept our air power in check for so long is mostly over, and he hasn't taken the base. I don't think he's going to try it now."

"Oh, sure," said Thompson. "I hope you let the colonel know the battle is over."

"That's not what I said. I said he's not going to try to take the base," Goddard repeated, suddenly positive of his assessment. "Not now. To do it he'd have to mass his troops, and without the bad weather to assist him, he won't be able to."

Thompson grinned. "That sounds good, if nothing else."

"You wait and see," said Goddard. "This thing's as good as over now."

A jeep roared up to the bunker and stopped. A cloud of dust engulfed it and then it backed out of the dust. The passenger put a hand up on the windshield and said, "Hey, Goddard, you're wanted at the gate."

"What for?"

"There's a whole gaggle of people out there, and the colonel wants a reading on them."

Goddard shrugged and stood up. He climbed into the rear of the jeep and waved at Thompson. "Hey, thanks for the coffee."

"Yeah. I hope you're right about the enemy and the weather."

The driver ground the gears, finally forced it into first and they rocketed off. Goddard was thrown against the rear of the jeep, nearly losing his helmet. He sat up and looked out the windshield. Like everything else on the base, it was broken, a bullet hole through the center of one side and a network of cracks on the outer.

"What's this all about?" asked Goddard.

"Don't know, Sarge, and don't care. We were just told to find you and get your ass over to the main gate area."

Goddard nodded and leaned back. They took the main road that paralleled the runway, passed the complex that included the CP, passed the control tower for the airfield and the edge of the ramp area and went through the TAFDS area. They finally rolled up to the gate, which was now defended by two Ontos and a company of Marines. Outside the wire were thousands of people, shouting and screaming and demanding to enter the camp.

As the jeep rolled to a stop and Goddard climbed out of the rear, a Marine officer approached. "Glad to have you here. Tell us what's going on."

Goddard surveyed the crowd. He could see Montagnards who had been at Lang Vei, Vietnamese soldiers from the CIDG and ARVN Special Forces, and members of the Thirty-third Laotian Elephant Battalion who had been driven from their homes by the NVA tanks only to arrive at Lang Vei for the armor to attack them there. Hundreds of men were armed with rifles, machine guns, hand grenades and pistols. They were a surly, unruly crowd demanding sanctuary inside the combat base.

Goddard stood behind the wire and studied them slowly. The officer was right behind him. "What do you make of it?" he asked.

Goddard shrugged. "A lot of people who've been displaced by the war."

"What should we do about it?"

"How the hell should I know?" Goddard demanded. "What did the colonel say?"

"He's not happy with all these people outside his wire. Says they could get caught in a cross fire if the enemy launches his attack. Hell, they could be part of the attack."

"You know," Goddard said, "there's probably five or six hundred men out there who have had some sort of military training. They'd make an extra battalion to throw into our defenses."

"Sure, if they could be trusted. But there could be a sapper company hidden in there. Hell, they could all be Vietcong. Not to mention the problem of feeding, housing and clothing all these people. We'd need double the number of supplies to survive, without doubling the strength of our defenses."

"Sounds like the decision has already been made."

The officer shrugged. "The colonel said to disperse the crowd before dark unless there was something there that suggested another decision should be made."

Goddard turned away from the wire and looked into the eyes of the officer. "You send these people away and you're liable to turn them all into VC."

"That's a chance we're going to have to take." He walked off, heading toward the guard shack where there was a land line back to the command post.

Goddard started toward the jeep, then stopped. There was more shouting and the Marines inside the combat base suddenly tensed, as if about to shoot. The officer ran from the guard shack and talked to one of the sergeants. He nodded once and turned, shouting orders.

The Marines formed a line, and there was a rattling of weapons as they chambered rounds. With grim-faced determination they started forward.

The officer stood behind Goddard, a bullhorn in his hand. He began shouting through it, demanding that the crowd leave the combat base. They were in danger from the enemy.

There was a roar from the crowd as the Marines advanced. The officer kept talking to them, telling them of the danger if the enemy attacked. Then he dropped the bombshell. They would have to leave their weapons. If they had weapons, they would be an inviting target for the NVA and the Vietcong. It was for their own safety that the Marines were taking the weapons. Without weapons, they would be treated as civilians by both sides. With them, they would be considered combatants and attacked. The officer didn't mention the fact that a third of them wore uniforms that would identify them to the enemy.

The Marines moved through the crowd, taking the weapons from the survivors of Lang Vei and other Communist actions. A few of the men, at the rear of the crowd, slipped away with their weapons, not wanting to give them up.

As the Marines collected the weapons, the people began to trickle away. They walked down the slopes toward the road and then to Route 9. The Laotians, who had already walked through the enemy lines twice, began the journey back to Laos, confused by the lack of assistance from the Marines at Khe Sanh.

Others, when they reached Route 9, turned east, heading for Quang Tri.

Goddard, his hands on the wire, watched as the crowd dispersed. The Marines stacked the confiscated weapons and ammunition in a huge pile, a motley collection of arms from World War II and Korea, even a couple of the new M-16s, as well as grenade launchers, LAW rockets and shotguns.

Goddard couldn't completely understand the order. It was forcing men and women who had supported them to give up their arms. It left them at the mercy of enemy soldiers, who had proved time and again that they had no mercy. It was a sad thing to watch, but then there was nothing he could do about it.

He turned and walked back to the jeep. When he saw that both the driver and the passenger were helping to disarm the locals, he walked on by, heading toward the bunker that housed the intelligence office. There had to be some kind of report he should file, but he was damned if he knew what it was. Besides, he just wanted to get the hell out of there.

IN WASHINGTON Lockhart sat in his cinder-block office in the basement of the White House and read the first of the after-action reports written by the survivors of Lang Vei. Lockhart wasn't an emotional man. After nearly twenty years in the Army, he'd seen, heard and ignored a lot. But this report brought tears to his eyes. Acts of individual courage had always affected him that way.

He dropped the report onto his desk and stared at the corner where the ceiling met the wall. He wondered how the cries for help from such brave men could go unheeded by those who could have helped, whatever the cost.

Lockhart knew a little about the camp, having studied the reports and descriptions of it when the President had told him to keep up on the developments at and around Khe Sanh. He picked up the report and looked at the map of Lang Vei attached to it. The map showed an irregularly shaped compound next to Route 9, only a few miles from the Laotian border. The bunkers were concrete-reinforced and better than anything at Khe Sanh. As the situation around Khe Sanh had worsened, extra troops, Montagnards, were sent from Da Nang to strengthen Lang Vei. When the survivors of the Thirty-third Laotian Elephant Battalion had arrived, talking of tanks, Captain Frank C. Willoughby had added them to his defenses.

Lockhart pushed the map aside and began to read again. As the Laotians arrived, so did Lieutenant Colonel Daniel Schungel, the commander of the Special Forces in I Corps. He

came in because the commander of the Laotians was a lieutenant colonel, and it was believed that an American of equal
rank should be at the camp.

Willoughby was set for an attack. He had two huge 4.2 inch
mortars, 81 mm mortars and nearly two dozen 60 mm mortars. There were 106 mm recoilless rifles and 57 mm recoilless
rifles and nearly a hundred LAW rockets brought in when the
reports of enemy tanks nearby began to circulate around Lang
Vei and Khe Sanh. He also had a couple of .50-caliber machine guns, nearly forty BARs but only two M-60s. For the
various weapons he had almost a million rounds of ammunition. Willoughby had bragged that it would take a regiment to
overrun the camp. But then he hadn't counted on enemy armor.

It was just after midnight when the tanks appeared outside
Lang Vei. Schungel ran out to take a look, saw them rolling
toward the northeastern corner of the camp and raced back
down the stairs into the command bunker. He told Willoughby to mass the artillery support in that area, to call for a
spooky for flare support, to call for air support and to call Khe
Sanh to get the artillery there firing for them. Then he ran out
to organize tank killer teams.

Another two tanks were on the south. The camp's mortars
were firing illumination rounds. The senior medic used a 106
mm recoilless rifle to set the tanks on fire. Three women, carrying American M-16s, leaped from the lead tank and ran for
cover.

A third tank rolled by the two burning hulks, used a spotlight to blind the Vietnamese defenders and then opened fire
on the bunkers. Corporal Jim Holt, who had destroyed the
first two tanks, hit the third and then ran off to get more ammo
for his weapon. That was the last anyone saw of him.

Two more tanks rolled in and opened fire. The defense along
the perimeter on that side of the camp collapsed, and the tanks
pushed on, coming up behind the Montagnards holding the
northeastern corner and facing two other enemy tanks. They
were caught in a cross fire and were forced to flee or die.

Willoughby called for more help. The Marines responded with artillery, but the first rounds landed inside the camp. Willoughby corrected the fire, but the eastern side of the camp was already lost, the enemy taking the bunkers, shooting the defenders who surrendered and killing all the wounded.

In the center of the camp Schungel used the LAW rockets to try to stop the enemy tanks. The first round hit the target with a fountain of orange sparks, but the tank kept rolling. He moved closer, tried again, but the LAW failed to fire. None of the tank killer teams had success with the LAWs. They either bounced off the lightly armored tanks, or they failed to fire altogether.

"Jesus!" said Lockhart as he read that. He turned away from the report and studied the wall, again thinking of dead cavalrymen trying to clear weapons and dead Marines trying to unjam M-16s. Corporate America had let the American military down again. Once before he had started to work on a report to the President about the problem with the M-16s, but had changed his mind, deciding that it wasn't appropriate for him to take that kind of action. He'd torn up the first draft and written no more.

It was hard for him to continue reading the report, knowing that he wasn't reading a work of fiction, but an actual account from the survivors. He turned his attention back to the printed words.

It was about that time, according to the report, that the ammo dump exploded. Thick clouds of black smoke, along with clouds of dust raised by the tanks and the explosions, obscured the camp. The FAC overhead lost sight of Lang Vei time and again and reported that the enemy was using flame-throwers to eliminate resistance.

Schungel and the men with him were unable to stop the armors, even when they rolled grenades under the treads or fired their M-16s into the eyeslits. They retreated to the command bunker near the center of the camp. As they raced across the compound toward the bunker, an explosion behind them lifted them and threw them to the ground. One Green Beret sergeant was blinded and Schungel was stunned. An LLDB lieutenant, Le Van Quoc, rushed from cover, gunned down a number of attackers with his M-16 and then helped the wounded men to safety. Safety for the moment.

With the defense collapsing, Schungel and an American lieutenant left the bunker and ran to the team house. They were chased from it and then hid in the dispensary. They could hear the enemy commander giving orders to his men. They watched a CIDG platoon try to fight its way clear, only to be caught by a cluster bomb unit from an American jet. A few minutes later, Schungel and the lieutenant took the same route to get out of the camp.

Willoughby was trapped in the command bunker with eight other Americans, five Vietnamese officers and two dozen CIDG soldiers. The tanks were now firing at them point-blank, and the enemy soldiers were tossing grenades and satchel charges into the vents. One of the tanks rolled over the top of the bunker, but the concrete held.

Willoughby knew it was almost over now. He called in the artillery from Khe Sanh, dropping it on his own position. He asked the Marines to execute the relief plan. The artillery began to fall immediately, but the Marines refused to send the relief force, fearing an ambush.

Throughout the night Willoughby and his men held on, with the enemy pounding away at the thick concrete walls. Even when radio communications were lost just after 3:00 a.m., Willoughby hoped there would be a rescue team. The enemy began to dig, and near morning tossed a thermite grenade into the bunker, setting papers, maps and wooden desks on fire. The men inside began to vomit in the thick, stinking smoke, but still they held out.

The NVA invited everyone in the bunker to surrender. The Vietnamese officers and the CIDG soldiers finally accepted and climbed the stairs to the outside. Minutes later there was shouting and shooting.

At 6:30 a hole was blasted in the bunker wall, and Willoughby with the last of his defenders waited for the final rush.

It never came. About the same time the defenders at Old Lang
Vei, half a klick away, Laotians led by Americans, attacked.
They fought their way into the camp, rescued a number of
Montagnards who had been wounded but missed by the NVA
and pushed toward the center of Lang Vei. They attacked four
times but failed to reach the command bunker where Willoughby and the Americans still held out.

Late in the afternoon Willoughby and the other Americans
used the timing of the strafing runs of the Air Force jets to escape from the camp. They were met on Route 9 by Le Van
Quoc, who had found a jeep. He escorted the Americans and
about forty CIDG to Old Lang Vei, where they were later rescued by Marine helicopters. There was no room for Quoc on
any of the choppers. He was told to make his own way to Khe
Sanh.

Sweating heavily, his heart pounding, Lockhart closed the
file folder. The story had numbed him. Of the twenty-four
Americans at Lang Vei, ten were either dead or missing and
eleven others were wounded. It was an unbelievable story.

Lockhart had to get up, had to move. His hands were shaking. He slipped around his desk, but stopped before he
reached the door. He looked back at the report. Once more he
thought about the failure of the LAW rockets, and his stomach flipped over. He opened the report again, rereading the
description of Colonel Schungel's fight with the tanks. The
LAWs had misfired or bounced off. An antitank weapon
hadn't been able to penetrate the relatively thin armor of an
Old Soviet-built amphibious tank. A useless weapon.

"Christ on a stick! How the hell can we fight a war with
weapons that don't work."

Lockhart opened the door and stepped into the corridor, but
then was lost. He didn't know whom to see, whom to call or
where he was going. He felt frustration and rage and knew that
it must have been worse for the men at Lang Vei. Plans had
been drawn up, weapons issued, but when it came right down
to it, the plans had been impossible to execute and the weapons next to useless.

The President had to be told, Lockhart knew. But how could he tell him that the American manufacturers and the Army procurement systems weren't giving the men in the field what they needed? It came down to the men in the field being twelve thousand miles away and unable to complain. Engineers, technicians and officers would all come up with the same self-serving explanations they had come up with about the problems with the M-16. Somehow it was always the soldier's fault that the weapon had failed.

Lockhart returned to his office and sat down behind his desk. He wished he could get a drink. He needed one after reading about Lang Vei. He needed something. It was an incredible story.

Again he flipped through the report, searching for the name of the South Vietnamese Special Forces lieutenant, Le Van Quoc, who had saved Schungel's life and then helped get Willoughby and his people to Old Lang Vei where they could be rescued. Surely something could be done for the man. Surely the United States could give him an award for bravery.

Lockhart made a few notes, and then decided he had avoided talking to the President long enough. He would have to head upstairs and tell the President what he had learned about Lang Vei. He would suggest that Lieutenant Le Van Quoc be singled out for some sort of recognition by the U.S. At the same time he would mention the weapon failures. Given Johnson's mood, and his long-standing concern that Khe Sanh was slowly turning into another Dien Bien Phu, he knew the President wouldn't be happy. He hoped the President wouldn't kill the messenger.

As Lockhart headed upstairs to schedule his appointment, he couldn't know that Lieutenant Le Van Quoc had managed to cover the distance from Old Lang Vei to the Khe Sanh combat base during the night. He didn't know that Quoc had hidden from enemy patrols and American artillery, and still in uniform and carrying his weapon, had reported to the combat base as he had been told to do. Lockhart had no way of knowing that the Marines at Khe Sanh, having no idea who

Quoc was, had taken his weapon away from him and then ordered him to get away from the combat base before he found himself in the middle of a battle.

Lieutenant Quoc disappeared shortly after that.

25

JUNGLES OF LAOS WEST
OF KHE SANH

Gerber and Fetterman retreated from the promontory and climbed back to the summit of the hill. They collected their security team and the patrol moved out, again with Fetterman on point. They worked their way down the slopes, sticking to the thick vegetation and avoiding the trails. They passed a few bomb craters, long shots, or short ones, that had destroyed a portion of the jungle but nothing else. The craters were fifty, sixty, a hundred feet across and twelve, fifteen and twenty feet deep. Dirt, blown from the ground, was scattered around the craters and the trees near them were shattered. Many of them were dying, the leaves turning brown and dropping off. The trunks were turning gray. The shrapnel was so thick in some of them that it looked like thorns on a rosebush.

It took them thirty minutes to get down the hill and begin the climb up the other. On the valley floor they had to be careful, dodging from crater to crater, using the thickest of the foliage for cover in case there were enemy patrols around. With the vegetation burned and shrapnel-riddled, it was hard to find a path across the valley that wouldn't expose them to the enemy on the hills, or the pilots in the aircraft overhead.

They stopped once as a flight of American jets roared over, dipping into the valley as if searching for a target of opportunity. They crouched among the broken, ruined jungle and watched the planes flash past. Once they were clear of the valley, the jets climbed nearly straight up, disappearing into the setting sun.

With the aircraft gone, Fetterman started out again, moving toward ground zero. It was near the summit of the hill, where the tall trees would have been, had any of them still been standing. The only cover there was the craters. The men moved slowly, carefully, until they came to the area of the worst damage. Without a command from Gerber, the security squad spread out, forming a half moon, facing back the way they had come. Gerber and Fetterman continued on, until they were in the center of the worst of the destruction.

Both got down on their hands and knees to search the ground. They tried to determine exactly where the center of destruction was, figuring that it would be the point where the Air Force was aiming. From there, they worked their way in ever-expanding circles, looking for evidence that the NVA had had a headquarters hidden somewhere in the area around there.

But there was nothing to find. Just the remains of trees, bushes and vegetation that had covered the hillside before the bombers had arrived. There was nothing that was man-made. There was no sign of the support facilities that would have been required, even if there had been nothing more than a radio relay point. Manufactured equipment would still have been used. Even the NVA and the VC, experts at turning American trash into weapons, couldn't relay radio signals with nothing at all.

They combed the hillside, crawling in and out of the craters, searching. And all the while Gerber knew exactly how exposed he was. There was no cover in the craters and anyone in the hills around them would be able to see him quite clearly. He could feel the skin at the back of his neck crawl. A sniper half a klick away could get off two shots, maybe three, before the sound reached him to give him warning. By that time he could easily be dead. He was as exposed as if he was standing on a parade field.

With that knowledge in the back of his mind, he still searched for a sign that the NVA had been there. Even on his hands and knees he found no sign. Nothing at all. Then all of a sudden Gerber realized that no matter how long they searched, they would find nothing—because he knew what had happened. If only someone in Saigon had bothered to ask a few questions, this whole problem could have been avoided.

Gerber glanced up and saw that Fetterman had crawled higher on the slope, toward the summit where the vegetation was thicker, offering some protection. Like much of the plant growth in the valley, it was dying, but there was enough there to protect them from the eyes of the enemy.

Gerber followed him up and into the jungle. The instant it closed around him, he felt better, safer. He stood up and turned to look back down into the valley. Even though he knew where the security team was, he couldn't see them. The men were good, but then there was no reason why they wouldn't be. All had been trained by the Special Forces.

Fetterman was searching the ground around the tallest of the trees, looking like an inspector who was sure something had been hidden from him. He was on his hands and knees again, probing at the dirt with his knife and then glancing up into the trees. Finally he stood up, grabbed at a vine that was wound around the trunk and grinned. He jerked on the vine and was showered with a cascade of bark and leaves, but the vine remained tightly wrapped around the truck.

When Gerber got to him, Fetterman was standing with part of the vine in his hand. "Here's the enemy headquarters," he said, his voice seeming too loud in the quietness around them.

"I thought so." Gerber nodded. "Assholes at MACV figured out where the radio was by intercepting the signal and triangulation and never thought that the antenna was separated from the site."

"And here's the antenna." Fetterman pulled on it again, but it still didn't come down. He turned then and yanked at it in the opposite direction. It came up out of the dirt, leading to the very summit of the hill. Fetterman followed it until he came to the end.

"That's why the signal quit. The antenna broke," said Gerber.

Fetterman went down on his hands and knees again and found the other end, then sat there for a moment, looking at the finger-thick cable. "You know," he said, "we get a direction and we might be able to trace it to the radio."

"And if the signals were as thick and heavy as they made out in Saigon, we just might find Giap."

"The antenna can't be that long," said Fetterman. "If it was, they would have too many problems maintaining it."

"Let's get the team and move out. We've got thirty minutes of light left."

Together they moved over the top of the hill down the slope. They signaled to the security squad and then covered them as they scrambled through the barren, crater-riddled hillside. Once they were linked, they spread out in the formation they had been using all day. Fetterman, at the point, led them to the tree that had been used as the antenna, found the cable again and began following it.

They started down the hill, staying close to the cable, until they came to another string of bomb craters, three distinct rows of huge, deep craters that were the remains of an arc light. The cable ended there.

"This explains why they didn't just repair the break at the top of the hill," Fetterman whispered as Gerber caught up to him.

The light was fading rapidly. "You think you can find it on the other side?" asked Gerber.

"Let's go."

They crossed the B-52 strike area, staying with the vegetation between the craters. In a city, such a bombing would have been devastating, but in the jungle, it just blew up trees and bushes and killed animals. Massed bombing just wasn't an effective weapon against a guerrilla force. The severing of the radio antenna was probably an accident.

On the other side, Fetterman, Gerber and the others spread out, searching the ground, probing at it with knives, until Hobbs found a bit of the cable. Ten yards away they found another piece and ten yards after that they came to the antenna where it was intact.

Fetterman picked it up and headed off again to the south and east. The light was almost gone and the jungle was dense again. They were on the floor of a valley, moving at a good clip. The heat of the afternoon was gone and the humidity seemed to have dried up, at least for the moment.

When the last of the light was gone, they halted for a moment. Gerber drank from his canteen and then passed it around to empty it so that it wouldn't slosh as they tried to move silently in the jungle. Later, one of the others would share his water.

After they rested, Gerber asked, "You think we can keep moving?"

"As long as I can hang on to the cable," said Fetterman, "there's no reason for us not to."

"Then take the point."

Again they moved out, this time more slowly than before. Fetterman held the antenna, using it to guide them through the jungle. Once they had to stop as the cable climbed into a tree, but they located it again. They came to another hill, a shallow slope that was almost flat ground, and kept moving upward until they reached the summit and the cable ended. Fetterman dropped back and told Gerber what had happened.

"It's no big thing," whispered Gerber. "We can use the rest, anyway."

They spread out into a defensive circle where they could keep an eye on one another. Gerber ordered every other man to rest for two hours. They were to spend the night, rotating the alert, so that everyone could get four or six hours of sleep.

As soon as they were in place, Gerber laid his head down on his arms and closed his eyes. He was lying on his belly so that he wasn't facing up into the jungle. He sometimes worried about insects, snakes and lizards dropping onto his face from the branches above him, but tonight that wouldn't be a problem.

He felt sleep creeping up on him and knew he would give in to it. Sometimes it was impossible to relax in the jungle, especially when there were calls from the big cats, or when the enemy had been dogging his trail all day. Ever since that ambush the night before, there had been no indication that there were any enemy soldiers around them. Maybe they were all in South Vietnam, waiting to attack Khe Sanh.

There were a couple of things he wanted to concentrate on, but sleep caught him before he had the chance. He didn't dream or move, and in what seemed to be seconds, it was his turn for watch.

The jungle at night was a strange place. The darkness hid so much. Some animals used the cover of night to search for food. The enemy often used darkness to cover their movements, and Gerber, with his Special Forces troops, did the same. The dark could be both a friend and an enemy, just as the jungle could be.

Gerber studied the landscape around him. There were no flares overhead and there was no moon, just a darkness that shivered and shook as the trees and the bushes vibrated in the light breeze blowing through.

And, as always, there was a reminder of the war, a rumbling felt through the ground as bombs and artillery exploded, quiet, almost inaudible detonations in the distance.

Gerber turned once and glanced at the man to his left, an indistinct shape in the darkness. Someone walking by would never have seen him, the cover was so good.

After two hours Gerber woke his relief and went back to sleep quickly. There weren't going to be many opportunities to sleep in the near future. If they found the headquarters and if they got a shot, the entire North Vietnamese army was going to be chasing them. They would have to nearly run to South Vietnam, where they might be able to call helicopters in to get them. But they had to get there first.

Just as had happened the day before, the jungle exploded at dawn when the animals and the birds awoke. They were so noisy that Gerber had to shout to be heard over them.

Gerber ate his breakfast of LRRP rations, a dehydrated, high-energy food designed for long-range patrols. He could carry more of it because the rations didn't come in cans. Fetterman was the first to finish breakfast and set off in search of the remains of the cable.

As Gerber finished eating, Fetterman returned and crawled up to him. He stuck his face in close. "Got it."

"You found the antenna?"

"No, sir. Found the radio."

AS GERBER AND FETTERMAN were getting ready to move closer to the enemy radio station, Marie was getting ready to leave South Vietnam. She was packing so that she could catch the late-morning plane that would land first in Japan, then Alaska and finally in California. Leaving Vietnam was something that both she and the people running the USO tour wanted.

When she had arrived back in the area assigned to them, she had noticed that almost no one talked to her. In the dressing room one of the women, whom Marie knew only as Maggie, told her that everyone was angry that she had disappeared for two days.

"But I didn't disappear," she had protested. "You knew where I was. Everyone knew."

"Makes no difference. They see it as you disappearing and they want you to go home." Maggie lowered her voice, as if planning a jailbreak, and added, "They say your talent is second-rate at best, and the only thing you can really do well is in a prone position."

Marie felt the rest of her world crumble then. All she had ever wanted was to do something for someone and be appreciated for it, but the politics and the petty jealousies got in the way. She sat down and began to cry.

Maggie sat next to her, and put an arm around her. "I'm only telling you what they said so that you can make an intelligent decision."

Marie sniffed once, then said, "Second-rate talent, hell. We're all second-rate here. If we weren't, we'd be on the circuit in the United States."

"Honey, you know how it is. You ruffle their feathers and they're all out to get you."

"Bastards!"

"It's the way it is. If you display a little more talent than they have, a little more intelligence, they have to take you down a peg. You gave them the chance."

Marie took a deep breath. "Do they have any idea what happened yesterday?"

Maggie stood up and moved to the other side of the room. She sat down at the makeshift vanity with the mirror ringed by light bulbs and said, "They don't care."

"I want to get out, then. I can't take it anymore. I just want to go home now."

Maggie turned and looked at Marie. "How old are you, honey?"

"Twenty."

"Well, there it is. You're smarter, prettier and probably have more raw talent than the rest of us combined. No wonder they don't like you."

Marie sat there for a moment and wondered why Maggie kept pushing at her. She suddenly realized she might not have any friends on the USO tour. First the organizers did everything to make her miserable, then Maggie, claiming to be her friend, kept hammering at her, telling her how rotten everyone said she was.

"I'm going home," she said again, and got up and walked out. She told the tour organizers that she wanted to go home, and not one of them tried to talk her out of it. They made calls to Air Force operations, got the flight schedules and made sure her name was on the list. They gave her the boarding time, told her she had to be there an hour early because she'd better not miss the plane and then they left her alone.

She'd spend the evening alone, even though a couple of people, Air Force officers and a few of the younger women on the tour, tried to get her to have a drink with them. Instead, she lay on her bed, a handkerchief clutched in her hand along with Whitmire's name tag, and tried to figure out where she had gone wrong.

She'd slept fitfully and finally got up. She showered and dressed in her best outfit and then packed. She was early for the flight and sat around the terminal waiting for the plane that would take her home. She decided that she wouldn't miss a thing about Vietnam.

GERBER STARED at Fetterman for a moment, then asked, "What did you see?"

"A camp, about halfway up the side of the hill opposite us, maybe eight hundred meters away. A couple of hootches, mud and thatch, a concrete building and the mouth of a cave. Looks just like you'd expect an NVA headquarters to look."

"How many men?"

Fetterman shrugged. "Depends on the size of the cave. Could be a company down there. A headquarters platoon and then three other platoons for security, or it could be a battalion. Just depends on the size of the caves."

"You see anyone?"

"Oh, yes, sir. Saw four or five guys wandering around. They're NVA and not VC. That much is obvious."

"Let's get into position," said Gerber. "You find us a place to hide?"

"There's an outcropping of rock where the hill drops away. Gives us a good view of the valley and the hill opposite. Put the security to the right, about three hundred meters behind us, watching the hill, and we should be in good shape."

Gerber dropped away to where Hobbs, Lawrence, Quinn and Rogers were eating their breakfast. He pulled them in close to him so that their faces were only inches from his. All four of them needed a shave and a bath, but at least the dirt helped them to blend into the jungle. The best designed camouflage in the world wasn't as good as a couple of days in the jungle. They camouflaged everything, from the skin color to the normal body odors.

Hobbs would be in charge of the security team. His job was to make sure no one came up behind Fetterman or Gerber once they were in position. The team would be watching for the enemy, and once a shot had been made, they would cover the withdrawal.

"Your job now," said Gerber, "is to sit quietly, not moving, until we initiate some action. You do nothing, unless there's an enemy unit coming up behind us. Then you take them. I leave that to you. But don't initiate an action unless there's no other choice."

"Got it, sir."

"Okay. Sergeant Fetterman and I will get into position. You watch so you'll know where we are." Gerber got out his map. Fetterman pointed to the area where the outcropping was located.

"Your best position," said Fetterman, "is probably in this area."

"Okay."

Gerber looked at the men. "I repeat, the one thing to remember is that once everyone is in position, we don't move. We stay put until a shot is made, or until I decide it's time to pull out. Questions?"

Hobbs studied the map, then peered into the jungle.

"Don't worry," said Fetterman. "Once you see the lay of the land, you'll see the obvious location."

Gerber looked from face to face, then asked, "Anything else?"

Each of the men shook his head. Gerber folded the map. "Good."

Fetterman got to his feet and moved away. Gerber joined him. They collected their gear and then Fetterman led him through the jungle, staying away from the crest of the hill, on the side opposite the enemy camp. Fetterman finally turned south, and they climbed the rest of the way, twenty or twenty-five feet to the summit. Then they got on their bellies and crawled forward slowly, Fetterman in the lead. He stopped once and pointed to the left, and they slipped into a dry streambed.

They followed it down for a hundred meters, then Fetterman stopped. He glanced to the rear and grinned. His face was covered with sweat as they crawled out into the sunlight. He kept moving, slowly, in a natural fluid motion. Jerky motions called attention to people in the jungle; fluid motion helped to hide them.

Fetterman crawled under the cover of the bushes and trees and then up out of the streambed. He kept moving, now along the side of the hill, rounding it to the east. Gerber was right behind him.

Again Fetterman stopped and pointed, then started down the hill and ended up on a plateau, a small grass-covered area. A single tree grew from the end of it, a log lay across it, and there were several piles of rocks to provide cover and protection.

Gerber nodded, telling Fetterman to go.

Together they crawled out of the cover of the jungle and into the sunlight that was beating down on the plateau. As he broke from cover, Fetterman started moving even more slowly. He slid a hand forward carefully, hesitated, then moved a foot and knee. He lifted his body from the ground and pulled himself out onto the plateau, using the knee-high grass to cover his movements.

Gerber followed, moving just as carefully. The sun was on his back, baking him. He felt the sweat form and drip. He knew his uniform was now black with moisture, but decided the darker, the better.

It took Fetterman more than two hours to crawl the twenty feet from the edge of the jungle to the log that lay across the end of the plateau. Once there he rolled slowly to his left and removed the sniper rifle from the camouflaged leather case. He set it down, then flattened himself behind the log.

Gerber reached the log, and Fetterman helped him slip off his rucksack. They pushed equipment up against the log. Fetterman laid out the rifle, set his canteen in the shade, then checked the weapon carefully. Gerber got out the binoculars and began to study the camp eight hundred meters away.

It was just as Fetterman had described it. There wasn't much visible from the air—a couple of mud-and-thatch buildings and one of cinder block that was probably the radio room, a dozen, maybe two dozen enemy soldiers. Gerber studied them. Each was in uniform, and fortunately, each wore the shoulder boards of his rank. Although Gerber couldn't tell much from the distance, he could pick out the officers.

Fetterman had taken the caps off the scope of the sniper rifle. He looked through it, then set it down. "Ready," he whispered.

Gerber swept the camp again. He studied everything, but didn't see anything extraordinary below him. A number of soldiers were going about their duties, paying no attention to anything else. No high-ranking officers were to be seen and certainly no one who even remotely resembled Giap.

There was motion to the north of the camp, lower on the hillside, and Gerber watched as a twenty-man patrol slipped out of the jungle, through the camp and into the mouth of the cave.

"Seems they have at least a company down there," said Gerber. "I've already counted about fifty men."

"Eight hundred meters is a good head start," said Fetterman. "Guess we'd better get comfortable because it looks like it's going to be a long wait."

Fetterman set the rifle aside out of the direct sunlight. "You know that Giap isn't going to be down there, don't you?"

"Of course," Gerber said. "It's too isolated, not close enough to Khe Sanh. But we might get lucky and see some general. Taking him out would be demoralizing to the NVA, proving we can get them anywhere."

"If there's a general down there."

"Tony, you're not usually that pessimistic."

"No, sir," agreed Fetterman. "But then we're not usually sent out on an impossible mission."

"All we can do," said Gerber, "is the best we can."

"Yes, sir."

26

JUNGLES OF LAOS WEST
OF KHE SANH

For most of the day Gerber and Fetterman lay in the hot sun, hidden behind the rotting log, moving only their heads and eyes. They studied the enemy camp below them, watching as the men and women of the North Vietnamese army rotated their duties. When one patrol came in, another went out, moving first to the west and then to the south. Soldiers disappeared into the cave mouth and didn't return. A few soldiers patrolled the perimeter of the camp as designated by their route of march rather than by walls or wire.

At noon the two Green Berets took turns watching the enemy camp through the binoculars while the other ate more of the LRRP dried rations and rested. Gerber was first, washing down the food with sips of water from his canteen. He drank no more than a capful, saving as much as he could for they might have to wait for two or three days.

Then it was his turn to watch while Fetterman ate. They switched jobs without saying a word. Gerber was trying to decide how long they should stay there. Now that they were in position, it was unlikely that the enemy would find them. Discovering six men hiding in the jungle wasn't an easy task, especially when there was no reason to suspect men were hiding in the jungle, and if the men didn't move.

Fetterman joined him again, but Gerber didn't give up the binoculars. He kept them on the enemy camp. Just after noon there was a commotion as men began to pour from the cave mouth. Gerber was afraid that someone had seen something in the hills, but the men didn't rush into the jungle. Instead they formed two lines facing each other near the cinder-block hootch and waited. It looked like an honor guard for a dignitary.

Gerber pointed it out and Fetterman shrugged. He pulled the caps off the scope of the rifle and studied the motion of the trees, trying to determine the wind direction and speed.

Below them, the men's lines were ragged which meant they were waiting for something. They had been put into position and then told to hang loose. Gerber had seen a hundred similar scenes at American military posts. The general was on his way, so the men formed up, ready to snap to attention when the general finally arrived.

Motion to the west caught his attention. There was a flash of sunlight off glass, and Gerber spotted a car driving toward the camp. He studied the jungle and finally located a patch of road. "I'll be damned."

The NVA had constructed a road that cut through the jungle, leaving the canopy intact. They had created a living green tunnel through the vegetation, and now that he knew where to look, he could see part of it.

In the camp the men came to attention. A color guard, holding the North Vietnamese flag and a couple of regimental colors, emerged from the cave. They took up a position at the head of the double rank of men, close to the radio shack.

"Captain?" whispered Fetterman.

Gerber knew the nature of Fetterman's question. It was highly unlikely that the man in the car was Giap. There was a very good chance, though, that the man was a high-ranking officer, possibly a general. Should they take him and head out, or wait for the unlikely possibility that Giap would either emerge from the cave or come for a visit?

The car was now no more than a hundred meters from the headquarters. Gerber could see it through gaps in the vegetation, a black sedan with flags on the front fender.

In the camp, several officers appeared, wearing dress uniforms, or at least as close to dress uniforms as the North Vietnamese ever got. They had pistols on polished leather belts and helmets that seemed to have been polished, too. One of them had a sword.

"Captain?"

Gerber made his decision. "As soon as you identify the main man, you take him. One shot. Then take out as many of the other officers as you can. As soon as all the targets disappear, we're out of here."

Fetterman stretched out, using the rotting log as a bench rest, and shifted around until he was comfortable. He checked the wind direction again, then settled down to wait for the arrival of the general.

Gerber packed up the binoculars, took a deep drink of his water and put the canteen away. He made sure he had everything he wanted either in his rucksack or fastened to him. After the shooting started, there wouldn't be a chance to search the plateau for equipment.

The car arrived and pulled to a stop so that when the right rear door opened, the passenger would be able to step between the two ranks of soldiers, who were forming an honor guard for him to walk through on his way into the headquarters.

One of the camp's officers came forward and opened the door. The man inside got out and stood there, his back to the car. He returned the salute of the man who had opened the door and then glanced at the troops. For a moment everything seemed suspended in time. For a moment Gerber believed they had stumbled onto Giap.

The man took a single step away from the car, halted, then started forward again. When he was halfway up the line of troops, Fetterman fired, the bang of the weapon echoing through the jungle.

For an instant it seemed Fetterman had missed. The man continued to walk in a steady pace toward the color guard. Then he pitched forward, facedown, looking as if he had been punched in the back.

There was a second shot from Fetterman, then a third and a fourth. The escort officer fell, rolled and ended up on his back. Another officer fell. Then everyone scattered. The two ranks of soldiers disintegrated as they dived for cover. Firing broke out: ripples of small arms, a hammering from a heavy machine gun. In the shadows around the camp there was the flickering of muzzle-flashes.

"That's it," said Fetterman. "Let's get out." He picked up the caps but didn't bother to put them on the scope, just turned and began to crawl to the rear.

Gerber hesitated, watching the response in the enemy camp. They were completely baffled, having no idea what had happened or how it had happened. It was perfect. If Gerber and his team could get out cleanly, it would scare the hell out of the enemy.

As he turned, the log was struck by machine gun fire. The soft wood disintegrated into brown fountains. Gerber flattened himself. There was a snap overhead, a single round that had passed close to him.

"You okay?" asked Fetterman.

"Fine. Go."

Fetterman reached the jungle and stood up, turning. He raised his rifle, using the scope to study the enemy camp. They were firing everything they had, pouring rounds into the jungle all around them.

Gerber caught up and crouched at the base of a giant teak tree. Another burst of fire came at them, slamming into the tree fifteen feet above his head.

"They've got no idea where we are," said Fetterman.

"Exactly what we want. Let's go."

They hurried up the hill, climbing straight for the summit, then turned west, coming up behind the security team. Hobbs saw them and Fetterman waved them forward, out of position.

As the men came closer, Gerber said said simply, "Let's go."

Fetterman took a moment to put the caps on the scope and then took off as the point. He led them north, to the summit of the hill, and then over it onto the northern face so that the hill was between them and the enemy camp. A third of the way down it, he turned east, moving rapidly through the thick vegetation.

Fetterman didn't hesitate or slow the pace. He kept pushing at it, waiting for some sign that the enemy was reacting to the sneak attack. He leaped one clear stream, not even bothering to halt at the bank as he normally did. The important thing was to put distance between the patrol and the enemy camp.

Gerber, as he had for two days, brought up the rear. He knew the confusion that had to be swirling through the enemy camp. They would be trying to figure out what to do. It was like a Vietcong assassination attempt at MACV Headquarters. Everyone would be running around, but no one would be there to organize patrols. No one would have a clue about the direction of the shots, and in the end the assassin would be able to get away. In the jungle the odds were even better.

Fetterman picked up the pace so that they were nearly running. They dodged around huge trees and bushes, leaping over holes in the ground, small bushes, fallen trees. They no longer worried about noise discipline. They were interested in speed and distance. The farther they got from the headquarters, the safer they would be.

They came down from the hill, through a valley where the vegetation was thicker and the vines grabbed at them. They tore through a veil of ferns and vines and out into a clearing. Fetterman didn't change course. He raced across the valley, playing the odds. No manned enemy bunkers and no booby traps. This was Laos and not South Vietnam. The enemy wouldn't be surrounding likely landing zones or booby-trapping them. That would do more harm to themselves than to the Americans.

They ran across the valley floor, slowing where the vegetation was thick, and sprinting where it was thinner. They didn't stop to eat or rest. They kept moving, getting closer to South Vietnam and safety, and getting farther from the enemy camp.

Still they ran, as the sweat soaked them and their mouths filled with cotton. They ran as the breath rasped in their throats and their lungs caught fire. They ran as the pain expanded out of their chests into their arms and down into their legs. They kept at it as the jungle closed in around them and then opened up again so that the sun could take its toll, too. They slowed only where the terrain and the vegetation dictated a slower pace. They ran up the hills, their legs suddenly leaden and the sky seeming to darken, and then ran down, trying to maintain their balance. They ran toward the east, away from the NVA base, until they came to a deep river that wasn't marked on the map. Fetterman slid to a halt on the bank, went down on one knee, his head bowed as he sucked in air.

Gerber caught up, stood there for a moment, then whipped out his map. He studied it and said, "We're either twelve miles into South Vietnam or this river doesn't exist."

"What do we do?" asked Hobbs.

"Fan out behind us," said Gerber. "Defensive perimeter and we'll take a twenty-minute break."

Hobbs got his men to their feet and scattered them through the trees. Gerber moved over, next to Fetterman. He glanced at the other bank and then down into the water. "Looks like there was a heavy rain in the hills. Twelve hours from now this will be gone."

"So we've got to cross."

Gerber mopped the sweat from his face. "We could rest here for an hour and see what happens. I think we're in the clear."

Then, almost as if to make a liar out of him, Hobbs appeared and said, "We've got movement in the jungle. A hundred meters to the north, heading this way."

"We'd better cross then," said Gerber. "Pull your people back to here."

Gerber moved out into the shallows at the edge of the river, and as he did, there was a roaring overhead. The captain glanced up and saw two American fighters screaming along no more than a hundred feet above the jungle canopy. He leaped back out of the way. He knew the Air Force pilots would roll in on any armed force they saw, never suspecting that the armed men were Americans. The jets continued north, disappeared and then suddenly were back, circling overhead.

"There must be a way for this to work for us," said Fetterman.

Quinn crawled over. "Those guys are coming right at us. I don't think they know we're here."

"They'll have stopped as long as the jets are overhead," said Gerber.

"We've got to get going," said Fetterman.

Gerber grinned. "Quinn, you think you can get close to them?"

"I can find them, yes, sir."

"Okay. Here's what you do. Don't press your luck, but get close enough to toss a grenade and then we'll hope the Air Force boys spot the detonation and roll in on the bad guys."

"Could work," said Fetterman.

"If nothing else, it'll give the men behind us something to think about."

Quinn nodded and shrugged out of his rucksack. With the sound of the jet engines drowning out the noise, he hurried into position. Crawling the last thirty yards, he kept his head up, searching for the enemy. He spotted them through gaps in the jungle. They were running around, one or two of them pointing toward the orbiting jets.

He had gotten close enough to them. He slipped behind a teak tree, flattening himself behind it. He took a deep breath, held it for an instant, then exhaled. Sweat dripped from his face and his hands were slick. He wiped his right hand on his fatigues, then pulled a grenade and yanked the pin free. As he peeked around the tree, he cocked his arm back, aiming. He threw the grenade as hard as he could, then flattened himself against the tree. The grenade crashed through the vegetation, hit the ground and blew up. Dirt and shrapnel rattled through the jungle. There were a couple of high-pitched screams and a single, drawn-out moan.

Quinn didn't wait to find out what had happened. He dodged away from the enemy, trying to keep the tree between them and himself. He didn't look back. He reached the rest of the team and threw himself onto the ground. No one had to ask how it had gone.

With the explosion, the jets suddenly rolled out of their orbit, raced toward South Vietnam, then suddenly climbed into the sky, rolling over so that they were heading back at Gerber and his men. They passed over and dropped two bombs that tumbled and then exploded into a flash of orange fire and black smoke.

Firing came from the jungle as the enemy soldiers shot at the jets. That didn't seem to bother the pilots. They turned and came back, diving at the point where the enemy was hiding. As the first jet broke away, there was a shattering explosion and a fountain of jungle floor erupted.

"Yeah," said Hobbs. "Get some."

A moment later the second jet rolled in and again the jungle exploded, but as it did, three NVA burst from the trees, running at Gerber and his men. Quinn and Lawrence were ready, firing with their silenced weapons.

The enemy soldiers were cut down before they knew what hit them. The first fell immediately, tossing his weapon out in front of him so that it looked as if he had stumbled. The second man stopped, turned and was shot. He screamed in pain and surprise and then fell. The last man tried to stop, but was shot several times, falling to the ground.

As they died, Rogers ran up to them and grabbed their weapons. He took them to the river and threw them in. The last thing Gerber and his men wanted to do was carry extra weight. All they could do was deny the weapons to the enemy.

Overhead the jets seemed to back off. They orbited the area, searching the ground for signs of the enemy unit, and apparently finding none, turned to head home. As they did, Gerber ordered, "Let's get across now."

Fetterman left the dry land and entered the water. The strong current pushed at him, and rather than fight it, he let it carry him downstream. The water reached to his waist and once tried to sweep him from his feet, but he managed to get to the other bank and pulled himself out.

Hobbs, Rogers, Lawrence and Quinn entered the water together. They walked quickly as the water climbed up until it reached their waists. They held their weapons over their heads to keep them dry.

As they reached the halfway point, with Gerber on one bank guarding their backs and Fetterman on the other, the NVA found them. There was a burst of firing from the jungle and the water around the men in the river began to splash. Hobbs dropped immediately, as if he had been shot. Quinn spun, blood on his shoulder. Rogers dived to the right and tried to reach the bank. Lawrence had grabbed Quinn and was trying to drag him across the river.

Gerber was up and running. He stayed close to the bank, running toward the sound of the machine gun. Fetterman tried to draw the enemy's attention to himself. Gerber glanced to the rear. Lawrence was close to the bank now, struggling to get Quinn out of the water, which churned around them as the enemy tried to kill them.

Gerber spotted the enemy machine gun about thirty yards in front of him. He pulled a grenade, whipped the pin from it and tossed it as hard as he could. He dropped flat, waited, and when the grenade exploded, was up and running. He leaped behind a tree, but the machine gun crew was down. One of them had lost an arm and was rolling around, trying unsuccessfully to stop the flow of blood.

Gerber turned, got to his feet but stayed near a tree. Lawrence had gotten Quinn under cover, and Hobbs and Rogers were now trying to cross the river. Gerber slung his weapon and dived into the water. He swam out as fast as he could, letting the current carry him along. Water soaked into everything he wore and flooded his boots. His rucksack filled with it, trying to drag him down. He stopped swimming and tried to stand. The current knocked him off his feet, but he finally got some footing. He dived forward once and his hands hit bottom, then he got his feet under him and stood. As he worked his way to the bank, the water poured from his clothes and rucksack.

As he got back onto dry land, there was another blast from the enemy. AKs on full-auto. Gerber dived for cover as the rounds smashed into the trees around him. He rolled once, ending up on his back, staring up into the canopy. He began to laugh because the situation was so damned ridiculous.

Firing began on his side of the bank. It was Fetterman's sniper rifle on single-shot. It was impossible to hear the other weapons because they were silenced.

Gerber rolled over and crawled to where Fetterman knelt, firing sporadically as targets appeared. When he was close, he asked, "How's Quinn?"

"Not good. A round through the shoulder tore up a lot of muscle and tissue. He'll be lucky if he can ever use it again."

"Can we move him?"

"I've sent him and Lawrence on, heading straight for South Vietnam. We'll cover."

Gerber moved around Fetterman to where Hobbs and Rogers were hiding. Both were firing carefully, trying to pick their targets. From the other side the enemy was putting out rounds from AKs and two RPDs. They weren't doing much damage, just shooting up the jungle.

Gerber took out his map again and checked it. He tried to spot a few landmarks and took sightings on them. He turned and looked over his shoulder. They had made good time from the enemy camp and might be something less than a klick from the border.

If they could pin the enemy down at the river for twenty or thirty minutes, they could probably get to South Vietnam before the enemy realized what had happened. Gerber moved forward and said, "Tony, hold your fire." Fetterman dropped back and looked at Gerber. "Let the others do the shooting," the captain said. "The enemy won't be able to hear it and that might work for us."

The firing from across the river slowed and stopped. Nothing happened for a moment, then a man appeared on the riverbank. Fetterman started to raise his rifle, but Gerber shook his head. "Let Hobbs or Rogers take him."

The man crouched at the edge of the water, as if checking it. He kept his head up, searching the jungle opposite them. A second man, his AK held in his hands, came out of the vegetation and knelt behind the first man. Hobbs took them, a burst low, into the water and then up onto the bank. There was no hammering of the M-16, just the dull popping and the quiet clatter of metal as the bolt worked.

One man fell into the water, struggled, then rolled face down, floating away from the bank. The second man turned to flee but was hit and knocked from his feet. He didn't move again.

The enemy opened fire again, but they seemed to have lost sight of the Americans. They were shooting randomly, trying to find where Hobbs was hidden.

Gerber moved toward Hobbs. "You and Rogers wait here for five minutes, then follow. Take anyone who shows himself. That'll slow them."

"Yes, sir."

"The thing is," said Gerber, "they're going to think time is on their side. They'll be waiting for reinforcements before coming at you. It's the same situation we always run into in South Vietnam. Before we get organized to attack, the VC slip away."

"Got it."

Gerber returned to Fetterman, and the two of them began to crawl away. As they cleared the area, they got to their feet. Fetterman stopped for a moment and asked, "Was that a good idea? Leaving those guys behind?"

"Hell, it gives Quinn a better chance."

"But we've scattered our men all over now."

"So that someone has a chance to escape. If one group is captured, the rest can get out."

They took off then, trying to catch up to Quinn and Lawrence. As they ran through the jungle, they heard more firing and then nothing. It was quiet for a while, three or four minutes, and then a burst of AKs and RPDs, followed by an explosion and then another.

"Mortars," said Fetterman.

"I hope Hobbs and Rogers got out of there before the enemy started using the mortars."

They kept going, running through the jungle, without knowing when they crossed into South Vietnam. When they came to a small clearing, they stopped short of it. There they found Quinn and Lawrence. Quinn looked bad, but he was still alive. With luck they would be able to get out of the field in only a couple of hours.

27

MACV HEADQUARTERS
SAIGON

General William C. Westmoreland stood at the head of the table, searching the faces of the men in the conference room with him. "I've called this meeting," he said, "to see if anyone can figure out just what the hell is going on at Khe Sanh. Any ideas, no matter how radical."

Jerry Maxwell, sitting at the end of the table, kept his eyes on the report in front of him and waited for someone else to speak up. Maxwell hadn't been feeling well for twenty-four hours, not since he'd received a report that Giap was in Hanoi, planning something new for the North Vietnamese war effort. Maxwell had a team in the field, hadn't heard from them for days and now knew that their target was absent, probably driven off by the Air Force raid he'd learned about after Gerber and Fetterman had been deployed.

A Marine colonel stood up. "There have been probes of the Khe Sanh combat base and there have been mortar and rocket attacks, but not once has the enemy made a real push to get into it. It's beginning to look as if they never planned to attack the combat base."

Westmoreland nodded and looked at the Air Force representative.

"Resupply by air is improving." The Air Force man stopped for a moment, then continued. "Or rather, maybe I should say that we're getting the supplies in there. We've had some trouble with the LAPES and the C-130s, but those are being worked out. A Marine aircraft on the ground was hit by enemy fire and blew up, killing the crew. We're not dropping everything onto the base. Ground fire around it is significant but not as heavy as it once was."

"What's the situation at the outposts?" asked Westmoreland.

Again the Marine colonel spoke. "Well, General, we've taken some heavy hits there, but we've thrown back everything that came at us. With the exception of Lang Vei, the enemy hasn't accomplished a great deal." The Marine looked down at his notes, then smiled broadly. "We have six tanks at Khe Sanh and their crews are praying that the NVA tanks come at them. It shouldn't be a contest."

Westmoreland sat down and wiped his face with his hand. He looked younger than he had when he had returned from Da Nang a couple of days before. Then the mood had been strained, with everyone worried about another Dien Bien Phu. Now they were upbeat, talking not like losers, but like soldiers who expected to win at every turn. The attitude had changed. The momentum of the siege had shifted.

"Operation Niagara is considered a success," said the Air Force officer. "We're confident our air power has reduced the likelihood that the enemy will mount a full assault on Khe Sanh. We're beginning to divert some of the assets to other problems."

"Mr. Maxwell?" Westmoreland said.

Maxwell shifted in his seat and didn't know what to say. The continued intelligence reports he'd received suggested the enemy was losing interest in Khe Sanh. The problem was the lack of success in overrunning any of the Marine outposts and the continuing rain of bombs from the air. The strategy of total air domination seemed to be working: keep the enemy from massing for the assault and you prevent the assault. Operation Niagara seemed to have done that, though there was no real evidence of it, other than the fact that the enemy hadn't attacked, even though it had seemed once or twice that attack was imminent.

Maxwell looked at the battle maps that had been taped to the wall of the conference room. Enemy units were shown around Khe Sanh, the Rockpile and Hue. In the rest of South Vietnam the fighting was tapering off. The grand plan had failed. The question was whether the NVA would push for one spectacular victory, or if they would get out to lick their wounds.

"We seem to have weathered the worst of it," said Maxwell. "The conditions at Khe Sanh, the early-morning fogs and the monsoons are tapering off and should be over in another two weeks, if that. The enemy will have to make a move before then or lose the initiative completely."

"What do you think will happen?" Westmoreland pressed.

Maxwell rubbed his eyes as he thought. Gerber and Fetterman were still out there, and they might have something to say about the next two weeks. Even if Giap wasn't around, they might take out someone and disrupt the enemy chain of command. There were so many variables. But Maxwell also remembered Westmoreland's parting words a couple of days earlier. "Sir, I believe there is no longer a real threat to the Marines at Khe Sanh."

"What the hell does that mean?" asked the Marine colonel.

"It means the enemy is still there but is no longer in a position to make an assault. There could still be some bitter fighting outside the wire, and maybe at some of the outposts, but Khe Sanh is safe from a major ground assault."

Westmoreland slapped the table and laughed. "That, gentlemen, is what coordination between air power, artillery and ground forces can do. Twenty thousand enemy soldiers around Khe Sanh and it isn't sufficient to attack."

"The battle isn't over yet," the Marine colonel said.

"It's as good as over," said Westmoreland.

HOBBS AND ROGERS came out of the trees and walked up to Gerber, who had been watching them for three minutes. Hobbs dropped to the ground and said, "I don't think they followed us. We got out just before the mortars began to fall."

Gerber looked over at Quinn. His face was pale and covered with sweat. There was a blood-soaked field dressing around his shoulder. He didn't look as if he could walk more than a hundred meters.

Gerber got out the map and studied it. They appeared to be due south of the Special Forces camp at Lang Vei. It couldn't be more than ten, twelve klicks away. Khe Sanh was no more than thirty. If Quinn hadn't been wounded, they could have gotten there in a couple of hours. "How you doing, Quinn?"

"Fine, sir. Just point me in the right direction and I'll get myself out of here."

"I don't think that'll be necessary. We'll all get out together."

"It's getting late," said Fetterman.

Gerber got to his feet and looked north. He folded the map and stuffed it into his pocket "Tony, take the point, and keep it slow." He turned back to Quinn. "You start to feel weak, you let us know. We're close enough for all of us to get out in one piece. Let's not fuck it up."

"Yes, sir."

"Hobbs, you stick with Quinn. Rogers, you and Lawrence hang back to cover the rear. Let's go, Tony."

Fetterman took off again, the pace slow and easy. He stayed inside the jungle, avoiding the clearing in front of them. They worked their way deeper into the vegetation. Fetterman now worked at not leaving any sign or making any noise. Now that they were in South Vietnam, they were among the NVA divisions that surrounded Khe Sanh.

They went down a hill, crossed a valley and started up again. Fetterman slowed, conscious that the heat of the afternoon, coupled with the loss of blood, was going to make it difficult for Quinn. When he reached the top of the hill, he stopped.

Gerber caught up with him and saw the problem. Once again it was as if they had reached the moon. Ahead of them were thousands of craters from the bombing of the enemy rally points. Much of the jungle had been burned away, leaving the blackened tree trunks standing in the barren country. There wasn't the look of a red scar because of the napalm that had been used. The land was blackened from fires caused by the bombing.

Then a light breeze blowing up from the valley washed over them. There was a stench to it, at first just a sickening undercurrent, and then something stronger. The patrol spread out and waited.

"Tony?" asked Gerber.

"There's a body around here somewhere." He stood up and faced into the breeze. "That direction."

Gerber nodded. "Let's check it out. Hobbs, you and the others remain here. Quinn, you've got an opportunity to rest."

"Yes, sir."

"Lead on, Tony."

They started down the hill and hadn't gone very far when they realized it was more than just one body. It had to be many—dozens, maybe hundreds. The smell was now overpowering, almost a living thing that pushed at them, but they pressed on. Gerber rubbed his face frequently and held his nose, breathing through his mouth, but that didn't help. It was like entering a slaughterhouse where the animals were allowed to rot.

The sounds of the jungle changed as the men moved lower on the slopes. The breeze was rippling the leaves. Then came a faint buzzing, like a power saw in the distance.

Fetterman halted and looked at Gerber. His eyes were watering and he was breathing through his mouth, too. "You want to continue?" he asked.

"Let's see what we've found," said Gerber.

They moved forward, the stench rising in front of them almost like a physical barrier that they had to fight their way through. They pushed past a group of ferns and found the first of the dead—one man, an arm and a leg missing, lying face-down in the dirt. The back of his uniform had been blackened by napalm.

Gerber moved beyond him and discovered the source of the smell. There were dozens of dead, both men and women, all wearing the uniform of the NVA or the VC. Or parts of the uniform. Some bodies lacked arms of legs or heads. Some had great holes ripped into them. Uniforms were blood-soaked and so were bodies, many of them burned.

And there were great black clouds of flies, buzzing, nearly roaring. Thousands of them crawling on and in the bodies and hovering over them.

"What the hell?" asked Fetterman.

"The bombings and artillery," said Gerber. He wanted to search through the stacks of dead soldiers and see if there were any documents or unit insignia. He wanted to know if all these dead belonged to the same battalion or regiment. He wanted to know if all the dead were enemies. If they were, it would mean that an American bombing had hit the right target at the right time.

But he couldn't move closer. The odor was too strong. It seemed to push at him, driving him back. From the bits of uniforms he could see, there wouldn't be much he could find out. Just that a couple of hundred people had been killed and that the NVA or the VC had hidden the bodies here—not hidden them well, but they'd tried.

Fetterman forced himself closer and then had to retreat. He shook his head. "Couldn't see any bullet holes. Looks like they were killed by artillery or bombs, but probably not around here."

"So Charlie wasted a great deal of energy to move the bodies out here where the Americans probably wouldn't find them."

"And if we don't know that we had such success, then we worry about enemy soldiers. This hides the evidence of a major defeat." Fetterman shook his head. "There might be five hundred people lying here."

"Let's get out of here," said Gerber.

Without a word, Fetterman turned and started up the hill. As they headed back to where the others waited, Gerber knew the intel boys wouldn't be happy with the lack of information. They would want exact counts, unit identification and weapon counts, none of which Gerber had. But then there wasn't much they could do, except note the location so that those intel boys, if they felt they needed more information, would know where to look for it.

As they approached their own temporary camp, Fetterman said, "If that happened to the enemy often, it could destroy their ability to attack."

"It could explain a lot of things," said Gerber.

When they reached the others, Gerber asked, "How's Quinn?"

"He's resting," Hobbs said, "but I don't think he has the strength to walk much farther. The heat's sapped the little he had."

"Lang Vei isn't more than five klicks. We could carry him that far in a few hours and arrive there about dark." Gerber studied his map. "That seems to be the thing to do."

The others nodded their agreement. Quinn, who had closed his eyes, as if he was asleep, opened them and said, "We make it that quick and I'll buy the beer."

THE PRESIDENT PACED the Oval Office, slapping the newspaper against his hand. He spun, struck the desk with the newspaper and demanded, "What the hell is going on at Khe Sanh?"

Lockhart, who'd already told the President about Lang Vei, which had been generally ignored by the press, was surprised. He sat in the leather chair and felt his face grow cold and his stomach turn over.

"The American press seems to think we're about to lose the base at Khe Sanh. They seem to think we have a real problem there. I want to know what it is."

Lockhart tried to take refuge in his leather folder, flipping through the papers and reports, but the trick didn't fool the President.

"Colonel, you better have a few answers for me."

Lockhart wiped the sweat from his face and shuffled his papers. "I'm afraid I don't understand the problem, Mr. President."

"The problem is the reports in the media comparing Khe Sanh to Dien Bien Phu. The problem is the constant comparisons and the suggestion we are losing there."

Lockhart took a deep breath. "The media are misinformed. They don't understand how the military operates. They see a massive enemy attack at Tet and assume we've taken a beating when it's simply not true."

The President dropped into the chair behind his desk and leaned forward. "I'm not at all interested in water that has passed under the bridge. I want to know the situation at Khe Sanh."

Lockhart smiled. "It's improving daily. More supplies are getting in every day and there's no indication the enemy's building up a force to attack. They've backed off from some of their old positions. There might not be a confrontation."

The President opened the paper and stabbed a finger at the headline. "It says here that Khe Sanh is in danger of being overrun."

"That's simply not true, Mr. President."

"The press is going to be asking me for some information about Khe Sanh, and I can't go out there and feed them a line like that."

"Why not?"

The President's head snapped up and he pointed at Lockhart. "Don't you ever question me again, boy. You're here to give me answers, not ask a lot of damned fool questions."

"Yes, sir." Lockhart pawed through his reports again as his heart hammered in his chest. He felt suddenly weak and thought he might be sick. Sweat popped out on his forehead as if it was suddenly too warm in the room.

Trying to cover his sudden distress, he said, "In the few major attacks on outposts, the enemy casualties have been significantly higher than ours. They weren't able to attack those outposts again. The comparisons between Khe Sanh and Dien Bien Phu are breaking down. There isn't the continuous shrinkage of our position as the enemy tunnels in. Our men are being resupplied. The wounded are being evacuated. The French were able to do none of that."

"But the enemy still surrounds the combat base."

"Yes, Mr. President, they do. But what difference does it make? In the past, if you had a fort surrounded, you had it cut off from help. We're putting supplies in there daily. We're flying in replacements."

The President wrote himself a note. "Good."

"If you're interested in destroying this Dien Bien Phu nonsense, you can point out that the French had no way to resupply and reinforce their men. They had no air power and they had very little artillery support. We have two divisions poised to thrust up Route 9, if we deem it necessary."

The President rocked back in his chair, finally looking relaxed. He reached out and touched the newspaper. "Reporters claim the enemy's massing for an attack."

"The media doesn't know about Operation Niagara," said Lockhart.

"All right, Colonel, I believe you now. What do you think is going to happen at Khe Sanh?"

Lockhart had spent two days preparing for that question, knowing someone was going to ask it sometime. He had read everything he could find, including the reports in the press, which missed so many of the subtleties of the battle. Missed the spirit of the Marines and the attitudes of the pilots who had to fly in the supplies. Lockhart had studied it all, including the destruction of Lang Vei, which wasn't the fault of the Special Forces defending, but of the weapons they had been given.

"Sir, I think we'll see the enemy hanging on there for another few weeks. There'll be some small engagements, and then our people will finish with everything that's diverting attention. We'll capture Hue, and the enemy who attacked all over South Vietnam will be gone. Without these diversions, the First Cav will roll up Route 9 and that will be the end of it. No Dien Bien Phu for us. Nothing.''

"You mean it will just end, without any attempt to overrun the base."

"That's how it's shaping up now. Any advantage the enemy might have held has been eroded. The weather that hampered our operations is clearing, so that it's becoming our ally as well. The best opportunity for the assault was during the massive Tet attacks when we would have had trouble providing assistance. That didn't happen.''

The President shook his head. "All that preparation for absolutely nothing.''

Lockhart misunderstood the President. He said, "If we hadn't made the preparations, then there would have been some real problems in holding on there. It was all necessary.''

"No, I meant on the part of the enemy. To work so hard to accomplish something and come up short.''

"That's the way it goes,'' said Lockhart. "Better them than us.''

The President turned and looked out the windows behind his desk. He studied the scene outside, then asked, "There really isn't going to be a Dien Bien Phu at Khe Sanh?''

Lockhart wondered what more he could say to convince the President. There was no longer any concern in his mind. Then he remembered something he had read in one of the reports, something that would show just how confident the Americans were.

"No, sir,'' he said, "no Dien Bien Phu. Hell, sir, we're even getting the men out of Khe Sanh in time for their DEROS. Not one Marine, one soldier, has had to spend an extra hour in-country. That's how well we're doing.''

28

THE JUNGLES OF SOUTH VIETNAM, SOUTH OF KHE SANH COMBAT BASE

They made a stretcher from a poncho liner and two seven-foot-long saplings cut from the jungle, folding the saplings into the poncho liner and then putting Quinn on it. Hobbs and Lawrence took the first shift carrying it while Fetterman had the point and Gerber brought up the rear. They moved quietly, knowing there would be NVA and VC patrols out. The enemy presence was everywhere. They found dropped and broken equipment, scraps of cloth, the remains of campfires and spilled food. It seemed that when enemy soldiers moved in large units, they were as sloppy as the Americans.

Only once did they have to dive for cover. They'd had plenty of warning, the voices of the enemy coming to them from more than a hundred yards. Voices talking quietly and then a piercing laugh. The patrol, twelve NVA soldiers in khaki, carrying AK-47s and RPGs, was just out for a stroll in the jungle. They walked by Gerber and his team and then disappeared into the vegetation. No one moved for ten minutes, and then Fetterman slipped off to scout in front. When he came back, they started off again.

Twice they passed piles of NVA bodies, once no more than two dozen and the second time as many as a hundred. These men and women wore the parts of their uniforms that were blood-soaked, but everything else was gone. The enemy had stripped the equipment, weapons and ammo and the clothing that was still good, and left only the dead as a mute reminder that not everything planned at Khe Sanh was going their way.

When Hobbs and Lawrence tired of carrying the stretcher, Gerber and Rogers took over with Fetterman left on duty as the point. Gerber had decided that in a jungle filled with the enemy, he wanted the best man on point, and that was Fetterman. There was no one who could smell out the enemy better than he. There was no one who could avoid ambushes or booby traps better, and with only a couple of klicks to go till they reached Lang Vei, Gerber didn't want to walk into anything.

The environment seemed to change as they approached Lang Vei. They noticed that the jungle in the vicinity had taken a real beating. Trees and bushes were stripped of their leaves. The bark was shredded by shrapnel and bullets. The trunks had turned gray as the trees died, and the bushes were deformed, leaves intact on one side and dying on the other. There were shell holes in the ground and in the trunks of the larger trees. There was the buzzing of millions of flies, feeding on the death around them. There were the cries of scavengers, which were flourishing in the suddenly rich environment of death. The air was no longer heavy with humidity, but with the smell of death.

They began to pass more bodies, singly or in pairs. There was a clump of five, all women, and another of ten who had been badly burned. There were naked bodies and those fully clothed. There were few weapons, mainly those that had been shot up so badly that they were of no use. And the closer they got to Lang Vei, the worse it became.

They were within a klick of Lang Vei when the sun set, leaving them enclosed in deep shadows and almost no light. Fetterman halted then and waited for Gerber to catch up to him. ''Sir, I don't like this.''

Gerber nodded and waited for Fetterman to continue.

"By now, we should be getting some indication that there's a camp close to us. The hum of the generator, flares overhead, maybe a mad minute. There's nothing."

Gerber turned and looked into the vegetation. "How close do you think we are?"

"Inside a klick, I'd bet. It's no secret that the camp is there, so there's no reason for them to be quiet. We should be able to hear something."

"Given the situation here, maybe they've imposed light-and-noise discipline to cut the advantages of the enemy in the field."

Fetterman nodded but said, "I don't think so."

"Let's move on ahead carefully, and then as we get closer, you can scout the situation for us."

Fetterman started forward again and Gerber hung back, thinking about what Fetterman had said. The stench of death was still in the air, maybe heavier than it had been, but that didn't seem to mean anything more.

They moved on another four or five hundred meters and halted again. Fetterman retreated to where Gerber crouched. "We're about to break out of the jungle and I see no sign of Lang Vei."

"Could be I didn't read the map right," said Gerber.

"When was the last time you made a mistake like that?"

"I think it was at Bragg about five years ago."

"My point exactly. So what do we do now?"

Gerber pulled the binoculars from his rucksack. They were still damp from the river, but that didn't mean they wouldn't work. He motioned Fetterman forward, then crawled to the edge of the jungle.

From there he could make out vague shapes above the ground. Nothing distinctive, just an abstraction of shapes created by the lights and shadows from the distant flares that hung over the Khe Sanh combat base. There was no shooting anywhere around. No artillery, no bombs and no mortars. It was strangely quiet.

Finally he slipped to the rear and shook his head. "Looks deserted. Maybe they decided their butts were hanging too far out and abandoned the camp."

"You really think that's a possibility?"

"Given the situation, I think it might have happened. We'll need to get closer to find out."

"Still that stink in the air," said Fetterman. "The worst it's been."

Gerber put his binoculars away. "Let's check this out. Thirty minutes at the most and then back here."

"Yes, sir."

Gerber crawled to the right and then got to his feet. He stood in a crouch, staring into the darkness, but could see nothing that would answer his questions. He moved forward slowly and cautiously, his eyes moving across the field in front of him, his ears pricked and waiting, searching for some sign that the defenders were there and alert. But all he noticed was the increasing stench of death.

As he neared the first strands of the wire, he dropped to one knee and studied the ground around him. He could see only vague shapes and irregular patterns. He reached out for the wire but there was no tension in it and no cans on it to rattle. He pulled on it and discovered that it was loose. He pushed it out of the way and then began to crawl forward slowly. He had designed enough camp defenses to know what to look for, but he found nothing.

Quickly, easily, he worked his way through the wire. There were no trip flares, no claymores. There were holes blasted, clearing paths, and Gerber knew what had happened. He didn't have to continue any farther, but he pushed himself on until he reached the berm.

To the right was the remains of a bunker, the twisted barrel of a machine gun poking up through the pile of sandbags and broken timbers. The odor of death was heavy near it, and Gerber felt his stomach roll and flop. He turned his head, afraid that he was going to be suddenly sick, but that didn't happen.

He crawled over the berm and dropped into the camp. There was little light, only the stars overhead, the flares in the distance, the moon just beginning to rise. But he didn't need much light to see the destruction around him. The ground was littered with bodies, many of them stripped. There were no weapons around, the victors having collected them all.

Debris from the fight lay everywhere—shell casings, chunks of concrete, broken sandbags, equipment and bodies. Since the dead lay where they fell, it was obvious the camp had been overrun. He didn't have to explore any farther to learn that. Still, he was drawn toward the interior.

He crossed over the redoubt into the center of the camp. Reinforced concrete bunkers, probably some of the best-built in South Vietnam, had been blasted open. In the rubble at the bottom of them were the bodies of the defenders. From the destruction, it appeared to have been a hell of a fight, but there was no way of telling for sure. The bodies of the enemy dead had been removed after the camp fell. The only evidence was the appearance of the camp. It had been blown to hell and gone.

There was nothing there he could do. He turned and started back the way he had come. He crossed the redoubt, then stopped. In the shifting, swinging light provided by the flares at Khe Sanh, he could see tread marks on the ground. That would explain how the camp had been taken. The enemy had used tanks.

Gerber wasn't sure the old Triple Nickel could have withstood an armor assault. The VC and NVA had used a full regiment and several additional battalions trying to overrun the Triple Nickel and had failed. It had been a near thing at the end, and a couple of tanks looming out of the rice paddies might have been enough to turn the tide.

"Fuck," he said quietly.

He got to the bunker line and studied the land beyond. Craters and blackening of the ground were mute evidence of the fight. It hadn't been easy for the Communists. They had to have taken a beating trying to get into the camp. But once they did, if they were backed by the armor, it wouldn't have taken long to overrun it.

Gerber hurried through the gaps in the wire and reached the jungle. He moved to the rendezvous point and sat down, his back to a tree. He gulped at the air, wanting it to wash away the stench that filled his head, but the air wasn't clean. He wiped at the sweat on his face and wished to hell he knew what had happened. Not that many Special Forces camps were overrun.

Fetterman loomed out of the darkness and crouched next to him. He wiped his forehead with the sleeve of his uniform and said, "Camp's overrun. Found a burned-out tank. Soviet T-76."

"Well, that shoots us down now."

"Let's continue on," said Fetterman. "Old Lang Vei is pretty much intact. We can hole up there and call for choppers at first light."

"What's it look like?"

"Not bad. Not shot to hell like the camp. We'd have a good defensive perimeter if the enemy stumbled on us."

"Okay," said Gerber. "Let's do it."

They returned to the men and told them what they had found. Then, with Fetterman leading, they headed north again, skirting the edge of Lang Vei and stopping at Route 9. They hesitated there. Gerber knew that a short walk, a few miles at most, would put them at Khe Sanh about dawn or a little before. He wasn't sure he wanted to walk up to the combat base at night. Either way, waiting at Old Lang Vei, or walking to Khe Sanh, would put them there at dawn. The easiest, and probably the safest course, was to sit tight at Old Lang Vei.

Fetterman crossed the road, stopped and then crawled forward again. He reached the outskirts and entered Old Lang Vei. A moment later he reappeared and waved the men forward. Hobbs and Rogers, carrying the stretcher, crossed first, guarded by Gerber and Lawrence.

Fetterman located a bunker that was in good shape and the men moved into it. Then Gerber slipped out, taking a look around. Satisfied that no one knew they were there, he returned. Fetterman had already set up the security and the schedule. Gerber agreed and they settled in to wait for morning.

The night turned out to be relatively quiet. There was some shooting around two in the morning. Small arms and then artillery, but that dropped off. Jets crisscrossed overhead for a while, then disappeared to the east.

At dawn Gerber got on the radio, calling for helicopter evacuation from Old Lang Vei. There were no helicopters available at Khe Sanh, but choppers were at Quang Tri. They would be alerted, and when they were ten minutes out, they would call for information.

The choppers arrived sooner than expected, not that Gerber minded. He tossed a smoke grenade, and as he and the others emerged from the bunker, two gunships passed low over them. Gerber waved at the door gunner, who waved back. A moment later the third ship dived out of the sky, landing with its nose over the billowing purple smoke.

Quinn was lifted in and the others scrambled in after him. The chopper spun 180 degrees, as if mounted on a pole, and the nose dropped. Then the aircraft raced across the open ground, popped up and climbed rapidly. From behind came the ripping of a single machine gun. The door gunner returned fire.

One of the gunships rolled in and fired rockets from the pods on its sides. There were twin explosions, and then the gunship broke away from the target.

The slick continued to climb out until they were two thousand feet above the ground. The crew chief reached around from his well and touched Gerber on the shoulder. "How bad's your man hurt?"

"Not too bad. Why?"

"We could land at Khe Sanh for Charlie Med there to patch him up, or take him on to Quang Tri."

"Quang Tri will be fine." Gerber glanced to the right and then asked, "Can we get airlift out of Quang Tri to Saigon?"

The crew chief ducked his head, nodding once, and said, "Might have to hop it down. Da Nang to Nha Trang to Saigon, something like that, but you can do it."

"Thanks," said Gerber. He sat back then, looking out the cargo compartment door as the Vietnamese landscape raced under them. So much had happened in the past few days. He had learned so much about what was happening around Khe

Sanh. It would be good to get to Saigon and let someone else have the information.

THE TRIP TO SAIGON wasn't quite the ordeal the crew chief had described. They took another chopper to Da Nang and arrived in time to board an Air Force C-130 to Tan Son Nhut. There was no time there for a shower or a change of clothes, so the other passengers stayed as far away as possible from Gerber and Fetterman. Hobbs and his men remained at Quang Tri with Quinn, figuring someone would find them in a couple of days and put them back to work.

In Saigon they took a taxi from the airfield to the hotel so they could shower and change uniforms. Within fifteen minutes they were in another taxi, risking their lives so that they could get to Maxwell and tell him everything.

They had no trouble getting into MACV and down to the iron gate that guarded the inner reaches of the headquarters, but the MP there refused to let them in and called Maxwell to vouch for them.

As Maxwell approached, Gerber said, "Sorry, Jerry, but he insisted on spoiling the surprise."

"You can let them through," said Maxwell. He was wearing his usual rumpled white suit and looked as if he was about to cry.

Gerber signed in and asked, "Not happy to see us?"

Maxwell shook his head. "You failed, didn't you?"

Gerber scratched his chin. "Depends on your definition of 'failed.' We might have something for you, something that will improve everyone's attitude around here."

When Fetterman finished signing his name, adding the date and time, Maxwell turned and retreated toward his office.

Fetterman pulled Gerber aside and asked, "Is there something going on that we don't know about?"

"Tony, I imagine there are a dozen things going on we don't know about. It just depends on whether any of them affect us."

Maxwell opened the door to his office and let Gerber and Fetterman enter. Gerber took the visitor's chair, dropping into it and hooking a leg over the arm. Fetterman moved to the row of filing cabinets and leaned against them.

"Let's hurry this up," said Maxwell. "I'm pretty busy."

"Jerry," said Gerber, "I don't think I like your attitude. You send us out on a wild-goose chase, make a snide comment about failure on our glorious return and then try to rush us out. It's just not nice."

Maxwell sat down at his desk and folded his hands. "Giap is in North Vietnam."

"That's certainly not our fault," said Fetterman.

"Especially not after the Air Force tried to blow him out of the jungle in an attempt that had no possibility of success," Gerber added.

"Now how the hell would you know that?" asked Maxwell.

"Because, dear boy," said Fetterman, "the North Vietnamese took the simple precaution of siting their antenna about ten klicks from their radio. SOP, for Christ's sake."

"How do you know?"

"We found the antenna and followed it to its source," Gerber grinned broadly. "We found their little headquarters, but of course Giap wasn't there."

Maxwell was suddenly interested. He grabbed a notepad and pencil and asked for details. Gerber filled him in, telling him about the officer and the car.

When Gerber finished the narrative, Maxwell said, "That's great. It had to hurt them. And you say there was no pursuit?"

"Not really. We had a few problems," said Gerber, "but I think that was more us running into a patrol than an actual pursuit."

"Good," said Maxwell. "Something positive to give to Westmoreland."

"We came across something else," said Fetterman. "Something around Khe Sanh that might be of interest."

"Tell me."

Fetterman described the bodies they had found, the piles of dead soldiers scattered throughout the jungle to the south and west of Khe Sanh. He told of the destruction at Lang Vei and the burned-out tank he had seen. He mentioned the one patrol, but that there seemed to be a real lack of activity there—

not what would be expected if the enemy was massing for a push.

"Intelligence puts ten or twenty thousand enemy soldiers into the field around Khe Sanh," said Maxwell.

"Not anymore," said Gerber. "We'd have run into more of them if there were that many people around. There's evidence that there was once that many, but not anymore."

"You're sure of this?"

"Shit, Maxwell, we just came from there. We saw evidence that there had been thousands of enemy soldiers there, but when we went through there they were definitely gone."

Maxwell waved a hand, trying to slow Gerber down. He wrote as fast as he could. He looked up and asked, "What about around the combat base itself?"

"Jerry, we were near Lang Vei and not that far from the base. My guess, from the evidence, is that the bombings and the artillery have caused the enemy to scatter. Maybe they pulled back into Laos. I don't know. I just know they're not around Khe Sanh and Lang Vei."

"You know what this means?" asked Maxwell. "It means the siege is over."

"No, it doesn't," said Gerber. "It just means the enemy has pulled back."

"Without even trying to take the combat base. They're slipping away. Oh, there'll still be trouble around Khe Sanh, but we don't have to worry about another Dien Bien Phu."

"Nice that we could cheer you up," said Fetterman.

"Your information about the bodies is the capper. That explains why they haven't hit the camp. They haven't been able to mass their troops. Each time they do, we hit them. It's beautiful."

"One other thing, Jerry," Gerber said. "I think someone had better find out who was flying the plane that took us to Laos, and get the crew a hatful of medals. They did one hell of a job."

"Meaning?" asked Maxwell.

"Meaning," said Fetterman, his voice deepening, "that they flew on straight and level, giving us a chance to get out while their airplane burned up around them. They didn't even try to get out of there. Gave us a good jump on the mission.''

"Okay," said Maxwell, nodding gravely. "I'll pass the word along and see what can be arranged. No one got out, huh?"

"We looked for their chutes, but there weren't any. Hell, they never really had the chance," said Fetterman.

"Okay," said Maxwell again, making a note to himself.

"So what's the next move?" asked Gerber.

"For you two? I'd say a steak dinner in Saigon. I'll even buy it for you. You might not have hit Giap, but the information you came back with is even better. There's going to be a bunch of happy people here tonight."

"What about the men at Khe Sanh?" asked Gerber.

"The worst is over for them. Harassment from this point on, but that's all. No big assault to grab headlines. Just a fizzling that will soon be replaced with more important news."

Gerber looked at Fetterman. Somehow he felt cheated. There should have been something more to it, but if he had been asked for an explanation, he wouldn't have had it. He knew Maxwell was right. The real trouble at Khe Sanh was over. There would be a few minor skirmishes, but the enemy had lost the initiative.

"Shall we meet you for that dinner, or are you going to give us the money?" Fetterman asked.

"Give me two hours," said Maxwell, "and then meet me at the Continental Shelf. Dinner and relaxation there."

"Got it," said Gerber.

29

THE WHITE HOUSE

Lockhart quietly read the latest reports from Khe Sanh. Minor skirmishes with the enemy forced to retreat before they were able to cause any real damage. Firefights that killed more of the enemy than the Marines. There had been a bad one on February 25, and the Marines still hadn't recovered the bodies, but there was nothing like the fear at the beginning of the year that Khe Sanh would be another Dien Bien Phu.

Lockhart closed the reports and sat back, feeling relaxed. He'd even gotten home for dinner the night before, and no one had called him back. Khe Sanh was moving from the front pages of the newspapers to the back, sometimes not even mentioned.

There was a tap at his door and Lockhart called, "Come on in."

A Presidential aide stepped through the door and glanced around. "Anything going on down here?"

Lockhart waved at his nearly clear desk. "A couple of reports, but nothing of significance. The Marines are behind their wire and the North Vietnamese aren't trying to get in. Rockets and mortars and a few ground probes."

"Okay, then, let's get this packed up and get it out of here."

"What?"

"Office space in the White House is at a premium. Every square inch is being used. You yourself just said things are winding down."

"All true," said Lockhart. He felt his stomach turn over and didn't understand why he was upset. Maybe it was the special status that an office in the White House had afforded him. Maybe it was having the President's ear. He knew the minute he walked out he would be nothing more than just another lieutenant colonel, and there were thousands of them in Washington.

"So," said the aide, "the priorities have shifted and someone else needs the office. This shouldn't put a burden on you. You have an office at the Pentagon."

"There's still the siege at Khe Sanh."

"You've told the President on several occasions it's winding down. Nothing but skirmishes."

"Still, you never can tell," said Lockhart, not wanting to move an inch.

"Listen," said the aide, "this happens all the time. People who have special knowledge come and go. I assure you the President is aware of your contribution, but now we have to put someone else in this office. Jessie, you still out there?"

A tall dark-haired woman wearing a skirt that ended at midthigh stepped to the door. "Yes."

"This will be your office now."

She glanced at Lockhart and smiled weakly. "I hope I'm not putting you out on the street."

Lockhart got to his feet and shook his head. "I think my tour is finished here," he said dryly.

"Will you need long to get your things out?" She laughed and added quickly, "That sounded simply awful."

"I'll agree with that," said Lockhart.

"I'm sure the colonel can be out of here by one. You can move in then."

Jessie came forward and held out her hand. "I'm Jessie Roberts. Sorry to be doing this to you."

"I don't mean to sound cynical, but you'll find yourself out of here soon."

Roberts continued to smile. "I have no doubt about it."

"We have work to do," said the aide. "Colonel, we'll leave you to finish clearing up your work here. There'll be a couple of men down for the safe in a little while. You're to remove any classified documents in it and take them to be destroyed."

"Fine," said Lockhart, dropping back into his chair.

Roberts stood there for a moment, then said, "I am sorry about this. Maybe I could buy you a drink, or lunch."

"No, thank you. Now I know how the fellow I replaced felt. My moment in the sun is over. I know it's not your fault."

"Well, if you're sure about that drink."

"Positive. Thanks for the gesture."

The aide touched her arm. "Let's leave the colonel to his own devices."

They left the office. Lockhart watched them go, then opened the middle drawer of his desk. He took out the yellow pads he had been using, sat back and laughed. The whole incident had ended with a whimper and not with the bang he'd expected.

CORPORAL WILLIAM DOBSON stood at the gate, waiting for the MPs to let the patrol out. It had been a long time since the Marines had run a patrol from Khe Sanh. They had been content to sit behind the wire and let Charlie come to them. Now they were going out in search of him.

The patrol leader, a sergeant who had been at Khe Sanh for six months, checked each of the twelve men with him. He worked his way along the squad, making sure each Marine had plenty of ammunition, water, grenades and a first-aid kit. Satisfied, he nodded to the MPs and they opened the gate.

The point man hurried out, then slowed when he was fifty yards ahead of them. As the rest of the patrol left the combat base, the point crossed the road and began to swing south around the base of a hill. He crossed through the waist-high elephant grass and then into a thick tangle of bushes, vines and ferns.

He waited there until the rest of the patrol closed the gap between them and then pushed on. Dobson reached the jungle and wished they could turn around and go home. He didn't want to enter the trees, but there was nothing he could do about it now.

He pushed on, and a vine grabbed at him. He shrugged it off and then ducked under a low limb. He stood up and slipped his finger around the trigger of his weapon, aware of everything around him—the colors of the vegetation, the shadows and the patches of sunlight, the heat and the humidity and the sounds. Under his flak jacket his uniform was soaked. He was nervous, feeling the strain of the first patrol out of Khe Sanh in weeks.

The squad slowed and then began to advance at a faster pace. Dobson kept his eyes and head moving, searching for signs that the enemy was close. He stooped once and picked up an AK round lying on the ground, but it was tarnished, as if it had lain there for weeks.

And then, just as he was beginning to relax, there was a single explosion at the head of the patrol. Dobson leaped to the right, rolled and came up facing the front. A machine gun opened fire and then two, three, four M-16s. Another grenade detonated and the shrapnel cut through the jungle overhead. There was a rattle as the dirt cascaded back to the jungle floor.

''Let's go!'' shouted someone over the sound of the hammering machine guns and blazing M-16s.

Dobson watched as two Marines got to their feet, glanced at each other and then ran forward, hunched over. Dobson didn't want to move, but he didn't want to be left behind, either. He got to his knees and listened to the shooting. The machine gun had stopped firing, but the M-16s hadn't. He could hear the rounds snapping through the vegetation, ripping at leaves and slamming into tree trunks.

On his feet finally, he ran forward, leaped over a log and saw three Marines lying on the ground, firing into the jungle. None of them was aiming. Each held his weapon up over his head and fired on full-auto. Dobson dived for cover near them, rolled and aimed his weapon. There were no targets.

Two of the others ran past him and dived to the jungle floor. One of them ripped off a burst that tore the hell out of the vegetation, but there was no response to it. The enemy machine gun was still silent.

"On your feet," shouted the sergeant as he moved forward, waving one arm.

Dobson got up slowly, and then knelt near a large tree trunk expecting the enemy to fire again, but it didn't happen. He worked his way forward and then spotted the barrel of the machine gun poking through a bush. He dropped, swinging on it, but the enemy still didn't fire. A Marine appeared from the jungle. He carried his rifle in the crook of his arm like a hunter in a farmer's field.

"That's got them."

Dobson got to his feet and walked slowly over to the machine gun nest. He kept his M-16 pointed at it, waiting for the surprise attack that never came. The enemy soldiers were sprawled behind their weapon. One of them had a bullet hole in his forehead, a neat little hole, blackened around the edges with very little blood. Another man was on his side, his stomach and chest ripped open, his blood staining the ground around him. The last man was missing an arm and part of his head and shoulder. The bone gleamed in the afternoon sun. Already the flies were beginning to gather, their buzzing unnaturally loud.

"Ambush failed," said the sergeant. "They were nervous and fired too soon. Way too soon."

"Now what?" asked Dobson.

The sergeant grinned. He had perfect teeth. Bright white. They didn't belong in the mouth of a soldier in the jungles of Vietnam. They should have belonged to a movie actor in Hollywood.

"I think we've done our job," said the sergeant. "Time to head home."

"Christ," said Dobson, "I thought we were about through with all this. I thought the enemy was getting out of here."

"Don't let this discourage you, son. These guys aren't regulars. Just three dummies, left behind for a few days. The best troops are gone. These are poorly trained irregulars and not the cream."

"You sure?"

"Two weeks ago we'd have lost half the squad in the first few seconds of the ambush. Maybe all of us would have been killed. Now none of our people are dead. All the VC are. That tell you anything?"

"Tells me they weren't very good."

"Right. Help police up the area, grab all the weapons and equipment around here and then we'll head back to the barn via direct."

Dobson picked up one of the AKs and slung it over his shoulder. As he did, he finally realized he had made it through the siege. He was one of the few Marines who had been at the base when the assault had started and who was still there at the end. The siege hadn't ended with the bang everyone had expected. It had ended with the whimper of the inexperienced.

EPILOGUE

KHE SANH COMBAT BASE JUNE, 1968

Sergeant Jim Goddard sat behind the wheel of the jeep and watched as the engineers set the final charges. The men ran across the open ground and leaped over a short wall of sandbags. A moment later there was an explosion and the last of the bunkers that had ringed the combat base was gone. Before the red dust had settled there was a rumbling, and then an OD green bulldozer appeared. The blade slipped down and pushed dirt into the crater where the bunker had been.

"That's got it," said the lieutenant who was standing near the jeep.

Goddard shook his head in disbelief. Not so long ago the Marines had fought and died to defend the combat base and now the engineers had just finished destroying it. They had blown up every bunker, knocked down every structure and carted away every piece of lumber, tin or steel that could be reused, and then had burned everything else. They had bulldozed the trenches and the bunkers and the airstrip. They had wiped out every trace of the combat base, making sure there was absolutely nothing left for the VC or the NVA.

"You about ready?" asked the lieutenant.

Goddard reached down for the ignition switch and started the engine. He turned back and glanced at the empty plateau. If it hadn't been for the damage done by the bulldozers as they covered over the trenches and the bunkers, there would have been no reason to suspect the Americans had built a base there.

"Two hundred and five Marines," said Goddard, shaking his head.

"What about them?"

"That's the official number of Marines killed defending the combat base. Now we're taking it apart. Bulldozing it."

The lieutenant climbed into the jeep and shrugged. "It served its purpose and now that purpose is over."

Goddard leaned forward, his elbows on the steering wheel. "You really believe that? You believe that in January and February the base is important but in June it's not?"

"I don't know," said the lieutenant.

"Well, sir, neither do I. It's just that I think about all the Marines who died, and that doesn't count the South Vietnamese or the Montagnards." He stopped talking, then added, "Or even all the Americans, like the men at Lang Vei and the Air Force people killed."

The bulldozer stopped, belched a cloud of black smoke and then turned. It rumbled up a ramp and onto a flatbed trailer and was shut off. There was complete quiet on the plateau, not a sign of the battle that had raged, not a sign that the Americans had ever been there.

"That really ends it," said the lieutenant.

"I guess it'll be up to the historians to decide if it was worth it."

"Them and the Marines."

"Yes, sir. Especially the Marines."

Goddard worked the gearshift and slipped into reverse. Backing up, he turned and joined the convoy as it moved down the road to Route 9. "So much for so little," he said as they reached the highway and turned back toward the sea.

GLOSSARY

AC—Aircraft commander. The pilot in charge of the aircraft.

ADO—An A-detachment's area of operations.

AFVN—Armed Forces radio and television network in Vietnam. Army PFC Pat Sajak was probably the most memorable of AFVN's DJs with his loud and long, "GOOOOOOOOOOOOOD MORNing, Vietnam!" The spinning Wheel of Fortune gives no clues about his whereabouts today.

AK-47—Assault rifle usually used by the North Vietnamese and Vietcong.

AO—Area of Operations.

AO DAI—Long dresslike garment, split up the sides and worn over pants.

AP ROUNDS—Armor-piercing ammunition.

APU—Auxiliary Power Unit. An outside source of power used to start aircraft engines.

ARC LIGHT—Term used for a B-52 bombing mission. Also known as heavy arty.

ARVN—Army of the Republic of Vietnam. A South Vietnamese soldier. Also known as Marvin Arvin.

ASA—Army Security Agency.

AST—Control officer between the men in isolation and the outside world. He is responsible for taking care of all the problems.

AUTOVON—Army phone system that allows soldiers on one base to call another base, bypassing the civilian phone system.

BISCUIT—C-rations.

BODY COUNT—Number of enemy killed, wounded or captured during an operation. Used by Saigon and Washington as a means of measuring progress of the war.

BOOM BOOM—Term used by Vietnamese prostitutes to sell their product.

BOONDOGGLE—Any military operation that hasn't been completely thought out. An operation that is ridiculous.

BOONIE HAT—Soft cap worn by a grunt in the field when not wearing his steel pot.

BUSHMASTER—Jungle warfare expert or soldier skilled in jungle navigation. Also a large deadly snake not common to Vietnam but mighty tasty.

C AND C—Command and Control aircraft that circled overhead to direct the combined air and ground operations.

CAO BOI—A cowboy. Refers to the criminals of Saigon who rode motorcycles.

CARIBOU—Cargo transport plane.

CHINOOK—Army Aviation twin-engine helicopter. A CH-47. Also known as a shit hook.

CHOCK—Refers to the number of the aircraft in the flight. Chock Three is the third, Chock Six the sixth.

CLAYMORE—Antipersonnel mine that fires seven hundred and fifty steel balls with a lethal range of fifty meters.

CLOSE AIR SUPPORT—Use of airplanes and helicopters to fire on enemy units near friendlies.

CO CONG—Female Vietcong.

CONEX—Steel container about ten feet high, ten feet deep and ten feet long used to haul equipment and supplies.

DAC CONG—Enemy sappers who attack in the front ranks and blow up the wire so that the infantry can assault a camp.

DAI UY—Vietnamese army rank equivalent to captain.

DEROS—Date Estimated Return From Overseas Service.

DIRNSA—Director, National Security Agency.

E AND E—Escape and Evasion.

FEET WET—Term used by pilots to describe a flight over water.

FIRECRACKER—Special artillery shell that explodes into a number of small bomblets that detonate later. It is the artillery version of the cluster bomb and was a secret weapon employed tactically for the first time at Khe Sanh.

FIVE—Radio call sign for the executive officer of a unit.

FNG—Fucking New Guy.

FOB—Forward Operating Base.

FOX MIKE—FM radio.

FREEDOM BIRD—Name given to any aircraft that took troops out of Vietnam. Usually referred to the commercial jet flights that took men back to the World.

GARAND—M-1 rifle that was replaced by the M-14. Issued to the Vietnamese early in the war.

GO-TO-HELL RAG—Towel or any large cloth worn around the neck by a grunt.

GRAIL—NATO name for shoulder-fired SA-7 surface-to-air missile.

GUARD THE RADIO—Term that means standing by in the commo bunker and listening for messages.

GUIDELINE—NATO name for SA-2 surface-to-air missile.

GUNSHIP—Armed helicopter or cargo plane that carries weapons instead of cargo.

HE—High Explosive ammunition.

HOOTCH—Almost any shelter, from temporary to long-term.

HORN—Term that referred to a specific kind of radio operations that used satellites to rebroadcast messages.

HORSE—See *Biscuit*.

HOTEL THREE—Helicopter landing area at Saigon's Tan Son Nhut Airport.

HUEY—UH-1 helicopter.

IN-COUNTRY—Term used to refer to American troops operating in South Vietnam. They were all in-country.

INTELLIGENCE—Any information about enemy operations. It can include troop movements, weapon capabilities, biographies of enemy commanders and general information about terrain. It is any information that would be useful in planning a mission.

KA-BAR—Type of military combat knife.

KIA—Killed In Action. (Since the U.S. wasn't engaged in a declared war, the use of the term KIA wasn't authorized. KIA came to mean enemy dead. Americans were KHA or Killed in Hostile Action.)

KLICK—A thousand meters. A kilometer.

LIMA LIMA—Land Line. Refers to telephone communications between two points on the ground.

LLDB—Luc Luong Dac Biet. The South Vietnamese Special Forces. Sometimes referred to as the Look Long, Duck Back.

LP—Listening Post. A position outside the perimeter manned by a couple of people to give advance warning of enemy activity.

LSA—Lubricant used by soldiers on their weapons to ensure they would continue to operate properly.

LZ—Landing Zone.

M-3—Also known as a Grease Gun. A .45-caliber submachine gun that was favored in World War II by GIs. Its slow rate of fire meant the barrel didn't rise. As well, the user didn't burn through his ammo as fast as he did with some of his other weapons.

M-14—Standard rifle of the U.S., eventually replaced by the M-16. It fires the standard NATO round—7.62 mm.

M-16—Became the standard infantry weapon of the Vietnam War. It fires the 5.56 mm ammunition.

M-79—Short-barreled, shoulder-fired weapon that fires a 40 mm grenade. These can be high explosives, white phosphorus or canister.

MACV—Military Assistance Command, Vietnam. Replaced MAAG in 1964.

MAD MINUTE—Specified time at a base camp when the men in the bunkers would clear their weapons. It came to mean the random firing of all the camp's weapons just as fast as everyone could shoot.

MATCU—Marine Air Traffic Control Unit.

MEDEVAC—Also called Dust-off. A helicopter used to take wounded to medical facilities.

MIA—Missing In Action.

MONOPOLY MONEY—Term used by servicemen in Vietnam to describe the MPC handed out in lieu of regular U.S. currency.

MOS—Military Occupation Specialty. A job description.

MPC—Military Payment Certificate. The monopoly money used instead of real cash.

NCO—Noncommissioned officer. A noncom. A sergeant.

NCOIC—NCO In Charge. The senior NCO in a unit, detachment or patrol.

NDB—Nondirectional Beacon. A radio beacon that can be used for homing.

NEXT—The man who said it was his turn to be rotated home. See *Short*.

NINETEEN—Average age of combat soldier in Vietnam, as opposed to twenty-six in World War II.

NOUC-MAM—Foul-smelling sauce used by Vietnamese.

NVA—North Vietnamese Army. Also used to designate a soldier from North Vietnam.

ONTOS—Marine weapon that consists of six 106 mm recoilless rifles mounted on a tracked vehicle.

P(PIASTER)—Basic monetary unit in South Vietnam worth slightly less than a penny.

PETA-PRIME—Tarlike substance that melted in the heat of the day to become a sticky black nightmare that clung to boots, clothes and equipment. It was used to hold down the dust during the dry season.

PETER PILOT—Copilot in a helicopter.

PLF—Parachute Landing Fall. The roll used by parachutists on landing.

POW—Prisoner Of War.

PRC-10—Portable radio.

PRC-25—Lighter portable radio that replaced the PRC-10.

PULL PITCH—Term used by helicopter pilots that means they are going to take off.

PUNJI STAKE—Sharpened bamboo hidden to penetrate the foot. Sometimes dipped in feces.

PUZZLE PALACE—Term referring to the Pentagon. It was called the Puzzle Palace because no one knew what was going on in it. The Puzzle Palace East referred to MACV or USARV Headquarters in Saigon.

RINGKNOCKER—Graduate of a military academy. The term refers to the ring worn by all graduates.

RON—Remain Over Night. Term used by flight crews to indicate a flight that would last longer than a day.

RPD—Soviet-made 7.62 mm light machine gun.

RTO—Radio Telephone Operator. The radioman of a unit.

RUFF-PUFFS—Term applied to the RF-PFs—the regional forces and popular forces. Militia drawn from the local population.

SA-2—Surface-to-air missile fired from a fixed site. A radar-guided missile nearly thirty-five feet long.

SA-7—Surface-to-air missile that is shoulder-fired and has infrared homing.

SACSA—Special Assistant for Counterinsurgency and Special Activities.

SAFE—Selected Area For Evasion. It doesn't mean the area is safe from the enemy, only that the terrain, location or local population make the area a good place for escape and evasion.

SAM TWO—Refers to the SA-2 Guidelines.

SAR—Search And Rescue. SAR forces would be the people involved in search-and-rescue missions.

SHORT-TIME—GI term for a quickie.

SHORT-TIMER—Person who had been in Vietnam for nearly a year and who would be rotated back to the World soon. When the DEROS (Date of Estimated Return from Overseas Service) was the shortest in the unit, the person was said to be next.

SINGLE-DIGIT MIDGET—Soldier with fewer than ten days left in-country.

SIX—Radio call sign for the unit commander.

SKS—Soviet-made carbine.

SMG—Submachine gun.

SOI—Signal Operating Instructions. The booklet that contained the call signs and radio frequencies of the units in Vietnam.

SOP—Standard Operating Procedure.

SPIKE TEAM—Special Forces team used in a direct-action mission.

STEEL POT—Standard U.S. Army helmet. The steel pot was the outer metal cover.

TEAM UNIFORM OR COMPANY UNIFORM—UHF radio frequency on which the team or company communicates. Frequencies were changed periodically in an attempt to confuse the enemy.

THE WORLD—The United States.

THREE—Radio call sign of the operations officer.

THREE CORPS—Military area around Saigon. Vietnam was divided into four corps areas.

TOC—Tactical Operations Center.

TO&E—Table of Organization and Equipment. A detailed listing of all the men and equipment assigned to a unit.

TOT—Time Over Target. Refers to the time that the aircraft is supposed to be over the drop zone with the parachutists, or the target if the plane is a bomber.

TRICK CHIEF—NCOIC for a shift.

TRIPLE A—Antiaircraft Artillery of AAA. This is anything used to shoot at airplanes and helicopters.

TWO—Radio call sign of the intelligence officer.

TWO-OH-ONE (201) FILE—Military records file that listed all of a soldier's qualifications, training, experience and abilities. It was passed from unit to unit so that the new commander would have some idea about the capabilities of an incoming soldier.

UMZ—Ultramilitarized Zone. Name GIs gave to the DMZ (Demilitarized Zone).

UNIFORM—Refers to the UHF radio. Company Uniform would be the frequency assigned to that company.

USARV—United States Army, Vietnam.

VC—Vietcong, called Victor Charlie (phonetic alphabet) or just Charlie.

VIETCONG—Contraction of Vietnam Cong San (Vietnamese Communist.)

VIETCONG SAN—Vietnamese Communists. A term in use since 1956.

WHITE MICE—Referred to the South Vietnamese military police who wore white helmets.

WIA—Wounded In Action.

WILLIE PETE—WP, White phosphorus, called smoke rounds. Also used as antipersonnel weapons.

WSO—Weapons System Officer. The name given to the man who rode in the back seat of a Phantom; he was responsible for the weapons systems.

XO—Executive officer of a unit.

ZAP—To ding, pop caps or shoot. To kill.

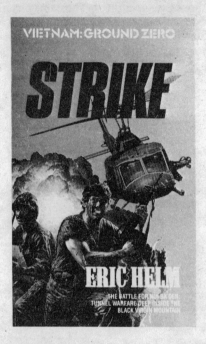

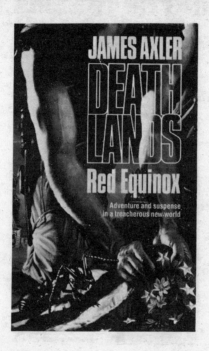